THE PINK HOTEL

The Pink Hotel

LISKA JACOBS

 MCD FARRAR, STRAUS AND GIROUX NEW YORK

MCD

Farrar, Straus and Giroux

120 Broadway, New York 10271

Printed in the United States of America

First edition, 2022

Title-page type by June Park.

Library of Congress Cataloging-in-Publication Data

Names: Jacobs, Liska, 1983– author.

Title: The pink hotel / Liska Jacobs.

Description: First edition. | New York : MCD / Farrar, Straus and Giroux,
2022. | Summary: "A newly married couple is confined inside an opulent
Beverly Hills hotel as wildfires rage through LA County and tensions
mount between guests and staff, testing social boundaries and hurtling
toward disaster, revealing the idle delusions of the wealthy and privileged
in times of crisis" —Provided by publisher.

Identifiers: LCCN 2021061245 | ISBN 9780374603151 (hardcover)

Classification: LCC PS3610.A356446 P56 2022 | DDC 813/.6—dc23

LC record available at https://lccn.loc.gov/2021061245

Designed by Abby Kagan

Our books may be purchased in bulk for promotional, educational, or business
use. Please contact your local bookseller or the Macmillan Corporate and
Premium Sales Department at 1-800-221-7945, extension 5442, or by email at
MacmillanSpecialMarkets@macmillan.com.

www.mcdbooks.com • www.fsgbooks.com

Follow us on Twitter, Facebook, and Instagram at @mcdbooks

1 3 5 7 9 10 8 6 4 2

For Jordan with love

Who hasn't asked himself, am I a monster or is this what it means to be human?

—CLARICE LISPECTOR

I'd rather smoke crack than eat cheese from a tin.

—GWYNETH PALTROW

THE PINK HOTEL

MONDAY

1.

If you had been on this morning's flight from Sacramento to Los Angeles, you'd have seen a pair of newlyweds on the commencement of their honeymoon. You would have overheard how proudly he said *My Wife* all through the short flight. Her voice muffled and timid, speaking into his shoulder, *My Husband*. After disembarking, oblivious to the heat and absurd humidity, they hovered at the arrival gate, then in front of the Terminal 6 Starbucks, where flies swirled in sluggish arcs. They're at the luggage carousel now, standing hand in hand. Her pretty sundress wrinkled from sitting. They are good-looking, you think to yourself. The full bloom of their youth like a flash-bang to your senses. But then a black Town Car pulls up just outside the sliding exit doors and they're whisked off.

Slowly, slowly, the newlyweds are shuttled along a jammed freeway, heading away from the busy beaches, where the sea is warm and the sand scorches bare feet. They won't get to see the Indigenous folks peddling mango and pineapple spears, or the sheriff's department patrolling them from atop their ATVs. Just as the surfers, out in the water, won't ever know the dappled pattern of sunlight along Wilshire Boulevard at this hour.

They're passing the university now, its students squabbling over politics and fair-trade coffee beans; its faculty checking their bank accounts, trying to figure out the math, *How much do I make an hour?* Meanwhile the Sav-on turned Rite Aid turned Walgreens is empty once more. Dust on a FOR LEASE sign is a very particular kind of sadness.

The ficus trees have become more numerous. Their gigantic, bulbous heads sprouting up and out across the street. Deeper and deeper the Town Car travels into Beverly Hills, into these landscaped expansive grounds, verdant and shaded and very green. This is where the sleek animals live. Everything expensive and pristine, the houses not like anything the couple has ever seen. Different from the mobile homes, the one- or two-bedroom apartments, the suburban neighborhoods— and there, springing up from this dense tropical jungle, is a stucco Mediterranean palace. Green-and-white candy-striped awnings fluttering in the hot dry wind, façade as pink and angry as a sunburn. This is the Town Car's destination, the Pink Hotel.

"Our reservation is under Mr. and Mrs. Collins," the husband tells the front desk.

The wife frowns. Her thumb slips into her mouth, the nail inserted between two pearly incisors. She repeats this new last name in her mind, over and over, but its meaning slips away. She chews harder, aware of Keith beside her, chatting up the hotel front desk manager, the assistant manager, whoever else might be nearby. His new panama hat tilted to the side for affected casualness, mustache trimmed to a neat little edge, his hand searching for hers. *They* are Mr. and Mrs. Collins.

The past twenty-four hours have been a series of rapid transitions for this newly minted Wife. She has not had time to adjust. Grains of rice are wedged into the dark corners of her purse from when the civil servant said, *You may kiss the bride*, and all their friends from the restaurant showered them with the bleached white grain. Then, like every proper wedding, even the small ones, there was champagne and cocktails and dinner and dancing. A Bloody Mary at the airport before their flight did nothing to ease this morning's headache.

Neither had the car ride from the airport. The Town Car's air-conditioning was no match for the heat outside. Little wife's legs are moist and tender from when they stuck to the leather seat. And the driver's buzzing voice, how Keith kept him talking in his persistent amiable way, runs on a loop in her head.

No one wants to take the bus or train when it's this hot.

Waves of heat wafting off the asphalt, the concrete, the other cars and trucks and eighteen-wheelers. Commuters at a standstill. So many knuckles gripping so many steering wheels as Santa Ana winds beat against their car windows. Dust devils spinning across construction sites, flapping workmen's shirts like flags, threatening makeshift tents beneath the freeway overpasses with collapse. All the while Keith was nodding along, asking, *How crowded are the beaches?*

The locals want their turf back, their driver told them. *You hear them say it under their breath, they say it to anyone who doesn't look like they belong.*

Keith's hand on hers became so sweaty, she pretended to

need something from her purse. Lipstick, wallet, pens—ah, yes. Her phone. She snapped a selfie. Husband and Wife in the backseat of a Lincoln Town Car.

The narrative of their wedding photographed well. The ceremony had been short, but the old courthouse had given it understated elegance. Our young couple promising each other that one day, when they had real money, they'd do it all over again. Have a huge party, with flower arrangements and party favors and a live band. Maybe a destination wedding, some other place that swam in their minds in vibrant colors like India or Hawaii or Thailand. Something to prove that marrying young had not been a mistake. They'd been together five years and had just moved in together, their first apartment without roommates. She was about to start a sommelier certification course, and Keith was moving up the ranks at his uncle's Michelin-starred restaurant. *Forge an empire*, they'd written into their vows. Because they were at the precipice, the beginning of their lives. Marriage as the next step in a life well planned.

There'd been no one to give her away, no one from Keith's family present to bless the union. A quick ceremony and then on to the next thing. Yet in front of the civil servant, entombed by the thick mahogany walls of the courthouse, beneath murals of California's forefathers panning for gold, missionaries looking to God, Native Americans harvesting corn and wheat, they became serious. Even solemn. Their friends from the restaurant, who had arrived laughing and jubilant, quieted down. Hands were folded in laps. Legs crossed and uncrossed and crossed again. Keith took a sprig of lavender from his almost-wife's bouquet and fastened it to his lapel. Someone rearranged her blouse so that it looked more appropriately prim. They pinned back her bobbed hair. Lipstick was reapplied. Her step became heavy, so did her gaze and the thumping in her chest. A new and unexpected transformation was taking place that she had not prepared for. No longer Kit Simpkins, she was to be Kit Collins.

Kit Collins. Kit Collins. Kit Collins.

The name ricochets off the walls of her mind. She cannot get its rhythm, has not been able to shake its alien feeling or understand why she bristles at its pronunciation. Who is this Kit Collins?

I now pronounce you man and wife.

The kiss that followed was *fine*. Somewhere in the courthouse an alarm went off. Somebody had exited through a wrong door. High and whirring, the sound reverberated through each of Kit's limbs. They were playing their roles, she told herself. Keith, the proud groom. Kit, the blushing wife. Rice raining down around them. Had she blushed?

On to the reception they went. His uncle's restaurant done up with votives, with tiny lights in all the oak trees and sycamores, crisp white wines chilling in silver buckets. They danced and danced, ties on the men's heads, the women barefoot and tilting. Kit's cheeks ached from smiling. Finally, Keith (not a good dancer) wildly swung his arm and the bottle of sauvignon blanc in his hand thumped his best man in the nose. Friends turned into employees once more, Keith directing them to clean up the blood, Kit softening his tone. *He just needs to get to bed.*

Back at their new apartment, the weight of the night embarrassed them. Made them like shy children. Keith joked about consummation. They were overwhelmed and exhausted. That they did not have sex on their wedding night seemed a bad omen. Kit stayed awake, a feeling of failure sweeping over her. The thrust of it surprising. She spent the night unpacking their wedding gifts. Spreading them out so it seemed like there were more. The fine bone china from her aunt laid out on the kitchen table. *Something to aspire to*, the note read. There were only two place settings. Her aunt had not been able to make it to the wedding. *Regretfully must decline.* Which was expected, they'd not seen each other in many years. Her uncle didn't even bother signing the card. It would have been nice if something of her mother's had been sent. Something borrowed, something blue.

Why did you take everything out of their boxes? Keith mumbled, harried, tripping over a blender her stepfather had given them. He, too, had been unable to make it to the nuptials. *Busy with the twins*, his email had said. A photo of his new wrinkly babies attached, both in powder-blue onesies.

Then it was a rush to finish packing for their flight from Sacramento to Los Angeles, Keith worrying about making a good impression.

This trip could change everything, he had said, rearranging his curls once more. And Kit wanted to ask, Hasn't everything changed already?

They're smiling at her now. The front desk employees. She must take her thumb out of her mouth and say hello. Their faces bright and merry from greeting the handsome young newlyweds. Sweat has collected at the back of her neck. Keith is busy signing paperwork. His signature slanted but solid.

The lobby of the Pink Hotel is a stark contrast from the boiling heat outside. Her bare arms are chilled from its sudden cool air.

"Welcome, Mrs. Collins."

She opens up her face so they are pleased. "Thank you," she says with a smile.

Around them a ballet of perfectly groomed bellhops, their costumes royal green, buttons polished gold, collects and disappears with their luggage. One of them hands her a bottle of water, emblazoned with the hotel's crest. Something to keep her from biting her nails. She twists off the top and catches a whiff of their apartment. Its new-paint smell has stubbornly clung to her summer dress.

"Congratulations," they tell Keith, and she knows what they mean. That slight clenched feeling returns to her jaw.

"It's such a beautiful hotel," she says.

Husband grins at wife. He's proud to have her beside him. She is an eager and breathless twenty-three-year-old girl. Cheeks rosy from the heat, brown hair tousled from the wind.

"And we get to spend a week here!" He sweeps his hat off, then, not sure what to do with it, puts it on again. "How lucky are we?"

He's giddy from having walked the red carpet at the hotel's entrance, which he'd seen in countless movies and photographs. The doormen smiling and welcoming. The heat outside forgotten as a cool blast of air was expelled from somewhere deep inside. A shiver had traveled over him. The same kind of anticipation as on their wedding day. As if standing at the mouth of a cave. How deep is it? How far does it go? The boy in him doesn't know. He must jump in to find out, becoming a man in the process.

The hotel's perfume struck him first. Made his blood hum. Everywhere massive flower arrangements loomed—birds-of-paradise, fuchsia anthuriums, monsteras, and elephant ears the size of an artist's canvas. Every type of lily. It was exquisite,

the mixing of tropical and floral. The sweeping carpet softening their footsteps, the curved walls unfurling them into the
grand foyer like a petal on a breeze, depositing them beneath
an elaborate Venetian glass chandelier. That humming height-
ened. He had to press his hands together to keep them from
shaking.

Luxury with a capital L. A bit naughty. Like the glossy
photos of the *Condé Nast Traveler* or *Town & Country* magazines he kept under his bed, hidden from his elderly parents,
who had expected him to follow them into academia. Into
denim and tweed, perhaps cotton twill for the new generation, but certainly not hospitality. How could he explain his
visceral reaction to velvet and silk? To them transformation
was about science. The sun turning nuclear energy into heat
and light, human bodies converting food into energy. Metamorphosis was reserved for caterpillars and tadpoles. Not for
boys with polyester sheets who pine for Egyptian cotton.

Their room is ready. Upgraded to a suite at Mr. Beaumont's
insistence.

"He didn't have to do that," Keith says, but he would have
been disappointed otherwise. He looks beyond the front desk
manager for Mr. Beaumont. The reason for the much-fussed-
over hair, the painstakingly trimmed mustache. He still has
his business card in his wallet, from when Mr. Beaumont
said, *I could use a man like you.*

"Is he here?"

The front desk manager holds up his hand, his supple suit
jacket falling away to reveal French cuffs.

"Let me check."

Keith watches him disappear into the back office, barely stifling a sigh.

Beside him, Kit is fidgeting. Her thumb in her mouth again. He takes her hand, rubbing his fingers over her cold ones to soothe her awkwardness.

"Can't we just go to the room?"

"Hang on for five minutes longer, I just want to thank Mr. Beaumont. Let him know I'm—that we're here." He squeezes her hand, the phalanx bones more yielding than the slim gold wedding band on her ring finger.

They'd met the Beaumonts two months earlier, when Mr. Beaumont and his wife, Ilka, were in San Francisco for the Western Hospitality Expo. It was the usual swarming of exhibits and cooking demos and seminars, bar tabs of brown liquors and wedge salads—Ilka Beaumont bored out of her mind, when out of the din of male voices droning on about industry trends and operational excellence, she overheard the wife of an executive raving about a small restaurant that had recently received a Michelin star. *It's in the boonies.*

And it's true, if you were driving Highway 128 at night you'd almost pass the quaint roadside hotel where Keith is general manager and Kit works part-time as a waitress. Except the restaurant has put lights in the trees, making you take a second look. Note the hand-painted sign, the unmistakable scent of a spa. Somewhere a creek trickles. Elk cross the road in herds. What's this, have you discovered something new? The patio is bustling with soft chatter, the patter of knives and forks and plates and spoons. Tapestries on the walls, touches of gold here and there to contrast the exposed beams and distressed wood. Different from the grid cities and hill cities and borough cities with their fine dining or food trucks or whatever. This is *authentic*. The Pink Hotel needs new and different to stay relevant, so Mr. Beaumont called the general manager to his table, asking, *How fresh is the venison?*

They'd brought Louie, their much-fussed-over bichon frise, and while Mr. Beaumont and Keith talked the little dog escaped from his mistress's lap, disappearing into the dark. Kit raced after him, eventually finding him in the parking lot. The Beaumonts insisted on treating them to a drink, which turned into two and then three. A bottle of burgundy was uncorked. Kit's cheeks turned a charming shade of pink. Her large eyes softened, her small, pouting mouth blossomed into something sensuous and ripe. They stayed until after closing, the older couple basking in the glow of the younger one, the younger couple seduced by the attention. Their espressos cooling in front of them, the tiny curled lemon peels untouched on the saucer.

Where are you lovebirds going for your honeymoon? the Beaumonts asked. They pooh-poohed Napa. *The grapes haven't been the same since the fires*, they said. *Come to LA*, they said. Mr. Beaumont offered them a substantial discount. Occupancy took a dive in the early autumn, plus this year, half of the 205 rooms would be undergoing renovation. Nearly a dozen of the twenty-three bungalows were getting what Ilka Beaumont called a face-lift. *We all need them after a time*, she sighed, and caressed Kit's rosy cheeks. *Oh, to be twenty-three again.*

Mr. Beaumont is not available.

"Meetings all afternoon," the front desk manager apologizes as he hands Keith a key card for Suite 220.

A baggage porter escorts them through the hotel, pointing

out the different ballrooms, the exit to the extensive gardens, the curving staircase that goes down to the mezzanine, where there are shops and a spa and the exit to the pool; Keith's head swiveling left and right.

"The Beatles once snuck in after midnight," the porter is telling him, his stiff band collar pressing into his brown neck. He grins at Kit, who is concentrating on the silk pink carpet under her ballet flats, her sinuses tight beneath the tender bones of her skull.

"They swam until dawn."

She meets his eyes and manages a look of eagerness.

They pass the Polo Lounge, where someone is playing jazz piano for the lunch service. Plates and glasses and bubbling laughter round out the scene. Keith crooks his neck to get a better glimpse of the room—how ornate and elegant it looks with its oak accents and mirrored walls and green upholstered booths. There are more potted plants, their waxy leaves dark green in the low light. He read somewhere that the Rat Pack only ever sat at booth 3, Steve McQueen had once been a regular at the bar—that Elizabeth Taylor preferred table 8, Marilyn Monroe always booth 6. A litany of celebrities swim in his head like stars in the sky.

The hostess smiles as they pass by.

"The Collinses," the porter mouths, and she runs out to say hello. Mr. Beaumont has made dinner reservations for them. Eight o'clock.

"Wonderful, wonderful," Keith repeats because he does not know what else to say. Again he sweeps his hat from his head and then puts it back on. He glances at Kit. She has had the same crooked smile since arriving. For a moment he worries she might not be up for dinner and drinks with the Beaumonts and what he imagines is a vast celebrity cohort. What if she doesn't fit in? But then the porter stands aside so Kit can step into the elevator, and Keith catches him looking at her ass and he's reassured of his choice of bride. Together they can do this. They are a striking couple.

"Sir," the porter says, remembering himself.

Their room is on the third floor with views of the gardens from the balcony. The grounds are so dense with tropical plants and exotic flowers that it looks as if they're staying in the heart of a jungle—but then the palms, a little ways off, their shaggy heads golden against the blistering sky, hint that this is Los Angeles still. If they'd been given a room facing Sunset Boulevard they'd have seen heat waves coming off the asphalt; heard the blaring horns from the slow-moving traffic; been able to watch the bus stop swell with nannies and maids and housekeepers, arriving on the ten o'clock bus that had inched them from a main hub that they'd taken a train to get to—sometimes two or more—from other jobs or maybe home, which is always where the weather is twice as hot, more concrete than green.

But that's *outside* the Pink Hotel. Inside, Kit has flopped across the massive California king, relieved to no longer be in the lobby with everyone staring. The room is quiet except for the faint hum of the air-conditioning.

"I only tipped that porter five dollars," Keith says, sitting beside his wife. "Do you think that was enough? I don't want it to get back to Mr. Beaumont that I'm cheap."

He pushes the pillows away so he can see her face. She's rolled over and is staring at the delicate curved molding on the ceiling, brow furrowed. Her sandals slip from her feet, silently plopping onto the carpet.

"This place is something else," she finally says. "It's nothing like the Old Boonville Hotel. Did you see the people in

14

the Polo Lounge? Their clothes, their jewelry—and that was the lunchtime crowd."

He stretches out beside her. "Don't tell me Mrs. Collins is intimidated."

She tucks her head in the hollow between his shoulder and pectoral. "It's just—what are we going to *do* all day?"

"Anything we want."

He reaches for her hair, brushing it with his fingers. Is now when Man and Wife consummate their marriage? It would make sense. They're alone in an opulent suite. The light slanted and gold, Kit's thigh warm against his hip. The word *union* swirls around his head. *Bless this union.*

He kisses the top of her head, and jumps up.

"Are you hungry? I still can't believe they didn't give us a snack on the flight. Not even coffee and a biscuit."

Room service is busy the first time he rings but he reaches them on a second try. He orders a turkey club and a bottle of champagne, then, because he can't shake the feeling of being judged, he asks about their famous soufflé and adds two to the order. Let them think he hasn't already added up the total in his mind and mentally gasped. He'll just have to increase his credit card limit. No big deal.

"Have you seen this bathroom?" Kit calls to him. It's tiled and marbled, everything pink and green. They can both fit in the shower. Everything is branded, all the products in the shower and by the tub. They riffle the minibar, which is filled with freshly pressed juices with names like Will You Berry Me? and Green with Envy. Everything monogrammed. They take selfies in front of the banana-leaf wallpaper. Unpack their clothes and put away their shoes. Kit slips one of the downy robes over her short sundress and turns the air-conditioning even lower.

"How decadent is this? Outside it's roasting and in here I'm wearing a robe as thick as animal hide." She parades around the room, relaxed now that it's just the two of them. Twice she teases him with kisses until he dashes toward her.

Around the bed, in and out of the walk-in closet, nearly tripping over their luggage. Finally he tackles her on the tufted chaise sofa. The sun coming through the window has turned everything silver. The palms, the banana and fiddle-leaf plants, the birds-of-paradise and bougainvillea. He kisses her laughing mouth, the hot, damp parts of her neck, the little mole on her collarbone. This he can do, this rediscovering of the familiar. But just as his hand slips beneath her dress, there's the chime of a doorbell, followed by a curt knock.

"Be right there," Keith huffs. He waits for Kit to retie the robe but she disappears into the bathroom instead.

A blond boy wheels in a table heaped with domed silver plates. He presents each item, the turkey club with french fries and tiny bottle of ketchup; the pumpkin soufflés in their porcelain ramekins. The chef has sent up a tray of chocolate-dipped fruit—strawberries and cherries and dried orange slices. *Congratulations* written in an elaborate hand across the plate in white chocolate.

"Would you like me to open the champagne, Mr. Collins?" He's holding the bottle of brut as if it were a newborn babe. Yes. Yes, Mr. Collins would.

Pop!

The heavy cut-crystal flutes are filled to the brim.

Keith makes sure to sign his name with flourish. He admires his smooth large hand. The gold band on his ring finger glints at him.

Kit has come out of the bathroom in her summer dress, the robe having been discarded. She runs her fingers over the

French-pleated pink cloth napkins, the buffed and shining silverware tucked within them. In the center of the table is a single calla lily, also pink.

"Congratulations," the grinning blond boy is saying as he hands her a flute of champagne. "Cheers to a wonderful honeymoon." His bushy brows rising and falling.

The bubbles loosen the stiffness in her neck, the tightness behind her eyes. She touches the calla lily's petals and thinks how pliable they are.

"If you need anything," the blond boy is saying to Keith as he backs out of the room. "Congratulations again."

The door clicks shut behind him.

"Where were we?" Keith asks, clinking his flute to hers. They gulp down their bubbly. The mountains, which had been dusty and yellow since their arrival, are clearly defined now. Parrots cry out as they cross the sky.

She munches on the french fries while he attacks the turkey club, which has some kind of aioli that impresses him deeply. He picks up the receipt, remembering how Mr. Beaumont had not even glanced at the restaurant bill when it came. Just held his card in the air. Ilka Beaumont glittering in her jewelry beside him. Keith had never seen anything like it. *He was like a sultan*, he had told Kit later, when they were in bed together in their apartment. *How do you get to that level? How do I get there?* He had wanted her to understand, promising her a diamond ring by their first anniversary.

He's studying his signature on the room service receipt. He'd thought marriage might change it somehow. But it looks exactly the same—except, no. There's maybe a firmer indentation, a slight bend to the K that was not there before. More of a shift, then, like a fracture in the earth's crust, creating new landmasses, entire continents. *This is metamorphosis*, Husband thinks, cracking the decorative wafer on the soufflé and digging into its molten center.

2.

Kit can't decide which bathing suit to wear. She's brought three. Keith has already gone down, eager to see if Mr. Beaumont is out of his meeting, *I should really thank him for the room upgrade.* With the distorted light the suite becomes extended. It's just Kit and the air-conditioning whirring. Lavish furniture does not count as company. Shadows from the jacaranda tree outside cross the plush carpet. The morning has been surreal and dreamlike. Walking past the Polo Lounge with its women like polished stones, smooth and ebony, delicate and shining. In spite of the low light, or the curved booths meant to shield them from prying eyes, some heat at their centers making them spark and light up the room. The effect of animals thriving in their natural habitat. Piano music all the way to the elevator. And then their room—their *suite.* A television in the bathroom mirror. The porter showed her how to turn it on. *If Miss would like to take a bath and watch her favorite shows.* The heated marble floors—the champagne, delicious and cold, Botox for the brain.

She chooses a rust-colored one-piece, cut low.

The bathroom mirror is still steamed over from her shower, which she had hoped would wake her up. Tousled hair will have to do. No time for makeup. Keith is waiting— her husband is waiting. *Mrs. Collins.*

"Enough of that," she says aloud to the empty room. A shiver traveling under her robe, down the length of her spine, the tiny blond hairs on her thighs rising.

She switches off the air-conditioning. Outside those green parrots screech in the coral trees. The wind whips the candy-striped awnings against the building. She stands there for a moment feeling the heat coming through the floor-to-ceiling window. The bathing suit warming over her flat stomach, the stripe of heat across her thighs. What will happen to them? She sometimes asks Keith as they lie in bed waiting for sleep. *What will happen?* The future as a blank spot—no, a dark cavernous endless thing. And Keith is the only thing keeping her from tumbling in. Perhaps marriage isn't a trick, only a necessary anchoring. No dark hole can get her now. A ring on her finger, feet firmly planted on this silk rug.

Voices in the hallway penetrate her thoughts. She adjusts her bathing suit and turns to leave. In the corner of the sitting area is the table that the blond laughing boy from room service had wheeled in. Those bushy brows wagging when he saw her peeking out from the bathroom.

Those dirty plates piled high, silver domes upside down. It's ruining the effect of the suite. With its ketchup-stained tablecloth and unfolded napkins, smudged with bits of grease and chocolate from their fingers. Silverware dirtied and dull. She moves it into the hall.

In the lobby everyone is well-dressed. Cell phones raised in front of faces, shopping bags dangling from jewelry-clad wrists. It was a mistake to wear the hotel robe downstairs. But this is how the women who stay at the Old Boonville Hotel do it. They show up from the city with their husbands, who haul their duffel bags and roll bags from their car while they handle the business of checking in. Always prudent, a little annoyed, going over the deposit—*How long will it take for the amount to go back onto my credit card?*—making sure their spa services and restaurant reservations and childcare or pet care

are booked correctly. *Could you send ice to the room now?* They think of everything, and then emerge from their room in the hotel's waffle robes. Spend their long weekends going from treatment to treatment in the spa. Husbands too. Although they sometimes duck into the hotel restaurant for a drink or hamburger, a quick glance at whatever game is on. *Take the shot, take the shot—damn!* Always a little self-conscious, tying and retying their robe. Which is what Kit is doing now.

It's a different hostess at the Polo Lounge than earlier. This one less polite. Lips pursed, she points Kit toward the pool, eager to shoo her away.

Down a carpeted, curving staircase—why hadn't she gotten a manicure before the wedding? It would have kept her from biting her nails, and the polished banister deserves a manicured hand gliding along it.

Past the Fountain Room, where Ilka Beaumont has celery juice and granola every Sunday morning.

While Louie feasts on a T-bone as large as my ulna, she told Kit during their dinner, her arm stretched across the table to illustrate her point. David Yurman bangles clanging together and catching the light. *Who's a spoiled brat?* she teased the little dog asleep on her lap. *You are, yes, you are.*

There are only old men in business suits in the Fountain Room now, each with a mug of coffee. They look up as Kit passes, their eyes following her as she continues down the long hall, silent but for the gentle slapping of her flip-flops. She stops to look at the memorabilia from films and photo shoots that have taken place here. A photo of Faye Dunaway lounging by the pool; Cary Grant being fitted for a suit. Katharine Hepburn on the tennis court; Rita Hayworth in a pantsuit. The gift shop is filled with trinkets monogrammed with the hotel's insignia. She touches these things, turning over their price tags and then hastily putting them back. There's a Cartier store, and she pauses to watch a couple browse. The woman presses a brooch to her breast. An emerald frog with rubies for eyes.

"Mrs. Collins," Keith says, wrapping his arms around her waist. His hands over hers so that she stops fidgeting with the robe belt. "Are you looking for the pool?"

He smooths her damp hair around her face, the ends almost touching beneath her chin.

Mr. Beaumont had been happy to see him, shaking his hand vigorously. He was exactly how Keith remembered. Tall and slim, lines on his face from smiling, fair hair receding in an everyman kind of way. It was the suit that transformed him. Immaculate, expensive. The material catching the Venetian chandelier light and shimmering. *Keith! Welcome, welcome. I was just talking to management about you.* Direct eye contact, introductions to hotel clerks, bellhops, concierge—anyone within arm's reach. It was a relief, a reiteration of what Keith had felt at that dinner two months ago. Mr. Beaumont *liked* him. A job offer seemed more and more likely. He hadn't wanted to tell Kit until he was sure. But Mr. Beaumont's smile was as broad as a drawn bow, insisting on personally giving him and Kit a tour of the hotel tomorrow. Telling him he'd comped a poolside cabana for the afternoon.

Ask for Coco in the café, she'll see to everything.

You didn't have to do that.

Nonsense, it's your honeymoon. It was my pleasure.

Their brief conversation buoyed Keith. His step across the lobby was light and confident, the other employees looking at him, some guests too. He'd practically floated down the curved stairs toward Kit, his beautiful young wife who was window-shopping—emeralds and sapphires, he realized as he got closer, a feeling of pride swelling within him.

"Oh, thank god you wore your robe too."

"What?"

"You left when I was in the shower, so I wasn't sure. Everyone's been looking at me."

"We're on our honeymoon," he says, kissing her. "Let them stare."

They cross into another hall. Kit looking around, taking in the mirrored light and pink-carpeted halls, the ribbon of banana-leaf wallpaper. Her eyes as wide as a doll's and just as brilliant. The women at the spa desk smile as they pass. Orchids framing them, their delicate blooms quivering beneath the air-conditioning.

"This place is so fancy," Kit says, knotting the belt tighter.

"You'll get used to it," he says, holding open the door.

The heat hits Kit like a weight. "I forgot how hot it is."

"See?" He smiles at her. "You've acclimated already."

The path meanders through a small garden, past a sitting area, rattan sofas with plush pink pillows shaded by palms and giant wild banana. Hummingbirds darting from flowering shrub to creeping vine, dragonflies droning in the tea roses.

Sweat has pooled between Kit's small breasts. She feels it drip down toward her navel. If only she'd packed a notebook. She could get up early, before anyone else was awake, and spend the morning in this perfect little garden. Reclining across the sofas, trying to capture the carefully pruned roses, how white their petals are against the pink cinder-block wall. Or the fig beetles, iridescent and as large as silver dollars, how they bump into hornets near the bougainvillea. She'd study the wind in the tops of the palms and write: *They bend like very tall reeds.* The beginning of a poem, maybe. *The heat is as thick as cream, scoop it up with a spoon.*

Her limbs have become heavy and slow. The ache to sit and scribble is so strong that she doesn't flinch when a hornet comes too close. Keith has to swat it away.

"I'm not used to the humidity," she breathes.

"Mr. Beaumont said the gardens create their own micro-climate." His voice sounding far away. "It's so dry everywhere else, in the city you'd get a nosebleed."

She squeezes his hand. "But here we have our own tropical paradise. Maybe I'll write a little."

"I'm going to keep you too busy," he says, tickling her sides so that she laughs and he can kiss her exposed neck.

They leave the little garden and descend a steep staircase to the pool and Cabana Cafe. Their senses awakening at the symphony of splashing and laughter, of piped-in music and cocktail shakers. The outdoor café is bustling with daiquiris and sparkling rosé. Ceiling fans swirling in slow arcs. Women in gauzy cover-ups. Waitresses in short tennis skirts and matching polos. Businessmen relaxing in angled alcoves. Kit watches as one of them drizzles maple syrup across his pancakes, sucking a bit that's gotten on his pinkie. She almost misses the last step. Keith gives her hand a squeeze.

"Mr. Beaumont said I should ask for Coco," he tells the pretty brunette at the hostess stand.

Coco tilts her head to get a good look at this Keith Collins, a little farther so she can see Kit, who is standing behind him. For a moment Keith is sure that she's looking at him the way all female new hires look at him. Posing so that he can admire their lips or eyes or whichever part of their face they think is their best asset. The beginning of a workplace flirtation. Except something flashes, very briefly, over her features, and although her lips remain soft, her name rolling out of her mouth with warmth, a glimmer remains in her dark eyes and Keith can't shake the feeling that Courtney Flores is laughing at him. "Call me Coco," she says.

She escorts them to one of the eleven cabanas, which are all in a row, constructed to look like Renaissance tents pitched beside an oasis. Their curtains swept and pinned suggestively to the side. Wall sconces above pink and cream couches, a circular daybed in the intimate corner. Brut rosé chilling in an ice bucket.

"This is where *West Side Story* was written," Coco is telling Kit.

Keith lets them chat. He's too busy admiring the back wall of the cabana, painted to look as if it weren't a wall at all. He could be on a villa balcony, a jungle of wild banana just on the other side, like the plumage of a giant exotic bird. The sound of splashing makes him turn back toward the pool, where a redhead in a turquoise string bikini has surfaced. Her pale arms glide through the water until she reaches the ladder. Delicate biceps and forearms flexing as she pulls herself up. The water cascades down those slender shoulders, waist, hips, thighs; water pooling on the hot concrete beneath her painted toes. A man rolls her into a towel, kissing the hollow cleft of her collarbone.

"Oh, the wedding was small."

He hears his wife. Coco is watching him with her dark eyes. He clears his throat and pretends to be interested in their cabana's flat-screen TV, flipping through the channels.

"Only a handful of coworkers and friends came."

"It was intimate," Keith says, abandoning the TV for an

apple from the fruit bowl. He can feel those dark eyes on him still. He looks up, meeting her gaze. She's gathered her mass of hair over one shoulder. The curve of her neck, how she stretches it so that he can see the muscles tense in her throat. Frowning, he puts the apple back.

"I'd much prefer an intimate wedding to some of the things I've seen here," she says to Kit.

The brut rosé is popped and two flutes are filled.

"Like what?" Kit sips, feeling those light, tingling bubbles rush to her head. That heavy feeling in her limbs has shifted to liquid once more. Humidity forgotten. She settles into the sofa, pillows fluffing up around her.

"A groom once parachuted into his own nuptials."

"No!" Kit guffaws. "What else?"

"One wedding party drank five thousand bottles of Mouton-Rothschild."

"Is that expensive?"

"One-point-five-million-dollars expensive."

Kit's eyes are huge. She looks at her flute.

Coco laughs, topping up Kit's glass. "This is Scharffen-berger, only eighty dollars a bottle. Don't worry, it comes with your cabana."

Kit glances across the pool, to where a stunning redhead is lying on a recliner. Her diamond ring could take out an eye. Husband stretching in his tight swim trunks beside her. They're so exposed, much too out in the open. She would hate that. Much better to have the privacy of a cabana. But then the redhead's sunglasses flash in her direction, the husband saying something in her ear to make her laugh—and the couple sitting on the edge of the pool, they're staring from behind their tropical drinks, legs splashing in the water. On the far end of the pool, where a group has pulled together recliners as if building a fortified wall, straws between their teeth, acrylic nails flashing like claws—everyone is watching her and Keith. The new arrivals. Even the parents, who should be watching their children in the water, look over.

Keith is asking Coco about the hotel's clientele.

"I run a hotel-restaurant up north," he's saying, and goes on describing the business of management. The polite smile on Coco's face is familiar. Kit has seen it often. It's the same as when Keith compares vintages to the female wine reps, or suggests a new dessert to the pastry chef. The practiced smile of a tired woman trying to get along with her day. *Grin and bear it*, Kit's mother used to say. *Like this*, and she'd demonstrate. That frantic energy that made her mother such a dynamic presence in Kit's childhood would disappear. She seemed a calm, rational human being. Eyes a little blank, smiling without showing her teeth.

"The owners wanted art nouveau but I knew French country chic was the way to go."

That *I* pricks Kit. She sits up.

"I'll let you two enjoy the cabana," Coco says. "I'm sure you get enough of talking shop at home." She smiles at Kit, who is biting her nail.

"Oh, we don't mind. Kit is used to it."

"I'll come back with some snacks."

From the hostess stand Coco observes them. They're entirely out of their element and anyone watching can see it—and here, at the hotel, everybody is *always* watching. It reminds her of those nature specials. Gators in the water, lions on the land, and here comes a dainty gazelle looking for a drink. Coco doesn't realize she's staring until Ethan pokes her side.

"Who're you gawking at?" He's pushing an empty room

service cart. "*Oh*, the new Mr. and Mrs. Collins. I talked to Bertie, he took them to their suite, and you know what? A fiver. That's what he was tipped. And he said the whole time the husband kept clearing his throat like he was about to make a speech. Made a show of signing the paperwork at the front desk. I had to see them for myself, so I brought up their lunch. The wife hums to herself, and you could not wipe the grin off his face. Poor country mice."

"Mr. Beaumont thinks Keith Collins might make an excellent protégé."

Ethan clicks his tongue. "Your pillow talk with the boss is so disappointing."

"Shut up," she says, slapping his arm with one of the lunch menus. "Besides, she seems sweet. I feel bad for them. Who gets married that young? Does she even look old enough?"

The Collinses are cuddled up now, drinking their free wine. Kit's foot tapping to a beat they can't hear, looking at something on her phone they can't see. They're giggling together, these young newlyweds. They watch as Kit reaches up to Keith's face, her fingers slipping into his curls, pulling his mouth to hers.

"Old enough." Ethan's brows rise higher.

A siren slices through the chatter, making everyone tense. The parents in the pool, the group on the recliners chewing the ends of their straws. An ambulance is stuck at the intersection in front of the hotel. It shrieks from the other side of the wall. Blares its horn at the cars blocking the street. One of the pool attendants drops a champagne bottle and it shatters on the hot concrete. Coco grips the menus in her hand tighter, blinking away grit that has blown into her eyes.

But then the bartender is making piña coladas, the blenders turned to high so that's all anyone can hear. When they're switched off there is only the piped-in music, the nearby fountain, laughter coming from the café, occasional noise from the hotel construction site. A little girl jumps from the side of the pool into the deep end. Her parents applaud.

"God, I'm on edge."

Ethan pats Coco's arm.

The pool attendant who dropped the champagne bottle has joined them. "This summer is fucking endless," he says. Coco helps double-bag the shards of broken glass.

"It's the heat," Ethan sighs.

"And the wind. It makes everyone crazy."

"I've never seen it this bad. Like a pressure cooker."

"I swear to god June was a decade long—but also somehow a blip? I don't know."

Several waiters and pool attendants have convened at the hostess stand. The casual banter of downtime. *It's fire season*, says one of them. *When is it not?* says another. *Did I tell you a fight broke out in my gym last night?*

Personal lives are discussed in broad strokes—How'd that audition go? Did you close on the condo? Breakups and make-ups and shock over how fast kids grow. *I swear you were just celebrating his first birthday.* But all conversations lead back to the Pink Hotel, to its customers and guests. They trade stories like war correspondents. *Jesus Christ, how much was the bill, can you imagine?*

"We're stressed out," Coco joins in, as she arranges truffle french fries beside two coconuts on a tray. "Every single one of us." She'd been only half listening to her coworkers, too preoccupied with watching Kit and Keith Collins. Already the hotel was beginning to have its effect. The husband adapting quicker than the wife. He was first into the pool, making a show of diving in. There'd barely been a splash. When he surfaced he tossed his head like a woman, wet curls flying back. Then teased his wife in a louder-than-necessary voice until finally she disrobed and waded, fidgeting and flushed, into the shallow end of the pool. They'd been swimming ever since. Rolling and splashing like seals in the sea. Now they're climbing out, toweling each other off. Breathless and elated and in need of a drink.

"Kit and Keith Collins," Ethan is telling the others. "Can you imagine? Probably the type to name their children all K-names, Katie and Kristopher and little Keith Junior."

Coco laughs. "You're terrible."

"He has a sweaty handshake. So clammy."

"Watch yourself, darling." She lifts the tray onto her shoulder. "That sweaty grip might end up your boss."

She crosses the pool area with the casual grace of someone who has done this thousands of times.

Kit Collins is indeed humming to herself. She's lying across the daybed, kicking her legs like a kid in a soda shop.

"Our specialty," Coco says, handing an excited Kit a coconut. "We mix two kinds of rum with the coconut water and crushed ice."

"Mmmm, it's delicious."

"Drink it slowly," Keith warns. "Rum isn't always your friend."

Kit wrinkles her nose at him. "Rum is my very best friend, thank you very much."

She likes it when it's like this between them—as if there were no restaurant with its Michelin-starred chef, no arguments about her needing to get her certification, no questioning of their future together. Just Kit and this person who, when he looks at her, smiles with his mouth *and* eyes. In these brief moments she feels confident in knowing Keith, in understanding the world and her place in it.

When Coco had first left them alone in the cabana there'd been a moment of awkward silence. Again Kit thought, *What will happen?* They clinked their glasses together and sipped their wine because that seemed to be the thing to do. So was lying across each other, looking out at the pool. From some hidden speaker French music pulsed. Kit's toes began to tap along, Keith stroking her collarbone. They imagined aperitifs in Parisian cafés. Of cobblestone streets and grand museums in the rain—balconies with views of the Eiffel Tower. That led to other musings. London, where they could see Big Ben, wander the gardens of Hyde Park. Or the Orient Express— Kit pulled it up on her phone. Verona and Venice joined the conversation. They had their whole life ahead of them. What an intoxicating thought. Glossy photos of art deco train cabins, of stewards in white gloves, of elegant stemware and delicate sterling silver sugar tongs. Women in gowns, men in tuxedos. It's fun to let yourself pretend. Maybe the Pink Hotel is just the beginning and she'll never have another cold shower or weevils in the flour.

Our newlyweds laughed louder, grew accustomed to being watched. Who are they? Everyone's eyes seemed to ask. Who could they be? Throw a dart in the dark because they could be anyone, and they might be on their way to becoming whoever they wanted.

Keith is talking to Coco about the truffle french fries.

"These taste like real shaved truffle, wow."

Kit smiles at her. "What would you do if you were staying here?"

"Exactly what you're doing."

"Here, sit down," Keith says, throwing their damp towels from one of the sofas.

Ethan pops his head in, Keith invites him to join them.

"We have this whole cabana for just the two of us. Kit—" He clears his throat and tries again. "My wife and I have been trying to decide what to do while we're here. What would you do?"

Ethan grins. "Well, I'd come down after dark and use one of the cabana phones to call room service, make them bring a bottle of champagne that I've been chilling in my room."

"You have to excuse Ethan," Coco says, shaking her head. "He's our resident savant. Has an answer to everything."

"What? I've given it a lot of thought. And it's so slow, it would give room service something to do. If you came a month ago this place would have been packed. But now with the remodel—"

"And this weather," Keith adds knowingly. He's tilting back on his heels a little.

Ethan grins. "It spooks even the regulars."

Kit stretches across the daybed. Coco and Ethan can't be much older than Keith but they seem so confident, so self-assured. Coco especially. Kit mimics the tilt of Coco's head, the arch of her back. Listens to her talk about the animals that have been coming down from the mountains in search of water. How at night bats swoop over the hotel pool. Coyotes calling in the canyons. *They make house cats skittish*, her voice drones. *Dogs too.*

"You're perfectly safe," Keith assures Kit, caressing her calf.

Had she looked frightened? Night soaks with coyotes in the distance, wind rattling the palms. It sounded exhilarating.

But she's missed the moment to object, to change the narrative. Ethan is telling them about mountain lions now.

"Groundskeepers saw one this morning."

"Don't tell Bungalow Sixteen," Coco says. "She'll flip out."

"Who's in Bungalow Sixteen?" Kit asks.

"Mimi Calvert," Coco says, taking her empty coconut. "She's been living here for twenty years."

"Twenty-two," Ethan corrects her. "Lives by herself with her pet capuchin, Norma Jean. Swear to god. She's absolutely bonkers, but in a delightful way where she tips everyone in fifties. All summer she's been convinced rattlesnakes are beneath her bungalow stairs. She only likes me bringing her breakfast so I have to check every morning."

Keith is helping load Coco's tray with their empty glasses and plates. "No one else can bring her breakfast?"

"He's just trying to impress you because we've heard you might be our new boss."

Kit blinks. "What?"

"Oh, it isn't a sure thing." Keith laughs, eyes shifting this way and that.

"Somebody should let Mr. Beaumont know," Ethan says, pushing himself up from the sofa. "He's talking like you're already hired."

Coco and Ethan are clearing out, taking the tray and wet towels with them. They're chatting about Egyptian cotton and bespoke patio furniture but Kit is thinking about when she and Keith were swimming. How he dived into the pool, and she waded in from the steps. They met in the middle, which had seemed important, and when they went underwater there'd been music playing there, too. Now the Cabana Cafe is closing and the music has shut off. It isn't even playing from the speakers hidden in the palms.

3.

The Collinses ride the elevator up in silence. It stops at the floor beneath theirs and the doors open to a girl barely nine- teen, dressed in a Diane von Furstenberg dress, the silk sleeves long and billowing. Her hair the soft color of whipped egg whites, skin luminous from youth but also full-time der- matologists and aestheticians. The young men with her look up from their phones. Identical twins. Mirror images of each other in their casual luxury streetwear, their green eyes sweeping over the Collinses at the same time.

"Going down?" the girl asks. Keith shakes his head and the doors shut like curtains on a stage. The last thing Keith notices is that both men are wearing limited-edition Piaget watches that retail for six figures.

Their suite is uncomfortably warm. And Kit, in her indeci- siveness, has left her bathing suits strewn across the room. Cover-ups and summer dresses lie crumpled on the floor. This emboldens Keith. He's not the one in the wrong. Kit's over- reacting. He did not trick her. It's still their honeymoon, but also he might have a few interviews. Why can't she be happy for him? For them? Had she expected they'd live in Boonville forever? He picks up each item of clothing with dramatic flourish.

"Why is it so goddamn hot in here?" he says, throwing them onto her suitcase.

Kit switches on the air-conditioning. "I turned it off. Don't look at me like that. It was freezing in here."

She begins rehanging the clothes, aware of his displeasure. She hates when he's upset with her. It's as if the oxygen has been sucked out of the room. In the bathroom she slips out of the robe, peels off her bathing suit, which has dug into the meatier parts of her flesh—around the thighs, beneath her breasts. A red stripe cuts across one buttock. She fills one of the crystal tumblers with water from the sink and gulps it down.

"It's cooler in here," she calls to him, but he doesn't answer. She turns on the shower, which hangs directly overhead. Her own little rain cloud. All the bath products smell delicious. She lathers her hair with grapefruit and mint, washes her body with geranium and pear.

"I just don't understand why you didn't tell me," she calls to him, hoping that if he sees her naked body he might forgive her for the scene she made out by the pool. *Our honeymoon is going to be one long job interview!* Guests in the pool had stared openly; the pool attendants closing umbrellas exchanged glances with one another. The bridge of Keith's nose turned white, then red, little blotches of pink appeared beneath his eyes. She embarrassed him, something she's always afraid of doing. *You've got to let me do the talking*, he told her once after a dinner with the Old Boonville Hotel owners. Kit had rattled on about remodeling with tapestries and exposed beams, touches of gold and bold wallpaper. *Like a chateau in the South of France*, she told the owner and his wife. *Have you been to the French countryside?* they asked, and Kit had to shake her head no. But she'd seen films, images in magazines. *I feel like I've been there*, she told them, *I can imagine it.*

"So," she tries again, the shower pulverizing her tender skin. "Has Mr. Beaumont offered you the job?"

Keith has gotten into the minibar and poured himself a whiskey. There's no ice but he doesn't want to leave the room again without showering and changing into his good suit. The gardens below are dark now, except for the gentle glow from Victorian-style lampposts.

It had been a good afternoon—the two of them fantasizing about their future like they used to, back in the beginning of their relationship, when he'd take her for dinner at an upscale Greek restaurant, which he couldn't afford, not really. But he had a credit card and he liked stealing Kit away from her blond phlebotomist roommates, who'd been pressuring her to follow suit. *I could do it*, she'd tell him. *I have very steady hands.* And he liked how after a few drinks the restaurant's whitewashed walls seemed to transport them; how the waiter brought little extras because they were young and good-looking and eager to learn how to pronounce things like *moussaka* and *souvlaki* and *spanakopita. You've got to roll it around in the mouth.* But most of all, Keith liked watching Kit transform from this unsure girl, an orphan really, to someone whose dreams matched his own. He'd listen to her talk about the Romantic poets on their Grand Tour, Hemingway and Fitzgerald, expats living abroad. How dreamy her face would become, her teeth stained purple from the agiorgitiko wine. *Ah-your-yeek-tee-ko.* He wanted her to have those things, to see those places, but that required work. Hard work. Planning, saving, *growing.* Once the wine wore off, the twinkling lights replaced with the regular blazing sun, he worried that Kit would never do anything more than dream.

"Keith," she calls from the shower. "Did you hear me? Did you get the job?"

"He's not going to offer me the job the minute I arrive," he shouts at her.

It isn't until after they're seated in the Polo Lounge, when the waiter brings a bottle of prosecco—compliments of the restaurant—that the Collinses begin to relax.

"Happy honeymoon," the waiter tells them, sabering the cork with a loud pop that makes the young couple jump and the tables nearby look over and smile. One or two raise their own glasses in solitary congratulations. *Welcome to marriage!*

Kit had a terrible time deciding what to wear, nothing looked right, nothing fit exactly as it should. The whole while Keith had been looking at his watch—which was not a Piaget but a simple Timex—mumbling that they'd be late for their reservation. Eventually he couldn't stand watching another outfit change and retreated to the bar in the Polo Lounge. This further put Kit out of sorts. Then the blow-dryer wouldn't work and she had to call downstairs for another. *Is Coco there?* she had asked the front desk, hoping she could bring it up. But no, of course Coco wasn't working room service. She was back at staff quarters—she'd heard from Keith that they all lived on-site, working in shifts. Like paramedics, like firefighters.

When she finally came downstairs Keith was talking with a group of men in gray suits, all of them with highballs in hand. On the television reporters were chattering about windstorms, the chance of dry lightning. Images of fallen trees on Westwood Boulevard. *Extreme red-flag warnings throughout the southland*, they said.

The men beamed at Kit, congratulated Keith on his choice of bride. Kit, in a low-back dress, fingering a string of false pearls her aunt had given her. She could tell their attention pleased Keith, so she smiled her woman's smile. She thought of Coco in the cabana, her mass of dark hair pulled over one shoulder to show off her neck. She turned her chin, angled her face so the light caught her jaw and cheekbones.

Keith was in a better mood, until they were seated and their audience of gray-suited men was replaced with sumptuously dressed and curious diners. The young blond girl from the elevator sucking down half a dozen oysters in the booth across from them, the twins on either side of her. Their eyes luminous in the low light.

The Collinses sat upright, their menus in front of their faces, Keith's knees bumping the table so that the dinnerware clamored. This sudden awkwardness made them silent. They lingered over the menu. *But this is nonsense*, Kit thought. *It's only Keith*, and she made some small talk.

Should we see if they have oyster shooters?

How quick his face changed to a frown. The blond in the booth craning her neck to try to overhear.

This isn't that type of place.

Things got worse when it came time to order. Keith wanted steak tartare—Kit was aghast at the prices. *We'll be broke by Wednesday*, she said, which made Keith angle his body so the giggling twins could not see his discomfort. *Close your menu, Kit, I'll order for us. What are credit cards for?* A knot in her stomach, she asked the waiter for water but Keith insisted on a bottle of prosecco. He ordered the steak tartare, Bolognese for Kit, the filet mignon for himself, and a Caesar to split. *What's wrong now?* he said once the waiter had left. *I thought you'd be happy, I could have ordered a salad for each of us.*

It's too expensive, Keith. She drummed her bitten nails. *I don't like how our honeymoon is starting out.*

Well, I could say the same.

I think you just did.

Then the waiter miraculously arrived with that life-giving bubbly, the word *complimentary* like a soothing balm. The flutes were crystal stemware, heavy and gothic, which to Kit meant romance and to Keith meant affluence. The bubbles

37

loosened those tight shoulders, smoothed the worry lines that had begun to work their way in between Kit's brows. She started to see Keith again as her rock, the one sturdy thing in her life she could rely on. Those curls, the thin mustache— such an angular, trustworthy face. Without his love she would be lost and alone. She had no one else, not really. And in exchange, she was privy to his secret. That beneath the golden good looks was an unsure boy. Look how he puts his hands on the table, then back at his sides, then on the table again. The way he tugs at his curls, how those blue eyes dart around the room, wondering who might be watching him. *You have to find your best friend and marry them*—that had been part of her vows. She remembers how Keith's eyes glistened at the words.

"You are my best friend," she says, leaning across the table, her face that becoming pink from her allergy to sulfites.

Keith gives in completely. All is forgotten. It's travel fatigue. Journeys are difficult. And Kit is being a champ, agreeing to let her honeymoon be bogarted by a job interview. Such a pretty girl, the men at the bar had said. This pleased him, made him feel bigger than Mr. Beaumont, larger than really any man in the bustling restaurant. Kit had something that made other men look. Even the gawking twins with their Piaget watches are staring, the platinum blond too. The cherry stem from an ice cream sundae between her teeth.

"My wife," Keith says, taking her hands. "Mrs. Collins." He tells her how gracious and welcoming Mr. Beaumont had been when he saw him in the lobby this afternoon. How he met the concierge, hotel clerks, shift and sales managers.

"It was as if I already had the job," he says, leaning back so the waiter can clear their dishes. "He's really something else. I wonder where he gets his suits."

Kit glances at the booth where the blond girl is shooing aside a group of friends who have just arrived, the gesture making her emerald ring splinter in the lamplight.

"I'm sure he'll tell you," Kit says, twisting her wedding band.

"I bet they're tailored. Wouldn't I look fantastic in a tailored suit?"

The chef sends out two more dishes, compliments of the house, and then brings the soufflé himself.

"For the lovebirds," he says, his accent thick.

The Collinses are enveloped in the warm light of the Polo Lounge. The green and white stripes, the scent of old polished leather—the piano music lulling them into drunken bliss. Across from them the blond girl and the twins have left with their friends. The booth is cluttered with cocktail glasses and plates of half-eaten hamburgers, bowls piled with mussel shells and french fries. All of them cackling and drunk as they filed out, the twins saying *Congratulations* as they puffed on e-cigarettes and disappeared in the direction of the bungalow gardens.

"Mr. and Mrs. Collins," the waiter says, bowing as he takes away the signed bill.

Keith's eyes are nearly slits. "Don't you love how they're always calling us that? It's so old-fashioned. You can't fake class like that."

They're sipping espresso, the delicate cups clinking against their porcelain saucers. He takes Kit's hand and touches it to his lips.

"Mrs. Collins," Kit repeats, and she thinks of Keith's mother. An elderly woman in upstate Washington unable to recognize her own son's face. "Who is this Kit Collins?"

"Anyone she wants."

In Suite 220 she lets him undress her. Their sex is familiar yet mysterious, like religious rituals and sacred rites. She stands naked before him. On the bed, he readies himself. Come here, he tells her. He isn't rough, but forceful, and Kit makes her body as pliable as that calla lily.

Love is a kind of possession, Kit believes. So she lets him possess her, gives herself over completely. And Keith—faced with this utter openness—becomes a schoolboy. He's a scientist after all, pinning open a butterfly. Examining its iridescent wings, the light soft fur of the body. If he could delve deeper he might discover some new unknown depth to this docile wife with her girl's body lying naked beneath him. But hunger is eager, and climax is quick.

Afterward there's dampness between her legs. She gets up quietly, Keith already gently snoring. In the bathroom she examines her body again. Gone are the lines from the bathing suit, there are other markings now. From her husband's hands, his mouth. "My husband," she says. *I am his wife*. She rinses again. When she's toweling off, the wind beats against the window, the trees and plants in the gardens lash about beneath the lamps like wild limbs. She opens the balcony door. The smell of smoke hits her immediately.

TUESDAY

4.

"I like to think of the remodel as updating art deco with a touch of Hollywood glam," Mr. Beaumont is saying to the Collinses as they traverse the garden paths the next morning.

A canopy of palms overhead—broadleaf lady, forster sentry, Mexican fan. The weeping evergreens and Brazilian pepper trees swaying in the wind; the wild banana and towering birds-of-paradise quaking and fluttering against the clear sky. Toadflax and cyclamen are bright against dark soil. Begonias and bromeliads as thick and waxy as if sculpted from animal tallow. Everything in bloom because the weather has become so confused. There are camellias the size of Kit's fist, petals splashed red and white. The jasmine is blooming too, filling the air with its perfume.

None of this adds up, cannot coexist with the images Kit saw on her phone. She had stayed up most of the night again. Scrolling through live videos of a quick-moving wildfire. Ash twisting in the wind. Entire mountainsides smoldering like coal in a furnace. How fast it happened. The world turning from calm to calamity. That fissure that existed at the center of life cracking open. You are always, always on the brink. How wide will it be this time, how far-reaching? A clear night sky—Vega, Ursa Minor, the moon impassive and bright. Then, suddenly, the Volvo veers into oncoming traffic and your mother is dead. Tectonic plates shifting. Change as quick as a car crash, or marriage vows.

When she had finally drifted off, it had been a heavy, all-consuming sleep. Twice Keith shook her awake. *I couldn't tell if you were breathing*, he had said, alarmed. He fell back to sleep but she stayed awake listening to the strange prattle of hotel noise. Doors opening and closing, footsteps in the hall, air-conditioning switching on and off. The bed, a California king, meant her feet could not find the bottom. The linens were light, the pillows puffy. She should have dreamed of fairy tales and clouds and things that soar high above. Instead she had felt faintly claustrophobic and frightened. A clock ticked with consistent menace somewhere in the dark. She was cold and then hot. Her nightgown twisted around her limbs. At dawn she jerked awake, went out onto the balcony. There was no blue in the sky, only a brown haze. The air was thick with smoke from the wildfires. She checked her phone again. There were two more fires in the foothills. Another in Santa Clarita. Freeways were shut down. Keith called for her to come back to bed. *What were you doing out there?* She lay beside him and he wrapped his arms around her. *There's a fire*, she said, but he was already snoring.

A few hours later, Keith and Kit are on Mr. Beaumont's promised tour, walking among the honeybees in blossoms. Butterflies flitting past.

Mr. Beaumont turns to smile at Kit, who is staring off. "There are twelve acres of gardens for you to explore."

"I can't imagine the upkeep," Keith says, nudging his wife so that she snaps to attention and smiles back.

Mr. Beaumont gestures with his manicured hand. "We have a very large team of gardeners."

"Can you smell the smoke?" Kit sniffs the air. "It's getting stronger."

Keith takes her hand, which had been creeping up toward her mouth.

"Don't worry." Mr. Beaumont is grinning a reassuring smile. "The Pink Hotel is invulnerable."

Nearby at the construction site, where they are erecting five more bungalows, there are jackhammers and saws, the bellow of men yelling to one another. A reminder that beneath the well-cut suit and practiced smile is a director of guest services under pressure. The bungalows have to be finished on time. There are already reservations. Management is anxious about the steady drop in laborers. Since the heat reached triple digits and the winds kicked up, construction has slowed. The foreman is concerned. *I don't have enough men*, he told Mr. Beaumont this morning. Maybe one of the porters or bussers has a cousin looking for work. Next Mr. Beaumont will try grounds, then housekeeping and valet. He'll take anyone, pay in cash.

He eyes Keith, but no. The slim build, the polo shirt and khakis. Eyes bright and eager. He is hungry for something else.

Already they've toured the back offices where Keith might assist him in guest services, shaking hands with management. Mr. Beaumont was impressed. Keith knew when to ask questions and when to listen and when to laugh at himself. *In Boonville there are no rooms over two hundred dollars.* There were promises of lunches later in the week at one of the cloistered tables in the Polo Lounge courtyard. *If you can get away from your pretty wife*, they winked. Kit quiet and polite, her bobbed hair framing her face in such a way that the men gazed at her openly and unabashedly. One even offered her a coffee candy from his pocket, which she accepted. The hoteliers watching her unwrap the candy, its foil crinkling in her soft palms, and then placing it in her mouth to be sucked on and then swallowed.

In the restaurant and kitchens they talked with the executive chef, the maître d', several of the longtime waiters. Keith rolling his Rs with so much flourish that Mr. Beaumont almost applauded. *Your Spanish is very good*, he said. *Muy bueno.* They've seen the secret valet area reserved for movie stars, high-profile financiers and producers, business moguls, and prominent nationals. This was really for Mrs. Collins because he had no coffee candies in his pocket. He overwhelmed her instead with anecdotes about royals drunk in the presidential suite, an aging Gore Vidal spending his final days by the lobby fireplace, David Bowie eating McCarthy salads in the garden.

The poor youths' heads were swimming. A glazed look about them. Like a baby drunk on breast milk. *Yes*, Mr. Beaumont thinks to himself. It's as if the hotel were suckling them. He knows that look. Had felt the same when he came to work here twenty years earlier. *Intoxicated*.

"You've been too kind," Keith is saying, as Mr. Beaumont unlocks one of the bungalow doors and ushers them in to view it before guests arrive later this afternoon.

"Are people not kind in Northern California?" He flips on the lights so they can admire the foyer, the newly remodeled living room with lacquered furniture and antique bronze fixtures. He points out the flat-screen televisions, the stocked fridge and bar, the crystal stemware, the modern paintings on the walls.

"They are." Keith smiles, running his hands over the leather sofa in the living room. "But I used to live in Los Angeles, and no one was ever this generous."

Kit looks up from the painting she'd been admiring.

"I thought you grew up in Northern California," Mr. Beaumont says. "Along the coast."

"So did I," Kit says.

There's an edge to her voice that Keith does not like.

"When I turned eighteen," he says, picking up a hefty crystal ashtray. "Hungarian? Beautiful." He puts it down. "I thought maybe I could make it in Hollywood."

Mr. Beaumont laughs. "Every eighteen-year-old thinks that. It's why I came here too. I'm actually from a small town outside of Omaha. Don't remind Ilka, she likes to forget the fact that she married beneath her." He pauses, looking out at the bungalow's courtyard, where a hot tub is bubbling and swirling despite the heat. "My parents ran one of those quaint motels you see along an endless stretch of highway. I thought I could be the 1980s Clark Gable."

"Tom Cruise," Keith says, laughing and pointing to himself.

"So, what happened?" Kit asks, sitting on the sofa. Her summer dress has slid up, revealing pale thighs and scraped knees.

Keith shrugs, the heat rising in his face. He refuses to blush in front of Mr. Beaumont and digs his nails into his palms.

"I lived in Koreatown for six months, spent another four on a friend's couch in Venice Beach. But I couldn't cut it and went home."

Never mind that it's morning, Mr. Beaumont has poured brandy into tumblers. Outside comes the muffled sounds of jackhammers and electric saws.

"I'll tell you a secret, Mr. Collins," he says, handing them each a drink. "We'll never *be* them. You've got to accept that first. Because once you do you'll realize we're the ones in control. They need something from us." He motions around the living room, the sunlight splashing across the polished marble floors, the chandelier above the dining room table scintillating. "Everything I've shown you today, they need it. *Need*, not want. It gives their lives context, purpose. They want infamy and in these walls that might just happen."

Both men have turned away from Kit and are silhouetted in the courtyard window. She drinks the brandy too quickly, stifling a cough.

"Of course," Mr. Beaumont is saying, "you can't let them know you're pulling the strings, that's the real feat. The invisible hand is the most powerful one in the room."

He clinks his glass to Keith's.

Just then housekeepers enter the bungalow. They let out a cry of surprise, apologizing for intruding. Mr. Beaumont switches gears easily. He knows each by name, asking about their families. He knows their children's names too.

This interruption has given Keith a chance to compose himself. The wet heat of the gardens, the peaty sting of the brandy—his nostrils are singed with leather and silk and magnolias. He is dizzy with it. He looks at Kit, his pretty wife, reclined on a sofa, flipping through a magazine in a twenty-five-thousand-dollar-a-night bungalow. In his mind a box is ticked. He is moving on to another. An uncle's restaurant in the boonies will not do—even if it does have a Michelin star. It's still just a family business, the place he spent summers

46

and came home from with mosquito bites and spider bites and a slathering of calamine lotion. *If you'd just read the botany book we got you*, his mother would lecture, *you'd recognize poison oak*. For the first time in his life, he admits freely to himself that he will do whatever is necessary to get what he wants. The sudden ferocity of this knowledge, the truth of it, makes him so light-headed that he pours himself another brandy and gulps it down.

5.

The sprinklers have just watered, or perhaps the gardens create their own weather system. Rain storms and fog and waterspouts. Sweat has gathered at the crown of Kit's head; she loosens the belt of her dress. Unbuttons the collar. Beneath her sandaled feet are veins of green moss, the crushed orange petals from an African tulip tree.

Keith and Mr. Beaumont are ahead, talking with Coco. She's missed what about. Her body may be standing in a tropical garden, but her mind is back in the bungalow, replaying when Keith said, *I used to live in Los Angeles*. Metal splintering against metal, the sudden impact of gravity. The velocity of the crash that killed her mother had given Kit whiplash but other than that there had not been a mark on her. Outwardly she remained the same. A girl standing in the garden with her new husband—the man she knew better than any other. Except she did not know he lived in Los Angeles for a year.

Mr. Beaumont's hand has moved to the small of Coco's back. They're talking about the hotel's general manager, who is about to leave for a conference in Paris.

"If he doesn't have time . . ." Keith is saying.

Coco shakes her head. "Oh, he definitely needs to meet you."

Her white tennis skirt flaps up in the wind, her painted nails splay out against its ruffle, pressing it over tan thighs.

Husbands still look, one of Kit's phlebotomist roommates had said when she announced their engagement. *And Keith looks more than most*, the others giggled.

"Shoot," Mr. Beaumont tells them. "But I've got to see about the Cabana Cafe—"

"It's under control," Coco says, brushing dried bits of leaves from Mr. Beaumont's shoulder. "Freddie's switching with Debbie. I told you not to worry. You'll need Botox soon." She touches the crease between his brows.

"Every hotel needs a Courtney." He smiles at Keith and Kit, his arm still around her waist. "She keeps this place running—and me sane."

"She's your Kit," Keith says, reaching for his wife. "The Old Boonville Hotel wouldn't be the same without her. She almost quit once. I told her I'd give her anything she wanted—and what she wanted was a ring."

Coco purses her lips. "I'd settle for shift manager."

The foursome smile as if this were gentle teasing, a joke among almost-colleagues. But there is grit in Coco's words; a vein pulses in the smooth meat of her neck that Kit understands. Her own blood beats along. They are speaking in another language, a primal animal recognition. Kit had not almost quit the restaurant, she had almost left Keith. The wandering eyes, the overt flirtatious remarks made to female staff and guests. *You know I love you*, he said one night after the restaurant closed and she was talking about moving back in with the phlebotomists. *It's my brand, a public persona, it's not me—please*, he begged. His chin wobbling, hands clasped together. And yet here she stands, placid and pert, her laughter an acceptance of a different narrative.

"Good thing you're already married," Kit says to Mr. Beaumont. There's a ringing in her ears. An ache at the base of her skull. The brandy has only made it worse. Her tongue darts out to meet the perspiration that has gathered above her lip.

Mr. Beaumont clears his throat. "Yes, yes," he says, dropping his arm from Coco's back.

The construction equipment has stopped, and with the parrots oddly quiet, they can hear water drip from fat banana leaf to fat banana leaf. There's the sound of a room service cart approaching, it's wheels rattling against the pavement.

"Hey-ho!" Ethan appears, a bottle of Bombay Sapphire and martini glasses knocking beside a bucket of ice. "It's almost time for Miss Mimi's breakfast medicinal. Note the number of glasses—she does not like to drink alone. The things we do for our guests, eh, Mr. B.?"

Coco loops arms with Kit. "I have an idea."

Her arm is shockingly cool. It snaps Kit out of her self-assessment. The headache, the fatigue in her limbs, the dizziness she was sure was coming next. For months after the accident her stepfather took her to specialists. *She's just not getting better.* Restless nights, pain, sudden numbness. They thought somewhere a nerve might be pinched. MRIs and CT scans turned up nothing. *Give it time*, the child psychologists said. A dormant illness, then. Like volcanoes and fault lines.

"Mrs. Collins and I can join Ethan and Mimi," Coco is saying, her eyes bright. "Let the boys meet with the general manager."

"I don't mind," Kit starts, but something about the way

Keith and Mr. Beaumont are looking at the two of them, indulgent smiles, glint in their eyes, makes her shut up.

"You look like you could use a cold martini," Keith says, leaning in to kiss his wife's cheek. "And it would be good for me if you got to know some of the hotel's regulars."

She takes his face with her hands, eager for the grounding sensation of his lips.

"I love you," she says, her brown eyes looking into his blue ones. "We'll have brunch afterward?"

He nods, and moves away before she can kiss him again.

"Newlyweds," Ethan sighs. "There's nothing sweeter."

Kit watches Keith walk with Mr. Beaumont back in the direction of the hotel, palms and ferns swallowing him up.

"You know she only likes a party of two," Ethan is telling Coco.

"Mimi will make an exception for me. I brought her Tylenol one morning when she was in a bad way."

The construction work has started up again. The roar of heavy machinery, intermittent jackhammering. The wind makes Kit shiver despite the wet heat.

"Hey," Coco says, taking Kit's hand. "You all right?"

"It's just so humid."

Ethan glances over his shoulder, the room service cart bouncing in front of him. What he sees: an insecure girl bride standing arm in arm with Coco. What he thinks: *What fun this will be.* What he says: "I'll get you a bottle of Voss from Mimi's room."

A helicopter beats overhead and then is gone. It's only dragonflies swooping over a fountain as they pass by gardeners on their knees planting perennials. They call out in Spanish, Coco replying in a teasing, lilting voice. Her arm never leaving Kit's.

"Is she famous?" Kit says as they reach Bungalow 16. She had meant to say more during their short walk, meant to have her voice take up space, if only to tell Coco that if she wanted to be shift manager then she should demand it, but the thought of Keith in Los Angeles, with friends and lovers—yes, probably, most definitely, lovers—crowds her mind. And the heat, it is pressing into her chest.

"I mean, will I recognize her?" She wipes her brow.

"Maybe," Coco says, eyeing Kit. "If you watched a lot of shows in the eighties. But you probably weren't born yet. Her marriages made her rich. Five of them."

"She has a daughter," Ethan adds. "But I've never seen her around."

"Maybe I should change," Kit demurs. Her head is pounding, there is little saliva in her mouth.

"Lesson one, little lamb," Ethan says. "The less you care about how you look, the richer everyone will think you are."

He taps Kit's pert little nose. "Wait here, I'll see if madam is open to receiving visitors."

"Mimi never leaves the hotel," Coco says near Kit's ear. Her breath soft and hot. "Despite owning a classic Mercedes-Benz 350SL. She lets Ethan drive it to get Norma treats at some exotic pet store in West Hollywood."

The lace curtain in one of the bungalow windows moves. Kit's first thought is that she's seen a ghost and she takes a step back, but then the door swings open. A petite woman with silver hair blow-dried into an extraordinarily curly coif appears from within the darkened foyer. Her face so pale it's almost translucent, her skin so tight that Kit can trace the skull beneath. She has on large sunglasses, which make her nose look even more fragile and delicate, much too small for the rest of her face. And the caftan—Kit has never seen anything so luxurious. Like delicate porcelain at high tea, or villa fountains in foreign countries. She watches it sweep around the woman's bare feet.

"Visitors," she says in a raspy voice. "Ethan, how could you, the sun is still up, for Christ's sake. Bring the gin and leave the girls."

"Bonjour, Mimi," Coco calls to her.

The old woman twirls around; her arms move in slow, languid movements. "Coco," she drawls, peering over the sunglasses. "I didn't recognize you. And who's that, someone new? Oh, I don't care. It's been a hell of a morning. Maybe tomorrow. Ethan?" She pats his face. "Be a dear and leave the cart. Just bring the tray. Norma is in one of her moods. She'll shit all over it and I'm not paying this damn hotel another cleaning fee."

She disappears back into the dark bungalow, the caftan trailing after her like billowing clouds.

"A party of two, then," Ethan says, smiling at Coco and lifting the tray onto his shoulder.

Coco makes a face at him.

"She enjoys Ethan's company," she says to Kit when it's just the two of them walking along the garden path, wind tangling the branches and shrubs around them. The air stinging their eyes.

"If you understand what I mean. No, I can tell that you don't. They drink together, and do other things—*intimate* things. Don't look so shocked. A woman of seventy needs to get her kicks too. I hope I have half her stamina when I'm her age. The things Ethan says she likes to do would make your toes curl."

Kit can hear Ethan's voice, he must have taken the tray into the bungalow's walled courtyard. There is ice clinking, and a high-pitched yipping from the pet capuchin. *Did Norma miss her Ethan?* she hears Mimi coo.

"Are you blushing? You're too much." Coco calls over her shoulder for her to keep up. "A quick detour so you can see the tennis courts."

Kit hurries to rejoin her. She's really sweating now, the armpits of her dress damp, the collar sticking to her neck. Somewhere drip irrigation switches on, the wet smoke smell is invading her throat, her nostrils. She coughs, tasting the brandy again. The new leaves of ferns are so tightly curled they could be a direct rejection of the world around them. No, I will not unfurl, they say. You do not deserve me.

"Are there orchids here?" she asks, reaching out to touch the vibrant green plant. "My mother used to take me to garden centers just to sit in their greenhouses. They had geraniums and petunias and chrysanthemums—but never orchids. We were always on the hunt for an orchid."

"In Boonville?"

"No," Kit says, remembering herself. "We were in Reno then—that was before my mother left us."

"Ah," Coco says, linking arms with her. "A broken home. I know that story. My dad left when I was little. How old were you?"

"Twelve."

"Me too! What a shitty age for parents to divorce. I knew there was something about you I liked. We're kindred spirits. The world is against women like us but we're gonna give it hell back."

"Women like us?"

Coco sidesteps a sign asking guests not to go any farther.

"Well, you're still young, but you'll learn soon enough. For instance, I bet Mr. Collins wants to spend all his time here at the hotel and you—" She pauses, that amused light flashing in her eye. "You probably want to go to the beach. You could use a day swimming with dolphins."

"Why does everyone think they know what I need?" Kit says, pushing her bangs from her damp forehead.

"I didn't mean anything by it," Coco says, and for the first time really looks at this girl with wide doll eyes and bobbed hair, cheeks pink like a child with a fever.

"I'm sorry," Kit says, shaking her head. "You're right. Keith—*Mr. Collins*"—she smiles shyly at Coco—"does want to stay close to the hotel."

"Well, the hotel can be fun too, we'll make it fun."

They've entered the area where bungalows are being renovated. Workers are fixing roofs, retiling entryways. They look surprised to see the two young women, a little embarrassed. Large swaths of plant beds are empty now, their dirt dry and gray. Buckets of thorny bougainvillea are waiting to be planted. Bags of manure give off a sharp earthy scent.

"Actually," Kit says, eager now. "I'd rather ride the Ferris wheel on the pier than swim with dolphins. Corn dog in one hand, a pink lemonade in the other!"

Gone is the laughing glint in Coco's eye; for a moment she's acutely aware of her Spanx cutting into her thighs, the osteoarthritis in her big toe. There's a deep ache in the soft organs of her stomach. She wants to tell Kit not to be so obvious, to hide some part of herself from the world.

"It will be packed with tourists," she says instead. "Especially in this heat."

The construction noise has gotten louder. Ahead is a large cloud of dust. The greenery has given way completely. They scramble up a small embankment, Kit puffing and loosening her dress belt even more.

At the top the lush jungle is gone. Kit is standing on Mars and it's under construction. Backhoes and crawler loaders and men in matching hard hats and vests. Several structures have already been erected, mostly of wood, metal studs, floor joists, and roof trusses.

"Charlie Chaplin and Buster Keaton played here every day," Coco sighs. "But no one plays tennis anymore so they tore it up."

All that's left are the lampposts, tall and ornate. Relics from another century. Kit shields her face from a gust of dirt and debris. Free of plants and solid structures, a dry wind pummels them. The construction workers in their orange shirts and khakis and heavy boots have spotted the two girls. They pull down their dust masks and whistle. Coco shouts back, laughing.

"I'm so thirsty," Kit says. The sudden dryness has turned her tongue into a heavy thing. Her lips are prunes. Her mother complained of this every day in Reno. *I AM SHRIV-ELING UP*, and off they'd go in search of a greenhouse or nursery.

Maybe the brandy has made her sick. Perspiration has gathered at the back of her neck. She keeps replaying the morning—the tour of the kitchen, the restaurant, the conference rooms, the bungalow. Keith saying, *I used to live in Los Angeles*. Mimi Calvert's entrance, how the stage door swung open and she stepped into the light, her hands flitting about as if she were trying to remember her lines. And nearby, honeybees pollinated citrus flowers; on Ethan's cart, beads of moisture had collected on the bottle of Bombay Sapphire; green parrots screaming in the eucalyptus trees, smoke tinting everything brown.

"This fabric doesn't breathe," she's saying, but Coco is

talking to one of the construction workers, who's walked over and is leaning on a piece of rebar sticking out of the dirt. He's tall, his shadow could block out the sun if he'd only move closer. His T-shirt is soaked through with sweat. Tattoos swirling across his chest. He's pointing at her. The fingers are tattooed too. His lips are moving. She moves her own, trying to form some kind of reply. Her breath is sickly sweet, nauseating. She unties her belt completely, unbuttons the dress so she can feel the dry wind, except the wind's too strong. She stumbles backward, is falling or perhaps the ground is coming up to meet her—but no, roots from the garden's tropical plants have caught her, holding her in their tattooed embrace.

"I'm here on my honeymoon," she hears herself saying, showing Sean Flores the gold band on her finger. "Keith's going to buy me a diamond later . . ."

6.

"You poor dear."

The waitress places another bottle of sparkling water at the booth where Kit is sitting with hotel guests she doesn't know, Keith looking on with a mixture of concern and embarrassment.

He'd missed the general manager, who was already in business class en route to Paris, but in looking for the GM, Mr. Beaumont was flagged down by a couple sitting alone in a booth in the Polo Lounge.

Tigran and his sister, Mr. Beaumont said in an aside as they crossed the dining room. His smile becoming wider and more luminous as they reached them. *Mrs. Lacey*—he beamed—*I have someone I'd like you to meet.*

A number of bangles, all encrusted with various green stones, chimed against one another as she extended her hand to meet Keith's. *Enchanté*, she said. And continued quietly in French to her brother. Her face vacant. Beautiful in an exquisitely delicate way. Like fine bone china or spun sugar works. Her skin completely smooth, brows dark and thick.

Now Mrs. Lacey is looking from Keith to Kit, the latter of whom is still pale and trembling from her fall. "Newlyweds," she says, her voice apathetic. "But you're so young."

Around her neck, incredible lengths of gold chains knot into a rope, a solitary emerald at the center. It bumps gently against her sternum as she tips her Bellini into her mouth.

"Sit with us for as long as you like." Her brother, Tigran, smiles. He's considerably older than his sister, broad and fit, with a neatly trimmed silvery beard and amber eyes. He is the type of man, Keith had mused upon first meeting him, who didn't want for anything. Keith could tell by how casually he dressed, the polite, tolerant smile—and when he ordered there was no pause, no adding of numbers in his head. No worrying of credit limits or the waitress's judgment. He'd waved to Mr. Beaumont about getting a third bungalow for his niece, Mrs. Lacey's daughter. *You know how Marguerite is*, he had said with a convivial wink. *Can't stand being cooped up with her cousins.*

Standing beside Mr. Beaumont, listening to him apologize and suggest a suite instead, something shifted within Keith. *The renovations*, Mr. Beaumont had said to Tigran. *All of our bungalows are booked.* Tigran never once demanded. An eyebrow raised here, an interruption there—to order another basket of pastries, to ask for oat milk instead of soy for his cappuccino, to inquire about spa appointments. *We could use an afternoon of pampering.* Then there was an invitation for

Keith and Mr. Beaumont to join them for brunch, which of course they accepted. Sliding into the booth beside them, cologne and perfume enveloping Keith into some other world, one of estates and manicured gardens and clifftop villas. Mr. Beaumont was wrong. Tigran was the most powerful man in the room.

The final proof came when Mr. Beaumont left to arrange Bungalow 5 for young Marguerite Lacey, leaving Keith alone with this grandiose pair. Tigran biting into a mini croissant, his sister sitting straight-backed beside him, sipping her frothy peach cocktail. They were so striking. Flawlessly tan. He was imagining them on boating trips all over the world—on yachts, on sailboats, or on a catamaran. Yes, a catamaran so Mrs. Lacey could lie out on the netting between the parallel hulls, watch the turquoise sea vanish beneath her. Fashion ads and film scenes blended together. A tanned toned couple, an unrecognizable sea. Not the Caribbean or the Mexican coast—something farther away, where the names sound as polished and rare as gemstones.

Tigran had turned his tiger eyes onto him, and Keith could feel the approaching conversation, he was climbing the hill, nearing its precipice. *Tell me*, Tigran said, sipping his cappuccino. *What made you want to work in hospitality?*

And then the construction worker appeared. Sweating and hulking, half carrying a pale Kit. *Fainted*, Mrs. Lacey repeated, her eyes illuminating for a brief moment. Tigran sent for the concierge doctor, signaled the waitress for sparkling water. They wouldn't hear of moving her. *She needs to regain her strength.* Their kindness and concern impressed Keith even more. They'd only been introduced and already they were treating him as if he were part of the club. If only that construction worker would leave. With his dirty hands and grubby work boots. He'd gotten Kit's pretty sundress dirty. He's with Coco at the bar now, the two of them speaking in Spanish with each other. Occasionally one or both glancing over. Some decision is being made, an argument between the two. On the bar television above them the fire chief is talking to reporters. Images of exhausted male and female firefighters, their faces smeared with soot.

"Really," Kit is saying to the concierge doctor, refusing his offer of a vitamin transfusion. "I feel much better."

A streak of mud has dried along her forearm, there is dirt in her hair. Keith watches his wife wipe the top of her lip with a shaky hand, sees that Mrs. Lacey and Tigran are watching too.

"Are you sure you don't want to go up to the room and lie down?"

She looks at him, eyes large and shining.

He clears his throat. "We can go up whenever you want."

"It was the heat," she says, lip trembling just as the construction worker returns with a bag of ice.

"Put this on your neck," he instructs. His shaved head glistening in the recessed lighting. The maleness of him—the distinct odor of manual labor, of processed foods and Red Bull, what Keith imagines must be his everyday life of toil and grime. He looks down at the basket of pastries the waitress has brought. The croissants and tarts oozing chocolate or raspberry jam, hazelnut butter or honey made from local purveyors. The kiwis have been carved into the shape of stars, the oranges spiraled into one continuous thread.

"With heat exhaustion," the construction worker continues, pouring Kit more sparkling water, "it's important to cool the body down."

Keith looks away. He does not want to see the thumb

sneaking up to Kit's mouth, chewing on nail or cuticle or both. Why is she talking with the construction worker? Literally anyone else at the table would be better—the waitress even. He focuses instead on Mrs. Lacey, her tawny beauty. She's talking with more animation now that Coco is at their table.

"First the gardeners," she says, her wide eyes distressed. "Then the maids, and now our house manager is leaving. I just don't understand, aren't we their family too? Don't we need them just as much?"

"You have us," Coco says, handing her another Bellini. "The Pink Hotel is always your second home."

Mrs. Lacey takes her hand, kissing it. "Merci, merci. Where would we be without you?" She looks at Keith. "I keep telling Mr. Beaumont she'll be running this place someday."

"Sit with us, darling," Tigran says, gesturing for Keith to make room on the bench. "The Cabana Cafe must be closed. It's disgusting outside. The air is absolutely hazardous."

Coco drops into the booth beside Keith. He can hear her bare thighs slap and slide against the leather, that tennis skirt riding up.

Tigran is talking about a new construction downtown, some trouble with the permits. *It's like they want to keep it low-end.* Keith nods but can't settle in. Not with Kit chewing away at her nail, and the construction worker still standing there—and Coco's thigh so near his own.

Coco reaches across him for the pastry basket. "Not eating, Mr. Collins?"

There's that look again. As if she knew his palms were sweating beneath the table and his feet were sore from walking in shoes purchased specifically for this trip.

"Mr. Collins is GM of a hotel-restaurant up north," Coco

says to Tigran, smearing jam across thick-cut brioche. "Has he not told you? We've got a young entrepreneur here."

She reminds him of his only cousin. She was a tease too. With the same thick black hair and soft brown eyes. She taught him how to count to ten in Spanish. Also the words for *belly*, *nipple*, and *foot*. He taught her how to say *please*, *thank you*, and *tongue* in Latin. They took turns being teacher or student depending on which part of their bodies they wanted to explore.

"Where up north?" Mrs. Lacey is asking.

"Boonville," Kit blurts out, and rambles about their small Northern California town known for redwoods and elk herds and how Clark Gable liked to fish at one of the old lodges along the river. Mrs. Lacey is staring at the tiny bubbles shooting up in her glass. Tigran asks the waitress to check on their brunch order. Keith clears his throat again.

Only the construction worker is listening. He gives her a small half smile.

"There's a brewery too," she tells him.

"You still haven't thanked my cousin," Coco interrupts. She adjusts her legs beneath the table, the sticking of one as it crosses over the other. *Muslo*, Keith remembers. *Muslo interno*—inner thigh.

She's smirking at him, lips pink and pressed together. "Mrs. Collins would have taken a bad tumble if Sean hadn't been there."

Keith can feel this Sean Flores measuring him up. Taking in the polo shirt and sport coat, the fresh haircut and slight build.

"Your cousin? Hey, man, yeah." He reaches out to shake his hand without getting up. "I owe you a beer."

"It was nothing," Sean Flores says, his hand dry and

calloused. "She should drink a lot of clear fluids. We see it all the time, especially in this heat."

Sean nods at this bizarre brunch group. His cousin, the cabana waitress shoving pastries into her mouth; the posh Mrs. Lacey and her brother, who are having a conversation with themselves; and the newlyweds who have avoided looking at each other, until now. Kit's dark-eyed stare has made Keith stand and take his hand again, repeating his thanks. And then Kit, the scent of her still ringing in his head, chlorine and sunscreen and an almost brutish musk, so unlike the petite girl now reaching out her own hand to shake his. How cold and small it is in his large one. A flush has returned to her cheeks.

"Take it easy," he says, just as multiple waiters push him out of the way.

The table is crammed with pancakes and waffles, the hotel's homemade gluten-free granola. Mrs. Lacey has ordered eggs Benedict with Scottish salmon, her brother the same but with Canadian bacon. There is celery juice and pomegranate juice and a bottle of champagne for the table.

"Dig in," Tigran tells Kit. Keith already pouring maple syrup onto a short stack.

On the bar television the sheriff has joined the fire chief. Images have switched to a Walmart ablaze. People in bandanas and face masks, arms full of diapers and cleaning products, shoeboxes and cases of beer.

They'll burn down their own city, someone at a booth nearby remarks.

Hoodlums, another utters.

Forks and knives clinking prettily against their porcelain plates.

Twice Kit tries to get Keith's attention but he's busy discussing investment opportunities and property taxes with Tigran. Coco is listening to Mrs. Lacey complain again about her staff. *I just don't understand why they'd abandon us.*

Kit's pushing yogurt around with a spoon when the platinum blonde from the other night bounds right up to her.

"Did you really faint?" she asks, taking one of the star-shaped kiwis. "I don't think I've ever fainted. Blacked out, passed out, but never fainted."

"My niece, Marguerite," Tigran says, eyes narrowed. "Marguerite, leave Mrs. Collins alone."

She ignores her uncle and places her palm against Kit's forehead. A diamond embedded in the nail of her pointer finger. "Huh, I thought you'd have a fever or be bone cold, or *something.*"

"I feel fine," Kit says.

Marguerite's laugh is high-pitched and fierce. "If this is what you look like when you're feeling fine—what, Maman, I'm just saying."

The sleeves of Marguerite's gown are flouncy and long, tiny pearl buttons fasten tight around her slender wrists. But then, the smeared purple eye shadow, the bluish circles under her eyes—there's a dirty smell coming from her hair, as if she'd been out all night and not bothered to shower or even wash her face.

Coco stands so that Marguerite can sit, but she plops down beside Kit instead.

"What is everyone drinking?" She examines the champagne bottle and clicks her tongue. "Always sparkling rosé."

Mrs. Lacey's lashes, black as soot, brush the tops of her cheeks. Her brother deposits a small round pill in his sister's palm.

"Marguerite," Tigran says, his tone at odds with his pleasant grin. "Your mother isn't feeling well. We're going to spend the afternoon in the spa."

Marguerite looks at Coco, then at Kit and Keith, rolling her eyes. "There are five fires, a mobile home park burned down, and Maman is spending the day at the spa."

Around them waiters are clearing their dishes. The Laceys and Tigran talking around and through the reaching arms, never once glancing up.

"Be patient," Mrs. Lacey is saying as she takes another pill with her champagne. "Mr. Beaumont is working on getting you your bungalow."

"I hate sharing with the twins, they're horrible. And the air outside is horrible, what am I supposed to do? There's no going to the pool. You two will be at the spa so that's ruined. Ouuu, Coco, let's bring the spa to us. Will I have Bungalow Five?" She turns to Kit, brushing that streak of mud from Kit's arm. "It's my favorite, you'll see why. Ouuu, manicures, pedicures, facials. I love, love, love a good manicure. Bring Ethan, he always has the best drugs—what, Maman, chill." She leans into Kit. "I can talk like that to Coco because she's known me since I was nine."

"That's right," Coco says, swiping the kiwi Marguerite had been playing with and taking a bite out of it, its juice dribbling down her chin.

Marguerite makes a face at her. "You should come too," she tells Kit. "If Maman needs a spa day because she doesn't know where the garbage goes—c'est vrai, we are terrible, absolutely useless without our staff—then a girl who faints in the gardens deserves a little pampering. What do you think, Hubby? Doesn't your new bride deserve a spa day? I can have her back to you in a few hours, or"—she claps her hands together—"come to our pool party this afternoon. The cousins are already planning it."

There's a fleeting crease in Coco's brow but it's so quick that Kit thinks she's imagined it. Coco's beaming and reaching to help the waitress clear the last of the plates. "I think the newlyweds want their privacy."

"Oh boo." Marguerite flops back against the booth. "How boring."

She perks up when Mr. Beaumont returns with a key card and spa reservations for Tigran and Mrs. Lacey.

Her only experience was temp jobs, Kit hears Keith say, and she knows he's talking about her.

She's missed the transition. Too distracted by Marguerite, who one moment has the mannerisms of a child, but then is speaking French to the waitress, asking for pour-over coffee. *A whole Chemex, s'il vous plaît. Kit, you'll have some, won't you? It'll do you good.*

"Front-office stuff." Keith's smile is familiar. The glance thrown her way filled with warmth and affection but something else too. Simple pretty girl, it says. His adorable naïve Kit.

It's a story she's heard many times before. The story of how a couple meets, how love follows, then marriage. Only this is their story, and she can't shake the feeling that the more Keith tells it—at dinner parties and hotel functions, right now, sitting here in the Polo Lounge—the less it becomes hers.

"A couple of months at a dentist office sterilizing equipment and processing X-rays. Half a year at a warehouse on the edge of town that was sort of a poor man's version of Amazon. And her résumé!"

Kit fidgets beside Marguerite, who is watching her from behind her cup of coffee. There's a sting in the back of Kit's jaw as if she were gnashing on bones, as if she were fighting the urge to grind down her own molars.

"It's typed out in this sort of Edwardian font, her name in bold: Kit Simpkins."

She can feel herself blushing. He has gotten to the part about first seeing her, how he fumbled his welcome, his sentences all running together. This is when she should smile and laugh, flattered because it means Keith had found her attractive from the get-go, but instead she reaches for a mini croissant, shoving it into her mouth so that she doesn't have to say or do anything.

"Of course I hire her."

"I would too," Mr. Beaumont says, who's pulled a chair up to the table.

Tigran agrees. "Anyone would."

Mrs. Lacey manages a small smile.

Plain. No jam or hazelnut butter or local honey. Kit is struggling to swallow the flaky pastry.

"You should really come to my bungalow," Marguerite says, offering her coffee.

"Thanks," Kit says, drinking. "I think that croissant had it out for me."

They smile at each other. Marguerite leans toward her. "A little break from husbands and uncles and *everyone* is probably a good idea, don't you think?"

Kit looks at her fingers, the cuticles raw.

"I could use a manicure."

"I should say you do, look at those. They're practically nubs. Then it's settled." Marguerite holds up the key card. "Hubby can come over when he's finished up here."

"Oh, but we haven't gotten the check."

Marguerite laughs a shrill giggle. "Maman's paying for brunch, aren't you?" She looks at Kit. "That was a yes. You don't speak 'Maman,' but that head nod means the Bellinis and the medication are making her acquiescent to all requests."

"That's enough," her uncle warns.

She ignores him and takes Kit and Coco by the hand. "Hubby," she calls over her shoulder to Keith. "Come over when you're done schmoozing."

Keith watches his wife exit through the courtyard doors, out toward the bungalow gardens. A nagging fear in his chest. His knee bouncing beneath the table. Kit isn't used to this type of place, these extraordinary people. Sure, he's taught her about grape varietals and terroir, handmade pasta instead of store-bought, how to send back a dish at a restaurant if she doesn't like it, how to carry yourself in a department store so the salespeople look at you like a possible sale and not some immature kid—but she's still just a girl from Reno. Loves gas station beef jerky. McDonald's hash browns. An occasional hard seltzer, always the ruby grapefruit flavor. She isn't ready for someone like Marguerite Lacey.

What if she doesn't get it? What if she never gets it? The thought makes his bones feel brittle and cold as if made of ice.

A small white bichon frise nips at his pants.

"Louie, Louie, Louie, King Louie," Ilka Beaumont coos. She's descended from her presidential suite on the top floor. A coral broach pinned to the lapel of a provocative jumpsuit, which she'd chosen knowing the Collinses had checked in and were somewhere on the hotel grounds.

"Coffee and cognac," Ilka Beaumont tells the waitress, who only just finished resetting the table. "I should have known Louie was after Daddy. He's always loved you more."

She kisses Mrs. Lacey and Tigran on their cheeks, just as they're rising to leave.

"We're spending the day at the spa," Mrs. Lacey repeats, her eyelids heavy.

"Well, don't let me keep you, enjoy it," Ilka Beaumont says, waving them off.

She takes Keith's face in her smooth warm hands. "I like the mustache, it's very Errol Flynn. Where's your lovely wife? I meant to come down earlier and shower you both with congratulations."

She bounces into the booth, hands still on Keith.

Mr. Beaumont touches her arm but she shrugs him off. "Oh, the boy doesn't mind, do you? What cologne are you wearing? It's divine."

Keith wipes his damp palms on the underside of the tablecloth. Ilka Beaumont is looking at him the way Coco should have. Lips slightly pouting because she believes those are her best assets. Her breasts too, he realizes, as she leans forward to adjust those David Yurman bangles. His confidence buoyed, he replies, "None, it's all me." She giggles.

Someone has turned up the volume on the bar television. A few of the kitchen staff have come out from the back. Evacuations remain in place. Several thousand more are expected. Another day of record winds. Expect red-flag warnings throughout the week.

"Christ," Mr. Beaumont says to no one in particular, watching the firefighters overwhelmed by ember assaults. He knows how his clientele gets when there's disaster in the air. They'll be demanding cocktails and music and distraction.

"We need a plan," he mutters under his breath.

Keith licks his lips. "If the wind changes we could do something out by the pool, dancing and margaritas."

"What about tonight?" Mr. Beaumont asks. The coffee and cognac arrive. The caramel-colored liquor in heavy crystal, the cream for the coffee in delicate glass. Outside, the wind gusts. The doors to the courtyard bang open and the waiters run to secure them.

"Oh lord," Ilka Beaumont huffs, Louie snuggled in her lap. "We're going to talk about the hotel, aren't we?"

"It's going to be one of those weeks," Mr. Beaumont tells his wife, shooting for calm. He sips his drink, smiles at Keith. "How shall we entertain our guests?"

"*We*—" Ilka Beaumont squeezes Keith's thigh beneath the table, eyes buzzing with kinetic energy. "Did you hear that? You're practically hired."

7.

In the Polo Lounge courtyard chairs are overturned onto tables, their tablecloths flapping wildly in the wind. Several waiters are folding napkins or stacking water glasses on trays. In their tailored white jackets, against the pink cinder-block walls that encircle the patio, amid the flowering hibiscus and towering bromeliads, they could be servants in a walled garden—and Marguerite their princess in a silk gown. She sends Coco on ahead to set up the bungalow the way she likes it. "Plenty of good vodka, and don't forget—"

"Find Ethan," Coco finishes. They laugh and kiss each other's cheeks.

The waiters smile as Marguerite and Kit pass by, elbowing one another. "Causing trouble?"

Marguerite flashes a haughty grin. "Always."

She glances at Kit, who's walking a bit behind her. Eyes

downcast, nail in her mouth. Dressed in something Marguerite can only assume was ordered online. No one would choose a cotton belted dress the color of a cabbage if they'd seen it in person first. Watching Kit, she's reminded of boarding school days when the scholarship girl would arrive with her plain clothes and earnest desires, and the daughters of rock stars and movie moguls and oil tycoons would argue bitterly over who would be the first to seduce her. She adjusts the sleeves of her dress so that they drape the way she likes and takes Kit's arm.

"Hubby will be with Mr. B. until well after lunch," she says. "Papa's good friends with the hotel owner, I practically grew up here. So I know the drill. Smoke in the air, freeways closed. Rumblings of protests—rioting already! Ouu, it's exciting." She clasps her hands together, that diamond in her nail flashing in the haze.

"Is that real?" Kit asks.

Marguerite touches the tip of her tongue to an eyetooth where another, larger diamond is embedded. "The quality isn't as good as this one. I'm a little pissed about it actually," she says, examining her nail.

"I have a gold crown," Kit replies, opening her mouth to show Marguerite. "And a silver one."

Marguerite giggles, a different sound than the shrill laugh in the Polo Lounge. This is excited and gurgling, a child discovering a new toy. "Ma petite chou has a mouth of precious metals."

She runs a finger through the bit of dirt that has crusted in Kit's hair. "Your hair needs brushing. And a different shade of blush, maybe a shock of fuchsia on the lips. Something to contrast all those innocent features. Otherwise Hubby will just keep railroading you like that."

Kit's about to object but then remembers how Keith had looked embarrassed by her appearance. How he had at first not stood to shake Sean's hand.

"He just really wants this job," she says.

But Marguerite's mentally scrolling through various outfits that might transform this new plaything. Mugler, Versace, Dolce & Gabbana, Balmain. There's a jaguar-print bathing suit that would be a riot.

She leads the way, silk dress undulating in the wind as a helicopter crosses overhead. Up in the hills, on the other side of Mulholland, firefighters are doing controlled burns. Hotshot crews cutting back brush and digging trenches. The wind carrying the sharp scent of brush aflame. The smoke stings the nostrils, scratches the throat. Makes their heads ache.

Kit gestures to the white-jacketed waiters. "Shouldn't they be inside?"

"You're funny," Marguerite says, pursing her lips. "Let's cut through here."

They enter the restaurant's private dining room from a sliding door. With the lights off, the tables covered in pink satin, the chairs made to look like gilded bamboo, dimly lit oil paintings on wood-paneled walls, it looks strangely impersonal. Like a diorama or a dollhouse. But then there are place settings with names written in calligraphy and crystal stemware and in the center of every table an intricate porcelain pot with tiny pink or blue roses.

"Ouuuu, I *love* when it's set up like this but empty." Marguerite sits at one of the tables. "What do you think? A bridal shower? No, those usually have balloons and catering has to do some lurid penis cake, and there was nothing in the kitchen this morning."

The lighting outside is strange. Muted and reddish, cutting through the windows like spotlights. Maybe the chairs are real gold and not lacquered wood; the ivy on the walls could be real too. Marguerite watches Kit touch the upholstered panels, running her fingers over the fabric. What must it be like to see this room for the first time? Excitement jolts through her.

"Come with me," Marguerite says. First she takes Kit to the mail room with its gold-plated mailboxes and Pink Hotel letterhead, then the boiler room because it's where she had her first kiss and she wants Kit to see how the corridors loop and bridge and end in mysterious ways. *Imagine playing hide-and-seek down here.* Or the secret entrance and exit to the garage that Mr. Beaumont had not shown them. Mimi Calvert's old roadster parked with its very own attendant; Marguerite flirting until he lets them sit in the car; Kit putting her nose to the creamy leather interior. *It still smells brand-new.* Then on to the koi pond, where hundreds of carp disturb the water's filmy surface, their mouths gasping. Marguerite slipping off her Prada sandals and letting the fish suck on her toes. Coaxing and teasing until Kit puts her feet in too. Two girls giggling and flushed.

In the Crystal Ballroom, Kit cannot hide her awe. Moon-eyed, mouth gaping.

You should see your face. Marguerite's diamond eyetooth twinkling.

Multiple balconies and chandeliers and in the center of the room one giant orb of glass roses, all of them crème and white. Various staff disassembling massive flower structures from a wedding the night before. They're derigging the stage lighting and taking apart the mirrored bar, fracturing light every which way. The girls exploring the balconies and stairwells and the secret area behind the raised stage. They find flutes with smudged lipstick and a bow tie stomped from a heel. *What do you think happened here?* They giggle.

Outside news helicopters circle freeway interchanges, traffic crawling to a halt. Multiple vehicles are on fire, the gray smoke billowing toward the wildfires in the hills. Schools are canceling classes, announcements will be made later in the day. Fire containment is at zero. Grocery stores are running low on bottled water and batteries. Those in the old neighborhoods feel that familiar tinge of dread. But in the Crystal Ballroom one of the employees has given in to Marguerite's pleading. She calls him Panda, and he lets her ride him around as if he were a horse. *They all have pet names because I can't remember their real ones.* Twice she whips him with a faux palm frond taken from the wedding arbor.

"Do you believe in the spirit of place?" Marguerite asks Kit once they've finally made it to Bungalow 5, hands and feet in bowls of warm water while small brown women fuss about them. "I want our nails to match those Damien Hirsts," she tells one of them, gesturing with her chin to two paintings above the fireplace. "Do mine like the yellow one and ma petite like the blue."

The palms outside the arched living room window flap violently in the wind. Shadows lash about the Spanish tile floors.

"What do you mean, *spirit*?" Kit asks. "Like ghosts?" She leans toward the Filipina working on her nails. "I'm sorry they're so chewed up."

"No, no, no—*spirit of place*." Marguerite's eyes get huge. She adjusts herself so that she's closer to Kit on the sofa.

"Some crazy things have happened in these walls. Where do you think all that energy goes? It builds up over time. You can't feel it?"

"I don't think so."

A pepper tree above the bungalow rakes its limbs across the roof.

"Maybe." Kit shudders.

But Marguerite has pivoted, she's telling the woman to add diamond dust to Kit's butterfly wings. "They aren't *real* diamonds," she assures Kit. "Well, they're real in the sense that if you took a hamburger and put it in a blender it's still technically a hamburger but now you have a smoothie."

Coco pops her head out from the kitchen, where she's mixing cocktails. "Are you telling Kit how your house is haunted?"

"I was just about to but you ruined it!"

Coco rolls her eyes.

"Shut up, it totally is!"

Outside, the wind howls. Leaf litter and dust twist in brief spouts and then disperse. Shadows stretch across the patterned silk rug, reflecting in the gilded mirrors and glass vases. Crooked as witch limbs.

Marguerite leans closer to Kit. "Okay, so our house was brand-new when we moved in, right? Tigran had it built for us. So it was completely clear of bad energy. Then last winter our maid cracked. *Devenue folle.* Had to go back to Colombia or Peru or one of those countries. She said the house had bad energy. You should see your face! Relax, ma petite, it was me. I kept spooking her. I tapped on the walls, ran my nails on the floorboards. Stuff like that. But then—this is the crazy part—things started happening that weren't me. I swear! Little things. Like the jacuzzi would be set to a different temperature than we left it. Maman swore someone had been in her closet, and once the oven door shattered and all the glass pieces were popping on the kitchen floor like they were possessed."

She likes the look of Kit's eyes. They're wide and deep and focused on her.

"Sometimes," Marguerite continues, moving even closer, "my room smells like someone else. I thought maybe our housekeeper had changed detergents or something but when I asked she said no. So I know whatever spirit that's there is from us. Ouu, what a monster it must be."

"Your cocktail, ma'am," Coco says, offering a tray of vodka and soda, little wedges of lime on the rim.

"Merci beaucoup. Now, *dis-le en Français*." She looks at Kit. "I'm teaching Coco French, I can teach you too if you want."

Coco rattles off a few words in a shy voice.

"You're getting better." Marguerite sips her drink. "But you need to say *mademoiselle* like this, *mad-moi-selle*, otherwise you sound Canadian and you want to sound Parisian. What are we doing for your nails, have you decided? Should we match them to Mr. B.'s bedsheets?" Marguerite looks at Kit and whistles. "*Oui, la maîtresse*."

"Behave or I'll tell Ethan not to come."

Marguerite blows Coco little kisses. "I love love love vodka and soda, don't you, ma petite chou? Drinks like water."

There is electricity in the air, the girls are skittish with it. Even the women working on their nails seem unable to keep still. They tap their feet in time with the music coming from the flat-screen TV. Twice the woman working on Kit's nails takes a phone call. Her tone is unmistakable.

"The fires?" Kit asks. "Is your family okay?"

"Yeah, fine." She smiles, working the dead cuticle from Kit's ring finger with casual expertise. "I live in Torrance. But it's exciting, isn't it?"

Marguerite drinks her cocktail quickly. She has a dull headache from being outside in the poor-quality air, and from dazzling Kit with stories of fashion shows in New York and Paris and Milan—summers spent on yachts, on private islands owned by wealthy expats. Her throat hurts from talking so much. Maybe she'd overdone it, had she overdone it? But no, Kit is in awe of this Marguerite Lacey, who has seen and done so much and isn't scared of anything. She'd slipped up only that one time. Wanting to hold Kit's hand when they entered the dark garage. But she recovered, even convinced Kit to pose in the bell tower, telling her, *I'm going to make you Instagram famous.* Her lips on Kit's, the mountains and palm trees behind them smoky and gray. There had been far-off sirens, and then gone. Swallowed up in the smoke. Only the blaring horns from the traffic on Sunset Boulevard and the noise from the construction site and the lingering taste of Kit's lips. Like the vanilla wafers you get in kindergarten as a snack.

Ethan arrives, his room service cart full of silver-domed plates. "There are seven fires now," he announces.

He reveals each plate, one at a time. A turkey club for Marguerite and Coco to share, a McCarthy salad for Kit.

"You're going to love it," Marguerite says. She's pleased with her nails. They are shockingly yellow, dotted and criss-crossed with green and gold butterflies, their wings shimmering. The butterfly on her left pinkie has two small diamonds for eyes. When she bites into her sandwich her nails pierce the toasted bread. She likes the violence of this too. Kit's nails are bluer than Marguerite would have liked, primary-color blue. Like something from an elementary classroom. *This is b-l-u-e.* But the butterlies' wings are iridescent and detailed, their bodies angled as if in midflight. She watches Kit wave her fingers to make them catch the light and flutter.

"And of course . . ." Ethan continues. Off goes another silver dome, and in the center of the plate is a pink box with letters in such flamboyant gold-embossed cursive that they're unreadable.

"These are the best chocolates in the world," Marguerite tells Kit.

"Do I get a kiss now?" Ethan asks.

Marguerite points to the corner of her mouth but Ethan kisses her on the lips.

"Naughty, naughty. You'll pay for that."

He unwraps the pink box and delicately removes the lid. Six perfectly square chocolates sit nestled in gauze, each of them flaked with sea salt and a tiny piece of gold paper that quivers in the cool, filtered air coming from the ceiling vents.

"Yes, please." Marguerite opens her mouth for him to feed her. He places a chocolate between his teeth and she bites the other half.

"Isn't there a baby shower you're supposed to be working in an hour?" Coco asks from the chair where she's getting her manicure.

"Canceled. Third event today."

"Then make yourself useful, since I'm immobilized. Make us another round of drinks."

Kit's toenails have dried too. She's dancing barefoot, admiring them against the pale pink carpet. Maybe this was where Elizabeth Taylor danced on her wedding night—or where Marilyn Monroe tiptoed to answer a call from the president. It doesn't matter. What matters is this is a room where things happen—where things *are* happening and Kit is part of it. How wonderful the carpet feels between her toes. This morning was just a bad dream. She thinks for a moment about Sean Flores and his comforting smile.

"Ma petite chou," Marguerite calls. "Come and have a chocolate."

She's put one between her teeth the way Ethan did, and waits for Kit to bite the other half. Vanilla wafers *and* chocolate.

"Is that lavender?" Kit asks, chewing. There's a dreamy look about her. Cheeks flushed, eyes serene and inky.

Marguerite shakes her head and spins her across the carpet. The music is turned up and for one song they are girls with pretty nails dancing barefoot on silk. The manicurists are being shuffled out the door, into the jungle of plants. The oasis of green in a city of ash and smoke.

"Let's go in our pool," Marguerite says, and pulls Kit into a bedroom, Coco just behind them. They undress Kit, arguing over which bathing suit will look best on her.

"I would kill for your breasts. Like two perfect brioches, I want to eat them." Marguerite makes a biting motion. Kit pushes her away, laughing and breathless.

"You turn into such a cannibal when you're high," Coco says. "Show us your model walk. Marguerite models, you know."

"Only if you take off that bra, it's hurting my feelings. What is it, Wacoal? Christ, take this one, Papa got it for me in Paris but the color is all wrong. Try it on."

Ethan bursts into the room with a bottle of champagne.

Coco and Marguerite pretend to be scandalized, but then all three are giggling on the bed and Marguerite reaches out for Kit, pulling her down to join them. Champagne gets everywhere.

8.

When Keith arrives at Bungalow 5, the door swings open and Ethan is standing there with a half-dressed youth on his arm.

"This one's wasted," he tells Keith, stepping past him. "Go in and enjoy yourself."

"Do you need help?"

Ethan shakes his head. "You're looking at a pro."

Inside there are young people everywhere. Many of them in bathing suits, studded with buckles and belts or Swarovski crystals. A spectrum of skin tones, of languages. The kitchen crowded with mezcal and grilled shrimp and little piles of caviar. A girl wearing cat ears is filling coupes with the clear liquor. She gestures for Keith to take one.

"What?" Over the music he cannot hear her. She holds the label out, waiting for recognition, and then points to the name impatiently.

"Right, fantastic."

She narrows her eyes but then prances away. Cat ears disappearing into the crowd.

Beside the record player, a pale girl, her hair and eyebrows a shocking white, changes the song. She's thin as a rod, and when she turns back to the tiled kitchen counter she stands on one leg, like a bird, carefully feeding herself sardines one at a time.

"If you're going to do a capsule collection for Macy's it's still got to look good," she's saying to the girl opposite her. They are a study in contrasts. A two-tone painting. Like exotic plants, flowering toward each other. "You know what I mean?"

"Do it on the cheap but make it look expensive," the Black girl says, smearing some of the oil from the sardines onto a cracker. A magenta bikini peeking out from beneath her oversized puffy jacket.

"Oh yes, ex-pen-sive. Otherwise what's the point?"

A rush of summer dresses as Keith returns to the living room—their fabrics light and flowy as if the girls wearing them are from another era. All of them flat-chested, with their hair parted perfectly in the center. But then he realizes some are boys. Their angular faces flushed, their lips large. Tattoos on their upper arms or necks. The Lacey twins brush by and smirk at his casual blazer and trousers. Never in his life has he been around such creatures. He drinks the mezcal fast, even though he's full from brunch, which had turned into an equally boozy lunch, Ilka Beaumont arguing with her husband over what would be appropriate entertainment. *There's a fine line between tasteful and garish*, she had said, adjusting the collar of her husband's checked dress shirt. They'd decided on a handful of events over the week. Keith made sure he was an integral part of each. Ilka tapping his wrist. *Keith Collins, you're a godsend.*

He leaves the empty coupe on a tray littered with crushed cigarette packs and tiny red straws and pushes his way through the crowd. In the sunken den, the redhead from the pool is lying on the living room rug, her head resting on the lap of someone not her husband, both of them watching the news with the closed-captioning on. Fires raging in the canyons, smoke billowing like cumulus clouds. Entire mountain ranges engulfed, the flames shrinking the horizon, condensing the sky into a black void. Requests for horse trailers, for larger evacuation centers, for donations of any kind. *People have lost everything.*

"The city is going to burn," the redhead says, and begins to laugh.

Keith follows a starlet he recognizes from TV out to the patio, where she asks the crowd where the fires will burn next.

"All the way to the ocean!" someone shouts back. Everyone cheering.

Is that his wife? *His* Kit? She's in a striking one-shoulder bathing suit, animal print—jaguar. Her nails are the color of lapis excavated from somewhere deep in the earth. Her hair is wet and slicked back so that it looks more couture, less country bob, and when she throws her head back to laugh, the jaguar spots on her breasts glitter. Flanked by Marguerite and Coco and a dozen young men and women he doesn't recognize. They could be nymphs and fawns in a lagoon.

He waits for her to notice him. Still buzzing from coffee and cognac and brandy, and now the mezcal, which has hit his stomach and settled there, smoldering. He can feel his blood in his temples. His hands shaking. He studies the blue veins in his wrists, snaking their way into his palms. Ilka had stroked them beneath the table. *Raised in Sacramento,* she had told him while caressing his little pinkie finger. *In a stuffy Victorian house, nothing but dust and loneliness and morals from a different century.* He'd made sure his smile touched his eyes, his mouth. Ilka Beaumont was the kind of woman who needed to *feel* a smile.

Thinking about this now, perhaps he should not have smiled so much. Flirting in hospitality is expected. Had he encouraged Ilka Beaumont's attention? Yes, of course he had. And Mr. Beaumont hadn't seemed to mind. In fact, he had seemed pleased. It was as if her flirting with Keith meant he'd been successful in choosing him as an apprentice. But toward the end of lunch, when Ilka kissed Keith's cheeks, lingering to tell him she enjoyed his aftershave, Mr. Beaumont became polite, even subdued. They shook hands, smiled cordially. His normally hyperexpressive face was tired and withdrawn. Perhaps Keith had not been as subtle as he imagined. Should he have mentioned Kit more, or less? *Her laugh*, he'd said when Ilka had asked what he loved most about her. *I fell in love with her hillbilly laugh.* Had he imagined a fleeting pain in her eyes? A tightening in Mr. Beaumont's shoulders? He'd meant to say "innocent," her innocent laugh. It was unabashed and open, something he could never be. But he said "hillbilly" because he had wanted the Beaumonts to know that he recognized Kit was not cut from the same cloth as them. She did not have Sacramento wealth, or even Nebraska motel money. No cozy craftsman near a university. Just a tidy mobile home outside Reno.

Kit has pushed herself up onto the side of the jacuzzi so that only her legs are in the water. She is saying something to Coco, who's facing away from Keith, so that all he can see is her mass of dark hair, the ends floating in the water like strands of kelp. Marguerite begins to gather it, a hair tie in her rosy mouth.

Do you think we can make the transition? Keith had asked Mr. Beaumont in a moment of weakness after Ilka Beaumont took her leave, Louie nipping at her heels. How resigned he looked when he motioned to the empty espresso glass that had been filled with foamed milk for Louie. *That dog*, he said, *had worms when we rescued it.*

"Keith," his wife cries. Her expression changes so abruptly that everyone in the hot tub looks at him too. "I'm sorry," she says, climbing out of the water and hugging him.

He removes her wet arms. "It's me who should be sorry, I've spent most of the afternoon with the Beaumonts."

"Hubby!" Marguerite shouts. "Everyone, this is our Kit's *mister*. Isn't he adorable?"

The girls in the jacuzzi nod and smile, their teeth dazzling white. A few of the boys reach up, their hands dripping wet.

Marguerite hoists herself onto the side of the jacuzzi. "Don't worry, we've taken excellent care of her."

He realizes then that she's topless—Coco too. She's emerging from the pool, her dark hair pulled back, breasts large. The left one hanging a bit lower than the right. She's laughing at him again, he can feel it tight in his throat, the way his stomach does a little unsure kick. She takes her time drying off. Stretching this way and that, breasts thrust forward.

"Lunch must have been grand," she says, before turning away.

Kit pushes her wet head into his sport coat. "Isn't it strange that the air is clear now?"

High above them, palms are bending in the wind, their trunks creaking. But here, in the walled patio, the potted and trellised plants are still. Their flowers bright in the silvery light. The only movement is the rippling across the pool's surface from where the starlet has just dived in fully clothed. Somehow she's managed to keep from spilling her drink. The crowd applauds.

"There's a dozen fires," Kit continues. "Animals are burning up in the hills. Did you see the carcasses? Not just pets." Her eyes are shining. "But here everything is fine, fine, fine."

"Are you drunk?"

"And a little high." She wipes her eyes. "I need a nap, can we go back to our suite?"

"Ma petite chou, stay a bit longer," Marguerite urges. She's wrapped herself in a magnificent chiffon robe. Prisms patterned all over it. "I want to introduce Hubby to all your new fabulous friends."

"And I'm sure he wants to meet them," Coco adds before taking Kit by the arm and toweling her off. "Let's get you out of the sun."

Time seems to speed up then. Keith is twirled around the courtyard like a debutante at a ball. There are stylists and producers, fashion photographers and entrepreneurs to meet. Kit is napping on one of the lounge chairs, Coco perched beside her while the white-haired girl and a brunette with Native American tattoos weave a flower crown for Kit's head.

An assault of conversation, everyone shouting over one another and the music.

Dad is a property developer in SF, but who wants to be up there? The sidewalks are ninety percent shit.

LA isn't much better.

At least it's condensed into one area.

I haven't been downtown.

I never go.

Liar, you were there last week, at G.'s gallery opening.

Oh, that was different, he can get the best coke.

He twirls and twirls, his feet growing lighter and lighter. Maybe with the next drink he'll float away. The mixture of laughter and cigarette smoke and the muddled sensation that something is happening, finally happening. To *him*. He's where the important people are, is maybe even important himself. Kit has been moved to Marguerite's bedroom, where it's quieter. Keith kissing her on the cheek. "Just a few more minutes," he tells her.

Then its fashion models and influencers and various people in public relations.

The fires are not great optics for the mayor.

The governor's got a plan.

Does he? This is America.

No one has a plan. Not anymore.

Keith can't seem to remember any of their names. He tries to list them in his head: Astrid, Etta, Paula, Flint, Gneiss, Leif, Nova—they could be colored pencils used to fill in the sky and sea, names of strata formations deep in the earth. Kimia, he remembers, is albino. Or maybe that was her Black girlfriend. The two are entangled on the couch now. Flowers grown into a two-toned vine.

Midconversation with a restaurateur and food stylist, Kit comes wandering back into the party. Everyone can see where the bathing suit cuts into her flesh, how her hair has dried wild. The offset stare and dulcet smile.

"What time is it?"

How quickly she's tanned. He takes her brown arm. "Time for home," he says, leading her back into Marguerite's bedroom. "Let's get you changed."

"Do we have to do dinner with everyone tonight?" She wraps her arms around him and pushes her face into his chest. "What if we ordered room service and stayed in?"

It's nice it being just the two of them. Door closed so that the party is muffled and far away. They are Kit and Keith of Boonville once more, comforted by the familiar smell and tender warmth radiating from each other's body.

Oh, antidepressants are awful, we only micro-dose. The Lacey twins have charged into the bedroom, Marguerite following behind with Coco.

The twins are in matching swim trunks, just as tan and toned as their father but with an impish hunger that makes Keith wrap Kit in the kimono so they can't keep staring at her.

"Have you ever shroomed, Hubby?" Marguerite asks. "My cousins are trying to convince me they do it all the time."

"It's true." They grin. "Shrooms are fabulous, *Margie*."

Marguerite frowns. Her pert little mouth no longer rosy but lime green. The same color brushed on the lids of her eyes. Small gold gems affixed along her brows.

"Kit wouldn't like it," Keith says, eyeing the twins. Can't they see his wife is indisposed? But still he smiles. "She's very straitlaced."

"I bet she is," one twin smirks.

Marguerite puffs on her e-cigarette, the smoke trailing from her green mouth up into her nostrils. "I'm all about natural medicinals."

"You take Valium," Coco starts. "And what about coc—"

"Oh, shut up, you take anything you can get," Marguerite says.

He watches Coco's throat work, the twins snickering. She's overstepped. Forgotten her place. Nothing more than a cabana waitress. Keith Collins is a guest of the Pink Hotel. Staying in a suite with his pretty new wife. He smiles at Coco, who looks away and begins folding the mess of clothes on the floor.

"We're staying in," Kit says from the bed. "Ordering room service."

The twins raise their brows. Teeth glistening in the low light.

"Can I get the bathing suit back to you tomorrow?" Keith asks Marguerite. "I can't find her dress."

Marguerite shrugs. "It's like a hundred degrees all week. Just keep it."

Somewhere in the bungalow a glass shatters, followed by collective cackling. Music is turned up. The bass buzzing the framed photos of Marilyn Monroe, the slender midcentury vases.

"Room service for breakfast," he promises his wife, squeezing her to him as he ties the kimono belt. In her ear he whispers, "Hang in there, sweetie. Do it for me."

She becomes more animated as they make their exit. Saying goodbye and hugging various people as if she's known them all her life. "Yes, we'll be there!" he hears her saying. "My husband planned the entertainment." She kisses a freckled girl's cheeks. *Bisous, bisous.*

Then it's just the two of them. The silent embrace of the landscaped gardens, a dull roar in their ears. The sky turning a stunning pink and orange. The wind pulling at the tops of the trees, dried leaves scratching the sidewalk as they tumble toward the grassy areas where azaleas and camellias and clematis are fluorescent in the queer light. Nearby, the construction noise quiets and then stops all together.

"Marguerite thinks her house is haunted," Kit says, tucking in closer to Keith. "Not by ghosts—by spirits. I'm not telling it right."

Crickets begin to chirp in the damp dark parts of the gardens. The lamps switch on, their faint glow haloed from the haze.

He can feel her trembling. She's wearing perfume, a scent he doesn't recognize.

"The news is relentless," she continues, pulling her phone out. "How will the construction workers get home if the canyons and freeways are all closed?"

"Babe, don't look at Twitter." He takes her phone and slips it into his pocket. "What are you wearing? Let me see."

She's so obedient. A tremor returns to his hands. He thinks of microscopes. How delicate you have to be when preparing a slide. Forceps to place an insect's wing or onion skin, or once he used scrapings from the inside of his cheek. A drop of water added, coverslip lowered slowly to avoid destroying the specimen. Always his hands trembled so that the forceps seemed unwieldy, the water too much or not enough, the glass forever cockeyed and a disappointment to his parents.

"Marguerite insisted I wear something expensive. I think it's Gucci."

She's turned to show how it rides a little high in the back.

"Things got a bit out of hand," she says, retying the kimono.

She tells him about the bedroom. About how there had been a moment with Marguerite and Coco and Ethan—when they were on the bed together, someone's leg, slim and strong (she suspected it was Marguerite's, but had kept her eyes closed), found its way between her own so that she gasped with pleasure. A hand cupped her breast, only held it.

"I was wearing a bikini top already," she assures him. "Bottoms too."

Keith listens, walking slowly through the darkening jungle, the smoke mingling with the dank plants and rich soil.

"I didn't touch anyone back. My hands didn't know what

to do—and then the doorbell, and Marguerite's cousins were there with all their friends—her bungalow has a private pool, and the party just kind of took over."

"Sit down, let's sit here," he says. The bench is wrought iron and a bit wet, cloaked in tropical plants and trees. "Are you cold? Come closer. That's my girl."

"Say something about what I just told you. Are you mad?"

A pandemonium of parrots screams overhead, fifty of them, all flying off toward the sea. The last orange hues in the sky ebbing.

"Did it give you pleasure?"

"But I love you."

"Pleasure and love can be two different things."

"I don't like it when you talk like that. I only want those things from you. Isn't that why we got married?"

He hesitates, imagining his hands are as steady as a real scientist's. They're holding forceps. He can see the glass slide, the microscope heavy and waiting.

"So what if Marguerite's leg made you feel good?" he says, finding his way beneath her kimono. "My fingers can do the same."

He studies his wife's profile. Eyes closed, lips parted. Her breath becoming irregular. Grasshoppers and crickets croon in the dark, a bassline for the noise from the hotel restaurant— the clattering of plates and forks and long stemware, the excited chatter of diners. He feels her relax and then arch into it. The wind has changed. Shrubs and trees and grasses shivering from a sudden gust, the reckless scent of wildfire pressing into them. Somewhere a coyote calls and her body gives a familiar little jolt, which is so reassuring he almost pants along.

"I love you," she sighs, her eyes brilliant in the sparse light.

For a moment he has the urge to leave. *Let's go home*, he wants to say. Not to the suite but back to Boonville. But then she blinks up at him, rubbing her eyes. "Is it snowing?"

Downy ash, silvery and fine, falls softly around them.

WEDNESDAY

9.

It's just before dawn, when it's coldest and darkest and no birds sing—and here comes Keith, newlywed that he is, entering his hotel suite drunk. He stumbles over the rug, bumping into the desk and love seat, leaning hard against an upholstered wall.

"Mrs. Collins." He stifles a giggle. "Are you up?"

Kit had heard him fumbling with his key card. She'd heard the elevator open and his footsteps. She hadn't really been asleep. The light outside was too strange. Pale and orange from the streetlamps, the smoke reflecting every which way like artificial sunshine, like postapocalyptic neon.

She'd left the party at the Polo Lounge last night when the fireworks started. Had someone really brought fireworks? Sober now, that seems ludicrous. But yes, the waiters had removed the patio tables, setting up chairs in rows. The Laceys' friends had sparklers—gone were the bathing suits and cover-ups and lightweight summer dresses. Everything was glamorous evening wear, sequined or studded or trimmed in furs. Never mind that it was a warm night. Or that more than a dozen wildfires raged across the city. Their mouths and noses were covered by couture face masks. Protection from the ash that had traveled from the San Bernardino National Forest; the Santa Ana and Santa Susana mountains; the Silverado, Yorba Linda, and Agua Dulce canyons.

Everywhere fires were pushing air up, up, the atmospheric instability accelerating the updraft's transformation. Kit read about it on her phone. Moisture condensed, water droplets mixing with ash to form a new kind of thunderstorm with even stronger winds, fanning the flames further, creating fire spouts that spiraled upward, tornado-like. The videos of it were surreal. Overwhelmed by ember assault, by smoke and heat, firefighters were forced to retreat. Dry lightning cracking overhead.

In the Polo Lounge the television played a nature show. A lynx in snow, macaws in the jungle, gray whales in the deep. Guests were given instant cameras. Movie stars and heiresses and CEOs of every kind snapping photos of their food or shoes or one another's faces. Wind blowing high above them, sending hot ash into the more densely populated neighborhoods, where an entire apartment building caught fire and burned to the ground in minutes. *Who's at fault?* Reporters want to know. The mayor and police chief and fire chief all looking at one another as the public flows down City Hall's steps, shouting, *Why did no one come to help us?*

But it's only midnight, Keith had said when Kit first wanted to go to bed. She recognized that look of disappointment. So she shut her phone off and stayed up. Played hostess to Keith's host. Drank the champagne offered to her, ate the caviar and chilled oysters, slurping the mignonette from a tiny silver spoon. She let Marguerite and her friends paw at her. *Ma petite chou is a waitress in Boonville.* What a novelty. She listened to them talk about the fires—about real estate prices dropping, about whether it was time to leave California for New York or Paris. Someone suggested Oslo.

But this is just something to say, to tweak the pitch ever higher. How boring would it be if the atmosphere were to stabilize? You want more, not less. Something to pierce the ennui. Maybe there will be blood—*Ooooh, how exciting.* You can sit back. Spectate. Blameless as Mother Nature burns it all down.

Around three in the morning Kit couldn't stand it anymore and left without Keith. He was with Ilka Beaumont and a group of housewives who ran some kind of Beverly Hills alliance. They'd been talking for over an hour about getting him into the Los Angeles Country Club.

Alone in the suite, she had willed herself to fall asleep. Orange light slanting across its pink floors, the forlorn furniture. Low voices in the hall, in the gardens below. She could hear the plants rustling outside, the groaning of their trunks and tendrils. Tropical flowers quivering in the hot dry wind. Once her mother had driven as far as Colorado Springs in search of orchids. Her stepdad had to come collect them. *Orquídea?* the nursery workers repeated, looking from mother to daughter. *A wild orchid, here?*

"Sweetheart," Keith says, his breath hot against her neck.

It's a relief to no longer be alone. To have him take up space in the room, whispering against the downy hairs at the nape of her neck, *Kit, Kit.* Kissing her skin, nuzzling lower. The heat of him, though, the oppressing rank of perfume and cigars and sulfur clinging to his clothes.

"You're drunk," she says, crossing her arms over her body. His shirt is damp, his blond curls and skin and everything sweaty.

He rolls onto his back, laughing. "*You're drunk*," he manages, wiping his eyes. "Do you know who you sound like?" He pushes a pillow beneath his head, his eyes already closed. "My mother."

She's unable to wake him. "Well, isn't this lovely," she says to the quiet room, pierced only by Keith's snoring. The sun is finally rising. She'd had an irrational fear that maybe it wouldn't and they'd be trapped in a world of pale orange and gray. But the strange light is gone. Replaced instead with something crisp and bright and almost blue. It's such a welcome sight that she slips out of bed and changes into her bathing suit.

The hallway is empty, the stairwell too. Somewhere a faint din of a vacuum. Downstairs the lobby is deserted and spotless. Everywhere the scent of fresh flowers—the floral arrangements have been changed to lilies and thistle and purple sprays of statice.

A pair of maids hurry toward the Polo Lounge, where banda plays low on a radio. Kit peeks inside. At the green leather booths littered with Polaroid snapshots and silver confetti; the empty bottles of wine and champagne, their labels as shiny as tinsel. The piano in the corner of the room sags. One of its legs is broken clean off. A housekeeper appears and waves her off.

"I'm surprised you're awake."

Kit swings around and there is Coco, in the same short skirt and blousy tunic that had caught the light as she and Mr. Beaumont ducked into the private dining room soon after the fireworks started. His collar unbuttoned, tie discarded, hand outstretched to find Coco's French-manicured one. Mrs. Beaumont had been standing right there, she'd watched them leave together. In fact, Kit was sure that Mrs. Beaumont had smiled at Coco or her husband or them both.

"Although, I haven't gone to bed," Coco says, shifting a large brown box against either hip. "Were you thinking of swimming? The pool is closed; grounds is having a hell of a time cleaning all the crap the wind blew into it."

Kit blinks. "Oh."

She could go back to the suite, roll around in the same twisted sheets that had trapped her during the night. And now Keith, passed out in his clothes. His hot arms trying to pull her close.

"Why don't you help me with these?" Coco suggests, handing her one of the boxes. "You can see staff quarters, and I'll make you a cup of coffee that isn't fifteen dollars."

They descend the curving staircase together, Coco talking about Mr. Beaumont tasking her with distributing air-pollution masks to staff. Kit glances down at her nails, at that shocking lapis color, the yellow, the shimmering diamond dust. They don't seem to belong to her; chewing on them would be akin to cannibalism.

Outside there's a strange chemical smell in the air, heavy and acidic. Everything is pink and blue, until it's not. Swallowed up by the jungle of tropical plants. She can hear the wind picking up, high above them tangled in the Chinese elms and southern magnolias.

"Did you have fun last night?"

For a moment Kit is sure Coco is asking a different question. If only she weren't so tired, the garden's warm wet perfume muddling her thoughts—hadn't the air just stung her eyes and throat, and now it's shaded and wet and heavy with plumeria and jasmine and orange blossoms. Maybe Coco disappearing with Mr. Beaumont while Ilka Beaumont watched had been a dream. What wife would smile?

"I don't know how you do it," Kit says, glancing at several gardeners, pads beneath their knees, pollution masks covering their noses and mouths, damp rags in hand to wipe ash from leaves. "The partying, all the champagne, and Mr. Beaumont—"

Coco looks away from her.

"I wasn't judging, I just noticed you and he—sorry, it's really none of my business."

"The Beaumonts have an arrangement." Coco sucks her lip. "Although I think he'd be faithful if that's what she wanted but she doesn't. Some women are like that."

"That's horrible."

Coco smiles at her. "Marriage is different for everyone."

They've walked to the same bungalows near where the tennis courts have been demolished. Potted bougainvillea still waiting to be planted, bags of manure stacked in the shade of the buildings. Roofing and painting materials, ladders and tools lean against their faded pink stucco walls.

When they enter there's music playing low. A steady line from the bathroom weaves between the dozen or so cots set up in the living room, employees hollering at one another from the second floor to brew another pot of coffee or, *Who has the blow-dryer?* One or two look over at Kit in her robe.

"Mrs. Collins," Ethan says from the half-refurbished kitchen, where he's buttering a slice of toast. Beside him Sean Flores is blowing on a steaming mug of coffee. The neck of his T-shirt stretched out so that she can see those tattoos. The colors duller than she remembered.

"Hi," Kit says to him. "You stay here too?"

Ethan leans against the linoleum counter. "Why would he stay at a motel when he can bunk with his cousin for free? It's all about the bottom line, ducky."

Coco's handing out masks. Kit stepping aside for girls with curlers in their hair, boys with towels around their waists, bodies still damp from showering. *I give these a day*, one says, fastening the paper mask over mouth and nose. *Ain't no way they're on-brand.* Kit's shoulders have relaxed. The quiet hum of ordinary people getting ready for work. This she knows. Ethan's handed her coffee and she's running a finger over the chip in the mug, thinking how different a room is when it's busy with purpose.

"How's the honeymoon going?" Sean Flores asks.

"Oh, that." She looks down and sees those nails—so out of place here. "The fires have put a damper on things. And Keith, my husband—"

"I didn't picture him with a mustache."

Ethan snorts.

"He's sort of here on a job interview," Kit goes on, her cheeks hot. "Do you know Mr. Beaumont? He gave us a really good discount, we'd never be able to afford a place like this. I'm just a waitress. Like Coco."

"You're not *just* a waitress," Ethan says. "*Mrs. Collins.*" He bites into his toast, sending crumbs scattering across the linoleum counter. Pleased that Coco's brought Kit to the bungalow. He likes how the hotel can take an average person and turn them into someone else—it never fails. Tourists from Albuquerque or Idaho or anywhere, it doesn't matter—plop them into a Polo Lounge booth, give them a cocktail in the proper stemware, and they're off and running. Let them spend a few nights and suddenly they think they're part of the fabric. But not Kit Collins. She had left the party last night. No one *leaves*. Not when they're from Boonville, California.

"Mrs. Collins," Kit is repeating, feeling the lips, tongue, teeth connect. The tiny force of air from her chest, or maybe lower. She's placed a hand over her diaphragm. How strange it is to have one name your whole life and all at once have another. "It sounds like someone else."

Ethan's blond brows rise. "Well, it's you, ducky."

"Where's the milk?" Coco is asking from the fridge.

"Pfffft." Ethan turns his attention to his friend. "Your gentleman caller drank the last of it. Why milk?" He looks at Kit. "Such a weird thing to want after sex."

"You're one to talk," Coco retorts. "Isn't Mimi waiting for her breakfast?"

Ethan clicks his tongue.

"Who were you before?" Sean asks. He's looking at Kit while lacing up his boots.

Somewhere in the bungalow a toilet flushes, a sink turns on. A shower shuts off. The music is turned up and the girls in curlers are swaying their hips while they apply eyeliner.

"Kit Simpkins," she says. Each syllable a root, a familiar tender thing.

"Is that a fresh pot?" one half-dressed youth asks, holding out a foam cup to Coco. His polo shirt draped over his dark brown arm. "It's gonna be one of those days," he says, pressing his lips together. "I can already tell."

"One of those weeks," someone lying on the cots calls out. "Don't I know it."

Coco tops up Kit's coffee too. "So what do you think of staff quarters?"

"You expected something else, right?" Ethan gestures at the pale green tiled backsplash, half removed. "They're replacing it with black granite. And the carpet, did you see it when you came in? Bubble-gum pink. Worn down by Prada slingbacks and Ferragamo loafers and all the rest. It'll be a more neutral pattern, silk rugs everywhere. What does Mr. B. say, 'Art deco meets Hollywood glam'?" His bushy brows rise and fall. "Of course, we won't ever see it. They'll move us way before then. Gotta air out the stench we leave behind."

"I've stayed in worse motels," Sean says from the doorway, hard hat under his arm. He nods at Coco, looks at Kit. "Try to stay hydrated today."

She sits up. "Absolutely, lots of water."

He tilts his head down to meet the hard hat. "Hasta luego, Kit Simpkins."

The door shuts behind him and the girls with curlers in their hair break out into giggles. "Your cousin is so hot, Coco."

"Did she really faint into his arms? *Jealous.*"

Ethan fans himself. "Muy caliente. Those tattoos."

"Come on," Coco says to Kit, rolling her eyes. "I'll walk you back. Maybe the pool will be open by now."

The pool water is dirty. Ash and leaf litter float at one end of it. Kit assures Coco she doesn't care. It's more familiar this way, like community pools, like the swimming holes at the end of hiking trails or trailer park rec centers. For several minutes she swims, forgetting about the hotel and the fires and the staff who have to live together, sixteen to a bungalow. She forgets to worry about Sean Flores and Keith, and who Mr. and Mrs. Collins are supposed to be. She does backflips and handstands—and then a groundskeeper is there with pool-cleaning equipment and she absconds with one of the pool towels, leaving a trail of water all through the lobby. Back in Suite 220 she rinses off and gets back into bed, breathless and happy. Keith rolls over to gather her in his arms and finally, finally she sleeps, dreaming of excavators and bulldozers and butterflies with bright blue wings.

Two floors below them, the hotel lobby is being descended on in droves. A traffic jam of luxury SUVs crowding the hotel driveway, valets sprinting to collect keys and tips, and *Welcome to the Pink Hotel.* Green-and-gold luggage carts cram the entry, brimming with Louis Vuitton luggage, pampered pooches yapping at one another from their plush kennels. The bellhops and porters and front desk managers breaking a sweat from this sudden assault.

Never mind that these new hotel guests have employed private hotshot crews, or that their fire insurance is full-coverage. Several don't have homes at risk at all. They've come for comfort. For the comped cabanas, the fabulous concierge doctor with his rejuvenation and vitamin IVs to combat environmental stresses. They've come for the endless Veuve Clicquot Rosé, for staff to smile and remember their names and how they like their room arranged; where they prefer to sit in the Polo Lounge, how they like their eggs at breakfast. Poached for the elderly blue-haired Mrs. Maison. Over easy for Mr. Petros and scrambled for his bodyguard. Omelets for the Smiths, gluten-free everything for the Daveys. The patio swells with residents from Beverly Hills and Malibu and every canyon in between. They chat with the servers, gape at one another, tense with anticipation. Then, all at once, their mimosas and spritzes and Valium kick in and jewelry-clad women and well-dressed men are leaning across booths, gossiping. Who's checked in, who's only just arriving, who might be joining later this evening. How the Oretas came straight from their private jet terminal, or the Rajovics took the last presidential suite.

The Sens had to get rooms at the Montage.

That's no Pink Hotel.

Not for times like these.

Have you heard? It was a downed LADWP power line.

Bill's on city council, he's going to have a long day.

Poor Bill.

Up in Suite 220, Kit turns over and burrows into her husband's side, where it's warmer and smells less of perfume and cigars and more just Keith. A familiar musk. He pulls her against him and they sleep deeply, entwined, through breakfast.

When Keith does waken, he's appalled with himself. He's still in his clothes from the night before. It's nearly one o'clock. He told Tigran they'd meet for coffee in the Fountain Room at eleven. Carefully, carefully, he removes Kit. When he stands he has to steady himself. His body is sore as if he'd run a marathon. There's an unfortunate taste in his mouth. How had things ended last night? He remembers only how close those Beverly Hills women were speaking to him. Ilka Beaumont twisting one of his curls around her finger.

He splashes cold water on his face, looks at himself in the mirror. There are bags under his eyes. He looks older—is that a strand of gray? Impossible. Only lighter blond than the rest. He steps into the shower and lets the water get scalding hot. He breathes in the steam. Remembers how he and Ilka Beaumont had watched her husband disappear with Coco into the private dining room. Coco looking right at them. Fireworks going off in the dark behind her. Thousands of tiny gold sparks. Ilka Beaumont smiling and nodding at the girl, as if giving her consent.

Are you okay? he had asked.

Oh, you're adorable, Ilka had said, tilting her face ever closer to his.

And how had he come back to Kit? Absolutely shit-faced, smelling like Chanel No. 5 and whatever floral-scented face powders they all used.

Ashamed of himself, he tries to think of ways to make it up to her. She must understand how much working here means to him. He's never wanted anything so badly in his life. How could he go back to Boonville? How could he possibly return to that life? If he cannot stay within the Pink Hotel's orbit—no. He doesn't want to think about that. Last night Ilka Beaumont implied she would make it happen. *You belong here*, she said, patting his leg. *Leave it to me.* He just needed to stay the course. Maybe not quite so much whiskey tonight, though. Then when Tigran offers him a Cohiba he won't fumble lighting it or clipping off its tip. He'll be familiar with Partagas and Romeo y Julieta, Montecristo and Plasencia. He'll do a quick search on his phone to learn the language. It's all about knowing the language.

A towel wrapped around his waist, he crosses the room to call the front desk. Maybe Tigran can meet for an afternoon drink. A little light on the phone blinks red. A message from the man himself, Tigran, who last night sashayed across the Polo Lounge, everyone wanting to hear him speak their name, for him to kiss their cheek because then it meant you were part of it. Part of the hotel, yes, but most important, part of whatever was unfolding here. You were going to be indoctrinated within its storied walls, imbibed by its lush jungle of ferns and palms and giant bromeliads. You were important and in the right place at the right time for once.

He's saying to forget about coffee. He'll send up breakfast

when Keith and Kit are awake. *With Mrs. Lacey's and my compliments. In-room dining can bring Tylenol, too.*

Hearing his easygoing voice, buoyed by the confidence that comes with—Keith doesn't know what, but he wants to. He swallows hard. Breathless with desire, hungry for it. How to have that which he lacks the language to even describe. Not just wealth or power or respect, but the world bending toward you rather than you chasing after it.

"We slept so late," Kit says, pushing the pillows away, untangling herself from the sheets.

Her hair is a mess. Like a child with a fever that broke sometime in the night. It sticks in clumps to her forehead. He goes to her, pulling the covers over them both. They are in their own tent of smooth linen, the light making everything pink—their skin, their limbs, their lips. She laughs her birdsong laugh.

"Kit, I'm sorry I was so drunk last night. Do you forgive me?"

His skin is cool and clean against her. The smell of grapefruit overpowering the lingering chlorine on her own.

"You know I can't stay mad at you. But maybe we should calm down a little, we probably spent a thousand dollars just on brunch."

Facts and figures. He can feel it dragging him back to that life where he will never be equal—not with Tigran, not even Mr. Beaumont.

"We're pretending, remember?" he says, smoothing her hair. "Let me worry about it. This is our honeymoon."

He kisses her, long and lovingly, because this is Kit, his Mrs. Collins. Her eyes are dazzling even beneath the covers. That feeling of possession, of her belonging to him and no one else, comes over him. He holds her close.

"Do we have to go downstairs for lunch?"

"I promised you breakfast in bed, we're staying right here."

He pulls back the covers to reach for the phone, returning them to Suite 220 with its plush-carpeted floors and rugs and large windows facing the gardens, where parrots screech as they cross from pepper tree to poolside palms, the cabanas and recliners below swelling with hotels guests who need piña coladas and rum coconuts and the pool attendants to get that spot—right there, where they can't reach. Otherwise they'll burn.

10.

"Is that live music?" Kit asks, as she and Keith step out into the little garden above the pool.

She takes his hand, satiated on brioche French toast and bacon and the fact that Keith had made her stay in bed while she ate. More coffee? He was up and fetching it from the dining cart. Milk? Just a splash, and he stirred it for her too. Tapping the spoon against the porcelain to make her laugh. He climbed in bed beside her, and she fed him bites from her plate, the afternoon light dappling the comforter with trees caught in the gusting wind just outside.

"The mariachi band was my idea." Keith grins. The image of his young wife in bed still fresh in his mind. How the breakfast tray slid a bit and coffee spilled. Those nails so blue and perfect, glittering against his chest, reaching for his curls. How her eyes shut and her mouth opened—and when he flicked his tongue she made a faint panting moan. "Mari-achi Son de Fuego," he says, a flourish on each word.

A solitary trumpet plays a mournful tune, but then strings swell, a Mexican guitarrón joins in, and a man's voice, smooth and mellow, croons.

"Beautiful," Kit sighs.

They descend the stairs together, toward the pool, where every cabana is taken, every pink chaise recliner, umbrellas standing open, tip to tip, their underbellies patterned with banana leaves. The Cabana Cafe is just as crowded. Each candy-striped booth, every four-top table is cluttered with bottles chilling in plastic buckets. Ceiling fans made to look like palm fronds circling overhead. Between the Roman-style columns, a mariachi band in Jalisco-style uniform is performing. Their gray-and-gold sombreros sharp against the laurel hedges and broadleaf lady palms, the jasmine and clematis, white as christening dresses.

"We were lucky to get them," Keith tells Kit. "So many freeways are closed."

The harpsichord meets the violins, swelling together, and reports of citywide unrest seem impossible. *Stay indoors*, city officials advised on social media. Household accidents have increased. Domestic violence up tenfold. Viral videos of fights breaking out in grocery stores, in parking lots. Costco, Walmart, Target—lines at the door before they open, shelves empty of water and toilet paper. Headlines of hospitals swollen with asthma patients, with stab and gunshot wounds. The mariachis belt a high note and the hotel guests applaud and whistle. One attempts a grito.

Some of the guests are wearing face masks. Fashionable with beading or sequins or fabrics that look supple and expensive. The staff are not wearing any.

"I thought you'd like a pink one," Marguerite says, looping

arms with Kit and steering her toward a cabana. "Maman won them last spring at a charity event. Who knew face masks would be in fashion this season, ça va!"

"Oh, but we wanted to lie out in the sun," Kit says, looking at the pool. Gone are the leaves and twigs and dead bugs. It is a tourmaline jewel, beneath its surface the same liquid silence, the essential blue solitude.

"But then you'll have to pay for everything," Marguerite says, making a face. "And it's much more fun to charge it to Maman. Hubby, here, so you can match Tigran and the twins." She hands him a black mask made from the same plush material as theirs.

She gestures to her cousins, who are stretched across the daybed. Dark-haired and svelte, each with the luxe face mask hanging around their wrist. Occasionally one or both will put it on and take a selfie.

"Is Tigran here?" Keith asks, looking around as a pool attendant hands him a glass of prosecco.

"Thank you." Kit smiles at the attendant, recognizing him from this morning. Dressed in the crisp white polo shirt and khaki pants—he could be about to board a yacht. "Looks like you were right," she says. "It's gonna be one of those days."

He smiles politely and moves away.

"Where's Coco?" Marguerite is looking around the pool. Her platinum blond locks smoothed back and glistening as if she'd already gone swimming. "Or Ethan? I know it's busy but they should check in."

She clinks her glass to Kit's. "I guess it's just us. *Salud.* Did you hear about the drama this morning? Where were you two anyway—never mind." She giggles, finishing her prosecco in one gulp. "*Newlyweds.*"

Kit blushes, Keith clears his throat.

"The hotel staff were all wearing these paper masks. The blue surgical kind you see at like ERs or urgent cares. Maman was horrified. I mean, the air isn't that bad. Maybe somewhere else, but not here." She's taken another drink from a passing attendant. "Only way to get rid of a hangover is not to sober up—anyways, my cousins made a big stink. They have fifteen million followers, and all the employees looked like they worked for FEMA. I'm just telling you what happened, personally I don't see what the big deal is. We're wearing masks—ugh, they're looking over. Wave."

The twins have their phones aimed in Kit and Keith's direction. Music swells again, drowning out the sound of a helicopter overhead. Marguerite is saying something to her cousins that makes them turn the camera on her. They're laughing and egging her on as she poses. Lips pursed, eyelashes batting. Across the way the pool attendant is taking a photo with a group of women giggling as they press their masked mouths against his brown cheek. *Besos*, they cry over the mariachis' crooning.

Mírame, miénteme, pégame, mátame si quieres, pero no me dejes, no me dejes nunca jamás.

Keith has spotted Coco. She's mouthing the lyrics to the bolero, weaving through the crowded café, holding a tray above her head, the drinks perspiring in the heat. Several tables try to get her attention but she sails right past them. The lone bartender wipes his forehead with a dirty rag, shaking his head. A busboy, who'd been running around refilling waters, collapses beside them.

"A break, my friends," the mariachi says into the microphone, his forehead damp. The hotel guests clap and whistle. That same woman attempts a grito, this one even shriller.

Keith calls to Mr. Beaumont as he passes the cabana.

"Everything running smoothly?"

"I'm swamped," Mr. Beaumont says, looking at his watch. "Half of in-room dining didn't make it into work. And the foreman and construction manager want to halt construction. Said if they can't get day laborers to the site they have to postpone. Postpone!"

He starts to turn toward the lobby, then the café, then abruptly drops into one of the cabana chairs, exhausted. His shirt collar a bit discolored from sweat. "The bungalows have to be finished on time," he mutters.

Keith glances at Kit, who is posing with Marguerite in their pink face masks. The twins filming them clinking their crystal flutes together in a toast.

"Let me get you something cold to drink," Keith says.

"Something with alcohol," Mr. Beaumont replies, rubbing his temples. "They trust you more if you take part."

Keith nods. "Then you're an accomplice."

"Exactly."

The mariachi band starts to play again, this time a lively polka.

"The hotel is at capacity," Mr. Beaumont confides once they're sequestered in a corner of the café, sipping mojitos. "With our most demanding clientele."

Keith surveys these elite evacuees. In the center of the café a man in a Brunello Cucinelli suit pulls a silk dress from an Hermès shopping bag. It hangs delicately from his pinkies by its straps. Tables and booths on either side hoot and holler, beating their hands on their thighs. The redhead from the other night begins to remove her cotton shift, the mariachis switching tempos so that she can sway her hips. She dances some kind of mock flamenco in her lace underwear. The man, when he's had his fill, slips the new dress over her head. It

catches on her panties, so for a brief moment while the mariachis begin to sing, one tanned butt cheek peeks out from
beneath a five-thousand-dollar silk dress.

*Eres mi prenda querida, mi prenda querida eres, la perdición
de los hombres, son las hijas, las mujeres.*

"Our guests need somewhere to unwind," Mr. Beaumont
is saying. "Somewhere they feel safe, and to them safety is
anonymity and consistency. I can drink with them, have a
cigar—by my being complicit they feel safe with me. But I
can't be everywhere at once. Standards are slipping and that
won't do."

A sudden gust of wind launches a pool umbrella high up
into the air. A Black pool attendant races to intercept it before
it can impale a woman in a Fendi bikini, who's filming the
whole thing. Never once does she look up from her screen.

"They need chopped salads and tapered palm trees and
blue-cheese-stuffed olives. It's the details that make the place.
Otherwise they might as well be at home. Fresh flowers in
the lobby, pecan sticky buns in the Fountain Room—the in-
room dining tables have to be perfect mirror images."

He gestures as if the table were in front of him. "A vase
with a calla lily in the center, rolled pink napkins on either
end, tiny salt and pepper shakers placed at a perfect angle."

"If you need help," Keith says, licking his lips, "I can certainly step in."

"No, I couldn't do that. What would Mrs. Collins say?
This is your honeymoon. I wouldn't be able to look her in
the eye."

Kit has taken off her robe. She's in the jaguar-print swimsuit borrowed from Marguerite. Keith watches her cross from
the cabana to the side of the pool. She doesn't jump in, she
gets down on her butt and scooches.

"We're talking about quality control," Keith says, finishing his mojito, the mint a cool blast to his sinuses. "That's my area of expertise," he tells Mr. Beaumont. "It could be a trial run, to see if I can cut it. Kit will understand."

Marguerite is folding Kit into a towel now. And there is Coco beside them with drinks on a tray.

"I'd be an idiot to say no," Mr. Beaumont says, shaking Keith's hand.

The mariachi players mop their brows and belt the final note to a norteño, helicopters crisscrossing in the heavy haze behind them.

11.

The sun has started to drop, making the sky neon. Or maybe it has already set and this is only the reflection of fire and smoke. If she stares long enough maybe the sun will break through and she'll know what time of day it is, how long she's been floating in the pool.

Kit saw the guilty look on Keith's face when he returned from talking to Mr. Beaumont. *I'll take you to Hawaii, to Paris, to Rome. We'll have a hundred honeymoons. I'll make it up to you.* How could she object? Keith wants to work here, he wants their life to resemble the Beaumonts'. She knows, too, that it's more than that. There'd been a moment when Tigran dropped by the cabana, cigar between teeth, and Keith had stopped trying to explain things to her—the importance of opportunity, his need to do this. Instead talking to Tigran about Mexican San Andrés cover leaf, binder from Honduras, filler tobacco grown in Nicaragua. When had he learned this? She imagined Keith on his phone, in between brioche

French toast and getting ready for the pool, researching cigars to impress Tigran. She felt further betrayed. Their intimate morning sullied. *Does it really have notes of leather and toasted vanilla?* he had asked, and Tigran, grinning, offered Keith one from his pocket case. The two of them walking off together. Probably with Mr. Beaumont now, discussing whatever entertainment they had lined up next.

She kicks her legs slowly in the water, careful not to hit any of the children swimming around her.

In this queer lighting, everything is muted. The lemon trees that separate the Cabana Cafe from the pool, the potted lavender, the bougainvillea-covered walls. Then the wind kicks up, the haze shifts and parts. The sun is coming out. Technicolor clicks on and Dorothy is in Oz once more. The lemons are yellow, the lavender purple. The sky the tranquil blue of surrender. Impossible that this afternoon a protest at City Hall turned violent. Riot police with their batons, firing tear gas into crowds, rubber bullets too. She had read it on her phone. The headlines and hashtags and live videos.

Here a dragonfly skims the water's surface. And other, stranger insects. Tiny green beetles no larger than a child's fingernail. Jewel-toned spiders, dusty white moths. *Of course*, she had told Keith. *It's fine*, she reassured him with a kiss.

A ladybug struggles in the water nearby; she lets it climb onto the tip of her finger.

After Keith left to meet with staff, Marguerite was determined to cheer her up. Out came rum coconuts, heaps of chopped salad, more sparkling wine than anyone could want. *Ma petite chou*, Marguerite cooed, petting her. But then one of the trumpeters from the mariachi band caught her eye. *I'm such a sucker for barrel-chested men*, she said, watching his lips on the trumpet's mouthpiece while touching her own.

Coco had come by a few times. *We're so short-staffed*, she said, apologetic. *Otherwise I'd stay.* Ethan delivered a box of gold-flaked chocolates. Tigran and Mrs. Lacey drifted in and out, now they were up on the terrace, smoking the hashish someone had brought from Morocco.

Adult guests, Kit realized, didn't swim. They only lounged with drinks and drugs and jewelry that caught the light and reflected like animal eyes.

Even the little girls in floaties, whom she'd been swimming with since Marguerite invited her barrel-chested mariachi into the cabana and pulled the curtains shut for privacy. Even they have diamonds in their ears, delicate Tiffany chain necklaces around their fragile pale necks.

I have to potty, one says to a nanny, who patiently waits for her to climb the stairs in the shallow end. *Let me do it myself.*

The water is oily, and when the wind picks up, Kit can smell the remaining children in the pool. They give off an aggressive equestrian scent. Like hay, like carriage houses from some long-ago century.

She gets out and the same attendant from earlier hurries toward her with a robe.

"Here you are, Mrs. Collins," he says. A drop of sweat weaves down through his fade. She wants him to call her by her first name, to know where he's from. Ask, do you have family affected by the fires? But he has that polite, plastic expression employees have when dealing with a guest. She recognizes it because she is usually the employee. How to signal to him that she is different?

"Does madam need anything else?"

"No, thank you."

The Cabana Cafe is closed now, there are two girls in

tennis skirts clearing ice buckets and half-eaten food and hundreds of coconuts. Neither one is Coco.

She doesn't bother letting Marguerite know she's leaving. The cabana curtain is shut and she can hear that forced artificial laugh, occasional chirping in French. Quickly she climbs the stairs, glancing at Tigran and Mrs. Lacey and a dozen others puffing on hookahs as the sun begins to drop into the horizon. Older women are gossiping over iced coffee drinks in the small garden above the pool, a plate of pecan sticky buns picked over on the table between them. One of their teacup Pomeranians begins to bark. *Hush, hush, who are you barking at?*

In the lobby she makes for the elevators, the bellboys and front desk staff smiling and calling out, *Good afternoon, Mrs. Collins.* She reaches the elevators but then stops. Housekeeping will have cleaned the suite. Pillows fluffed and bed remade, towels stacked or folded. All traces of their morning spent in bed together erased. Soon, turn-down service will bring cookies and cold milk for two. She can't stay here.

The wind is blistering until the tropical gardens swallow her up. Then it's quiet except for the pollen and seeds and tiny flowers that tangle around her flip-flops. A sudden blaring slices through the silence. The roar of heavy machinery, the shrill turbulence of electric tools. She walks toward it. Repetitive hammering, beeping, the gravelly rumble of tractors and diggers. Sounds of earth being pulverized, of trees being dug up, of asphalt breaking apart. She recognizes Sean Flores even with a bandana around his face. Wind flapping his vest open, his boots slipping as he slides down a gravel pile. Oh, lost little wife, you want to be on that gravel pile with the big white sky turning pink behind you, don't you. Boots crushing anything that gets in the way. Confident in your anger, not embarrassed and impotent. *Of course*, she said to Keith. *It's fine.*

Limbs shaking, she ducks behind a eucalyptus tree just as Sean looks up. She hurries back to the main garden, where it's landscaped and perfect. The aloes blooming, despite it being September. The hydrangeas too. Everywhere azaleas and honeysuckle and jasmine vines. She breathes in, remembering how relieved Keith had been when she said it was okay. How he'd kissed her and said, *You are the best wife.*

Kit Collins, Kit Collins, Kit Collins. She's walking along, that name beating in time with the jackhammering, when she sees it. Beneath an overgrown bauhinia are dozens of feathers, bloodied and yellow. Here a little bone, there the torn wing. A finch, she thinks.

"Kit!" Coco cries, taking her by the arm. "Thank god you're here. Mimi hurt her knee and I need help getting her back to the bungalow. What are you looking at? Don't touch it. I told you all kinds of animals are coming down from the hills."

She lets herself be steered away.

"It's the damn gardener's fault," Mimi Calvert laments from the ground where she's lying, grass and mud smeared along her side. "Always overwatering."

Her dress is magnificently large, it balloons over her feet, her arms. It's so oversized that Kit at first can't find Mimi's outstretched hand.

"What do you expect?" Coco says, taking her other one. "It's been a hundred degrees for weeks. If they didn't water, everything would die."

"Oh, pooh-pooh, I don't need a lecture. Help me up. Careful, I might have sprained my ankle."

"I thought it was your knee." They pull Mimi upright.

"Are you a doctor, Miss Courtney? No. Just get me back to my bungalow, please. This child is going to help you? My god, aren't there any men around? Child, go to the construction site and get one of the brawny fellows. A cute one, for the love of god. No? All right, all right. I marched for women's rights. Let the women do it."

"Ready?"

"Careful, careful."

They reach her bungalow at a slow pace, Coco shouldering most of Mimi's weight. The most difficult part is navigating the stairs, but eventually they make it inside, which Mimi keeps blissfully cool. The rooms are dimly lit, most of the light coming from a dozen or more candles. There's the strange, impersonal scent of a hotel—commercial cleaners—but also a bouquet of other scents, all of them clashing. Dried hay, turpentine, tobacco and cedar, bitter orange and verbena.

"Norma Jean can do a lot of things," she says once comfortable on a plush all-white sofa, her leg propped up on an ottoman. "But she's still a monkey. What I mean, children, is that she shits a lot. The candles are a necessity."

"Mr. Beaumont has told you before not to leave them lit."

"Are you going to tell on me? Don't be boring, please. I have such a headache. Call the concierge doctor, or better yet, get us some gin from the kitchen."

"Mimi, the hotel is very busy—"

"You can't let me drink alone, it would be rude. Plus you work for me, so you can't say no."

"I work for the hotel."

"I said *don't* be boring. Now humor me, dear. That's a good girl."

Coco disappears into the kitchen. Kit can hear ice breaking.

"Child, I forgot your name."

The name is still hammering away in her brain, pulsing in her limbs. It comes out louder than she meant to say it.

"Kit Collins," Mimi repeats, her lips pursed. "Dear, you're making me nervous hovering like that, sit down, please. You were here yesterday, or was that the day before? They all run into each other, have you noticed? You will."

The sofa sinks deeply. Kit has to adjust her robe so that it covers all of her. She's self-conscious and crosses and un-crosses her legs. In this light the sequins on Mimi's dress shimmer. She looks like a painting of a duchess or a queen despite the fact that she's smeared with mud.

"You're newly married," Mimi says. More a statement than a question. She's fanning the dress out on either side of her. "We're worse than an English village around here. Everyone knows everything about everyone. Isn't this dress lovely?"

Coco returns with a tray of martinis, to Kit's relief. But then even Coco in her uniform looks less out of place than Kit feels. She doesn't belong in this lavish bungalow, with its rose-pink carpet and fine art in thick gilded frames.

"The only reason Coco came to my rescue was because she thought someone had thrown out a Lanvin, and came to have a closer look," she says, pressing those thin lips in Coco's di-rection. "You know it's true."

"Oh, for heaven's sake. You were asking about Kit's mar-riage," Coco says, handing her a martini. "Mimi was married five times, isn't that right? She's an expert in matrimony."

"Each husband richer than the last, god bless them." She raises her glass, sipping with her eyes closed. The crease be-tween her brows relaxes, her nostrils flare slightly. She sighs. "Would you like some advice?"

Kit steals a look at Coco, but she's using her pinkie to push the lemon rind in her gin aside.

"It's advice for you both." Mimi smiles when Coco looks up. "Yes, even you, Miss Courtney, who has all the answers. Has this place dialed in." She leans back into the cushions, lightly fluffing her silver coif with her free hand. "I see how you and Mr. Beaumont behave. I know that Ilka allows it— for the sake of her marriage, she says. Always we do things for the sake of our marriages."

The light is fading, the room is growing darker. Mimi Calvert is glowing, from the gin, from the sequins, from some inner wisdom that comes with age and heartache.

"I loved each of my husbands, truly. Not the marriages, I couldn't stand being tied down—being tied *into* a man like that. You can get lost in a marriage, my dears. You can lose yourself."

"Isn't that the point?" Kit says. "Two people becoming one."

"Oh, child, lose yourself in love by all means. That's all we have in this hideous life. But don't confuse love with marriage. Marrying someone doesn't mean you know them any better. You can be married to someone and think you know them intimately, and then, well, it's hard enough to know yourself."

Coco downs her martini and places the glass sharply on a Louis XV gilt bronze side table. Overworked and hungover, she is not in the mood. Yes, she's Mr. Beaumont's *mistress*, but that's just a label. A lot like *wife*. Or *niece*, or *cabana waitress*. That isn't who she really is—yet at the moment she can't think of any other way to describe herself.

"It's a fantasy to think love exists at all." Coco has risen from the wing-backed chair where she'd been sitting. "Best to enjoy yourself before the apocalypse. Haven't you heard, the whole world is burning. Another round?"

She marches back into the kitchen. This time the sound of ice breaking is vicious. It could be bones splitting, ligaments snapping. Kit remembers the torn little bird beneath the wilting bauhinia.

"I hope I haven't depressed you," Mimi Calvert says, leaning toward her. "Young and romantic is a terrible combination for a girl nowadays. Always has been, I suppose. But now more than ever I worry—"

Outside on the patio Norma Jean is making a terrible racket. She hollers and shrieks, trying to get her mistress's attention. Mimi gets up easily and walks to the bay window, wrapping her knuckles against the glass.

"Ignore her," she says, turning back to the living room, the dress rustling against the carpet. "She's being a brat because I put her outside. She broke my last Herend—a precious little box turtle. I had my own little menagerie of Hungarian porcelains. A peregrine falcon, a Sumatran tiger, an elephant—my fourth husband gave them to me every year on our anniversary."

Coco returns with three more martinis, this time with olives, the liquid nearly sloshing over their rims.

"She hates being in her cage," Mimi continues, taking the fullest one. "But look, it's almost the size of the entire patio. Larger than the apartment I grew up in. Are you surprised? It seems like a different life now. If I never smell Ralphs fried chicken again it'll be too soon."

Coco joins Kit on the sofa. In the kitchen she cracked the ice out of the tray with real violence. Twice she hit it against the counter and didn't care if it broke in half. She would have preferred that. Why can't she think of other words to describe herself? She had wanted to be a singer, but that was years ago. She gave up on that around the same time things heated up with Mr. B.—she'd thought, here's someone who needs her. Not just him, but the hotel too. How many years has it been? She doesn't want to count. Her hand was steady when she measured the gin and vermouth, though, steady too when she stabbed the olives with garnish picks. Always the consummate waitress, she observed bitterly.

"Oh, you do make a good martini, Courtney. Better than Ethan, but don't tell him I said so. He has other—attributes."

The capuchin has settled down now. Its tiny head tilted as if considering them.

"Why were you in the gardens anyway?" Coco asks, raising her drink toward Mimi, then to Kit, who looks completely out of place. In her robe and bathing suit still, face pale from the gin, from hearing that marriage is not all that it's cracked up to be. Well, good, she thinks. Time for young Kit Collins née Simpkins to grow up. But then something wet and shining rolls down Kit's cheek, and Coco realizes she's crying.

Mimi has turned back to the bay window, studying her reflection in the glass. It's nearly dark. Parrots shriek as they cross the sky, settling in for another night. She wraps an arm around herself, feels the bones and sinewy muscle beneath all that fabric.

The young women sip their cocktails, waiting for their elder hostess to remember their presence. But she's lost, gone somewhere else entirely. For a moment Kit feels her sadness, it is palpable. Alone in her bungalow, in this hotel. The dining room table already set for dinner for one: bone broth in a rimmed soup bowl, crudités on a salad plate, the hotel's insignia engraved at the bottom of both ceramics in pink and green. Norma Jean joining her to finish off the basket of rolls that in-room dining always sends but Mimi Calvert never eats.

Finally, looking at her watch, Coco clears her throat. "Were you looking for Ethan? I can have him paged, if you'd like."

"Can't an old woman walk in her gardens?" She's still facing away from them. Her voice has lost its charming lilt. "Tell me, girls," she says, finishing her martini. "Do you ever get lonely? I think I've felt it all my life. With every husband, even when I had my child—especially when I had my child. Isn't that horrible?" She presses a manicured fingernail against the window, Norma pawing at it from the other side of the glass. "I feel it most when the hotel is full. It becomes very loud."

All at once the patio lights up. The sconces on the walls, the lamps in the gardens, the tiny strands of lights around trunks of majesty and Mexican fan palms. Her reflection in the glass is gone. Gathering her dress, she goes to the corner of the room, to an exquisite mahogany encoignure, and removes a cigarette case inlayed with pearl from one of its cupboards.

"A present from my first husband. You love your first the most. They're all dead now, of course. Every single one. I'm all that's left. Cigarette?"

12.

Never has Keith felt such fabrics. Silk that yields in his hand, cashmere as soft as Kit's cheek; ties in bright prints or pinstripes, their boxes stacked atop one another, a colorful wall towering above him. *These came in from Venezia just last week*, the salesman said when Keith and Mr. Beaumont arrived, opening one box after another for them to admire. Dozens of orchids decorating the room, their blooms cascading like the Hanging Gardens of Babylon, like a courtesan's hair unpinned. More than once Keith had reached out to feel their soft petals, rubbing them between his fingers, hoping it might leave a trace of their scent. Kit would adore him smelling of orchids. And the cream marble floors, the mirrored walls that made the cozy shop seem twice its size, the enormous chandelier in the center of the room that set everything ablaze. He was swathed in luxury, cocooned in it.

If you're going to work for the Pink Hotel, Mr. Beaumont had said after they left the pool area, the mariachi band still playing, *you need the right uniform.*

Keith was prepared to accept whatever starchy fabric Mr. Beaumont had in mind. But they breezed past the laundry room, where rows and rows of staff uniforms hung in plastic garment bags. Industrial washing machines whirring. Up a flight of stairs, they nodded at security in their plain black suits, and then through a side door, which brought them into the long mezzanine hall where the suit shop glittered, classical music replacing the live mariachis.

"A perfect suit size thirty-eight, eh?" Mr. Beaumont says, looking Keith over just as the salesman returns from the back, his heeled loafers click-clacking on the marble.

"What about dove gray?" he asks, holding the suit out for Keith to inspect.

How wonderful it is to slip his arm through the jacket sleeve, the fabric caressing his skin. How perfectly it hugs his shoulders, his sides. He stands taller, tilts his chin so the light in the fitting room draws a hard line along his jaw. He thinks of kings and sultans and presidents. They're all clients. When he was being measured the tailor let slip stories of crocodile shoes for princes, vicuña sport coats for Bollywood stars.

Cary Grant had his suits made here, Mr. Beaumont added from the case of cuff links where he was inspecting a pair of chalcedony cameos.

Businessmen fly in from China, the tailor went on. *Spend two million dollars in a single afternoon.*

On what? Keith had asked, which made Mr. Beaumont laugh.

If you have to ask the price, the tailor said with a teasing smile, *you're not one of our clients.*

Yet here he is, Keith Collins, dressed in a mohair-lined suit. He tousles his curls, pushing them one way and then the other. He smooths his narrow mustache. Dabs at the sheen on his forehead with a silk pocket square. Above the lip, back of the neck too. He breaths in, shakes out his wrists, shifts his weight. It's the Timex that isn't working. He takes it off and shoves it into his trouser pocket.

"Now you look the part," Mr. Beaumont says once he's emerged from the fitting room. "How do you feel?"

He'll be spending the next several hours running point for in-room dining. The role of food-and-beverage manager is a difficult one. The employees will have to feel he's one of them, but also a cut above. They'll be reluctant. Who's this guy? Some twenty-seven-year-old flown down from Hicksville who silently yelped at the suit total and signed the receipt with a shaking hand. The guests would be even more difficult to navigate. Unsure and suspicious of anything new. They'll spot a fake and snuff it out.

Mr. Beaumont has removed a pair of Italian loafers from the front window.

"I couldn't," Keith starts, but then he remembers how Tigran had snipped the tip of his cigar with such casual violence. And he just held his hand aloft until a pool attendant appeared with a box of matches and then Tigran was puffing great clouds of toasted vanilla and leather without ever pausing their conversation, never taking his eyes from Keith because it was all expected. Like lunar phases and ocean tides.

The shoes complete the outfit. Metamorphosis has occurred. He can tell by how the salesman no longer has that teasing smile, Mr. Beaumont is no longer laughing. He's moved on, listing off what needs to be done to prepare for tonight.

"Shall we see how our guests are doing?"

Keith almost does a shuffle step out of the shop. He'll win the staff over. Slim and blond and authoritative in his lustrous suit, able to speak Spanish and a little Italian too. Soon he'll know the kitchen staff by name, have special handshakes with the waiters and bussers, and the old-timers will joke with him. *Jefe, el jefe.*

He'll go into overdrive with the guests. Flatter the men, flirt a bit with the women. He'll ingratiate himself with their children; a bosom pal to every pet.

The Polo Lounge is already humming with dinner guests.

Keith still has an hour before he has to meet Kit. What will she think of this new Keith Collins? He tugs a bit at his tie, loosening the knot.

Together, Mr. Beaumont and Keith do a walk-through, surveying their domain. Waiters in white or red jackets pick up their pace. Bussers and runners are quick to refill water glasses, even quicker about flutes of champagne, glasses of pinot noir or Sancerre.

Ilka Beaumont is drinking gimlets at the bar with her clique of Beverly Hills wives. She cries out when she sees Keith.

"Don't you look delicious," she says, caressing his lapel.

Tigran and Mrs. Lacey call them to their table.

"You and Kit should dine with us," he suggests. Mrs. Lacey, unusually alert, reaches for Keith's jacket sleeve. "What a gorgeous color." She smiles, her lips painted red. Nearby another table is eager to make this newcomer's acquaintance. Introductions have to be made. He and Mr. Beaumont work the room. He's Gene Kelly pulling off a tap dance, mesmerizing his audience.

"This is Keith Collins," Mr. Beaumont tells table after table.

Anything you need, I'm your man.

All is right at the Pink Hotel.

Absolutely, yes.

More mineral water at booth six.

Keith is captivated, he's forgotten the time, that Kit is waiting for him in their suite. Mr. Beaumont is telling a group of Hollywood elites about tonight's entertainment.

"Ukrainian synchronized swimmers," he says as he prepares their tableside steak tartare. The guests at the nearby booths craning to listen.

Keith touches his mustache. "The lead is a descendant of Catherine the Great."

There are oohs and aahs. Other tables want the same attention.

"Insatiable monsters," Keith quips after another hour of cajoling. They have talked to every guest, checked in with each waiter, exchanged jokes with the chefs and prep cooks, and laughed with the dishwashers. He is a dove-gray moth now, shimmering and lovely and full of confidence.

Mr. Beaumont grins at his protégé. "But if you know what they feed on, you've got nothing to fear."

13.

Since returning to Suite 220 from martinis with Mimi Calvert and Coco, Kit has received two room service deliveries. First was a pair of stilettos and a dress that Keith had picked out especially for her to wear tonight. The salesman in the suit shop had talked him into it. *So your wife can complement your suit.*

A Saint Laurent minidress in metallic silver crepe, as short as the tennis uniform Coco wears. With a V-neckline that plunges from collarbone to the base of the sternum. The fabric ruched at the center to draw the eye.

Wear with the stilettos, the note instructed. *Will be up soon xx K*

She took a bath, expecting he'd come in any moment and join her. They'd stay in the water until it cooled, talking over the day's events, like they did at home. Resolving any arguments, misunderstood remarks. It would be a rejection of what she'd felt in Mimi Calvert's bungalow, when that distance between her and Keith became an almost tangible thing. An expanse so wide no marriage vows, no amount of love could bridge it.

Surrounded by dissolving bubbles, she thought of Norma Jean stuck in a cage as large as a Los Angeles apartment, asking her mistress from the other side of the glass, in sad squeaks and grunts, *Love me, please love me.* And when the capuchin was ignored, left wanting, how it tore up its cage, breaking this and that, shitting and screaming and baring its tiny fangs.

Keith was still not back after her bath, so she wandered the room in a robe, opening and closing drawers she had not explored before. All of them empty, except for the bedside one, which had the requisite hotel Bible. She flipped through its onionskin pages with the same feeling she got whenever she held a Bible: a slight curiosity, quickly overtaken by her ignorance and fear of religion and God. Her mother had been suspicious of all religions, group sports, anything with what she called *herd mentality.* Kit had to beg to be in Girl Scouts, and even then her mother embroidered *Kit Simpkins* across her sash. *So you don't forget who you are,* she had said. And then she met Kit's stepfather and seemed to transform into someone else entirely. Suddenly she liked beer, didn't mind the television on during dinner. She made five-layer bean dip and whooped during basketball, hockey, and football games. Sure there were cracks in the façade, how many times had Kit seen her mother cry in the car? Or, later, her interest in gardens, in orchids, specifically. *Some will only bloom for a few hours.* By the time they went all the way to Colorado Springs in search of one, the marriage was struggling, twelve-year-old Kit unsure how it had worked in the first place when her stepfather had never known her *real* mother. It was soon after that road trip the Volvo swerved into oncoming traffic.

This was when room service arrived the second time—Kit thinking of her mother suddenly saying, *Put your seat belt on.*

No note from Keith, he had not even thought of sending dinner. No, it was from Mr. Beaumont. A tray of chocolate-dipped strawberries and cherries, delicate marbled caramels, and guava jellies. *We hope you are enjoying your stay*, the note read. *Love, your Pink Hotel family.*

She had nearly eaten them all when the phone rang.

"Keith?" The edge in her voice surprising her. "Is that you?"

Marguerite's shrill laugh. "Ma petite chou, has he still not come up? Well, forget him. Come to my bungalow and we'll go down to the aqua ballet together."

She hears others in the room. Someone saying something that makes Marguerite put on that exaggerated gaiety.

"Really, ma petite, don't wait for Hubby. We're much more fun."

"I'll meet you there, when does it start?"

More pealing laughter.

"Start? It's been going on for hours, just come to the pool when you've given up on *Mr. Collins.*"

Kit hangs up, annoyed and furious with Keith. Where is he? She dials the Polo Lounge and is immediately assaulted with noise.

"Yes, hello? Mrs. Collins?" the hostess shouts. "I'm sorry, I can't hear you."

"Never mind." She slams the receiver down.

Dressed and ready, she paces the room, her stilettos making tiny points in the carpet. Too much sun, too much gin—too much something has emboldened her. Before Keith—life before Keith, she cannot recall. Would Kit Simpkins descend into the hotel alone? She feels like yes. At what point did she start *needing* Keith?

Guests in the hallway are growing rowdier and rowdier. She can hear their laughter, their fumbling feet on silk carpet. The rattled excitement of unbridled anticipation. Like children without a bedtime. Shrieks, hushed conversations come from the other side of the suite door, from the gardens down below. Sounds that are faintly animallike. It could be a nighttime safari.

She's about to forget the whole thing, but then catches sight of herself in the large darkened window. The bobbed hair, the shimmering dress, the way her large eyes recede into the black sky beyond.

The suite door bangs shut behind her. The hallway is now surprisingly empty. Cautiously, she makes her way toward the elevator, the banana-leaf wallpaper waving on either side of her. Several times she almost turns back but the sweet, beguiling scent of night-blooming flowers entices her forward.

The light fixture in the elevator is askew from some brouhaha that had happened earlier in the night when a group of couples swapped partners from the fourth floor to the mezzanine. She adjusts it just as the doors open and the muted noise from the lobby is assaulting and boisterous. The screeching laughter of girls, like those green parrots that cross the sky. A swarm of male voices, as they cross the lobby for the stairs to the gardens. Pack animals, always. There are other sounds too, the kind that make up jungle canopies and cannot be deciphered from one another.

A chorus of *Good evenings* from the bellboys in the lobby as she passes by, from the attendants at the front desk, the hostesses at the Polo Lounge. *Mrs. Collins, Mrs. Collins, Mrs. Collins.* The name rings out, directed at this long-legged girl in a two-thousand-dollar dress, tottering in stilettos as she descends the curving staircase toward the pool. Lapis-blue nails, butterflies gilded in gold so that they cannot fly away.

On the mezzanine that intoxicating, punch-drunk scent is stronger. Someone has propped open the doors to the pool. Otherworldly and bewildering. Hotel guests mill about the small garden. Electronic music pulses. Chinese lanterns sway in the palms above, tiny white lights wink in the birds-of-paradise and bromeliads below.

The pool area has been transformed. On one side are the cabanas, but the other, where the recliners had been, is a makeshift amphitheater. Strobe lights rippling across the crowd. In the water girls swim in unison.

Twice Kit thinks she spots Keith, but then he's gone, or was never there at all.

"I like the way your legs go up, up, up," a man says, taking her by the arm.

They stand watching the swimmers for a moment. The electronica and strings are joined by a chorus chanting. One swimmer is held completely out of the water by the others, her muscular body taut in a nude swimsuit, crystal beading over the parts that matter. Hands sliding along her sides. Limbs moving in unison. Legs, toes, arms, fingers. The water moving around them as if it were alive. Applause from the amphitheater.

Could this be the same pool from this afternoon? From this morning? Kit looks up at the sky for some sign that this is the same place. But there's only the bright impartial moon, a smattering of stars. *Luminous spheroid of plasma*, her mother taught her about stars when she was little. *Held together by its own gravity.*

Do fires still rage? When she was in the bath waiting for Keith, she'd turned on the TV in the mirror. Nine thousand structures had burned. Not in any neighborhoods she's heard of—Silverlake and Santa Monica and Culver City were all safe. It happened south of the 10, east of the 110 and 210 freeways. In areas where there are more police in combat gear than firemen. Live feeds of protestors in air-filtration masks, in bandanas and makeshift balaclavas, using their bodies to block traffic. EAT THE RICH, their signs read.

This gentleman who has secured Kit's arm is done watching the show. He's steering her toward the Cabana Cafe, saying something in her ear. There's a large gold watch on his wrist, its hands two sword-shaped sapphire crystals.

Coco in her tennis uniform is at the hostess stand, menus in hand. She smiles blankly until Kit fidgets, her nail sliding between those pearly incisors.

"Kit?" she says, staring at the dress, the strappy stilettos. "Mrs. Collins, if you're looking for your husband—"

"What are you waiting for?" the man beside Kit says, his watch hands glinting at pearlescent Roman numerals. His forehead shining. "I can see an open table right there."

Coco leads them across the rowdy café. Every table in possession of a chilled bottle of vodka, piles of caviar, trays of crostini.

"Mr. Collins is in cabana number eight with the Beaumonts and the Laceys," Coco says, waving an approaching waitress away and pouring the vodka herself. "Do you want me to let him know you're here?"

Kit sits up straighter. "He can come get me."

"If you were my wife," this man is saying—how sweaty he is, even the bridge of his nose glistens—"I wouldn't let you out of my sight."

She feels his hand on her leg and shifts away from him. The music has changed. Gone are the strings and chorus, which had made it less hostile and aggressive.

"Sit closer," the man says, shooing Coco away. "That's right. Drink your vodka. You're a placid little thing, aren't you?"

He pinches her thigh. She doesn't slap his hand away. She's thinking about Kit Collins being *a placid little thing*. Does Keith think this too? She's going over all the times he's chosen the restaurant and ordered for her—but he knows more about those kinds of things. She'd never have ordered osso bucco herself, or known to eat the marrow. But then there are larger things. Like the apartment, or the wedding, the sommelier course. Now their honeymoon.

"There you are, ma petite chou," Marguerite cries, her mariachi in tow. She's refused to let him change out of his Jalisco costume and forbidden him from speaking English.

"I like it better when I can't understand a word," she explains. She's in a high-necked halter dress of metallic brocade silk, a slit revealing a large swath of thigh.

The mariachi says something to her in Spanish, motions to their drinks and stalks off toward the bar.

"Come with me, ma petite, we can do better than this. Junior, how dare you, this is my meat." She taps the man's greasy nose with her green-and-gold claw and pretends to bite him. He laughs, throwing back his head.

"My mistake." He holds up his hands. "I forgot, this is the Lacey playground, we're all just visiting."

"Damn straight," she says, smiling so that her diamond eyetooth catches the light. "Goddamn, look at those legs. Kit Collins, you are delectable. Let's get you to the cabana before these hyenas tear you to pieces."

Kit does not recognize any of the pool attendants by the cabanas, except for Ethan, who winks when they pass by.

"They're from the construction site," Marguerite says over her shoulder, a ribbon of silk waving from the back of her neck down the length of her bare back. She's holding Kit's hand, pulling her through the crowd. "We had to make do, short-staffed and all that. Mr. B. is paying them in cash."

In her cabana are a dozen hotel guests, surrounded by vodka and empty satin pink boxes, their chocolate wrappers crumpled on the floor.

"Don't you look gorgeous," Ilka Beaumont says from the sofa, Louie on her lap.

The dog raises its fluffy white head, tiny pink tongue hanging out. It jumps down and trots toward Kit, sniffing her stilettos.

Tigran whistles long and low. "Turn for us, dear."

"Saint Laurent?" Mrs. Lacey's shawl slips from her shoulder, Tigran stroking her arm. "I used to have legs like that."

"An ass too, Maman." Marguerite laughs. She picks up Louie and presses her face into his corkscrew curls.

"There's my wife."

It's the right voice, the same curls and pencil-thin mustache. But this Keith Collins, rising from beside Ilka Beaumont on the sofa, is all flash and sheen. The suit, even in this dim light, is reptilian. Kit steps back when he approaches her.

"I missed you," he has to shout over the music. He takes her hands. "Sweetheart." He kisses her hard mouth.

This she recognizes. The warmth of his lips and hands. Even the pleading—especially the pleading. *It's a public persona, it's not me—please.* She has a choice to make. She could tell him off right there, everyone shocked, Keith embarrassed. Or she could lean into him. Let go of her anger and let the distance between them dissolve. A placid little thing, this Kit Collins.

"Don't be angry, please," he whispers against her. "I've very nearly gotten the job."

She accepts the chilled cordial of vodka he offers. Tossing it back in one gulp.

"Someone's thirsty!" Marguerite has laid down on the pink daybed, two brunettes on either side, both of them in slinky tight dresses. They're playing with Louie, mocking his yipping. *Awoooooo*, they howl.

Keith draws Kit deeper into the cabana, eager to show her off. She looks exactly the way he wanted her to. How long her legs must look to Tigran and Mr. Beaumont, how smooth and lithe.

"Your husband was a great success today," Mr. Beaumont is telling her. "I could not have pulled this off without him."

"Nostrovia," Tigran says over the thumping music.

Awoooooo the girls on the daybed howl at the dog, at each other. They're a mess of limbs, play-fighting until dress fabric has ridden up, exposing slender curves, pale lines where underwear should be—now they're only playing with each other.

The daybed is in the middle of the cabana, in full view of Ilka on the sofa, Tigran and Mrs. Lacey on the love seat. They, all of them, are watching as if this were part of the show.

"Kit," Marguerite says, pulling her onto the bed to join them. "Come here."

Keith looks at Mr. Beaumont for some signal, some sign that he will not have to sacrifice Kit in this way, but he's lighting Mrs. Lacey's cigarette.

"Merci," she breathes, touching her lips to his cheek. Her hand tense and white on Tigran's leg.

Keith goes to Kit, who is looking at him with her wide large eyes.

He kisses her as if it were just the two of them, as if they were up in their suite beneath the covers. French toast on its way. Afternoon light making their skin pink. Marguerite has sat up on her knees, hungry for a taste. So he shows her. They're on the daybed now, Keith moving to watch Marguerite kiss his wife.

It's easier if Kit pretends this is a dream. The vodka shots help too. She keeps her eyes shut as hands that are not Keith's travel along her body.

"Quiet or Maman will hear you," Marguerite tells one of the girls, giggling. But behind her Tigran and Mrs. Lacey are busy themselves. The curtain to the cabana is not shut and outside are hotel guests with pool attendants, lights swirling around them.

The string instruments have returned, the choir too— only they're singing a religious hymn now. It starts small, then it's loud and fierce. Kit can't imagine anyone dancing to this, it's aggressive and ugly and she's thinking of that goddamn Girl Scout sash again. An object of ridicule to the other girls in the troop but Kit didn't care. She wore it anyway. Kit Simpkins was not a placid little thing. When one of the girls slips her hand between her legs she pushes her away. Marguerite too. She waves Keith off when he tries to stop her from leaving.

"Kit," he calls to her. "Kit, come back!"

Someone is screaming. Then multiple people. Glass shatters. Hundreds of heels, loafers, dress shoes stampede across concrete. Guests trip and fall, some dive right into the pool. The music still grating, lights blinding so at first Kit can't tell what's happening.

A path has cleared for it. Such a thick neck, its shoulders and muscles working as it pads forward. Strobe lights catching its muscled body. Louie between them, barking and snarling.

She's watching it breathe, mouth slightly open. Larger than she would have imagined—how ludicrous Louie looks in comparison, like a toy for a child. She's imagining it crushing her chest, teeth peeling back flesh.

There are shots. Distant, Kit thinks. But then her ears are ringing, and the mountain lion is dead, close enough that she can see its ragged fur ruffle in the wind. Hotel guests come nearer to it. A girl in a salmon dress kicks it with her Louboutin heel. Mr. Beaumont is there with Keith, who pulls Kit to him, shaking her gently. She doesn't hear him, though, she's focused on the redhead who is sprawled on the ground just behind him. Her Hermès silk dress trampled with shoe prints, that murderous diamond ring twisted oddly on her finger. There is crimson coming from her skull, leaking into the pool.

THURSDAY

14.

"I've got to take this down to laundry," Keith says, laying his dove-gray suit out on the bed. He looks at Kit in her night-gown, sitting up in bed with a pink cloth napkin across her lap. The cup of coffee beside her untouched. "If you get dressed you can come with me."

She sinks lower into the bed, pushing aside the breakfast tray that in-room dining brought at the exact time that Keith had specified. *Thank you, Mr. Collins, sir.* Keith signing the bill without looking at the attendant or the total.

She had watched him eat, unfolding and refolding her napkin into a French pleat, a trifold, a cardinal hat. The poached eggs in his corned beef hash gooey so that when he cut into the yolk it oozed onto the pinkish brown meat. He wiped his plate clean with buttered rye toast. Then moved on to a yogurt parfait, crunching on the granola while reading headlines out loud from his phone. *Why do protests always turn violent? A hundred people arrested, what good will that do them?*

His breakfast dishes have given the room a funk. The bits

of dried egg, the ketchup from his hash, the yogurt turning hard in the glass. Beside them, on a small ceramic plate, are two pecan sticky buns. Absently, Kit picks at one of them, the orange-brown sunlight streaming in through the window. Smoke has blown in again, twice as thick as before. Occasionally she can smell the burning; it's an acrid, skittish scent.

She keeps thinking about the redhead. How Mr. Beaumont had directed Keith to remove the unconscious body. How swift and efficient her husband had been. How the music had never stopped, the DJ playing on, the hotel guests drinking and dancing. Mrs. Lacey was agitated but then a concierge doctor gave her an IV infusion right there in the cabana while the Ukrainian swimmers finished their performance and the brunettes switched their attention from Kit to the mariachi, who had arrived with tequila shots. *Caballitos.* Marguerite wearing his sombrero. Kit did not know what happened to the redhead in her trampled Hermès gown. Part of her doesn't want to know. There were no sirens, no ambulance was called. And now Keith is acting as if the stain on his suit isn't someone's blood.

"Come on, babe," he says, sitting on the bed beside her. He caresses her arm. "You can be my assistant. No more being apart. I don't want any of that. I want you with me all the time. Okay?"

He does not like the glassy look in her large dark eyes. Or how when he reached out in his sleep she rolled away.

"The pecan sticky buns are made with real Ceylon cinnamon," he says, cutting into one. "From Sri Lanka."

He offers her the bite. The fork hanging in midair between them. His smile is too wide, watching Kit chew, her eyes still not meeting his. "You can't have cold coffee with a fresh cinnamon roll."

He goes to dump out her cup in the bathroom sink. That is a gray hair, he can see it clearly now in the mirror. There are several.

"The cinnamon roll is cold too," she says from behind him. "Just let me shower, I'll be ready in ten minutes."

She's surprised when he joins her. Tries to remind herself that this is what she wants. Reassurance by way of his possessive mouth. Distance bridged by those exploring hands. The thick steam, the shower walls closing in on them. She has to mimic the sounds, playact the spasms and expressions of pleasure.

"You're so beautiful when you come."

She busies herself with buttoning her sundress to hide her shame. Her disappointment that he couldn't tell the difference.

He kisses her shoulder. "I'd be jealous if anyone else saw you like that. You know that, don't you?"

"Would you? I thought pleasure was different from love."

He frowns. "I didn't say that."

"Yes, you did. You said it almost verbatim."

She's gotten ready quickly. There was no trying on various outfits and asking what he thinks, no switching shoes three, four, five times and posing in front of the mirror. It was as if he weren't in the room at all. She's standing in a blue sundress, dotted with little yellow flowers, purse over her shoulder as if she were leaving the hotel without him.

"I don't think you need your purse."

She shrugs. "I want to bring it. Are you ready?"

Down in the hotel last night's fervor had given way to a general malaise. At breakfast guests milled about aimlessly, restless and disappointed. Was a dead mountain lion to be the apex of their drama? They were like those in the city who saw the fires and protests and riots and began to stockpile groceries. Buying carts of water and toilet paper, frozen foods and diapers, milk and eggs, every type of bread and cereal and flour—their fevered, delirious excitement increasing at the sight of emptying shelves. Only to find that they were plenty stocked the next day. *How anticlimactic*, they all thought. But aloud they said, *How reassuring*.

There was chatter of leaving for estates on the East Coast, ranches in Idaho or Wyoming, chalets in Switzerland, penthouses in Manhattan or Paris. Then one of the waiters let slip that a home in Hancock Park had been vandalized by rioters and burned to the ground.

Doesn't Peggy Nasar own a couple properties in that area?

I think it was one of hers.

No! Well, that area has always been iffy.

Poor Peggy. Can you imagine?

Their skin begins to prick. Elation and dread rekindle in their stomachs. The TV in the bar is switched on. Multiple fires burn across the Angeles National Forest, effectively blocking travel north. Hearts skip a beat, chopped salads are ordered, oysters shucked. Nearby, a wildfire burns from Topanga to Malibu, embers catching parts of Kenneth Hahn, blazing into Crenshaw and Inglewood. Smoke plumes turn the sky inky black, shrinking the mountains, collapsing space and time. *How small we are*, one of the younger hotel guests says to his mother, who asks if she can smoke her cigarette inside. *The air is terrible out there.* Images of firefighters exhausted and defeated, of stucco homes consumed by flames, of singed palms and burned-out cars and leveled apartment buildings and convenience stores. Live clips from the mayor's daily briefings with his task force in dark suits standing united behind him. Face masks on because the air has turned toxic.

Tiny American flags pinned to their lapels, shiny as new pennies. The hotel guests are breathless and quivering once more. *Turn up the volume*, they shout to the bartender. No one will be leaving the Pink Hotel.

By lunch politicians have joined financiers, Hollywood executives, and CEOs in the bar. Tigran buying the first, second, and third rounds. Gone are his linen pants and casual dress shirt, replaced instead with an impeccable suit, the bright patterned tie knotted at his throat, a fuchsia pocket square pulling the eye to his broad chest.

I've donated five million to relief funds.

We've donated twenty-five.

A toast to our contingent.

Here, here, to the private fire crews.

I don't know what I'd do if Benedict Canyon burned.

A pair of tourists in a booth nearby crane to listen. Self-conscious in their department store clothes and Birkenstocks. "This is no time for outsiders," Tigran says to Mr. Beaumont, who nods in agreement.

By the time Keith and Kit arrive in the lobby, security has increased and the hotel has closed to the general public.

"There you are," Mr. Beaumont says, walking briskly toward them. "On your way to laundry? They can get that stain out. Then I need you in the kitchen—the guests are quite excited this afternoon. We're overrun with orders. Ah, Mrs. Collins." He takes her hand. "How are you feeling today? We were concerned you'd be too frightened to leave your room."

"Why would I be scared?" Her voice is sharp.

"Babe," Keith is saying, squeezing her arm. "I think Mr. Beaumont is joking."

"Right," she says, forcing a smile. "Because of the mountain lion."

Mr. Beaumont's smiling that gracious, impersonal smile. "Not many women are brave enough to stare one down."

"Sorry." Kit forces a chuckle too. "I might be a little hungover."

"Haha, well, you aren't alone. We definitely enjoy a party around here. Marguerite was asking about you, Mrs. Lacey is having a late luncheon in her bungalow and you're invited."

Keith tightens his grip on his wife's arm. "I was going to show Kit the back of house." He glances at his wife. "There's massage chairs and flat-screen TVs, even a frozen yogurt machine in the cafeteria. We have nothing like that in our hotel back home."

A slight arch in Mr. Beaumont's brow is all that's needed for Keith to second-guess himself.

"If that's okay," he adds quickly.

A prick of disgust. Does he really need to ask for permission? She removes her arm from Keith's grip and pretends to look for lip gloss in her purse.

"Of course it's okay," Mr. Beaumont says, his expression back to being one of eager acquiescence. "You're guests here. Anything you want you shall have."

He lowers his voice.

"You know," he says, gesturing to the Polo Lounge behind him. "Don't tell anyone in there, but a lot of us prefer the food in the staff cafeteria. Same chefs, same kitchen. So you can imagine how well we eat. And the pies and cakes— those pecan sticky buns everyone loves so much—whatever isn't eaten, goes to the staff. I gained fifteen pounds when I first started working here, Ilka was not pleased. Ha!"

A howl of male cries comes from the Polo Lounge. The news has long since been switched to a golf tournament and one of the players has sliced it. A hostess runs out looking harried and shows Mr. Beaumont her tablet. Keith looks too. The three of them trying to figure out some seating fiasco.

Mrs. Marasco always sits at that table.

Her cocker spaniel prefers the lighting there.

What if we moved the music producers?

Kit snaps her purse shut. "I can go to Mrs. Lacey's luncheon if you're needed here."

"No, no," Mr. Beaumont says, finishing up with the hostess, who scurries away. "We can manage without your husband for an afternoon. Perhaps a couples massage in the spa afterward?" He pauses. "Well, not *this* afternoon, Tigran is determined to throw a black-and-white ball—something to divert us from this hideous business happening in the city. We have meetings lined up with event planning, food and beverage, security."

"Of course." Keith nods, finding Kit's hand again.

"Coco should be downstairs," he continues. "The Cabana Cafe and pool are closed. The air quality is just shameful."

A front desk assistant has hurried toward them with another urgent matter. Someone of great importance has just arrived. Mr. Beaumont listens, taking a tissue from his pocket and dabbing his forehead.

"I'm being pulled every which way today." He grins. So many white teeth. "But have Coco show Mrs. Collins the ladies' locker room. Fair warning, though." He winks. "You'll want to work here too. Keith, I'll see you in an hour in the Emerald conference room?"

He doesn't wait for an answer, he's already striding across the lobby to the front desk, where he gets down on his knees to greet two regal greyhounds on long red leather leashes. That megawatt smile never slipping from his face.

15.

The small garden area above the pool is empty except for an elderly blue-haired lady letting her Pomeranian pee on a half-crushed Chinese lantern that's fallen from the palm trees. The air is so thick with smoke, the tiny coiled lights around the wild banana and kumquat trees are as bright as if it were dusk.

"Who's this little guy?" Keith asks, bending down to pet the dog.

The woman looks at Kit for a brief moment, her eyes sweeping over the bobby pin in her hair, the blue dress with the tiny yellow flowers, the no-name, faux-leather purse.

"We made quite the mess," she says, returning her attention to Keith. "Didn't we, Mr. Collins? You must be shocked by how we behave."

Still petting the dog, Keith grins up at her. "Mr. B. wouldn't want you to see this area until we've properly cleaned it up. I'll have to swear you to secrecy."

Her smile is slow and languid. She touches the tip of her finger to Keith's curls.

"I swear," she says, glancing at Kit again.

The gate to the pool stairs is locked. Keith has to use a master key, which he shows Kit, thinking it will impress her.

"With this I can go anywhere in the hotel."

She nods. There's an ache behind her right eye. Maybe she should have eaten more at breakfast or maybe Marguerite is right and the trick is not to sober up. The light is playing tricks on her. It could be late in the day or early. They could have been here three days or three years. The plants, the pink stucco, the wind in the palms—she has known it her entire life or else it's completely foreign. Keith too. He is part of the scenery. Woven into the space surrounding them, exactly where he wanted to be.

"The air out here is awful," he's saying.

Out come the face masks Marguerite had given them. The material soft and luxurious. How nice it is to have half her face covered, to have only eyes available for communication. She does not have to talk or smile. Not at the groundskeepers replanting a bed of begonias, which have been trampled by a careless pair of Jimmy Choo heels. Or the maids in the cabana, in black uniforms instead of pink, white ruffles at the shoulders as if they were from another era. Their mops and brooms and other cleaning materials in wheeled trash cans to better push around the concrete, sweeping shattered bottles, mopping sick from beneath the booths. The café waitresses in their tennis skirts are collecting dishes of half-eaten things. They load tubs and roll them away. Napkins have blown into boxes of cyclamen, cigarette and cigar butts pushed into their soil. Garbage floats in the pool too, joining leaf litter and ash from the fires and someone's silk stocking.

The employees are all wearing flimsy paper masks, but still they must smile with their eyes, saying, "Hello, Mr. Collins. Hello, Mrs. Collins." Asking Kit, "Are you enjoying your stay?"

Yes, yes, she assures them. The mask hiding her guilt at having been part of the mess they are so diligently clearing away.

She follows Keith into the Cabana Cafe kitchen, surprised by how many people he knows by name, embarrassed by their elaborate handshakes, the smattering of Spanish he uses as they travel deeper into the belly of the hotel.

He introduces her over and over. *This is my wife. Mi esposa.*

Now that they're inside she's had to remove her mask, wearing it looped over her wrist like a corsage. She smiles. Feels her tongue flat against her molars, a puff of air coming from a tightening chest, a stiffening jaw. *Kit Collins*, she repeats.

In the laundry room, Keith hands his garment bag to a petite brown woman, unzipping it to show her the stain.

"Sí, sí," the woman says, smiling at Kit. Her cheekbones sharp beneath the fluorescent light. The hundreds of plastic garment bags hanging behind her, gleaming like teeth.

"It's dried brown," Kit says, pointing. When it had been so red.

The woman waits for Keith to translate, but he just smiles, shaking his head. *My wife does not speak Spanish. No habla español.*

They're making their way down a long hall now, Keith pointing out the carpet and green-and-white candy-striped ceiling. "It's just like the hotel's entrance." She nods, he babbles. Onward they travel, husband and wife arm in arm. He's most definitely, maybe, always has been, part of this place. That other life in Boonville was a dream. The kind you can poke holes in because none of it adds up. Keith Collins, with his slim-fit jeans and collared shirt and big ideas. Why would he marry a waitress from Reno? A girl four years younger than him, who left Reno for Sacramento as soon as she was old enough. She didn't know Hermès from Hanes but she was industrious and capable. Worked diligently at entry-level jobs to pay for community college. Found roommates online. Girls her own age, all of them golden-haired and lightly tanned. She suddenly misses them terribly. Those girls. That part of her life over. Phlebotomy books always open on the kitchen table, words highlighted, pages dog-eared. Flash cards in every color carpeting the living room floor.

"She's worked here for almost forty years."

"Who?"

"The woman in dry cleaning that I just introduced you to. She's been pressing and cleaning our uniforms for forty years—have you not heard anything I've said?" He turns to look at her. "Kit, are we okay?"

How searching his eyes are. Calming blue, reassuring blue. They do not want her to be lost, they want her here with him. *Be part of me*, they ask. Remember that night when the wine rep had left sample bottles and after the restaurant closed, when it was just her and Keith, how he laughed when she mispronounced their names.

This one tastes like sea-foam and silver fillings, she said, excited by his attention.

You have a natural palate. He smiled. *If only you could remember the grape varietals.*

"Why didn't you tell me you lived in Los Angeles?"

He lets out a little puff of air. "Is that what this is about? Sweetheart, it was a blip. I don't know everything about you. But we've got the rest of our lives to find out."

He kisses her. The heaviness that had been in his chest since breakfast loosening because he thinks he's solved it. A little checkbox beside this particular problem. Kit ☑.

In the staff cafeteria there are a dozen or so tables. Employees look up from their food. Some start to stand.

"Please, don't get up," Kit says. "Don't let us interrupt your lunch."

But they're interested and curious and proud. They want

to show her the flat-screen TVs, which the hotel's owner, a sultan, had installed.

We can watch games on here whenever we want.

He takes excellent care of us, we pay very little for our health insurance.

We can go to any of our sister hotels all over the world.

I haven't been yet, but soon.

Maybe next year. Paris or Italy.

There are trays of hot food, a salad bar in the middle of the room. They are watching her every reaction, to each little thing.

"Wonderful," she manages. "We don't have anything like this at our hotel."

Which is true. The waiters at the Old Boonville Hotel make minimum wage. They scarf down a staff meal before the restaurant opens each night. A trough of fettuccini alfredo, lengths of pizza, and some kind of salad on the side. Then 150 covers a night. There are no breaks, not really. Sometimes standing eight hours or more. At the end of the night tips are pooled. Rinse and repeat. Turnover is high. Waiters come and go. *On to better things*, they'd say. And everyone hopes it's true. All of them. Nothing is quite as tragic as when a waiter is rehired.

The Pink Hotel staff want her to eat something. They will not let this end until she has eaten something.

"No, I couldn't, I just had breakfast."

"Go on," Keith says, handing her a waffle cone.

She gingerly pulls on the frozen yogurt handle. It dribbles out, getting everywhere. Someone hands her a napkin.

Keith takes the cone from her. "Let me help." He fills it properly, with expertise and precision. "Perfect for a hot day. Who else wants one?"

Kit takes her frozen yogurt and moves to a corner of the room where one of the kitchen preps is talking about how many pounds of beets he chops for the McCarthy salads in a week.

My weight in beets. Forget about the bacon, and the chicken . . .

Kit tries to get the attention of Coco, who's just walked in with Ethan. She looks tired, older. The usual half smile at her lips strained, strands of hair slipping from her ponytail. Shoulders slumped. Her tennis skirt wrinkled as if she slept in it. But then she recognizes Keith and her face adjusts itself, gone is the weary thirty-year-old. She surveys the room and sees Kit in her little corner, frozen yogurt melting down her wrist.

"Marguerite has been looking for you," she calls, grinning.

Ethan takes one of the cones that Keith is still busy handing out. "Who could have guessed you'd be down here with the rest of us?" His tongue bright pink against the vanilla.

"I heard Mrs. Lacey is hosting a luncheon."

Ethan waggles those blond brows. "There's a very special guest of honor."

He leans against the wall, close enough that Kit can smell aftershave. He's so young and boyish, though. Like an impish Pan. She looks closer for stubble, which makes him lean toward her so that she blushes.

"Ethan, leave her alone," Coco says from the salad bar.

"What? We were having a moment."

"Sit with us, Kit, we've been on our feet since breakfast."

Keith joins them at one of the cafeteria tables, glancing at Kit, who has not eaten her frozen yogurt. She's peeling the paper away from the cone. Every last scrap. When she's done she tosses all of it—the paper, the cone, the frozen yogurt—into the trash. That heaviness returns to his chest.

"Oh my god," Ethan says, scrolling through his phone. "Marguerite's photos on Instagram from this luncheon are *hilarious.*"

"As soon as I'm done here," Coco says, gesturing to her salad, "we'll head over."

They're looking at the photos together now, all three of them. Heads bent over the phone. Kit laughing at something Coco has said. Keith has missed what about, he's remembering how on the flight here she had fallen asleep on his shoulder. The flight attendant smiling at them. This woman, still a girl, really, fast asleep, hair tangled, a bit of drool at the corner of her mouth. The wedding ring on her slim hand caught the cabin lights and blared at him. Her head became heavy on his shoulder. *I'm someone's husband.* The responsibility nearly choked him. He waved the flight attendant over and asked for a whiskey. But since last night—when *his wife* was in the arms of others, when Kit had calmly looked into the face of an approaching mountain lion and did not blink—the pressure shifted. Instead of suffocation he felt only fear that she might leave him.

16.

News of the citywide curfew has spread as quickly as the rioting. Beverly Hills is on lockdown. National Guard patrols the streets. Police have increased their own patrols. *They're ransacking homes,* someone says at Mrs. Lacey's luncheon, where the guest of honor is a French bulldog named Matilda. She's in a polka-dot ruffle dress, sitting at the head of a long dining room table covered in pink satin, arrangements of dried flowers parading down the middle, a silver candelabra in the center.

One of the photographers adjusts the tiny gold crown on Matilda's head.

"Bark for the camera," he instructs.

Beside the French bulldog is Ilka Beaumont's bichon frise, Louie. He's dressed in a classic blue-and-white striped sweater, giving him the look of a fluffy miniature yachtsman. Also in attendance is a Yorkshire terrier named Moose, posh in a cable-knit Ralph Lauren; a no-nonsense Maltipoo in a puffer jacket and hood; and an Afghan hound in an olive-green Temellini cashmere cape, who will not keep still so that its owner has to keep calling in French for it to *coucher*. The Pomeranian from earlier is in a piqué dress and a glittering matching bow; his mistress, the blue-haired woman, is no longer in slippers and loungewear but a belted Carolina Herrera and vintage Italian loafers.

"Aren't they darling," she says to Mrs. Lacey, who is supine on a sofa watching the scene unfold. Surrounded by women in divine ensembles, their skin as smooth as the precious metals around their throats and fingers and dainty wrists. All of them of a particular age, with similar sloped foreheads and shaved noses and skin tones.

Waiters present each dog with a menu, turning the pages so that they can choose from tuna and brown rice, ground beef stew, or chicken and oatmeal. Their mistresses calling out:

But no chopped spinach, it will make him gassy.
A side of bacon for Monsieur.
Ham hocks from the kitchen.
Do you have pig ears? Those too.

Mei-mei is vegan.

Kit has been introduced to each woman and dog. The moment she arrived she was separated from Coco and Ethan. First by Marguerite, who wanted her to pose for photos, thrusting a flute of champagne into her hand. *Where have you been? Everyone wants to meet ma petite chou, the lion tamer.* Ilka Beaumont was quick to cut in, making the introductions herself. *This is Kit Collins, Mr. Collins's wife—yes, the one you met yesterday, our new addition to the team.* She's kept Kit close beside her, occasionally whispering some tidbit of information about Mrs. Lacey's guests, or explaining the intricacies of playing hotel hostess.

"The dogs must behave themselves with dignity and decorum," she's telling Kit now, her breath heavy with nicotine and mint. "Or they'll end up like poor Rocko."

She points to a banished border collie who has been stripped of his three-piece suit and dressed to look exactly like one of the waitresses from the Cabana Cafe.

"That seems mean," Kit says, looking for Coco. She's across the room adjusting an LED ring light for the photographer.

Look here, look here, hold still. That's a good boy.

"Courtney doesn't mind," Ilka Beaumont says with a shrug. "Do you, darling?"

"Not at all." She smiles, walking to them.

Ilka Beaumont takes Coco's face in one of her hands. "I like your hair long like this, it suits you."

"Dogs in hotel uniforms are tacky," Kit mutters.

"What was that?"

"Nothing." She might be more patient, more amused by the dogs and their owners if she weren't so exhausted. The wind beating against the windows and rattling the door. The coffee and pecan sticky bun from this morning are not mixing with the salmon canapes and champagne. Thank god she did not eat the frozen yogurt too. Keith standing there as if it were an olive branch. His face when she'd thrown it away. That distance between them widening.

"Tell us again about the mountain lion," one of Mrs. Lacey's guests is saying, a bit of salmon mousse on her lip.

Retreat: her blood hums the word. Get somewhere far away before they realize you're faking it. Instead out comes a string of sentences. The tone in her voice contrary to the rapid beating of her heart. The words concealing the current beneath. From their gasps and rapt attention comes a vague outline of the girl telling the story—she can almost see her. This young newlywed, unfamiliar with orgies and mountain lions and hotel etiquette but willing to learn—her husband her mentor. In this version a hero too. *He pulled me out of the line of fire.*

You're lucky he was there, the Beverly Hills wives simper. *We could all use a Keith Collins.*

Peggy Nasar, Matilda's mistress, is frowning. Her tragic mouth quivering, an unfortunate chin implant making her face look like a half moon. "Maybe he could have stopped those heathens from destroying my house."

She hadn't been home. From what Kit could gather (and the stories varied), she was in Malibu or Montecito recuperating from a procedure or *procedures*, plural, when her Hancock home was vandalized.

Did the police use deadly force? The women are consoled by tales of rubber bullets, flash-bangs, sting ball grenades. Tasers, mace, choke holds—*resisting arrest*, an aphrodisiac. The women lick their plump lips.

"I heard a lot of the protesters are in the hospital," Kit says, but no one is listening.

And they say defund the police.

At least we're safe here.

"Damage in the millions." Peggy Nasar is dabbing her eyes. "Matilda hates it when I'm this upset. My poor little refugee."

"Now, now," Ilka Beaumont coos, taking her by the arm. "There's champagne in the kitchen, Courtney can get yours topped up."

For a moment Kit thinks Coco will curtsy or bow, but she doesn't do either. That immovable grin remains pinned to her face. Then she's disappeared into the kitchen, where Ethan is helping the waiters uncork more Veuve Clicquot.

The dog owners have stopped fussing now that their pets are busy eating. Several are persuaded to go out onto the patio, *Tigran hates it if you smoke inside.* The rest retire to the living room, which is larger than Marguerite's bungalow. Everything cream and beige so that their gowns are a vibrant contrast. One of them begins to play something on the baby grand piano.

Ilka Beaumont has stayed behind in the dining room, directing Coco to mop muzzles, brush bits of tuna from vests or jackets. *I know they can photoshop it out later but it's about dignity.* It's Mrs. Lacey's bungalow, but Ilka Beaumont is directing waiters by name, the photographer too. She's asking waitstaff to ring for more champagne, to see about the house doctor dropping by. *Mrs. Lacey is worn down from all the attention. Peggy Nasar has that look about her.*

Kit has moved to the far side of the room, somewhere between the dining room, where the dogs are making a mess of silver place settings, and the living room with Mrs. Lacey sitting stoic and pale, checking her watch every so often. Watching Ilka Beaumont, wondering if she's glimpsing her future. A dizzying sensation of déjà vu, but then Marguerite has taken Kit by the arm.

"Finally," she says, "I get you to myself. I thought Mrs. B. was going to ask you to start taking notes." She smoothes Kit's hair where it had begun to stick up. "You look tired, do you need a little bump?"

Kit shakes her head no, then nods her head yes. Maybe Kit Collins does cocaine at dog parties.

"Marguerite," Ethan interrupts them. He's balancing a tray of cocktails in one hand, his phone in the other. "Your maman has lost her goddamn mind. This beats Sean Combs's bunny brunch last Easter."

"Make sure you tag him."

"Where's your uncle?" Kit asks.

"Probably with the menfolk. They like to do things old-fashioned like this." She pops one of the smoked salmon canapés into her mouth, the cucumber crunching between her teeth. "Ladies to the drawing room and all that. Or in this case *bitches*."

The Pomeranian starts yapping at the Yorkshire terrier. The blue-haired woman comes running over, clapping her hands violently.

"*No, no, no,*" she yells at the dog.

The Pomeranian is growling at the terrier, who barks back. Both lunging for the other, baring their teeth. Kit jumps back just as a tray of chicken and oatmeal crashes onto the carpet. All the dogs are barking now, plates and silverware and flower arrangements crashing about the table. No one is quick enough to catch the candelabra, which falls onto its side, the decorative twigs and dried flowers catching quickly. The hydrangeas are fully engulfed by the time Coco produces a fire extinguisher.

Dog owners have poured in from the patio and living room to see what the fuss is about. *Only a minor fire*, one of them says.

The dogs are back in their chairs, their bow ties and tiaras adjusted, the candles relit, a new flower arrangement formed—this one all fresh flowers—and luncheon resumes. Except for the Pomeranian, who is led out of the room on a leash, a Cabana waitress outfit waiting for it.

"You did this to yourself," the blue-haired woman says.

Ilka Beaumont points to the mess on the carpet. "Courtney, please make sure it doesn't stain."

There's a faint twist to Coco's mouth that Kit recognizes. Before they came to Mrs. Lacey's luncheon she'd shown Kit the women's staff locker room. They were in the carpeted dressing area with Hollywood vanity lights around all the mirrors. *These shifts are catching up with me*, Coco had sighed, eyeing her reflection. When she opened her locker for her makeup bag, something sparkling caught Kit's eye. *Is that Marguerite's diamond nail?* And that slight twist of the mouth appeared in the mirror, her eyelid pulled flat so she could draw a smudge of black across it. *If you told someone they threw away diamonds here*, her distorted image said, *they wouldn't believe you. But they do. They do it all the time.*

But that sour look is gone. There's only a docile nod of the head and then Coco is on her knees.

"Kit, you don't have to help her," Marguerite says. "Come get some champagne with me."

"I've got this," Coco says, when Kit has crawled beneath the table. "You should enjoy the party."

"Everything's on fire and they're having a luncheon for dogs," Kit says. "*Dogs.*"

Coco scrubs at the carpet, the smell of dog food and carpet cleaner making their eyes water. "Rich is a country to itself."

"I don't belong here."

Coco plops the gray chicken mash into a bowl, some of it splattering onto her tennis skirt. "Well, Mrs. Collins, you're a guest, so you kind of do."

She starts to work on a pile of mushed green beans, and Kit remembers the massage chairs in the locker room. They were the kind you'd find in a nail salon. There were only two, a weathered woman from housekeeping reclining in one, the other empty. Coco insisted Kit try it out. She used a remote control to make a knob climb up and down her ropy spine. *Doesn't it feel nice?* Kit nodding, yes, yes. The woman from housekeeping smiling at her. *Suite 220, right?* Kit flushed. She hadn't recognized her—was sure she'd never seen her before—and yet she must have cleaned her room at some point. She would know what facial products Kit used, because she was the one who arranged them into neat rows instead of cluttered around the sink—or changed the linens because she'd eaten French toast in bed and the sheets were sticky. How she leaves towels on the floor or clothes strewn about the room, knowing someone—this woman probably—will pick them up.

The entire sky is orange sherbet, parts tinged pink where smoke has climbed high into the atmosphere. Dander and flowers and ash whorling like a snow flurry. Hotel guests have gathered on the lawn. Their faces covered in exquisite air-filtration masks. Swarovski crystals, chain mail, camo, skull and crossbones. They take photos of themselves. They wander pathways through the tropical gardens. They find partners. They swap partners. That skittish scent of burning not that far off. If they were sensible animals, they'd flee.

Keith worries when he doesn't find Kit at Mrs. Lacey's luncheon. He calls her cell but no answer. She is not in their suite. He tries the pool, even though it's still closed. All the garbage from last night is gone, the area is clean, the stadium seating still like a medieval coliseum. The tiny flags atop the cabana tents whipping in the wind. The pool water is murky. A beach ball floats at one end. That silk stocking sunk near the bottom. Only a few employees in groundskeeping had shown up for work, and maintaining the bungalow gardens was priority number one.

He wanders the Crystal Garden, which opens up to the Crystal Ballroom, where preparations for Tigran's ball are well under way. Thousands of flowers will be wired into abstract sculptures. *The idea is to bring the outside gardens in*, Tigran had explained in their meeting with events and food and beverage. Inside, the air is clean and cool and filtered. Palms and wild banana will dominate the room. Tigran requested colossal monsteras towering over the dance floor, which is currently being fitted with parquet. The paneled walls will be covered with large mirrors. An infinity jungle. Mr. Beaumont is spending the better part of the day trying to find a bandleader who the hotel guests know and trust.

No outsiders. Tigran was firm.

An easy request now that Beverly Hills is in lockdown. No one will be going anywhere.

Keith takes his time getting to the construction site. Part of him knows Kit will be there, but he doesn't want to believe it. That weight in his chest doubling. Dread mingling with fear. He's uncomfortable here. Dust and debris, men in busted jeans and work boots and sweat-stained T-shirts. A reminder of an outer world, the one waiting for him if he doesn't get this job. He'd prefer to stay where the men are elegant in silk and satin, where the martini olives are stuffed with blue cheese, and hats aren't allowed in the Polo Lounge after eleven.

But his Kit has left the silks and satins for a mound of dirt where she watches the crawler loaders cut into a hillside as if it were room temperature butter; the excavators digging deep into the earth exposing the strata, proof of time passing. The sound of drills and hammers and saws, the noise of crushed granite beneath heavy tires. Men shouting over the turbulence. Bandanas covering their noses and mouths, goggles over their eyes. The wind whipping all sorts of things into their faces.

Keith recognizes the blue dress with its dainty yellow flowers. Her purse still over her shoulder as if she were going somewhere.

He watches her raise her hand, follows where she's looking. The tattooed construction worker waves back. It means nothing, not really, but Keith's mouth goes dry. He's sweating despite the dry wind.

The day laborers can work in the back of house, Mr. Beaumont had said during their meeting with the kitchen staff. Many were pulling double, even triple shifts. *Out of sight*, Mr. Beaumont assured the head chef. *Where they won't make guests nervous.*

Dishwashers would be moved to prep, prep cooks would be moved to bussers, busboys would become runners, and so on. Those who had experience in restaurants could assist on the floor on a trial basis. Sean Flores would be a bar back for the evening.

Are you sure? Keith objected.

But Ethan and Coco had both vouched for him and management was already congratulating Mr. Beaumont on a job well done. *This is a tricky situation*, they said from their home offices, unable to make it into work. Even staff was pleased. Many of them had, essentially, been given promotions.

"Keith," Kit says, startled. "How long have you been standing there?"

"It was rude to leave Mrs. Lacey's party without saying goodbye," he says, taking her hand and pulling her back along the path toward the bungalow gardens.

"A party for dogs. You should have seen it. They were dressed like people and when they didn't behave they stripped them of their Gucci or whatever and put them in hotel uniforms. It was disgusting."

Giant ferns and monsteras and wild banana envelop them back onto the hotel grounds. Somewhere, in one of the bungalows maybe, a group of girls are chanting along to a song.

"If it doesn't bother Coco then it shouldn't bother you."

"But I think it does bother her, that's what I'm saying. How are you not freaked out by any of this? Not even a little? The dogs ate at a *dining room table*. There was a candelabra and waiters—"

"So they're rich and out of touch."

"They practically orgasmed over police beatings."

"Kit, stop." That dryness has returned to his mouth. He has the distinct feeling that she is sunlight slipping away. That he cannot hold on to her. "Why don't you want this for me? I'm working my ass off and you're hanging around a construction site, why?"

She turns to look in the direction of the construction site, which has grown quiet. The men have cleared out for the night.

He abruptly kisses her. He wants her to respond to him how she normally would. Open up to him, let him savor her the way a child savors a special treat. But she's restless in his arms. She even smells different. That acrid scent of flame retardant has permeated her clothing, her hair.

"Kit," he says, cupping her face with his hands. "Why did you come out here?"

"I don't know," she says as the lampposts flick on. "I don't know."

17.

Just as there's a lull during the dinner rush Ilka Beaumont asks Coco to assist in-room dining. She's about to refuse, the Polo Lounge is bustling around them, the word *no* building inside her. *Have someone else do it*, she wants to scoff.

Dinner had turned into one giant supper party. Everyone either knew one another, or wanted to be introduced. And Coco, who's worked at the Pink Hotel for ten years, is more than an employee to many of them. She was called to tables, pulled aside, whispered questions and shared gossip.

"You *are* underdressed." An emir is frowning at her from over his highball.

It's an observation of the facts. She *is* underdressed. Her Cabana Cafe uniform with its irrationally short skirt. The Polo Lounge has its rules. Yet it feels like a betrayal. She has done her part, listened to them cackle and guffaw at the news, agreeing that the police could be more rigorous—when asked about her abuela and traffic and where in the city is the best panadería she smiled and said, *Delicias has the best pan dulce, but don't tell abuela.* Her laughter shrill. That prick of guilt softened because someone had ordered her another martini and they were all laughing along too.

"It's past their bedtime," Ilka Beaumont explains, gesturing to the children running around. And Coco nods her head, yes, yes. She files out of the Polo Lounge, herding the children as if they were goats.

"But I don't want to go," the little ones whine.

She is wrangling the broods of politicians and CEOs, venture capitalists and hedge fund managers, celebrities and foreign aristocracy, the progeny of well-to-do literati— thinking of those hotel employees who don't "live in." Always they arrive before dawn. The housekeepers and groundskeepers, the bussers and prep cooks and porters. They come by carpool or bus, from as close as the Valley or as far as Victorville. Coco will overhear them in the women's locker room as they change into their uniforms. Their makeup bags open on the bathroom counter, smudged with mascara and face powder. They'll shout in Spanish over the blow-dryers, and if they see her, their expressions change.

They'll ask if she slept well, always with a pronounced accent as if they were speaking to a child still learning the language. Even if they're her own age. Always a polite wall of civility but with the faintest twist of the lips.

I don't know why you try so hard with them, Ethan always tells her. Unable to understand why she goes out of her way to get them to smile at her. *They're just jealous. Don't think they wouldn't chew off your foot if it meant they'd get your job.*

This morning there had been no shouting over blow-dryers, the cafeteria at lunch was empty of their easygoing chitchat. Instead, Keith Collins was handing out ice cream cones as if running for mayor, Kit Collins tucked into a corner of the room like a folding chair. How to explain to Ethan—to anyone—that these women are her buoy.

Without them there is no disruption to the show. It's a continuous seesaw of Coco the waitress and Coco the mistress. Either she's cleaning dog vomit off silk carpet or it's like tonight—the option of pork chops or prime rib, every kind of tartare and oyster. Bottles of red, bottles of white. Cocktail shakers going full tilt. Four-figure bills seeming quaint. The jazz band letting the guests' children join in with their cellos and trumpets and whatever other instruments they're learning to play. The professionals smiling at the missed notes. *You're more than a waitress*, Mr. Beaumont will often tell her. *So, so much more.*

The children press every button in the elevator, drag their feet down halls toward their suites; kick shrubs on the garden paths to their bungalows. One plucks an azalea in protest and, showing it to Coco, crushes it in his hand. They terrorize their waiting nannies until gift baskets arrive. Teddy bears, plush slippers and robes, bubble bath, and a branded rubber ducky. *Compliments of the Pink Hotel.*

"If I have to deliver one more of these," Coco tells Ethan as they leave a bungalow where twins of a baroness are now fighting over who gets the pink teddy bear and who gets the green, "I will fucking lose it."

Ethan scoffs, "Tell me about it."

It's sometime past midnight, the ruckus from the Polo Lounge spilling out into the night.

"Did I tell you that the Weinsteins' kid refused to sleep until he had the soufflé of the day? Except he didn't like today's flavor. He demanded funfetti."

They push their carts down the dark garden path, back toward the hotel. Moths flitting around the lampposts. Crickets chirping in the damp soil. The only suggestion of fire is the sting in their eyes, the rasp in their throats. Otherwise it's another night of gardenias and night-blooming jasmine.

"Did the kitchen oblige Monsieur?"

"Of course. He only took one bite, the little shit."

Even Ethan's impish laughter sounds strained. How tired they are. How sore their feet are, their calves swollen and throbbing. She should ask him about that job he was going after—that thing he wanted outside of this place. What was it again? She can't remember. And her too, what was it that she wanted? A singer, yes, but that seems so long ago now. A child's fantasy. She is an almost-thirty-one-year-old Cabana Cafe waitress. They turn the corner, riotous laughter from the Polo Lounge dulling their senses once more.

Inside, the hostesses exchange excited looks with them.

"How's it going in there?"

"Mr. Beaumont wants you to join him when you're done. And Mimi Calvert requested Ethan's presence as well."

"No! She actually left her bungalow?"

Coco cranes her neck, peering into the restaurant. Even with the courtyard doors thrown open the restaurant is warm and humid. Every booth and bar stool is taken. The tables in the main dining room too. Guests move in packs, from table to table in grazing herds.

"She's brought Norma Jean." The hostess points to Marilyn Monroe's favorite booth, where Mimi Calvert is drinking lemon drops with her pet capuchin, who's in a sequined harness. The blue-haired woman beside her, asking the waiter to make their second order of steak tartare spicier. Her Pomeranian on her lap in a silver bow tie.

Mimi brandishes a brass fireplace poker, the gold knob polished and gleaming. The end as sharp as a spear.

"I refused to leave my bungalow without some sort of weapon, the animals have gone crazy."

There's a break in the music. A rush to the bar, where Sean Flores is taking drink orders, Marguerite on the bar stool across from him. She leans toward him, tracing one of the tattoos on the back of his hand with her little pinkie.

"Who is this Ruby, should I be jealous?"

She tongues the cherry from her drink, the strap of her bustier dress slipping from her shoulder.

"Another working-class hero for her collection," one of the hostesses says.

"She's really something else," the other replies.

Ethan has taken a tiny plastic bag from his breast pocket. They pass it back and forth, dipping their pinkies into the white powder.

"She's not half as bad as some of the others," Coco says, shaking her head when he offers her some. "I blame her family."

Ethan rolls his eyes. "You're still thinking of her as that sweet kid who brought you back a puka shell necklace from Hawaii. I bet you still have it."

Coco doesn't say anything. She watches him snort cocaine with their coworkers. How easy it is for him to be flippant with youth on his side. Cocaine is only for the most difficult shifts. The last couple of years she's tried to stick to clear liquors. That hangover she can handle. They've become as familiar as the hotel with its pink stucco walls and gilt mirrors.

The ebb and flow of its guests. The small corners only she knows, where early in the morning, after Mr. Beaumont has returned to his wife, she can watch the flower delivery truck arrive with today's arrangements. The air on that side of the building always cool, smelling strongly of lilies.

"She's had to stop posting," one of the hostesses is saying. "They've really been giving her a hard time."

"Well, what does she expect? Posting photos of a dog party while people suffer."

"We're lucky there aren't pitchforks at the gates."

Across the dining room, Mr. Beaumont raises his rocks glass, gesturing for Coco to come back to him. *Soon*, Coco mouths.

"Have you seen our little country mouse?" Ethan says, pointing to the cove of booths where Keith has an arm around Kit's waist.

"Mr. C. isn't letting her out of his sight tonight."

"Are we calling him Mr. C. now?"

"My number one rule," Ethan says, waving coyly to Mimi Calvert, who has seen them standing at the door, "really my only rule, is to make nice with the boss."

Coco watches Keith Collins work the room, gesturing to his wife in her backless black dress, a strand of pearls around her pale neck. It makes Coco think of those male guests who like to show her photos of their sports cars, who sometimes buy her things just so they can see her wear them. It can be a kind of exchange of power, if you know how to conduct the transaction properly. How has Kit Collins not learned this? She's a waitress and a woman too. Look at how she lets Keith parade her around, using her beauty for his own advancement, getting nothing in return.

And how far he'll go! Mrs. Lacey is laughing with him,

Tigran too. Ilka Beaumont groping his backside. Coco's entire twenties were spent toiling at the Pink Hotel, and Keith Collins has slipped in with his blond good looks and charming smile. *All-American boy.* The words whir about in her mind, taking shape in the form of boys from her youth. Assholes so confident that success is inherited through the Y chromosome that anything less would be an outrage. The world is theirs to do with as they please because the exchange is always rigged in their favor.

Keith catches her observing him then. She recognizes that look, what it means.

"Who's pissed you off?" Ethan asks, slipping the baggy back into his breast pocket. "You've got that scorched-earth vibe."

"I was just thinking Keith Collins is the kind of man who thinks he's untouchable," she says, smiling across the room at him. "And that maybe someone should remind him that he's not."

Those blond bushy brows rise. "I just remembered to never cross you."

She changes her mind about the coke. It's definitely one of those shifts. Out comes the baggie once more.

The cocaine kicks in quick. She's changed into something more appropriate and is twirling around the Polo Lounge dining room, martini in hand.

Where did you go? they shout over the music.

Does it matter? I'm back. Clink, go their glasses.

There's a whispering in the blood, a tingling in the timber of their bones. Something is going to happen, something always happens at the Pink Hotel. The anticipation has made them insatiable. Their demand for food increases. In the kitchen the executive chef is calling out orders, the sous chef scrambling to get control of a bevy of new fry cooks and grill cooks and line cooks who have never worked a restaurant quite like this. Meat is overcooked, tuna is underseared, the asparagus is limp. Twice a restaurant expediter comes back to ask about a soufflé for table seven.

"They're working as fast as they can," Coco reassures him. Then turns to the kitchen staff once he's left, "*Pinches gabachos no quieren trabajar.*" They laugh along with her and it's almost like those women from the locker room are here.

The third time the expediter comes back nothing can be done. He shouts at one of the newly appointed dishwashers who has gotten in his way. There's a confrontation, a threatening with a carving fork that sends the expediter running back into the dining room, the construction-worker-turned-dishwasher chasing after him.

They slam into the bar crowd, sending a group of Marguerite's friends scurrying for cover. A table is knocked over, bowls of house-cured olives and roasted almonds are sent flying. A bottle of Dom Pérignon falls to the floor with a heavy thud. Phones are up and recording. Several businessmen urge the fighting on. A supermarket chain CEO puts a thousand dollars on the winner. A group of television executives meet his ante. Tigran doubling the purse.

The two men rumble into a booth of actresses who flee, screaming with excitement. Mimi Calvert has her brass poker raised above her head. Norma Jean behind her jumping up and down in her sequined harness, panting and hooting. The blue-haired woman embraces the poor Pomeranian, who is shaking from the commotion, his bow tie crushed on the floor.

For a moment the expediter has gained the upper hand. His tailored red jacket is ripped, his lip has split, but he's grabbed one of the gilded lamps from a booth and hit the dishwasher over the head. The crowd is in a frenzy now. The expediter raises it again, the cord dangling near his fattening ear. Sean Flores catches him by the wrist. There is protesting from the businessmen, from the actresses and television executives and politicians. The emir boos loudly.

Tigran is indignant. "They're grown men, if they want to fight let them fight."

"Look at the mess they've made," Coco says, stepping forward. "Who do you think is going to clean this up?"

A potted fern has been trampled, framed photographs of the Rat Pack have shattered, someone has thrown a heel clear across the room. There is dog hair in the butter dish and napkins stained with wine or maybe blood. Norma Jean has shit on the booth where Marilyn Monroe enjoyed her ice cream sundaes.

Something in Tigran's face twitches. Kitchen staff has poured out from the back. They're shaking the dishwasher, trying to rouse him.

Marguerite flicks bits of broken glass from Sean Flores's vest. "They've ruined all your nice cocktails, haven't they?"

The dishwasher has regained consciousness. He touches the tender spot on the back of his head and when he sees his own blood he starts for the expediter again. There are cries of female glee, hoots of male adulation. Coco moves to hold one of them back but Keith Collins steps between them.

"The Polo Lounge is no place for a fight," he says, grinning that sly grin at the two men. "Not a proper one anyway."

Tigran catches on and plans are made to put that stadium seating to good use. One way or another they will have their entertainment.

18.

"You've done good here," Tigran is saying to Keith in front of Mr. Beaumont as the hotel guests file into the stadium seating.

Next to the pool Keith has overseen the quick construction of a makeshift boxing ring, the rigging swaying in the wind. The fighters are eager now that they will get a cut. Bets have been made in the hundreds of thousands. They shake hands beneath the spotlight, the crowd cheers. Waitresses are serving everyone prosecco. Keith had taken the initiative here too, suggesting Coco reopen the bar. *They all love the sparkling rosé, just serve it.* A gust of warm wind blows up their short tennis skirts, a chorus of hoots and hollering.

Tigran hands him a cigar. "You're a regular entrepreneur, Keith Collins."

"Thank you, sir." He laughs, a little drunk and pleased with himself. "Thank you."

He's about to follow him up into the stadium seating, but Mr. Beaumont takes him by the arm.

"Why don't you get us a bottle of grand cru," he says.

The match starts just as the wind kicks up. That beach ball in the murky pool spinning.

Keith signals for one of the waitresses.

"It wasn't a suggestion." Mr. Beaumont's voice is hard. "I want you to get it. Then stay at the bar. Make sure Coco has everything she needs."

Keith cannot make him out. The stadium seating was left intentionally dark. *Our guests appreciate privacy*, he had said, not noticing the look on Mr. Beaumont's face. The only light is the spotlight over the boxing ring. Insects flit about it, casting shadows over the two fighters.

"Did you hear me?" Mr. Beaumont repeats, feeling the meat in his jaw tense.

"Yes, sir."

That boundless energy, the relentless charisma, his blond curls—the way he knew just what to do in the Polo Lounge, how he uses his pretty young wife as if she were an accessory to show off or pass around. Mr. Beaumont was sick of his face. It won't always be so easy, he wants to say. She'll push back eventually, maybe realizing she never should have married you. Maybe she already has. It can happen that quick. Maybe Keith sees it coming and that's why his arm is always around her waist, why he's been talking faster, laughing louder, drinking more. Swaggering around like he owns the place. Maybe that's why the veneer slipped when Kit had said she'd attend Ilka's supper party instead of his little boxing match.

In the ring there's a solid gut punch.

The audience applauds. Mr. Beaumont watches Keith's figure, shoulders a little slumped now, duck behind the Cabana Cafe bar. He turns to Tigran, rearranges his features into those of a gracious, enthusiastic host. Accomplice and subordinate. *Whatever you need, isn't this great?*

"I had Mr. Collins fetch us a bottle of the good stuff."

He wipes his brow. It's a tropical heat. The air perfumed with hibiscus and gardenias coming from the gardens, where his wife is encouraging guests to change into more appropriate attire—breezy chiffon and silk blends, loose, forgiving linen.

For a moment the smell of chaparral burning confuses the matter but with an exaggerated frown and a flick of Ilka

Beaumont's Tank Française–clad wrist, the wind seems to change direction and then there's only honeybees in the honeysuckle as if it were the middle of the day and not the middle of the night.

"I've got the perfect dress for tonight," Marguerite is saying, arm looped with Kit's as they navigate the heady jungle toward her bungalow. "I love it when Ilka is game, usually she doesn't like it when Mr. B. throws *jobs* at her. Thinks she's above all that. But it's like, you married the boss, what did you think was going to happen?"

For a moment they can hear the ruckus coming from the pool area. Then it's quiet once more.

She tosses her head and looks back at Sean Flores, who's behind them on the garden path, her cousins on either side of him.

"Are they being completely annoying? You can tell them to shut up."

"You shut up, we're just asking him where he's from."

Marguerite makes a face at them.

Sean's taken off his vest, rolled up his shirtsleeves.

"Those tattoos," she whispers to Kit, gripping her arm. Then louder so Sean can hear: "It's a sheer devoré djellaba dress. Completely see-through."

She leans closer to Kit. "Do you think he'll be able to control himself? He's got such an animal vibe about him. Maybe I won't wear a bra. You'll have to help me choose shoes. It's white, so I feel like something bright."

In her bungalow Sean sits forward on the sofa, arms resting on his knees. Marguerite brings him a beer.

"I don't drink," he tells her.

"Oh! Are you a recovering alcoholic?"

She runs her green-and-yellow nails across her delicate neck.

"No, I just don't like the taste, never have."

"What do you like the taste of, I wonder." She giggles, and leaves her bedroom door open while she changes. Kit takes the beer and pours it down the sink. When she looks up her eyes meet Sean's and she loosens the pearls around her neck, then takes them off completely.

"Are these real?" one of the twins asks, taking them from her. "They don't look it." He winds them around a giant inflatable unicorn meant for the pool, pretending to choke it.

"What's Reseda like?" the other twin asks Sean. "Does your apartment have cockroaches, shit like that?"

"Don't record me."

"It's cool, I'm not. This is live."

"We get water bugs sometimes."

"What are those?"

"Basically cockroaches."

Kit's relieved when Marguerite calls for her. She doesn't want to be alone with Sean Flores. Not after Keith found her at the construction site. She'd felt so out of place at Mrs. Lacey's party. Not just out of place, but alone. And it was comforting to watch the construction workers, to pretend they weren't building more bungalows but tearing them down. How could there be a need for more of them? And then there was Keith, saying all the wrong things. Making her feel even more alone than she had at Mrs. Lacey's dog party. That kiss an attempt to sidestep the rift between them. She could taste their desperation, his and hers. Like the monogrammed towels his cousin had sent them.

She was feeling less agreeable, less tolerant of this whole

thing, which was the opposite of what she knew he wanted. That rift was widening. She wrestled with herself all through dinner. Pretending to laugh at a real estate tycoon's jokes, smiling and nodding as a banker told her about his eight-million-dollar bunker. *For when the economy finally collapses.* They were on their fourth round of martinis. How was Keith enjoying himself so much? Who was this person with his arm tightly wrapped around her waist, waltzing her around the room as if he'd known the steps all his life. When someone ordered a bottle of Château Mouton-Rothschild, he didn't send for proper glasses. There was no long story about the winemaker or why the terroir was special. The bottle was passed around the table as if it were a jug, people practically swigging out of the bottle, everyone smacking their lips together and laughing.

To the rioters! he cried, and she wanted to shake him.

You know those rioters would live like us if given the chance, the daughter of a famous director said. Her husband cracking open a prawn and sucking out its meat.

Here you go, Kit, Sean Flores had said, handing her a wineglass. No one had spoken her name in hours. Only *Mrs. Collins* or *my wife.* She stared after him.

Marguerite makes her reappearance in a floor-length gown, the sleeves long and wide, the back open with a chain draping around her neck, a seashell at one end. It's completely sheer and she's forgone a bra, as promised. Her breasts, pert and small, the nipples the color of sand dunes, peek out from behind patterns of crescents and stars and stalks of wheat.

But Sean Flores is watching Kit, who has gone to the other side of the room to untangle her aunt's pearls.

"Let me help," he says, getting up.

"Thanks," she says when he manages to get the final knot out. She lifts her hair so he can fasten the clasp.

The twins click their tongues. "Maybe don't be so try-hard, *Margie*."

"Isn't ma petite chou adorable?" Marguerite says, her throat working. "We're all obsessed with her."

They can smell cooked meat the moment they step out of the bungalow. The kitchen has prepared not only prime rib and filet mignon, but braised lamb shanks; whole chickens roasted in garlic, their gizzards sautéed with onions; classic veal Oscar, the béarnaise sauce still warm; creamed sweet-breads and mushrooms; venison bourguignon with baby pota-toes boiled in their own skins. There are mountains of broccoli rabe and steamed spinach and roasted brussels sprouts. There is no silverware. Not a plate in sight. Only round slices of ba-guette, small spoons made out of bone for the caviar. The tablecloth is covered with butcher paper, vases filled with cit-rus and pale roses for centerpieces.

Our own beefsteak banquet, Ilka Beaumont says. Explain-ing to those not in the know about the underground supper clubs during the Depression, how high society ate steaks with their fingers and drank until sunrise.

Already Mrs. Lacey is seated near the head of the table, Peggy Nasar on one side, the blue-haired woman and her Pom-eranian on the other, a smattering of philanthropists and politicians' wives and CEOs' wives and real estate moguls' girlfriends making up the rest of the party. They have very sensibly been given chef aprons to cover their Tom Ford, Val-entino, and Saint Laurent gowns.

"Didn't he make me a Manhattan earlier?" Peggy Nasar asks, thrusting her moon chin at Sean Flores as she tears a piece of meat with her fingers.

"Woodford Manhattan, up, no cherry," he says.

"Thought so. I never forget a face." She sops a piece of baguette in béarnaise sauce and stuffs it into her mouth. She leans over to Marguerite. "You do like to pick up strays, darling."

"Sit here beside me," Marguerite is directing him. "And, Kit, here on my other side. Do we have to wear aprons?" She sighs, disappointed that her dress will be hidden.

Mrs. Lacey is busy scraping salmon flesh with her nails, revealing its tender spine. She smiles serenely.

A woman in a caftan cackles. "We're eating with our hands, like isn't it *so* cathartic?" She wipes her fingers on the butcher paper, waving to Ilka Beaumont, who's at the head of the table. "The Pink Hotel is such a balm."

The courses are brought out on gold trays, surrounded with lemons and herbs. Dozens of candles have been lit. Never mind the wind, which seems to be caught high in the trees. Kit can hear their branches bending, leaves beating. But down here they're protected by patterned cinder-block walls and garden suites and the forest of trees and shrubbery. It's almost still, except for the gurgling fountain and the party guests attacking the haute cuisine.

"Aren't you hungry?" one of the twins asks Kit.

She takes a piece of broccoli rabe and chews on the end.

Someone passes a bottle of burgundy around. There are no glasses, they've sent them away.

"I feel like a pirate." Marguerite laughs, and drinks from the bottle. "Arrrrg."

"Don't be embarrassing," her cousins sneer.

"She's always been difficult," Mrs. Lacey sighs.

Film producers and production execs drift between the poolside fight and the party in the gardens, taking notes.

Call Reed, he'll eat this shit up.

Beattie can whip up a treatment like that.

Mimi Calvert arrives with her fireplace poker and Norma Jean on a ruby-encrusted leash.

"I wasn't going to come," she announces. "But I couldn't sleep. Not when y'all are out here having a ball without me."

Ilka Beaumont peels the last chunks of meat from a lamb shank with her teeth and tosses the bone to Louie and the other dogs playing on a patch of lawn. They nip and growl, louder than the cheering that drifts up from the boxing match. The concierge doctor is on hand with cocktail infusions to aid digestion.

It's mostly alpha-lipoic acid. But with a hint of ketamine—to mellow the mood.

In the flickering candlelight, the women look saintly. Meat under their nails, blood on their aprons, their minds at peace with all below. The candles have burned down, the wax a sea of scalloped waves. Somewhere in the canyon coyotes begin to yip and howl.

Did you hear that?

The dogs are barking now.

Come, come here, their mistresses command.

Mimi brandishes her poker, holding Norma Jean so tight that the monkey claws her dress.

"We're safe here," Ilka Beaumont reassures her guests.

"We're safe, we're safe," Mrs. Lacey repeats, eyes shut.

Kit gets up from the table. That forlorn crying. It is shimmying up her spine, making her feel chilled. Reminding her of desert nights on long dark roads, a vacuous mother at the wheel. The moment Kit Simpkins became all alone in the world.

Sean stands too, Marguerite clutching his arm. *Stay*, she pouts.

The howling carries down to the pool, where the expediter hits the ground with a heavy thud. Knuckles bloodied, the dishwasher is triumphant.

FRIDAY

19.

"I'm glad we finally get some time alone," Keith whispers as they wait for their couples' massage. She's flipping through a rack of glossy magazines, her back to him. He drums his fingers on his thighs. If he could just see her face, read her expression.

After the dishwasher's win, a party had erupted in the Cabana Cafe that lasted well into the early hours. Keith did not return to Suite 220 until after four. Kit was already fast asleep. He'd climbed into bed imagining they'd lived this way for many years. An elderly couple with separate routines. It made him sad, sadder still when he reached out to hold her and she did not stir and return his caress.

He watches her fingers turning the magazine's stiff pages. He sighs, smacking his lips together, a sign that should alert her to his anxiety. He wants her to ask about last night. A question that would mean they were still on the same page. Priorities aligned, souls in tune. She could tell him about Mrs. Lacey's party, and he would tell her how Mr. Beaumont had banished him to the bar. She'd reassure him that he hasn't blown it. The job could still be his. He sighs again, bending his neck left and then right. Cracks on both sides but Kit isn't paying attention. A spa attendant is offering her infused water.

Cucumber again, Mrs. Collins? Or would you like to try rose this time? They're Bulgarian rosebuds.

He'd been careless and overstepped. Mr. Beaumont had made that clear last night. There was a food chain and Keith had sauntered up thinking he could eat with the lions. It was just he was used to the type of hospitality at places like the Old Boonville Hotel. Where guest and employee were interchangeable because they existed on the same plane. Here the guests possessed a kind of absolute wealth that made them untouchable. Keith was not one of them, of course, he knew this. Yet Tigran was seeking him out at parties or in the Polo Lounge, and Kit had befriended Marguerite Lacey with such ease, and he and Kit were living in a suite with brocade-paneled walls. Wouldn't it be nice? *Nice* isn't even the word. To always live like this—silk robes for Kit, Italian suits for himself. One in every shade. A house, an actual house. Fuck apartment living. Jesus, maybe they could own more than one. A summer estate, a winter one too. Maybe an apartment in Europe. He is getting excited, drumming his thumbs on his thigh.

He wants to tell Kit about the after-party too. How the prostitutes were attractive in an ordinary way that surprised him. Not like Marguerite's friends, who were an exaggeration of contrasting angles, wild-eyed and slim; or Mrs. Lacey and her ilk, their skin buffed and shining, lips as exquisite as tulips. Even Mimi Calvert's clan of blue-hairs and spectacles had a certain elegance, reminiscent of intricate ironworks with their impeccable craftsmanship. No, these women were more pedestrian. Large mouths, always wide open and laughing. Their dresses tight and inexpensive, balayage hair all exactly the same length. They sat on the men's laps, fed them with their mouths, slipped off into the dark hand in hand. Everyone took advantage except himself and Tigran, who had been impatient to find his sister. All the while the construction-worker-turned-dishwasher-turned-celebrity-prizefighter had this satiated look that made Keith gnash his teeth until his jaw was sore. He would tell her all of this except he's sure Kit wouldn't understand and that rift between them would widen.

"Are you all right? You keep sighing," Kit says, looking at him from over her cucumber-infused water. Magazine discarded.

"Just tired," he says, instead of all the things he should.

She nods. There is frankincense burning, the lulling soundtrack of the sea playing, the attendant has given them eucalyptus towels and little lavender mint candies—still she cannot relax. She'd spent twenty minutes in the sauna hoping to sweat it out. Whatever *it* is. She emerged dizzy and red and, for a moment, felt weightless but then there was Keith in his robe, those blue eyes looking around the room, telling her what he liked and what he thought should be changed. *Where do you think this marble is from, Italy? Probably Italy . . .*

She had walked back to the suite last night alone, the coyote calls growing closer and closer so that she picked up her pace and jogged through the gardens. That burnt scent from the fires choking the already humid air. Her sandals slipping on wet ash. She could still hear them from her room. Through earplugs and pillows and the noise machine she had the front desk send up. If it wasn't coyotes then it was the men down at the pool, the women in the gardens. The smell of meat and blood and smoke permeating the carpet and rugs and banana-print wallpaper. It singed her nostrils. She could taste its metallic bite. Her skin sensitive to every shift in temperature. Was the fire here? Had it reached them? Sleep was impossible, except she must have slept because Keith had shaken her awake. He was already showered and dressed. *Spa day*, he said, kissing her. He tasted metallic too.

"I'm glad we're doing this," Keith repeats himself.

"So am I," she replies.

The couples massage room is just large enough for two massage beds. Whales sing to one another, seabirds caw, waves crash against some imaginary shore. Kit takes off her robe, hanging it on a hook.

"Babe," Keith whispers. "You're supposed to take off your underwear too."

He helps unhook her bra, his fingers warm against her skin. She tosses her undergarments near her robe, then, not liking that the first thing the masseuses will see is a matching lacy bra and underwear she bought specifically for her honeymoon, she gets up and stuffs them inside her robe pocket. When she turns back, they are standing naked in front of each other.

It's foolish to feel shy, she tells herself, but still she does. His penis is slack and wrinkled. The short curly hairs above it trimmed. His thighs strong and sinewy, calves like a horse's. Slightly narrow hips and a flat, muscular stomach. Not a hair on his chest because he waxes. A smattering of freckles on his curved shoulders. What is he thinking as he looks at her? It's too dark to clearly see his eyes. She has the odd sensation she's standing naked in front of a stranger. When he turns to climb onto his massage bed, she catches sight of his balls drooping and exposed. How soft and vulnerable are parts of men. And his butt is still that of a boy. High and round, with a mole on one cheek. She's flustered and embarrassed for being flustered and has to press her cheeks into the face cradle so as not to do something silly like laugh out loud or cry.

"Ahhh," Keith sighs, feeling the weight of his body press into the bed. He reaches for Kit's hand, kissing it.

He doesn't let go, and when she doesn't pull away, the vibrating in his blood settles to a hum. Her fingers are so cold and delicate. Maybe he can transfer some of his own warmth. An offering of recompense.

"Hey," he says, lifting his head so he can see her. "I'm sorry, I know this wasn't the honeymoon you imagined. Let's just try to relax, okay?"

She smiles but it doesn't reach those big dark eyes. And her hand is still cold. His blood is vibrating again. Neck tight. Why doesn't she understand? He's trying to get them the life they deserve. He drops her hand when the masseuses enter.

Are you enjoying your honeymoon? they ask. *How did you two meet?* they want to know. But soon it's only ocean sounds and Kit's masseuse occasionally telling her to relax. *Breathe in, breathe out.*

Keith groans. "That's the spot."

His legs ache from standing behind the Cabana Cafe bar all night, Coco showing him how to make one of the hotel's signature cocktails. *Salt the rim, like this.* The stadium roaring on the other side of the pool. Her dark hair pulled into a ponytail, a few loose strands curling around her pretty face. A surge of heat in his groin makes him adjust himself. He concentrates on those crashing waves. Searches for Kit's hand again but she's pulled her arms beneath her sheet.

The masseuses press into their shoulders. Stretching the meat connecting clavicle to scapula. They do pressure points on their skulls. Reflexology on their feet.

"My calves are very stiff," Keith is saying.

The masseuse is working the same area on Kit. There's an ache in her own calves that had not been there a moment ago. Some kind of transference is occurring. Her body has become an extension of his.

"Relax," the masseuse says.

The little room is warm, the incense stifling. Like a campfire in a tent. Or maybe the wildfires are closer still. Keith's searching for her hand again. She knows this would comfort him, that he needs that reassurance, but lying here motionless is the most she can give. Eyes shut, she tries to imagine being outside this room.

At first it's difficult: every time a whale moans or waves crash and recede, Keith sighing, she wants to kick off the sheet and run out of the spa. But then her masseuse has put a towel over her head and everything is muffled and quiet and she's picturing herself walking down the carpeted hallway where Cary Grant in his gilded frame mugs for the camera. Past the hotel gift shop, the salon, the boutique that outfitted Keith in his prized gray suit. Up the carpeted stairs, her hand skating along the railing.

Past the Polo Lounge, where late this morning, at brunch, Tigran and his fellow titans of business had devoured turkey clubs and coffee while concocting this afternoon's entertainment. A hostess suggested she wrestle Mona from housekeeping. *In a pool of crème anglaise*, someone suggested. Now that they were anticipating rolling blackouts, it would go bad anyway. The hostess laughed, the businessmen joined in. Bets were made.

"Turn over," the masseuses say.

They roll onto their backs. Keith still thinking of last night—his thoughts leading him like a funnel to Coco's teasing smile. *What'd you do to work the bar—get too big for your britches already?* How when she stopped to retie her ponytail the Santa Ana winds had mixed the scent of her shampoo with the hot tar smell coming from the hills. Now he's wondering how far the fires really are, whether he could see them if he went to the highest point of the hotel. What it might look like to see this city burn.

Kit is lying there breathing evenly, somewhere else entirely. Outside, in the gardens, the smoke blowing in again. No matter, she is gliding past the Lacey twins' bungalow—where later this afternoon an infamous pop star and her fiancé will fuck on a painting canvas for charity. Marguerite had told Kit all about it at brunch. *For the fire victims,* she said. *The painting will be auctioned off for a monstrous sum.* Snippets will be recorded for social media. A postcoital selfie will be taken for the cover of a well-known fashion magazine.

"Are you enjoying the massage?" the masseuses ask.

Husband and wife keep their eyes closed. "Mmhm," they say.

The masseuses tackle their necks.

While Keith imagines flames gobbling up Hollywood Boulevard, Capitol Records a burned-out husk, Kit's walking through citrus trees. Honeybees buzzing overhead. Lemons lying overripe in the dry soil. Pockets full of loquats. A shipping mogul had complained this morning about a loquat tree that was sagging with overripe fruit. *It's blocking my bungalow door,* he told Mr. Beaumont, who had been at their brunch table too, celery juice in hand, a parfait half eaten. *At night I can hear little animals eating.* Mr. Beaumont had apologized, explaining that nonessential hotel staff had to choose between home and the hotel. If they left they could not return until Beverly Hills was safe. *We're operating on a skeleton crew.*

As she nears the edge of the hotel lawn, her mind goes blank. It might as well be the end of the earth. Everything is black. That feeling of being untethered returns. She is unmoored, a faint tremor beats in her breast as she rises higher and higher—but then the masseuses are talking, they're saying her name, and the incense hits her like a gust of car exhaust.

"Keith and Kit Collins," they're saying. "It does have a nice ring to it."

"I thought so too," Keith replies.

She can tell by his voice that he's smiling. Her name materializes in front of her closed eyes: K-I-T. She sees it written in her own looped handwriting, the frenzied leaning hand of her mother, the bubble letters of a forgotten elementary school teacher. Always with SIMPKINS after it. But then SIMPKINS is replaced with COLLINS. How easily KIT can be changed to KEITH. That E appears, an H too: K-*E*-I-T-*H*.

"I just can't get this knot out," the masseuse tells her. "I did my best, you might be sore later."

Keith helps Kit dress, kissing her cold fingers.

"What are your plans this afternoon? I've got to assist Mr. Beaumont with Tigran's ball—can you believe we get to go to a ball? Two kids from Boonville at an actual black-and-white ball, crazy. You could go to the Crème Anglaise Tournament—four more girls have signed up. It'll be messy but entertaining." When she doesn't say anything, he clears his throat.

"Or Ilka is setting up a theater in the Sunset Ballroom. They're screening every film set at the hotel. Popcorn in little retro boxes, pink and white stripes instead of red, with the hotel's crest. This place thinks of everything."

The sea soundscape has changed to Tibetan chanting.

"A nap," Kit says, pretending to yawn. Then adds, because it's true, and she knows it will please him, "Later, Marguerite is having another party, to unveil the new painting. Her bungalow is the only one with a private pool so the twins talked her into hosting. She's invited us."

He squeezes her hand. "Perfect. I'll meet you there."

20.

Mr. Beaumont is worried. There's a throbbing ache behind his right eye as he watches the wrestling tournament between the Polo Lounge waitress and her girlfriend from housekeeping. Timid in their bikinis, they've become even more bashful now that they're standing before the stadium of hotel guests. Before they can even grasp each other, one slips and brings the other down with her, crème anglaise slopping over the sides of the inflatable pool. The hotel guests, drunk on strawberry and mango daiquiris, yell at them.

Get up, a financier shouts.

Five thousand to the winner! his wife screams.

This animates the girls, but they're giggling so much, it isn't much of a show.

Sweat has collected beneath Mr. Beaumont's suit jacket. The wind does little to dry it. This is not his best work. It's tacky and repulsive, but what else could he do? The Lacey twins had latched on to the idea, dubbing it the "Crème Anglaise Tournament." There they are, across the way, filming it for whatever social media platform they use. He dislikes this new generation, or maybe he just dislikes those twins. It's moments like these when Mr. Beaumont's usually easy smile becomes forced. He does not like to be reminded of his guests' darker whims, of basic human ugliness. He much prefers when they behave with the decorum befitting that of millionaires and billionaires. An inflatable pool, for Christ's sake. What will management say? It isn't "on-brand," certainly not up to the hotel's luxury standards. But the rolling blackouts—the gallons of crème anglaise that would go bad. And his guests were bored, a dangerous thing. The ennui of the elite wasn't some abstract concept. Their boredom can shift landscapes, collapse entire economies.

He rubs his temples. Then there's his quickly thinning staff. Irritable from working doubles, triples, in some cases all week without much of a break. Something will have to be done to make amends, he needs his crew smiling and ready to serve filets and oysters and whatever else the guests might demand.

A free round at the end of their shifts would help—except the goddamn bar is running low on alcohol. The endless to-do list expands. Figure out who on the diminishing staff is available to do an inventory check; and then there's the Sunset Ballroom–turned-movie-theater, check on that; and the ongoing monstrosity that is Tigran's vision in the Crystal Ballroom. *Don't you dare forget about Tigran, the most influential guest of all.* That ache is behind both eyes now, pulsing at the base of his skull.

He digs his nails into his palms, thinks of family summers spent on Lake McConaughy. How his mother spent weeks making meticulous lists, planning out their meals, their clothes, what activities they'd do each day. And every year his father on the first day would decide he wanted to barbecue burgers instead of hot dogs, swim instead of hike. All his mother's careful planning would seem for nothing, except she planned for this too. *The invisible hand*, she'd say, winking at her son and producing hamburger buns and swim trunks.

He can do this. It might not be the work of an invisible guiding hand—the girls in bikinis is tasteless and he should have never allowed it, but he's managing. At this morning's employee meeting he sat with staff and swapped shifts, negotiated time off, and even persuaded some of them to stay on instead of returning home. He begged Ilka to act on his behalf in the Sunset Ballroom, the only one he could trust to do the job, even knowing that her pursed lips, the raised brow, the near stranglehold on Louie meant she was pissed and he would hear about it later. He stationed an overeager Keith at the loading dock to await Tigran's delivery of macaws and cockatoos and a variety of exotic cats. *Whatever you need*, he had said, dashing off. If Mr. Beaumont had been in a more generous mood, he'd have told him not to be so obvious. A desperate man can be easily exploited. No matter, the work is getting done. The invisible hand may be pushing and pleading but it has not yet lost control.

Mr. Beaumont makes a show of clapping his hands together. "All right!" he says to the girls, who are still giggling and slipping in the cream. He can feel his smile in the meat of his cheeks, piercing the backs of his eye sockets.

"I think we have a tie!"

Humdrum cheers followed by polite applause.

"We're getting low on rum," Coco whispers to Mr. Beaumont. Thank god he still has her beside him.

"Switch to the brut rosé, do you know where it is?"

Coco nods and he watches her hurry off, his confidence buoyed by her loyalty to him.

"The final match," he shouts in his most animated voice, "is our lovely ladies from the pastry kitchen."

Two plump girls step out from one of the cabanas, hairnets still on from having just finished working the lunch shift.

"Missy One from Eagle Rock, and Missy Two from Loma Linda. Girls, would you talk a little about what it is you do? Tell everyone how our famous soufflés are made."

He drags out his little introduction to give Coco enough time to find the crates of brut rosé in cold storage. Tigran isn't even watching. He and a trailer park magnate are studying something on an iPad. The Lacey twins have already left. After all of the cajoling, the careful manipulating, the tactful shepherding, his guests are restless. He can see them shifting in their seats, calling sharply for more alcohol, more food. This oppressive heat, how dry his nostrils are, his throat too. He loosens his tie, is about to break protocol and remove his jacket when Coco returns to cheers. The sounds of dozens of corks popping at once sets his jaw on edge.

Santé!

Prost!

The girls get right to it. Missy 1 yanking Missy 2 by the hair. Quickly they're a mess of limbs slathered in cream, each trying to pin the other down. The crowd screaming exorbitant numbers. *Ten, twenty, fifty thousand.* Missy 2 has Missy 1 in a headlock, her face turning pink.

Take her out, the financier yells.

Mr. Beaumont's hands are clammy now. He cannot seem to unbutton his coat. Missy 1 slips out of Missy 2's arms and swipes her legs from beneath her. No, buttoned is better—he buttons his jacket again. Missy 1 is holding Missy 2's face in the pool of cream. Why has he never thought about the animal who gave up his horns for these buttons? Was it cow or deer or maybe something more exotic? They are so smooth and lustrous in the beating sun. Missy 1 is not letting Missy 2 up. Their struggles are getting too vicious. One of them is bleeding, or maybe both of them are. Small clumps of hair float on the cream's surface.

Seventy thousand! The crowd are shouting over one another. *A hundred!*

"Okay, okay," Mr. Beaumont hears himself say. How jolly he sounds, how unperturbed he is at the spit projecting from the roaring stadium. Unfazed that some have crushed their flutes in their hands, their blood mixing with the champagne, while Missy 2 is being drowned in crème anglaise.

"I think you've won, my dear," he says to Missy 1.

There are cries of discontent. Perspiration gathers on his forehead.

He offers his hand but instead of shaking it she pulls him in. Missy 2's head pops up gasping for air.

The hotel guests laugh and cheer and point.

Mr. Beaumont joins in, even lobbing some crème into the crowd. Pool boys come out with towels for him and the girls. He bows to his guests, who are standing now, their applause thunderous. Cream drips from his hair, his nose, the tips of his suit jacket. He can feel it squishing in his loafers.

Keith arrives then. He whistles as if he were at a ball game.

"Well, this is a shit show," he says to Coco, who is resting against the side of the stadium, the wind flipping up the back of her tennis skirt so he can see where her Spanx cuts into her thighs.

"Think you could do better?"

"Definitely." He winks.

The Missys are surrounded by hotel guests. The financier and his wife offer more money if they can lick the cream from their arms. *Come into our cabana*, they say. Other guests stroll off toward the hotel, a few let their pets sample the cream that has puddled around the murky pool.

Mr. Beaumont is trying to wipe the cream from his face. "Did Tigran's delivery arrive?" Already it's drying, sticking in his eyebrows, the roots of his hair.

"The caracal cats and pygmy elephant are delayed," Keith tells him. "But security will sign for them later."

"Wonderful, thank you." Mr. Beaumont spots Tigran yawning in the stands. "I was hoping this would entertain them for longer."

Coco takes the towel, wiping a spot he missed on his cheek. "You know at this hour Tigran would be at one of his country clubs, on the golf course."

"The second floor," Keith interrupts. "In the south wing. It opens up onto a stretch of flat roof, and since the only traffic allowed on Sunset Boulevard are police cars and fire trucks, we could set up a driving range. Courtney," he says, grinning at Coco, "could do a Bloody Mary bar."

It's a cold sweat now, chilling even with hot wind tugging at his hair. He's about to send Keith away. He wants to tell him he isn't needed, he's got everything under control, but his wife's clipped voice is coming from his radio, telling him of some scuffle in the Sunset Ballroom. Mimi Calvert has gotten into it with Mrs. Lacey.

Mrs. Lacey called Mimi new money.

Ilka sounds upset, and just like that, Mr. Beaumont will have to see to the matter personally.

"I'm counting on you, Keith," Mr. Beaumont says, dabbing at his forehead with a handkerchief. "Keep Tigran happy. We can get through this."

That *we* is such a relief. All morning Keith had been trying to get back into Mr. Beaumont's good graces. He'd managed the arrival of Tigran's growing menagerie, and was reserved and subservient during the staff meeting, even when Mr. Beaumont asked for his opinion. *Whatever you think is best.* And it's paid off. Here he is being entrusted with Tigran and his group of industry titans. The exact group of men he most admired. They lived in their own world, in a delicate ecosystem that required careful handling. If you wanted to become part of it yourself, you needed to find a way in.

He knew it was possible, he'd seen a dishwasher do it. Last night's impromptu party had been in his honor. Champagne and whiskey and enormous amounts of red meat cooked extremely rare, its juices staining the tablecloths pink. *Viva El Lavaplatos*, the hotel guests saluted his victory. Keith thought about suggesting a match between himself and Tigran's valet just so he could be the center of all that attention. He wanted *his* glass overflowing with champagne, everybody wanting a picture. But this was better. The dishwasher could keep his fifteen minutes of fame. This was an opportunity for a more permanent infiltration.

"Aren't you just the cat that swallowed the canary," Coco says when Keith joins her on the south wing's roof. She's already set up the folding table for the bar and found the rolled putting green in storage.

She helps unload his cart of Bloody Mary ingredients.

"Jesus, this view is something else," he says, walking to the edge of the roof. A sea of palm trees stretches out beneath him, the horizon a patch of brown where the smoke has blown out toward the sea. He turns to see if he can see the fires but the hotel is blocking the mountains. If he leans far enough, though, in the distance is a cloud of black rising up into the sky. He stands there waiting to see what he imagined during his massage. Flames leaping over the mountains, palm trees engulfed, buildings collapsing. But there's only the wind whipping up dust devils and dispersing leaf litter across the flat roof. Beverly Hills stretching out, a green canopy buffering them from the rest of the city. He snaps a picture anyway and texts it to Kit.

> Check out this view! Mr. B. put me in charge of a driving range on top of the hotel.

He's disappointed when she doesn't respond. This morning's couples massage wasn't the healing balm he had hoped it would be. He did not feel any closer to her than before; in fact that distance between them seemed wider than ever. She'd kissed his cheek when they parted. Not his lips, his cheek, as if they were friends or siblings. He can feel the weight of his phone in his coat pocket. What a useless bulky thing it is. He takes it out again, making sure there's service. This time he sends her a photo of the makeshift cocktail bar, Coco posing with a Bloody Mary.

> Want to join us?

He hits send and then stares at the screen.

"She's probably just busy," Coco says, watching him. "Marguerite requires a lot of attention."

"I wasn't worried," Keith replies, shrugging and sliding

his phone into his pants pocket. He ignores her smirk. Tigran and his friends are arriving and there are handshakes and banter and Bloody Marys already perspiring in the afternoon sun. No time for mocking waitresses or his good-for-nothing phone, which is sitting in his pants pocket like a pebble in the tip of his shoe.

21.

The sun beats down the moment Kit steps out onto the rolling hotel lawn. The street shimmering in the heat, dirt and dust swirling in small bouts. Without the protection of the gardens the sun is blistering, the wind pouncing first here and then there and then in every direction at once, blowing like mad across the street. By now she's used to the rasp in her throat, the sting in her eyes from the smoky air. Amazing what a person—what a woman can get used to.

It's the waiting I can't stand, her mother would say. *Everything else is fine, fine, fine.*

How small their hotel suite seemed when she returned to rinse away the massage oil. The late afternoon light cramming its way into the room; the gold hands of the desk clock gleaming. *Ticktock, ticktock.* Laughter in the hallway, someone crying next door, a heavy crash somewhere in the building. She showered and dressed but could not find anywhere to walk to. There was nothing nearby. No shops or cafés, not even a grocery store. And the streets surrounding Beverly Hills were all closed. Little dotted red lines fencing her in. She was biting her nails, spitting flakes of blue nail polish from her mouth, when housekeeping knocked on the door.

May we clean? And it was either join Marguerite at her cousins' bungalow, where the pop star was fornicating in paint for
charity, or venture out into the unknown.

Another eddy whips ash and dirt up Crescent Drive. It's
so strong she has to cover her eyes, her shorts and tank top do
little to protect her from this sudden assault. Pebbles and
brush pelt her bare limbs.

A woman can never be on her own, her mother had said.
They'd just finished their weekly grocery shopping, which
was just a restocking of Kit's stepfather's favorite snacks and
beer, when they came upon an accident. The police and ambulance had yet to arrive. Her mother pulled over, Kit got out
too. They joined a small group that had formed around the
woman lying twisted in the street. Pants dirty, shirt and coat
too. A hit-and-run. Her cart of empty bottles had launched
across the intersection. The metal warped from impact. The
bottles rolled into traffic, crunching under slow-moving tires.
A couple of teenagers pointed at where the woman's shirt
wasn't covering her full breasts. Her nipples large and dark.
Some big fucking titties, they snickered. Kit's mother was furious. They waited until police arrived, standing guard, and
then she marched back to the Volvo, slamming her door shut.
A woman can never be on her own, she said, jabbing the key
into the ignition. *Not in this world.*

Kit steps onto the sidewalk and all at once her heart is
rattling around in its cage, her muscles and organs as buoyant
as if filled with helium.

She's experienced this sensation twice before. The day her
mother swerved their Volvo into oncoming traffic, she went
weightless, the seat belt holding her in place. She should have
been killed too, they said.

The second time was on her wedding day. In the Sonoma County courtroom smelling of dust and pencil shavings. More like an elementary school than a city hall. It was not the kind of place Kit had imagined getting married. And there were so few guests. Only Kit and Keith, her phlebotomist ex-roommates, and their friends from the hotel. Someone was streaming it so Keith's parents could watch from their nursing home. It happened when the official paused between the words *woman* and *wife*. The sensation of weightlessness came over her so suddenly, she thought she'd float right out the window. But there was Keith, his warm hand taking her cool one. At the time she'd been thankful, even relieved. He'd anchored her back to earth.

As if summoned, her phone vibrates with a text from him. It takes a while for the photo to load; service away from the hotel is not great. Then a large expanse of flat roofing—what must be a tower antenna, various ventilation systems. What Keith means, though, is look how high up he is. Look how he's become part of it all. The hotel encompassing him, the rooftops of other mansions in the distance with their sea of palm tops and pine trees. This is what he wants, where he thinks the two of them belong. She only has to text him back and she'll be anchored once more. Instead she slips the phone into her pocket and crosses the street.

At first she's jumping at every dried leaf or twig. She worries Marguerite might have seen her sneaking past her cousin's bungalow—the sound of bodies slick with paint, moaning and grunting that made her blush. Editors from the fashion magazine racing past, their feet slipping on the damp path. *We don't want to miss the climax!*

She turns onto Lexington and the hotel is out of sight.

The wind is less violent here. It does not beat at her ears or pull at her hair. The sidewalk is shaded, almost pleasant. She breathes in and out, stretches her arms skyward.

News reports had her imagining chaos in the streets, but here in Beverly Hills there's only sprinklers switching on and off, the wind high in the pines. No traffic noises, no leaf blowers, not even dogs barking. There's no one anywhere. Not behind the diamond-paned windows in the large Tudors, or standing on the Spanish Colonial balconies. Abstract mobile sculptures in front of midcentury modern estates creak in the wind. Kit's twisting her hands together now. If only a car would drive by—or no, maybe that would be bad. She holds her breath when a sedan approaches and slows. But it's only security.

I'm staying at the hotel, she tells them, but they just look her over and continue on.

She passes several run-down estates. Old Cadillacs parked on their circular motor courts. Others are hidden behind huge shrub walls, at the end of long, twisting drives. She can only make out their tiled roofs. Another vehicle is approaching, this one a large tank. "SWAT" on the side. The men on the back in full military garb, their helmets glinting in the sun.

A gust picks up, carrying with it that rank scent of fire retardant. A fire truck speeds down Sunset Boulevard but the thick canopy of trees, the lush vegetation softens its siren and then it's gone. Quiet once more except for the ash skirting around the tires of parked cars, fluttering across their hoods. Another gust blows a cloud of ash and dirt down the street, making Kit cover her eyes. Except it isn't ash, or dirt. Thousands of butterflies swoop and dart around her. Wings shimmering orange and gold.

The desire to capture this moment, its odd juxtaposition.

If she only had a notebook and a pen, the words would come. She can feel them budding in her chest, they're filling her lungs—knocking at the tips of her fingers. *Mot juste.* Kit Simpkins would fill pages and pages trying to find the right word. She thought she could write herself some friends, maybe a boyfriend, or a family if she just got the words right. That lingering loneliness, the chasm between us all, could be bridged.

I love it, Keith had said when Kit had first let him read her scribblings. *I mean it's a little old-fashioned—orchids and bumblebees and the wind—but then you're my old-fashioned gal.* Kit had mumbled something about how the Romantics lived during the French Revolution. Art as a reaction to human suffering, beauty amid inexplicable chaos. Maybe a more confident girl, one of her ex-roommates perhaps, could have made him understand. *How can you apply this to the real world?* he said, and soon the notebooks were put away. She enrolled in a sommelier certification course instead. *We'll be an unstoppable team*, he liked to say, and she nodded yes, yes. She believed they would face the world together—if that's not love, then what is?

She's reached a gorgeous manicured park. The playground equipment brand-new and shining, the picnic area sprawling beneath large sycamores; a shallow man-made creek curving through the vast lawn. Girls in pinafores are dancing barefoot in the water. Boys too, their pants rolled up as they jump from fake rock to fake rock. Butterflies fluttering past them. Their smiles hidden by face masks, which cover their noses and mouths. *To keep out the bad air*, the nannies explain to one another. *They really shouldn't be out here.*

They speak in Spanish or Portuguese, shoulders tight, throwing looks around the playground, glancing at the far side of the park where a group of men in construction vests and blue jeans are lunching in the shade of a bougainvillea-covered pergola.

"I can't believe you made eight grand kicking the shit out of a waiter," one of the construction workers is saying.

"Expediter," the dishwasher from last night replies, crushing potato chips in his hand, throwing them onto the lawn. "There's a difference."

"Well, excuse me, la-di-da."

"I'd fight one of those nannies for eight grand," another says, waving at them so their backs straighten and they look away.

"They'd beat the hell out of you."

Laughter.

"All I'm saying is eight grand is enough to get the hell out of here—before shit really hits the fan."

"We can't work a site with half a dozen dudes anyway."

They watch finches hop around pecking at the crumbs.

"That settles it, then. We're not coming back next week."

The construction workers nod in agreement, all of them except for Sean Flores.

"Hey, Earth to Flores. You with us?"

But he's watching Kit. She has taken off her sneakers and socks and is splashing in the little creek. Splashing and hopping and laughing as a golden retriever joins her and then has to shake itself dry, sending water everywhere.

"He's watching that Collins girl again."

They heckle him.

Sean looks down at his half-eaten sandwich. "She shouldn't be out here, is all. It's dangerous."

"You gonna save her?"

Just then a revving of an engine, shouting. A van with

blacked-out windows peels around Coldwater Canyon and blows right through the intersection. Teens in balaclavas leaning out the door.

"EAT THE RICH," they shout. They throw firecrackers and colored smoke bombs—*pop-pop-pop*.

The older children shriek, smaller ones begin to cry. The van has raced up the side of the park, screeching in a circle before racing back through the thick cloud of blue and pink smoke. The teens launch bottles at the picnic area, cackling as the nannies shield the children with their bodies.

"SEE YOU SOON," they howl as their van swings back onto the main street and races away.

The nannies are a flurry of activity. Children are gathered and ushered into waiting black Suburbans. Toys are left behind, a rumpled picnic blanket lies abandoned in the grass. The golden retriever is shoved into the back of a Mercedes. The construction workers have moved toward their trucks.

"Where's Flores?"

They spot him heading toward Kit.

"Leave him, man, that's his problem."

Soon it's just the two of them. The swings in the play area still creaking from their tiny inhabitants' quick departure, the smoke from the firecrackers and smoke bombs swirling up into the sycamores.

"Are you hurt?" Kit asks him.

"I was going to ask you that."

He'd watched her chase after the van, barefoot and armed with a fistful of rocks. Her voice had been drowned out by the van's engine but she was red-faced and panting.

"I don't know why I did that," she says, looking up at him.

She had hobbled back to the creek, the bottoms of her feet tender from the hot asphalt, when suddenly her limbs went gooey. If Sean hadn't been there she'd probably have fallen face-first into the artificial stream.

"I thought they were shooting at us."

"So you just ran after them?" He spins her around as if checking for a gunshot wound, which is irrational, but he does it anyway.

"Where are your shoes?" He sits her on a bench. "I'll find them, okay? What do they look like?"

"They're black Converse."

Water from her feet has ruined a chalk drawing of a rainbow. She blinks away tears. "It was such a nice afternoon, almost normal. Why did they have to ruin it? Why scare children at a park?"

"They're pissed at everyone with money."

She watches a pinwheel spinning on the lawn. He finds her shoes in the bulbous roots of a large ficus tree.

"But I'm not rich." Her socks are missing. She puts on her Converse without them. "Really, I don't have any money," she says, because she caught his smirk. "I know I'm staying at the hotel but I'm just a waitress."

"Ah, but you're still a guest. Those kids probably grew up on welfare."

Her face is hot. "It's just the smoke bombs," she says, wiping her eyes. "They're worse than chopped onions."

"Hey, I'm sorry." He helps her up. "It shouldn't be a contest of who's worse off. Come on, I'll give you a ride back. Try to forget about those guys, they were just some jokers. Probably the same ones who set up a guillotine in front of Saks."

"There's a guillotine in front of Saks?"

He chuckles. They're crossing the park together, the wind stronger now. Sun at their backs. "You should've stayed at the hotel."

"I had to get out of there. You saw them last night, eating meat with their fingers like animals but in gowns that cost more than my rent. And today there was going to be a wrestling match in crème anglaise—you know the stuff they put on the soufflés? A whole tub of it. Some girls from the kitchen were going to wrestle for money. I know," she says, laughing because Sean is laughing. "It sounds insane—"

"No, no, I believe you. I've been working that site for months. Things have only gotten slightly crazier since you've shown up."

She glances at him. Away from the hotel he seems less imposing. His build is actually slight, there are lines around his mouth and eyes, and when he opens the passenger door for her, she notices he bites his nails too.

"Yeah." She smiles. "I bet you have a ton of stories."

He mimes zipping his mouth. "It's all going in the memoir."

She notes the crumbs on the floor, the receipts shoved into the door. How familiar this is, her mother's car had been the same. Only room for two. Books on the back seat, energy drinks in the cupholders.

"Plus they make you sign an NDA," he says as he climbs into the driver side.

"Of course they do."

They laugh again. He turns the key and the truck rumbles to life.

"Sorry about the mess," he says.

"Don't be." She leans against the seat and closes her eyes. A loose piece of sheet metal beneath the truck rattles as he reverses. "When I was a kid we had a car just like this."

He's rolled down his window. The air hazy and thick, those empty Tuscan villas and Tudors passing by in a blur. They catch whiffs of rose gardens and wisteria, murmurings from fountains, but no voices. No sounds or signs of human life.

"When I walked this way before," she says, looking at the passing houses, "there were hundreds of butterflies—now there aren't any. I swear, hundreds, maybe thousands."

Already they can see the hotel. It's so grand the sky could be resting on top of it.

"Doubtful, it's too late in the year for that."

"Well, I saw them, I'm pretty sure I saw them."

"Maybe you did." He shrugs, switching gears. "Everything's out of whack. Nothing makes sense anymore."

"I saw a military tank too. It passed right by me."

"Let's hope we don't run into them."

He parks his pickup at the far end of the construction site. The engine rattle is replaced with the noises down at the site, the revelry at the hotel. Kit's phone buzzes in her pocket.

"Here we are," he says, keys in one hand, the other on the door.

She's staring at her phone, at the second text and photo from Keith.

"Everything okay?"

"I have a suite in a five-star hotel," she sighs, putting the phone away and looking at him. "And I don't want to be in it."

The humidity from the gardens wafts toward them.

"You've got to," he says, gesturing with his chin. "Nowhere else to go."

She hesitates. From here she can see the wooden skeletons of what will be very grand and expensive bungalows. "Do you like working here?"

Sean shrugs. "I feel bad for them."

"Coco and Ethan?"

He shakes his head. In the shade with the truck windows

down, a light breeze replaces that musty old-car smell with whatever perfume Kit is wearing. It's pleasant and familiar and he settles into his seat without realizing.

"No, the hotel guests. People like Marguerite and the Laceys."

He gestures to the hotel, where sedans and SUVs are parked along the street. Their occupants roaming the lawn near the Laceys' row of bungalows. The X-rated painting must be old news, there's a bunch of people smoking cigarettes and posting on their phones. The girls all cheekbones and jaw-lines, the boys too. Dressed in slinky summer jumpers or bil-lowing satin trousers. Face masks half on, some dangling from their wrists like expensive jewelry. Ethan standing there with a tray on his shoulder, probably supplying uppers, down-ers, and everything in between. *Whatever they want*, he had explained to Kit one night. She can't remember which. Mimi Calvert was right, the days do blur together. Kit sighs.

"I'm serious," Sean continues, his eyes soft in the late af-ternoon light. "You see how they are, nothing's enough. The Laceys live on a compound in the hills—not one but two mansions, fucking palaces with their own security and pool and tennis courts and live-in help. And here they are at the Pink Hotel, taking up three bungalows, throwing parties, every horrible whim being catered to."

"You've been to their house?"

He runs a hand over his shaved head.

"Oh." Kit makes an awkward crossing of her fingers. "You and Marguerite . . ."

He shakes his head, laughing. "Is that what you think of me?"

He reaches across her to open the glove compartment. There are papers and an old map of California, folded badly.

Also a pistol. Steel gray and matter-of-fact. He finds an old pack of cigarettes and shuts the glove compartment with a snap.

"You know, I haven't had a smoke in almost a month," he says, putting one between his lips. "I promised Coco I'd try to quit, but you, Kit Simpkins, are going to make me start again."

She watches the lighter click, the small flame wavering.

"Me? What did I do?"

"How many times have you fainted this week?"

She laughs, shifting in her seat to better see him. "Heat-stroke is real!"

"Chicks in fairy tales faint less than you," he says, blowing smoke out his window and grinning at her. "No, Marguerite and I aren't whatever you just did with your fingers. I don't know what that was, but no. I'm sure you've noticed how the Laceys treat my cousin. If they forget something they send her to their house. A bikini, a pair of heels. Once Marguerite wanted her Polaroid camera, and I guess she has a bunch because Coco went three times before she came back with the right one."

"I don't know how she stands it."

His grin widens, smoke trailing from his nostrils. "Sometimes she moves things."

"What do you mean?"

"A sculpture, the salt and pepper shakers—or she'll rearrange the clothes in Mrs. Lacey's closet, change the temperature of the hot tub."

"No, that's you guys? Marguerite thinks her house is haunted. I swear, she told me she created a house spirit."

Sean starts to laugh. It's an openmouthed, whole-body kind of laughter that makes Kit laugh too. She's laughing so hard her ribs hurt.

"Fuck, that is hilarious."

Now would be the time to say goodbye. An easy silence has nestled between them. His cigarette is almost down to the filter. Instead she asks about Marguerite's house.

"What's it like?"

"I've only gone with Coco a few times over the summer, but it's huge. And the views are insane. You can see from the Pacific to downtown. The pool is one of those infinity ones, on a cliff so it looks like it just goes right over the edge."

Kit is picturing it: the water cool and blue, the city far below.

"You should see your face." He takes a final drag from his cigarette, then opens his door, and crushes it with his boot. "I was like that the first time I saw it. Then, I don't know. Every time I was there, their kitchen smelled like broccoli water; the maids were always cleaning up ants in the bathroom. Once I was there when a plumber unclogged Mrs. Lacey's shower drain." He shows her with his hands. "The hairball was this big."

She giggles, seat belt still on. The sky brightening now that the sun has dropped low. Bass thumping from somewhere within the hotel grounds, Marguerite's bungalow probably. The twins are out on the lawn now, mingling with their guests as more arrive for tonight's party.

"It was just humans being humans." He shrugs, taking another cigarette from the pack. "But in a larger space."

"It's weird how they're treated," she says, watching the twins mess with Ethan before snorting something from his tray. "I mean, I get it. Keith and I are both in hospitality but if someone asked us to put together an outdoor meat party in the middle of the night or a boxing match for money, we'd say no. Or I used to think we'd say no."

"Ha, I don't think *no* is a word they hear very often."

He thumbs his lighter, trying to get it to work again.

Out on the lawn, Marguerite has appeared in a silk chiffon lamé dress. It's much too mature for her, the print like something her mother might wear, or even Mimi Calvert. She's following her cousins and their friends around like an eager puppy.

"Coco loves that girl," he's saying, still trying to light the cigarette. "For the life of me I don't know why."

Kit takes the lighter and gives it a good shake. The flame leaps out. "Thanks," he says, careful to blow the smoke away from her.

Kit's watching Marguerite link arms with first one, then two, then three girls. All of them older than her. "Because she's alone," Kit says. "And she's just a kid."

Cigarette smoke swirls between them. The pert nose, the bobbed hair, the large dark eyes—he did not expect such a knowing look. He glances away just as she turns to him.

"Check out those getups," she says.

They watch as new partygoers arrive. They alight from their car hires, the twins waiting like princes to greet them, like rulers of a hotel kingdom. They form a royal procession. Their couture billowing behind them as they cross the lawn together.

Kit slouches in her seat but too late. Very slowly one of the twins waves at them. His laughter is real. It's brusque and biting and makes Kit's skin tingle. He jabs his brother in the ribs and points. Now they're both laughing. They wag their fingers. *Tsk-tsk*, they shout before disappearing into their bungalow.

"Don't worry about them," Sean Flores says. "They're less intimidating if you've seen where they shit."

Kit smiles. "I'd better go."

"Or," Sean says, turning the key in the ignition. "We go pee in the Laceys' pool."

22.

Keith shouts *Fore!* as he cracks the golf ball toward the hazy sky.

"He sliced it," a renowned plastic surgeon hiccups.

"No way," Tigran says, shading his eyes.

"A rock says he won't make it over Sunset."

"You're on."

A Hollywood exec sits up to see better, his Bloody Mary sloshing over the brim of his glass.

The ball ricochets off various roof vents and air-conditioning ducts—pool attendants pause from cleaning the last of the crème anglaise mess to watch it soar overhead, valets catch sight of it as it whizzes by—it flies across the empty intersection of Benedict Canyon and Sunset Boulevard, dropping smack at Rodeo and rolling into the gutter.

"Ha!" Tigran fist-bumps Keith. "Pay up," he tells the others.

They've forgotten what they were aiming for, which had been an abandoned camper van parked on Canon Drive. The window covered in tickets, a boot on the back wheel. The fact that he made it across the boulevard is enough for money to exchange hands, calls for another round of drinks. Keith has had to ring room service three times for more Bloody Mary mix, twice for hummus and pita bread, and another time for a crudité plate. He's acted as course marshal, golf caddy and golfer, and bartender when Coco had to use the bathroom. It has been a lengthy, sweaty few hours and he could not be more pleased with himself. Except Kit's phone is going straight to voice mail.

"Put your phone away," Coco whispers to him. "We're not supposed to have them out when we're working."

He slips it back into his pants pocket before Tigran and the others can see.

"Just checking the time." He grins. "Hey, make my drink as spicy as yours. I can handle it."

She rolls her eyes and adds more hot sauce to the glass.

The wind is blocked by the curve of the building, trapping the hot air beneath their angled umbrellas. The men are wiping their brows, dabbing their upper lips.

"Make yourself one too." The plastic surgeon pinches Coco's arm. "Men drinking alone is depressing."

She swats his hand away. "I've got one right here, thanks very much."

"You'd better behave," Tigran warns as he sets up his shot. "Coco's practically family."

She's produced her own drink from beneath the folding table. The celery stiff and green against the tomato juice.

"Good girl." The plastic surgeon winks.

Keith leans across the bar, watching her mix his drink.

"Just remember you asked for this," she says, pushing the glass toward him.

One sip and he's coughing and sneezing. He loosens his tie, that charming smile never faltering despite tears streaming down his cheeks, laughter coming from Tigran and the other golfers.

"You got me," he chokes out. "That's too spicy."

"Drink some water," she says, handing him a bottle. "You'll survive."

He excuses himself, ducking inside the suite to use the bathroom. Sneezing and coughing the whole while. He's splashing cold water on his face when his phone slips out of his pocket and hits the pink tiled floor with a thud. Maybe Kit forgot to charge her phone. That would be like her. A charger next to the bed and she's neglected to take advantage of it. He's scrolling through their messages. She's barely responded to any of his texts all week. Something twists uncomfortably inside him. He splashes water on his face again.

"Hey," Coco's voice comes from the other side of the door. "You all right in there?"

"Yeah, fine," he calls over the running water. "Why? You can't handle them without me?

"Do me a favor, just call Marguerite's bungalow and talk to Kit."

When he comes out of the bathroom she's already stepped back onto the roof. He can hear her low teasing drawl, the businessmen roaring.

Keith takes a seat at the Makassar ebony writing desk and picks up the receiver. No answer in Suite 220. That's all right, that's fine.

"Bungalow Five please," he tells the operator, watching the wind blow back the curtain, revealing Beverly Hills. It looks as if it stretches all the way to the horizon. Just a sea of green. You'd never think anything was wrong, not here. But every so often the wind switches direction and he can smell the wildfires. He has to resist the panic. Tigran isn't worried. None of them are. Not even Coco. They holler and laugh at the passing fire trucks and police cars below. *Our little fortress*, Tigran said when the National Guard rolled by.

He doesn't realize he's twisting the telephone cord around

his finger until Marguerite's voice chimes *bonjour* on the other end.

"Hubby, is your golf thing over yet? The twins' painting was just messy and kind of gross. I mean, what girl wants paint *there*? When are you and Kit coming over?"

"Uh." He clears his throat. A pain in his chest. "We'll be there soon. I just wanted to see if you needed anything for the party."

"I *need* Kit here."

He reassures her they'll be there soon. "Kit's just napping," he hears himself say.

"I don't think so." Marguerite giggles. "My cousins saw her with Sean Flores. They were in his truck."

He hangs up, hot and cold all at once. That pain in his chest doubles. It's as if the room's air conditioner was pumping out hot air. Maybe he's sunburned, or coming down with something. He loosens his tie, resisting an urge to kick off his shoes and bury his toes in the thick carpet.

"Did you get ahold of her?" Coco has popped her head in.

He nods, feels the reflex of a smile.

"Great, now get your ass out here and help me."

Below them the palm trees are dancing wild and ancient. The sky golden. A cloud of butterflies blows through as if on their five o'clock commute. The golfers beating them back with their stalks of celery and reams of bacon.

They go their whole life without seeing their wings.

"What?" one of the golfers says, looking at Keith.

Nothing, nothing. He hadn't realized he'd spoken aloud. Better sip this Bloody Mary slowly. Little husband is getting mushy in the head. So what if Kit hasn't texted him back. Or that she's not at Marguerite's like she said she'd be, but instead out somewhere with that goddamn construction worker.

It's fine, really it is. Kit wouldn't betray him. She wouldn't. Concentrate instead on how impressed Tigran is. Sure, Keith looked up golfing tips while on the loading dock, waiting for his menagerie to arrive. He still knew to compliment Tigran's Titleist wedge, his Ping driver. That Tigran was a member of eleven different clubs all over the world.

Someone has suggested Coco take a turn, the men helping her with her swing. *You've got to loosen up your hips.* The CEOs and Hollywood execs each have a go. Arms around hers, crotch to her backside, the sky draining of color beyond them. "Like this," Keith tells her when it's his turn. Mouth close to her ear. She smells salty. As if she'd jumped in the ocean, her skin cool to the touch.

She drives the ball straight into the camper's back window. Even from this distance they can hear its glass shatter. "A rippin' dinger," an old famous rocker proclaims. The tips of his hair bleached white, skin the color of prime rib.

"Boooo!" one of the billionaires' progeny says. "I lost a hundred K on you."

"Serves you right." She laughs. "Never underestimate a bartender, I'm the only sober one here."

"Haha, all right, a bet's a bet," he says, weed pen in his mouth. "Dad, pay them."

Keith can hear bass coming from the other side of the hotel. A DJ testing his speakers. Their soft thumping rattling the roof. The hotel lamps flick on, the streetlights along Sunset Boulevard, Canon and Rodeo Drives. Worn out and drunk, the golfers settle their bets.

"For your hard work," Tigran says, tapping a stack of cash at Coco and Keith. He's checking his watch, which is the size of a softball. The face carved opal, dazzling even in the dull light. Everything about him is bronzed nonchalance. Not a

213

silver hair is out of place, he hasn't had to mop his brow or adjust his jacket.

"We made the most of it today, didn't we?" Keith says, shaking his hand. His phone is heavy and hot in his pocket, making his leg sweat. Maybe there's something wrong with the battery. Maybe Kit has been trying to call all day and can't get through.

"You're a sharp kid," Tigran is saying as he steps over the railing, reentering the suite with ease. "I see great things in your future."

He wishes Kit were beside him. He wants to hear her say, *Of course he does, my husband is going to do great things.* Without her unwavering belief in him he fumbles his reply, almost stuttering Tigran's name.

Now the plastic surgeon is trying to hop over the railing. His face slick with sweat as if he just exited a sauna. Keith catches his arm just in time.

"Let me help you," he says, trying to focus. *The afternoon's been a success, don't screw it up now.*

A stack of hundred-dollar bills grows on the makeshift bar, each bill includes a kiss for Coco, a handshake for Keith. The CEOs and their kin, a cloud of cologne and body odor as they take their leave, the politicians talking with them in hushed tones.

"A little extra for you," a Hollywood exec says, holding out a folded bill for Coco to take.

She exaggerates her accent. "*Gracias, señor.*"

"*Muy en fuego!*" He tries to kiss her but she turns her head. One of his buddies has to pull him toward the suite.

"*Ay, ay, ay,*" he sings.

It takes a while for them to break down the table and umbrellas. Keith huffing a little too hard, cracked pepper and

Worcestershire haunting his mouth. Twice he spits when Coco isn't looking, the third time she catches him and her laughter slices right through him. *Should I get you some milk?*

One of the waiters from the Polo Lounge retrieves the folding table, a porter takes the cart of Bloody Mary mix and assorted accoutrements back to the kitchen. It's nearly dark by the time they're loading the putting green and umbrellas onto a trolley cart.

"I'm not getting them out of storage again," she says. "Let's put them in the panic room—that's the storage space off to the side of the jacuzzi."

"Why do you call it that?" Keith asks.

They're riding the staff elevator down to the pool area. Coco rubbing her neck, Keith touching the phone in his pants pocket.

"It's where we keep the backup fridges of Pepsi and Veuve Clicquot. Plus old recliners that we could use in a pinch, bits of pool equipment if something needs swapping out. Stuff like that."

The elevator doors open and they roll the trolley cart across the empty pool area. Keith pushing it at an angle because one of the wheels is cockeyed.

"It's also where overworked cabana waitresses go to have a good cry."

Keith chuckles. "Oh, you're serious? That's horrible."

"You saw them this afternoon. There's only so much pawing a girl can take. It wears you down."

It's too dark in the panic room to see her face but when she reaches past him to flip on a light he glimpses the hot pink bra beneath her shirt.

"Just shove it wherever there's space," she's telling him.

The room is filled with random things that the cabana

waitresses might need on a busy day. Extra ice trays, packs of paper drink umbrellas, tubs of sunscreen. The beach ball that had been floating in the pool all week is on top of the boxes of plastic margarita glasses. Keith takes his gray suit jacket off, folding it carefully over a cold storage fridge, when he catches Coco rolling her eyes.

"You're unbelievable," she says, lifting the lid of one of the backup fridges and taking out a Pepsi. "One Italian suit and you think you're one of them."

She's sipping it, watching him work. Legs crossed, a teasing smile on her lips. So he makes a show of it. Lifting two umbrellas at a time instead of one, hefting the putting green onto an overhead shelf even though he could make room on the floor.

"Maybe you're used to nice things," he says when he's done. "I'm sure you've earned some *nice* gifts from Mr. Beaumont."

"Wow," she says, crossing and uncrossing her legs. "You're a real piece of work, Keith Collins."

He grins, stealing her Pepsi for a sip. "I'll take that as a compliment."

This is a language he understands. Coco's exasperated smile, her reaching for the soda and his keeping it from her. Her light hand on his chest, his own hand touching her hip then her arm, now her wrist. Much better than unanswered texts, the awkward couples massage, the twisted sinking in his core.

He holds her by the wrist, finishing her soda.

"Ah." He smacks his lips together. Tossing the empty can. "Just what I needed."

She pulls away and points to where he's sweated through his shirt. "You're working awfully hard for a man not getting paid."

"You forget"—he follows her to the fridge, leaning against it while she roots around for another soda—"I'm back to being Mr. Beaumont's right-hand man. Pretty soon I'll be running this place."

"The difference between you and Mr. B. is that this is his vocation." She lets the lid of the fridge drop and sits on top of it. "He thinks of his job as a duty."

"So do I."

"No, you don't. You see it as a stepping stone to something more. I've seen it before and it never happens. They'll never let you in." The soda cracking open sends a tingle up his spine.

"So you're happy being *practically* family?"

"Fuck you. I've known Marguerite since she was *nine*. When I met her she was crying because her mother was ignoring her. Mrs. Lacey wouldn't say a word to her." She's taken out her ponytail, dark hair falling around her shoulders. Its damp salty scent filling the cramped space.

"Can you guess why?"

Keith shakes his head no.

"They wanted Marguerite's French to improve, so they wouldn't let her speak in any other language. To anyone. And they told the staff here to do the same. She had no one to talk to, not at home, not here."

"Why not just take her to Paris?"

"That would have defeated the purpose. There's power in understanding a country's official language but speaking in another."

Perspiration has slid down her long neck. He watched its slow journey as she spoke. Gathering in the small divot of her collarbone.

"I was the only one she could talk to for three months, and I had to do it in secret."

He leans closer, grinning. "Still not quite an aunt or cousin."

How many men has she known like Keith? They could blend into one. Nothing but a shit-eating grin and swagger. So in control, so very much the master of his own destiny. She should teach him a lesson, bring him down a peg or two.

She hops off the fridge, pushing past him. "Tsk-tsk, litter-bug," she says, bending over to pick up the empty soda can he'd tossed. It's a deliberate and slow movement. Is he look-ing? Of course he is.

"I stopped wearing the issued Spanx. I figured they can see what a real woman looks like. Thighs are dimpled, see?"

His eyes are very dark. Poor Kit Collins, she thinks when his phone vibrates and he doesn't answer.

"Not going to get that?" She smiles at him. "Could be important."

He's standing there like an animal caught suddenly on a very fast-moving highway. She can see his jaw muscles work-ing. For a brief moment she pities him.

Outside parrots screech as they make their final descent from eucalyptus to palm. But Keith Collins isn't listening. He's lost in the blue fluorescent glow of Coco's skin. How nice and cool it would be to touch it, how soothing it would be for her to touch him. He reaches out, grabbing her much too roughly. She laughs into his face.

"Mr. Collins!" She feigns surprise, shoving him away. Hard enough that he stumbles and falls back onto the floor, onto something hard and jagged. It presses into his back, his ribs. The air has been knocked out of him.

"You'll bruise," she says, straddling him. "You'd like that, though, wouldn't you? If I roughed you up a little?"

The weight of her on his legs is making him dizzy, she will not let him touch her.

"Hands to yourself. Open your mouth." She takes him by the face, thrusting his head back. He's a baby bird, beak open to receive food from its mother.

Her tongue lightly touches his lips. She swats his hands away again. Then spits into his open mouth.

"What the fuck?"

But she's already standing, smoothing her tennis skirt over her thighs. "Give my best to Kit," she says, and leaves him alone in the panic room.

23.

The Lacey house comes upon them suddenly. They'd been climbing the canyon road, passing compounds with helicopter pads and decorative follies, sun-bleached tennis courts, entire hillsides of terraced vineyards. Kit catching glimpses of deep aquamarine swimming pools, more like lagoons. *They really are palaces*, she thought, in awe of their towering gates and imposing shrub walls, even the kitschy sculptures of children playing on the lawn.

It'd been quiet except for the truck rattling, then a scrub jay called out as it swooped over them, and loud, thumping music echoed off the mountains—the humidity gave way to dry heat, chaparral replacing wet lawns and tropical gardens— and there across the canyon was the Lacey compound.

Slick and boxy, like something a child might build with Duplo. Cut right into the hillside. The façade a series of floor-to-ceiling windows. A smaller house below, and higher up, along the ridge, a large swath of mountain cleared and leveled for a third. Lights and people, and was that smoke? But then the road twisted again and the house was gone.

"Did you see that?" Kit asks, but Sean is concentrating on the hairpin turn, the downshifting of gears.

"There must have been hundreds of people there."

"At the Lacey house?"

They're turning onto a private road, the gate propped open with spare tires. That raucous music growing louder.

"Sounds like someone's having a party," Sean says. He catches Kit chewing her nails. "We can turn around."

She shakes her head. "I want to see this place."

It's a steep drive, the tumbled granite cobblestone bouncing Sean's truck from side to side, imposing aloes and flowering succulents on either side. Then, in the middle of the drive, stretched out on recliners, a group of teenagers. They stand up, holding out their hands for Sean to stop.

"You'll have to park here and walk," the tallest of them says. They're wearing ill-fitting valet uniforms, and impossibly giggly. *Park here and walk*, the others echo. "You gotta leave your keys with us," the tall one is saying.

"Like hell I do," Sean says. "I'll park here, but you're not touching my keys."

They back away when he gets out of the truck. Animals sizing up other animals, Kit thinks as she follows Sean down the rest of the drive, past dozens of cars parked along the side.

"Aren't you worried about your truck?"

He snickers. "Those tykes? Nah. They're too high to do shit."

There are people everywhere. Filtering in and out of the house, meandering around the driveway, climbing rocks in the rock garden, splashing in the huge sculptural fountain.

They are every age, from various backgrounds. Some born in Los Angeles, others blow-ins. Social media managers, architects, librarians, screenwriters, editors, marketing consultants, graphic designers, union lawyers, kindergarten teachers, critics, high school counselors—so many minimalist shift dresses and skinny chinos. The girls Kit's age, the alt bloggers and college students and project managers, have borrowed cropped animal-print bomber jackets from Marguerite's closet, their bikinis and one-piece bathing suits peeking out from beneath. Their combat boots shiny and loosely tied. The boys are shirtless beneath Cavalli and Givenchy army jackets, the rhinestone designs flashing in the late afternoon light.

A museum curator welcomes them at the front door, her novelist girlfriend on her arm. *Santé!* they cry, crystal cut glasses heavy in their hands. *Bienvenido.*

D-list actors and actresses laugh on the landing with low-level producers and professors from a nearby film school. There are people swimming in the infinity pool, picking over platters of cold cuts in the marbled kitchen, stretching out in the sunken living room, drinking vintage ports from the wine cellar.

"Some party," Sean says as they stand on the landing. A ballerina dances by, swirling a ribbon around him.

"Drinks are downstairs." Her voice is lilting and sweet. She does a little pose and then prances off to where a DJ in a gas mask is playing EDM.

Kit is having trouble taking in the house and the party all at once. A girl in a blue sequined dress has a parrot on her shoulder.

"Doesn't that hurt?"

The girl hasn't heard over the music. Kit motions to the bird's talons.

She shakes her head, puffs on her e-cigarette. "Shoulder pads."

Everywhere smells of perfume and cologne and something yeasty and warm. It's stuffy despite the open floor-to-ceiling windows. Sean has gone to find drinks, telling Kit to wait there. But those huge open windows are calling. The balcony overlooking the pool, the city far below. Even in smoke, the Pacific Ocean is a shimmering line. Like a mirage, the flat surface of a fogged mirror. She breathes in the noxious air, watches the trees far below in the canyon bend in the wind, the grassy hillsides pulled this way and that. Proof this is still the same world. She has not fainted. She isn't in Suite 220, in bed, sick with a fever. Just in case, she pinches herself.

"Pretty surreal view, right?" A young IT technician in plaid swim trunks leans over the railing beside her. "When the sun sets you'll see just how many fires there really are. Make sure your phone's charged."

Emerging from the green of Beverly Hills at the base of the dry canyons is Los Angeles, a circuit board of concrete buildings and palm trees. Already she can see smoke plumes, like geysers. A twinge of panic presses into her.

She turns away. "Do you all know Marguerite?" A group of MFA students are twerking in the living room. One has crutches, the pads beneath his arms covered in faux fur.

The IT technician is beating his palms on the railing in time to the DJ's beat.

"Nah, some buddies and I were at a party nearby. No one's home in any of these houses. They've all left for New Zealand or fucking Ibiza or wherever. Did you see the setup they have in the office?" He whistles low, adjusts his glasses, which have slipped on his damp nose. "Here comes the fuzz. Say hi!"

Overhead a helicopter appears, circling above the house. No one is frightened, they coolly wave, some shout and pump their fists at the sky.

The curator who had been at the front door cups her hands and yells, "*Heyyyyyyyy!*" Her whiskey splashing on her Eileen Fisher jumpsuit.

She laughs. "They can't tell the difference."

"Cheers to making it," the IT tech says to her. Their glasses clink together.

This is when Kit's phone vibrates with a missed call from Keith. She must not have had service in the canyon.

Keith, *her husband.* For the last half hour she'd pushed him from her mind. He's down there, in the city below. Swaddled within the Pink Hotel's palm-printed walls. He wouldn't understand why she'd left. Just as she can't understand how he can be so attracted to people like Tigran and Mrs. Lacey. He would love their house, she realizes. With its clean lines and views and soaring property value. He'd want one just like it, maybe even bigger.

So much of her has been wrapped up in Keith. On the drive here, she'd seen purple needle grass along the hills and knew it was California's state grass because Keith had taught her about the native flora and fauna. How to tell the difference between the canyon and coastal live oak, or the Norway spruce and Douglas fir—where the best hot springs were and the best time of year to sit in them and drink expensive white wine pilfered from the restaurant bar.

When the curator offers Kit a bite of bruschetta from a little party plate she knows to pronounce it properly—with a hard *sch* instead of a soft *sh*. This is because of Keith. As is her preference for Sicilian olive oil. San Marzano tomatoes instead of Roma. Campari over Aperol. Holy basil over sweet.

Kit Collins is really just an extension of him. Their new apartment, the sommelier course, even the wedding and their honeymoon—they'd been his decisions. He'd ask her opinion, but more as a matter of confirmation. *Yeah, babe, it's a great idea.* And onward they went, and probably would have gone if they'd never come to this place. It's fine to be the passenger when you trust the driver. But now, now doubts have reared and questions gnaw.

Sean finds her on a recliner by the pool, staring at her phone. Wafts of smoke drifting from someone smoking brisket on an elaborate outdoor setup.

"Some guy in a horse mask just gave me two beers," he says, handing her one. "He said he's *Maggie's* house manager. I don't think anyone here actually knows Marguerite or any of the Laceys."

"I missed a call from Keith," she says, sipping the beer, which after all the champagne at the hotel tastes refreshingly bitter. "I don't have service, I can't call him back."

Sean shrugs. "He's probably refereeing a mud wrestling tournament."

"Ha ha," she says. "He isn't normally like this."

Her eyes are so large and searching that Sean moves to a different recliner. He wants to make clear that this is not a romantic excursion. Just then the pool lights switch on, giving the water and those swimming in it an ethereal glow. As do the lights strung in the trees, the recessed lighting on the balconies, the landscaped lights beneath the ocotillos and paloverde trees—the whole lavish house is suddenly twinkling like a small constellation. The partygoers let out a cooing cheer.

A girl in a rainbow halter has swum up to them.

"God, look at these palms."

Kit strains to look at the darkening canyon below.

"I mean on my phone." She's holding it out to show Kit and Sean a photo. It's Marguerite's courtyard pool, from her bungalow at the hotel. There's a spread of magnum champagne bottles and various delicacies ordered from room service. A group of celebrities posing in front of a gigantic canvas of smeared red and blue and silver paint. The caption reads: *Just 'cause Rome did it first, doesn't mean we can't do it better.* Looking at the photo you'd think Marguerite was a confident It girl. Surrounded by beautiful people, in charge of her world. Never mind her cousins in the background slightly sneering, or that Mrs. Lacey is not there. Neither is Tigran or anyone else who might protect Marguerite from herself, or the older businessmen that Kit knows must be just outside the picture frame.

The girl in the rainbow halter is enlarging and shrinking the image with her fingers. She seems to know everyone in the photo. She's listing them off, one by one.

"Can you imagine being at *that* party?" She swoons, tossing the phone onto an empty recliner beside them. "Have you seen her bedroom? It's on the third floor. You've got to see it. Her bathroom has four different shower heads. There's like six people up there showering right now. And her closet is an entire separate room. The real expensive stuff is on mannequins. Someone said that her uncle is building a third house, for him and his sister, and this one will just be hers. Can you imagine? Nineteen and this is *your* house." She falls back in the water and then resurfaces, mascara dripping down her freckled cheeks.

"My sister's boss went to one of her summer parties," she

continues. "She got to see *the* chain-mail dress—you know, the one Marguerite wore to the Met Gala. And afterward they all got marmots. They're illegal, of course, but you get them in Arizona and then register them as service animals. Then the state can't do shit."

"Yeah, fuck the state," Sean says, tipping his beer into his mouth.

"Right?" she says, oblivious to his sarcasm. "Like what are they doing for any of us? Fuck 'em. I don't blame anyone for rioting."

"You should be down there with them," he says.

"Me?"

"Yeah, all of you should. Instead you're up here pretending to be Marguerite Lacey."

The girl's mouth hangs open. She practically spits. "I have more in common with the Lacey family than someone living in a mobile home. I don't mean to sound classist, but that's just a fact."

"You're all poor to the Laceys, I can promise you that."

"I don't like you. You're a drag."

She swims away to join a group doing handstands in the shallow end. Dragonflies darting over the water. A young accounts manager for a talent agency does a backflip from the diving board. When she surfaces, a mixed-media artist in flamboyant gauchos, head half shaved, bends to give her a kiss.

"Come on," Sean says, launching his empty bottle off the cliff. "Let's get out of here."

He helps Kit up, her hand cold and dry in his. He wants to rub lotion into it, warm her fingers with his breath. Instead, he leads her around the house, back up to the circular drive. Up on Tigran's construction site, Kit can see the slim silhouettes of journalists drinking twelve-packs as they monkey around on the wood framing under the guise of reportage.

"What a gentleman." She laughs when they reach his truck and Sean holds open the passenger door for her. He plays along, bowing his head.

Then they're driving away, the sky behind them orange and yellow. The teenage valets don't look up when they pass. Heads exactly where they should be, bent over their phones, scrolling through social media. Joints in hand.

"I forgot," Kit says, relieved to be back in the canyon with Sean at the wheel. Dusk, warm and fragrant. A delicious shiver travels over her. "I was going to ask you to point out where you lived."

The truck climbs out of the private lane, Sean relaxing into a turn.

"You wouldn't see it on this side."

As they come to the main road the sky is nearly drained of color. The canyon below is gray and blue, but there's a sliver of orange over the horizon.

"If you want, I can take you to the top of the canyon. From Mulholland you can see where I live. But you'll be late to Marguerite's party."

Finally she has service again. "I don't want Keith to worry," she says, trying his phone. It rings and rings and then goes to voice mail.

"Told you," Sean says, lighting another cigarette. "Mud wrestling tournament."

She forces a laugh, pushing that sharp tick of sadness away.

"Top of Mulholland it is."

24.

That uneasiness Keith's felt all afternoon has solidified into something heavy. Its weight is nauseating. He's pretty sure he can't stand, not with it pressing down on him. He strains to see if Coco has really left. From where he's lying he can make out a swath of dark sky, a solitary star laughing down at him.

He gets up slowly, holding his side. Boxes crushing beneath his weight. Sure enough, a missed call from Kit at 6:58 p.m. The photo for her in his phone is from the week they spent in Lake Tahoe, hiking and kayaking and playing the casinos. A toothy grin, pink-cheeked from brisk mountain air. It's one of his favorite photos of her. He likes the way she's looking at the camera, at him. Full of love and trust. The thought of hearing her voice increases his discomfort, but at the same time he's hurt and angry that she didn't leave a voice mail. There's no text saying where she is, explaining why she'd gone off with that construction worker.

In his haste to get his jacket on, retuck his shirt, he gets a grease mark on his pants.

"Goddamn it," he swears. He'll have to get it out himself, he doesn't want to see the old woman in dry cleaning. Not because she's already cleaned his suit once, but because he does not want to see anyone, least of all staff.

He peers around the wall. Bubbles in the hot tub swirling, underwater lights making them look as clear as glass. All the cabanas are empty, each an exact copy of the others so that he could be in a hall of mirrors.

Female laughter cuts through the air. He takes a step back, unsure if it belongs to Coco, his face hot. Then it's silent except for the fountain and jacuzzi. He realizes he's holding his breath and lets out an audible sigh.

If he can just make it to Suite 220, he can shower off this horrid afternoon. Recalibrate for Marguerite's party. From here the music coming from her bungalow is faint, but the bass is unmistakable. It rattles his teeth, his fillings. Or maybe it's guilt making the ligaments in his jaw tight, keeping his steps heavy so that he has to concentrate on the tips of his shoes. One foot in front of the other, back straight.

Anyone in the stadium will think he's a very important man in a hurry. Places to go, people to see. Was that a man's voice? A woman's whisper? Do not look up.

He presses the staff elevator button several times. Then worries the doors might open and Coco will be standing there with one of the Cabana Cafe waitresses, laughter on her lips. He takes the stairs, climbing them two at a time. The gate at the top is locked and he fumbles with the master key Mr. Beaumont gave him. His face flushes again. What if Coco is already telling him? He could kiss this precious job goodbye.

His hands are sweaty. He can barely get the key into the lock.

In the small garden above the pool, those greyhounds are reclining on the wicker furniture, kumquat trees on either side of them. They whimper and sniff him as he passes, their masters busy chatting up the Lacey twins' friends, many of whom Keith recognizes from that party at Marguerite's bungalow. When was that? This week, last month. Yesterday. It doesn't matter, onward he marches, pretending not to notice when someone in the shadows waves to him.

Inside is crowded with guests. Fewer and fewer of them want to stay confined to their rooms. All the shops in the long hall are still open. Blow-dryers buzzing in the salon; men combing the suit shop for statement socks or a tie that will outdo their fellow hotel guests. Even the tiny gift shop is packed.

"My kid's birthday is Monday. Can you get it to Hawaii by then?" a businessman inquires, his security detail admiring pens and phone cases emblazoned with the hotel's crest.

At the base of the carpeted staircase, Keith can hear Mr. Beaumont's voice.

What seems to be the matter here?

He climbs a few stairs, squatting behind a potted palm. There he can see Mr. Beaumont standing at the hostess stand. That easygoing confidence radiating from his smile, from how he stands, hands clasped together as if waiting for a train but with all the time in the world.

I'll tell you what's the matter, a woman in a jeweled turban shouts at him. *What table you're at decides the pecking order and you want me to sit at table FOUR?*

Keith can see it in his relaxed shoulders, in every gesture. Seating in the Polo Lounge has become a high-wire act; the hostesses are close to tears from trying to juggle so many expectations and presumptions, but Mr. Beaumont is unfazed. He knows better than anyone the seating preferences of his clientele, the history of every booth and table—where famous celebrities sat or presidents drank is ingrained in him as if it were his own family history. *Ah, yes*, Keith hears him say in that soothing voice. *But Michael Jackson and Bubbles enjoyed root beer floats at table four—they preferred it because it has the best view of the action but the most privacy.*

Keith retraces his steps, heading for the mezzanine elevator. He cannot see Mr. Beaumont, not when he can still taste Pepsi and sea salt. He's quite sure now Kit must be asleep in their suite. A sob escapes him. He'll wake her up with kisses, beg her to take a bath together. He won't do anything more than wash her body, as if she were a goddess. Why had she not replied to his texts?

He'd been the one to propose, the one to push for a quick wedding. *Marriage*, he thought one night when they'd worked different shifts and Kit came home laughing about something a new busboy had said to her, eyes as brilliant and dazzling as they were in that Tahoe photo on his phone. It made him ache, panicky and suddenly starving, as if there were no food left in the world.

His parents had a dry, professional relationship. Everything revolved around their work. He remembers their excitement at dinner one night, ignoring the eight-year-old at the table. They were discussing how the mutated yellow gene in a fruit fly could in turn mutate a normal one. *It can spread quickly*, his mother said, her glasses catching the overhead light and flashing. *You know what this means?* his father replied, hands grasping the table as his mother nodded, licking the last of the soup from her bowl. *If the right gene were to mutate, an entire population could self-destruct.*

He's passing display windows, the abstract outline of a man reflected back at him. He'd thought Kit's *I do* would ease that ache. Reassure him that she was his.

A few of the window displays are of sterling silver children's hairbrushes and combs and sippy cups. Maybe a baby would settle them. He loosens his tie then takes it off completely. Another display case has chiffon dog pajamas monogrammed with the hotel's insignia. *Don't forget about your puppy child!* the window dressing reads. Or maybe, when they get home, he'll surprise her with a dog. Something small and playful. A terrier or a beagle.

The television in the gym is blaring. Protests stopping traffic on the 110 freeway; police in riot gear. A fire engulfing a high-rise. Keith sneaks by undetected. The young blond women on the treadmills and ellipticals too busy trying to change the channel.

If he's lucky the elevator won't stop on the lobby floor. He'd be in full view of the Polo Lounge, of Mr. Beaumont and the Laceys and whoever else. He's impatient, pressing the button repeatedly. Kit had better be in their suite. *Please, God, let her be in the suite.*

"Where have you been?" Ilka Beaumont cries.

The elevator doors have opened and she's standing, arms outstretched toward him. Her mass of blond hair dyed golden brown. It's been blown into waves, framing her round face.

"Do you like it?"

"Stunning," he manages.

She takes his arm. "You flirt. I did it because I know how you *love* brunettes. Dine with me. I always come up the staircase, I like to make an entrance. And with you on my arm, the girls will scream."

She's turned him around. Her lips wet and shining as she beams up at him.

"Today has been a nightmare," she continues, petting his arm as if it were Louie. "Thank god you impressed Tigran with the driving range. He was singing your praises, by the way. Let me kiss you for that. Just a little one on the cheek. Was that so bad? Another for this side, just to even things out. No one's looking! You're so jumpy. If it weren't for you, Tigran wouldn't have helped smooth things over with Mrs. Lacey. She was furious with Mimi, you know. Wanted to ban her from their black-and-white ball."

Her perfume has embalmed Keith in its sickly vanilla scent. He can feel where her lips flamed against his cheek. They're passing those window displays now. The children's gifts are as polished and gleaming as knives.

"A part of me wishes she'd go back to being a recluse," Ilka Beaumont rattles on, those animated brows arching and then lowering. "But let's keep that between you and me. It's just there's no one here to clean up after that monkey and it's shitting all over the hotel."

"Everyone's a little on edge," Keith says, turning to look back at the elevator, its doors open as if waiting for him.

"Yes," she sighs. "You look awfully pale, darling. Was it very hot on the roof? Coco mentioned it was sweltering up there."

Keith has stopped at the bottom of the carpeted stairs. Mr. Beaumont's boisterous laughter thunders toward them. He jerks away when she places a hand to his forehead.

"Why don't you take the evening off." She's turned him back to the elevator now. Keith lets out a sigh, relieved. *Yes, yes*, he nods.

"I'll have room service bring you a bottle of bourbon." She's patting his arm. At the elevator she kisses him lightly on the mouth.

"Or if you like, I can bring it up myself?"

"No." He's shaking his head. "Thank you but no."

She's staring at him, so he adds something about Marguerite's party.

"We'll see you there," he says as the elevator doors shut, those brows arched skyward.

He slumps against the elevator walls, relieved to be alone. The hallway feels excruciatingly long, its meandering patterned carpet stretching farther and farther until finally he's at the door of Suite 220.

It's a shock to flip on the lights and see their room perfectly tidy. Pillows on the bed fluffed and chopped, their clothes folded and put away, shoes in a neat row. No one has been here all day. The impressions from housekeeping's vacuum are still in the carpet.

"Kit, are you here?" he calls out anyway. His voice cracking. The room sounding even emptier with his voice bouncing off the palm-print wallpaper. "Kit?"

That heaviness twists into something ugly. His hands fold into fists and he punches a throw pillow across the room.

Nothing he's done is as serious as this. He didn't run off with Coco—in fact, if Kit had just answered his texts, if she'd come up to the roof like he asked her to, that whole incident would never have happened.

In the bathroom he strips naked in front of the mirror. The shower filling the room with steam, the pink marble floor cold against his feet. He can only make out his long, hairless torso. The sculpted limbs, those exaggerated lines. The squareness of that body doesn't feel like his own. He showers quickly, thinking of what he'll say when he sees Kit. Because she'll be at Marguerite's—she'd better fucking be there. He stifles a sob.

Halfway across the hotel lawn, beneath the soft glow of lamplight, the wind gusting above them in the dark, the sprinklers switch on and they have to run—Sean catching Kit when she slips on a pile of wet leaves.

"You gotta watch where you step." Sean's laughing, still holding her arm. The wet grass fragrant in the dark.

The day's events blur together. When was the couples massage? When did she walk to the park—had that been only a few hours ago? And the drive up the canyon? It has come and gone so quickly.

Sean's truck reached the top of the canyon when almost all natural light had drained from the sky and the city below was a sharp gleaming plane. The ocean a silver wall. She could just make out the colored lights of the Ferris wheel on the pier.

But which way to face? On the one side she could see from Santa Monica to downtown, dotted with small fires, and in the other, the San Fernando Valley, stretching out in a vast grid of stoplights and streetlamps and strip malls all blinking with suburban life.

And then farther, the foothills and distant mountain ranges, their ridges a seared orange line, smoke larger than any cumulus clouds. There was no sound, she could not hear the popping and hissing, its ceaseless roar.

It wasn't just Sean and Kit up there. A couple sat arm in arm on the hood of their Honda Civic eating sushi takeout. Huddled in the back of an El Camino, a group of twenty-somethings passed a phone around, trying to find a way into the empty rich neighborhoods. Bandanas over their noses and mouths, the patterned fabric damp from their sweat. A gang of bikers used an abandoned camper to block the wind as they barbecued hot dogs. *Do you guys want one?*

There were Nissans and Toyotas and Acuras parked on the side of the road in the dirt, their inhabitants in silhouette against the vast city sprawl. Music blasting from their cars, the skunky scent of weed lacing the air. The darker it got, the more fires showed themselves. Sean pointing out where he lived, where he'd gone to school, his favorite burger shop.

Ray Bradbury used to eat there, he said, finishing his hot dog. She'd had one too. So different from caviar and steak tartare. The grease making her fingers slick so that she could not zip the windbreaker he'd loaned her.

Next time, I'll take you to try their steak burgers.

The comfort she took in hearing these words. Maybe her world was not in free fall. How could it be when there were still barbecued hot dogs and shared joints and lukewarm beer? *Next time* was sure of itself. The future was not yet carved out for her. Setbacks happen, like natural disasters, often the seed of something new.

Regeneration follows the fire, one of the twenty-somethings had said, his buddies nodding along.

Their adventure ended with a helicopter beating overhead, its searchlight sweeping over them. *Curfew*, bullhorns crackled, sirens approaching in the distance. A Toyota and a Nissan almost reversed into each other trying to escape. The twenty-somethings threw beer bottles. *Fuck you*, the bikers yelled.

Fuck you, Kit joined in.

They'd raced back down the canyon, a blur of black, Kit babbling about her mother and her wedding and *Can you believe I flipped off the police?*

There's music booming from Marguerite's bungalow. They're walking toward it now, or maybe Kit's on a conveyor belt and being sucked back in—and there, at the end of it, is Keith. He'll want to know everything and she can't tell him about going to the Laceys' house in the hills. He'd be furious.

He's watching her and Sean cross the lawn together. Dressed in the same button-down shirt he wore the first day they arrived. The same twill pants cuffed at the ankles, even the panama hat has returned. The look on his face is very different, though.

"Sean Flores," he sneers. "How nice of you to return my wife. Did you have fun with her?"

"He just took me to the top of Mulholland," she tries. "So I could see the fires."

His mustache twitches. "I bet he did."

Sean's lit a cigarette. "I'll let you two talk," he says as Keith steps toward him, but then Marguerite is there.

"Ma petite chou!" she cries out, throwing her arms around Kit. "I thought maybe you weren't coming."

Her gown blows about them in the breeze.

"What are you three doing out here anyways? And, Kit, what are you wearing? It's one thing for Sean to look rugged." She giggles. "But not you. Come with me, I bought a whole new collection for us. Sean, you'll make me a martini? Or are cosmopolitans fashionable again? My cousins and their friends were drinking them all afternoon but I couldn't tell if they were doing it ironically or not and no one would tell me."

It's no use trying to preserve that Kit from atop Mulholland. This other Kit Collins is here now. She's in the way Marguerite swings her hand back and forth as if they might skip down the garden path; Keith's phony grin, the expectation that Kit will follow suit.

Nothing wrong here, everything is fine, fine, fine.

The air has grown thicker, more perfumed—so different from the dry canyons and burning plastic and hot dogs popping on charcoal. Paper lanterns give off a dull glow, partygoers mingling in the shadows. Fireworks bursting over an orange moon.

They've reached Marguerite's bungalow. Guests exchanging their face masks for plastic animal noses, the kind found in children's party favors. The elastic string pressing into their cheeks. Pigs and walruses, elephants and sharks, toucans and rhinos. They're dancing barefoot in the sunken living room, snorting lines of cocaine the length of the art deco coffee table. Most remember Kit from parties earlier in the week. They raise their arms and oink and growl and run their fingers over her skin and in her hair. Someone is there with champagne and a handful of colorful pills for Kit Collins to partake of.

Keith watches as his wife disappears into one of the bedrooms with Marguerite, a magnum bottle in her hand, smiling at something a walrus is saying. Marguerite Lacey had arrived just in time. It was one thing to arrange a boxing match for entertainment, but a brawl in the Pink Hotel gardens with a construction worker—it would have been the end of Keith's ambitions. He'd be just like *him*. Sean Flores, who's posted up across the living room. A blot on this affluent party. With his ripped and dirtied jeans, and faded T-shirt, the chain around his neck.

Ilka Beaumont is offering Keith more champagne. Why not? He holds out his flute for a refill. A faint knot in his stomach loosening with each sip. Kit is with Marguerite Lacey and her friends, which is exactly right. She'll come out dressed in something that will make everyone gape and awe and congratulate him. More pills are consumed. Ethan is an alligator offering ecstasy-laced chocolates. The music is quaking in his blood, in the pink bungalow walls. Ilka Beaumont with her pack of Beverly Hills wives, pawing at him.

Keith is laughing, an odd heedless sound. Maybe he should take it easy.

"I've always wanted to be at a party like this."

"Like this?" Ilka Beaumont looks around the room, pouring him another drink.

There are celebrities and models, tycoons and captains of

industry. He rolls these words around his mouth, feeling their sharp edges. Mutters *mogul* aloud.

Her hot breath tickles his ear. "I've been to better."

Kit returns, dressed in leather and a black Corvidae headdress, boots that go up to her thighs.

Oh bravo. Everyone applauds. *Encore, encore!*

SATURDAY

25.

On the morning of the Laceys' black-and-white ball there is a brief respite from the Santa Ana winds. Its sudden absence is less a relief and more of an intense standoff. Residents peer out their windows. The jacaranda trees that flowered despite it being the wrong time of year have dropped their flowers. Palms are as unmoving as if on a postcard: *Wish You Were Here.* Police on patrol pop chewing gum, tap their batons against their cruisers. Children are provoked by this new silence. National Guardsmen patrol Rodeo Drive, the Beverly Center, the car dealerships along Wilshire. *Take Their Money Take Their Power,* the graffiti says.

The wind returns almost as quickly as it disappeared. Those fallen jacaranda flowers swirl into electric purple eddies. Palm trees are wild-haired once more, camphor and pine trees shiver with anticipation. That breathless sensation returns. You will not have to wait much longer.

The residents of the Pink Hotel are only just stirring. Some, like Ilka Beaumont, have not slept at all. She watched the sun rise from one of the recliners on the balcony of her presidential suite, wrapped in a sheet from the bed. From here she can see the high-rises downtown, where news helicopters had hovered late into the night, her iPad playing their continuous coverage. She could see, too, the police helicopters, their spotlights sweeping over the city.

During that brief stillness when the wind stopped she had drifted off. Now the candy-striped green-and-white awning above her whips and snaps again and Louie is barking at nothing.

"Shut up, shut up!" she cries, rubbing her temples. The fluffy white dog trots to the far end of the balcony.

Helicopters in the distance again. She reaches for the matches and lights a cigarette. Then, not liking how withered her hand looks, stubs it out.

God, how she hates this city. The crap air quality, the traffic, the *fucking* Dodgers. How spread out it is, how so many arrive thinking it will be different for them. *Their* dreams will come true. A city of disappointment, no wonder it was on fire. And Richard—Dickie, as she used to call him—had brought her here, saying it was temporary, promising that it would be a brief stop on his trajectory to success. She should be living in London, in Paris. Richard working in management instead of kowtowing to hotel guests. Her grandfather had been a banker in Sacramento; her grandmother entertained presidents and ambassadors, writers and artists. Artie Shaw and Rita Hayworth had once picked her mother up from school in a Cadillac Coupe de Ville. *Their car smelled of lace and cigarettes*, her mother liked to say. *Rita bought me an ice cream.*

"Louie," Ilka Beaumont calls, patting her lap. When he doesn't stir, she whistles. "Louie, come here."

She lights another cigarette and then throws the little box

of matches across the balcony. It slaps against the tiles, making the dog leap up.

"Poor Louie, did something frighten you? Come to Mama, come here. That's a good boy."

She nuzzles her face into his kinked soft fur, thinking of the framed portrait of Rita Hayworth in the mezzanine hallway. Often she will stop and study it. *The Love Goddess*, the caption beneath reads. She's posing by the hotel pool in billowing slacks, skin radiant, a youthful impish grin on her painted lips.

Dozens of celebrities are enshrined in these pink walls. Everywhere are artifacts from a bygone era, displayed in glass windows. This is Milton Berle's cigar; a line drawing on a napkin by Andy Warhol. There is the bungalow Howard Hughes lived in for thirty years—did you know he requested a roast beef sandwich to be left in a nearby tree each night? Too often she's heard her husband recite this anecdote to hotel guests. The clientele is still famous, some far wealthier than their predecessors, but they only play at greatness. How can they do anything else? The originals did it first and better. Then there are those who come for the spectacle. They make the pilgrimage. Spend money they don't really have, just to be enshrouded in the celebrity mausoleum that is the Pink Hotel in the hopes some of it might rub off on them.

She hears the click of the presidential suite front door. The familiar padding of her husband's long strides across the carpet, toward the office where she's put all of his things.

"Ilka?" comes Mr. Beaumont's voice. "Where are you?"

"On the balcony."

"I need a shower."

The water switches on, his belt buckle banging against the bathroom floor. Until recently the convenience of their marriage had not bothered Ilka Beaumont. Her parents and grandparents had been public figures, who privately led separate lives. *Love fades, empires endure*, her father liked to say.

But then that dinner in Boonville some months ago. She witnessed love with a capital L. She'd forgotten what it was like, in the beginning. A tenet on which to build a life.

It was why she suggested the Collinses stay at the hotel for their honeymoon. Their Love had awoken a yearning. Like a cold-blooded creature suddenly finding warmth, she wanted to be near it. Only, since their arrival she'd been unable to stop herself from testing it. A caress here, a flirtatious remark there. If it broke, well, that's just proof it doesn't exist. Not for anyone. Last night she had her hands on Keith Collins for most of the evening, searching for some part that might give in.

Occasionally he'd look around the room for his young wife, who every hour on the hour emerged from Marguerite's bedroom. Diamonds dripping from her ears, her throat, rubies on her fingers. Such a becoming flush on her cheeks and neck. She was as pink as a rose. Her smile like Rita Hayworth's in that photo. Marguerite escorting her around the bungalow living room. Everyone applauding enthusiastically except for the tattooed construction worker. He looked like he wanted to spit. Several times she saw him head for the door then stop and turn back to the room.

At some point a game was devised. The guests each stripped something from their body—undergarments, jewelry, watches—and tossed them into a pile in the center of the room. They then took turns guessing which item belonged to whom. *Ten out of ten*, Peggy Nasar said when one of the Lacey twins took her satin panties from the pile, held them to his nose, and guessed correctly. *Pour plus tard*, he said, stuffing them into the back pocket of his Balmain jeans. Ilka Beaumont had seen them later, outside on one of the teak chaise lounges, his dark head nestled in Peggy Nasar's breasts, her half-moon face thrown back in ecstasy.

She had hoped Keith would choose her Bulgari bracelet; she'd shown him the rose-gold pendant set with carnelian before adding it to the pile. But he never got his turn. Marguerite wanted the construction worker to play and made a fuss until he finally agreed. *I'm just a simple niñita*, she cooed over the DJ's music. From silk bralettes, gemstone cuffs, Cartier watches and tiaras, he drew a strand of false pearls. Beneath Ilka Beaumont's hand, Keith's thigh tensed. The construction worker walked the pearls to Kit, placing them around her neck, where they dangled over chains of gold and diamonds and an emerald frog brooch. Kit began to cry, and Coco had to take her to one of the bedrooms. Keith got up and followed them. Then the construction worker disappeared too and the game ended soon after. Ilka waited, hoping Keith might reemerge looking for comfort. She considered a proposition from an elderly shipping magnate—Richard had already slipped away with Coco. But what she really wanted, more than anything, was *Love*, and the shipping magnate could not give her that.

The DJ's music lasted until the moon turned big and yellow, finally blotted out by a hazy dawn. By then Ilka Beaumont was on her balcony with Louie and a carton of Virginia Slims, wondering how love, capital L or otherwise, could exist in a time such as this. Flash-bangs in the distance like thunder. Tanks rolling down the city streets.

Mr. Beaumont comes out onto the balcony toweling his wet hair.

"The construction site manager texted to say they aren't coming back next week. Texted! We're in an absolute crisis."

She calmly sucks her cigarette, studying him. The gray at the temples, the hawkish nose, those withered smile lines and lethargic eyes. It all comes together in front of others, bright and refined for everyone but not for her. *Why won't you try?* she wants to ask him. *I'm still your wife.* She adds this to the list of grievances built up over their twenty-five years of marriage.

"Thank god the banquet team has everything under control for the Lacey party tonight," he goes on, not really seeing his wife, lying there in a sheet, a bit of cigarette ash between Louie's ears. There's a thin band of sweat developing on his upper lip, his dress shirt is already sticking to his arms. He reaches out for his wife's cigarette.

"Things must be bad," she says, arching her brows. "If you're smoking."

He frowns. "Did you do something different to your hair?"

"You noticed I'm not blond anymore. Such an attentive husband."

"I can't do this with you right now. Will you shower and come down to the Polo Lounge?"

"Am I working in the kitchen?"

"Don't be daft, we still have our core staff."

She takes back her cigarette. "Did you wake up with our core staff?"

Every presidential suite has porcelain ashtrays, the hotel crest emblazoned in the center in pink and green. Ilka Beaumont prefers the ashtrays in the bungalows, which are heavy cut Hungarian crystal. More like a vase than an ashtray, and perhaps in Hungary that's what they are used for. She can imagine a dozen gardenias floating in them instead of the dozen or so Virginia Slim cigarette butts.

She makes a show of crushing her cigarette in the one she took from Marguerite's bungalow as she left—at that hour the party had spilled out into the gardens and no one gave her a second glance. They were busy taking advantage of the anonymity their face coverings provided them. The mobile home magnate might have been with a girl from room service or one of the thin boys with enviable bone structure who always seemed to be at Marguerite's parties once the sun went down.

"Is that from Bungalow Five?" her husband says, tossing the towel inside. "Goddamn it, don't I have enough on my plate without you stealing?"

The little dog hops down from his mistress's lap and darts through the open sliding door. Ilka Beaumont stands up, letting the sheet fall away. The sight of his wife in a silk negligee embarrasses him. It's much too short for a woman her age. He can see the stretch marks on her upper thighs, her low-hanging breasts. An intimidation tactic, he thinks, and retreats into the living room, where the dog is lapping at a bowl of spring water.

She follows him in, emboldened by the crease in his forehead, the fear in his eyes.

"When you said we had to move on-site to oversee the renovations, I told you I wouldn't be an employee. Didn't I say that? And what have I been doing all week?"

"These are extraordinary times," he says, concentrating on picking up around the suite. "Why are there bathroom towels everywhere?"

"They stopped bringing new ones a couple days ago. I'm throwing them on the ground in protest."

"Oh, for God's sake," he says, dialing housekeeping from the room phone. A busy signal. He hangs up and calls again.

He listens to it ring and ring, the sweat above his lip becoming more prominent. "Why is no one answering?"

His wife has gone to the sofa. She pushes Louie from the cushions and stretches across it. Mr. Beaumont focuses on calling the front desk, jabbing the buttons with his finger.

"Why isn't housekeeping picking up? No one? Not one person? I'll be right down."

He hangs up, perspiration dripping into his mouth. It's salty, a little rancid from the cigars he smoked last night, the scotch he consumed. The taste of Coco's mouth. His invisible hand is slipping—no, it's tightening around his neck.

"Dickie." His wife is standing between him and the door, Louie in her arms. "What if you didn't go down? What if we left? We could go to my sister's in Christchurch."

He reaches around her for his suit coat. "Don't be absurd, I can't handle it right now." He gives Louie a quick pat between the ears. "Put on some clothes and come down. I promise I won't work you too hard."

The suite door opens and up goes the smile, the eyes bright and alert. Then her husband is gone. The presidential suite silent once more except for the awnings, which continue to slap in the wind. She drops Louie, who goes sniffing and pawing at the door.

The closet is large, the size of another bedroom, with a tufted ottoman in the center. Indecisive and exhausted, she gives up and slips the hotel robe over her plump nakedness. She thinks of Kit Collins, how she saw her wandering the hotel grounds that first day in a similar robe. A silly child, but rich in adoration. It's a bittersweet comfort that *Love* exists, even if not for her.

When the doorbell rings, she assumes her husband has

sent up fresh towels. She opens it without wiping the mascara from beneath her eyes.

There, in the same button-down shirt and cuffed twill pants from last night, panama hat cocked to the side over his golden curls, is Keith Collins. He does not wait to be invited in, he pushes past, then turns and pulls her against him. Hands inside her robe, his hot mouth on hers.

"What are you doing? What are you doing?" She trails off.

He mistakes her tears for happy ones.

"Put the Do Not Disturb sign on the door," he says, and she does.

26.

They are a mess of limbs. Keith tripping over the dog, a pile of towels, feet slipping on the negligee, which Ilka Beaumont had left on the hallway floor. She's an attractive woman with plenty to grab on to, but he's unable to quiet his mind. He remains alert, hyperaware of her pale round ass, the knobby bumps of her spine, her hand dipped inside his pants. None of it can drive away the image he saw this morning—his wife in the arms of that construction worker.

How many gowns did Kit model for them last night? His memory is fuzzy, each had been more extravagant than the last. Marchesa ombré tulle with rosebuds along the bodice, a black Alexander McQueen embellished at the collar, Valentino couture with a hot pink wig and exotic face jewelry.

He never went into the bedroom where she was being stripped and re-dressed by Marguerite and her friends. He and the rest of the party saw only the result. They were gods witnessing evolution in hyperspeed. Time ceased to matter. Mockingbirds sang outside. A meteor shower began and ended. Each mutation of Kit drew her further and further from the original. *What will she become next?* the wife of a pro footballer cried with enthusiasm, her toucan beak quivering. A slim petite creature in a latex bodysuit emerged, iridescent and shimmering. She was a goddess, she was an insect. He heard someone, Mr. Beaumont maybe, say, *Birds are the evolutionary descendants of dinosaurs.* And Keith remembered the last time he visited his parents at the nursing home. *Butterflies spend their whole lives never seeing their wings,* his mother had said, more to the doctor than to him.

Was it soon after this that Sean Flores pulled Kit's pearls from that pile of treasures? Yes, and metamorphosis reversed. That pale, incandescent goddess became Kit once more. Girl bride who did not know Manchego from Iberico cheese, did not care except that Keith preferred Manchego, so she'd learned to prefer it too. Kit Simpkins who wanted a wedding in the redwoods or on the beach but was persuaded to marry him in a dusty old courthouse.

What hurt most was not watching Kit break down in tears. It was that the construction worker had seen that she was on the verge when no one else had noticed. Until those pearls were placed around her neck and she crumpled onto the plush carpet, Keith had thought she was enjoying herself. He'd even despised her a little for it. But the tattooed construction worker had seen through the costumes, had seen they *were* costumes. Disguises that had pushed Kit to the edge. He had walked in to Coco tucking Kit under the covers as if she were an overly tired child.

Keep her safe, Coco said, giving Keith a hard look.

He fell asleep beside his wife. Feeling the weight of his

responsibility, the crushing guilt at having failed her. There was something else too, just out of reach. He passed out trying to figure out what it was, dreaming of the flycatchers he watched as a child swoop over his front lawn, clapping insects in their beaks, the sound so loud it was like an electric shock.

Ilka Beaumont is sighing and moaning but he cannot get hard. He shuts his eyes, trying to concentrate, but this morning—when he woke, Kit was not there.

The wind had stopped. The pepper tree above the bungalow was no longer scraping the roof. No dirt and pollen and dried leaves pattered against the windows. Only light voices in the hall. One that could have been Kit's.

In the living room half-naked toucans and lions, rhinos and elephants had mated together. Those still awake were silently dancing, eyes closed, headphones in their ears.

His zipper is stuck. They've fallen back onto the unmade bed, Keith's hands fumbling to get his pants down, Ilka Beuamont's Cartier watch ticking much too loud. *Why isn't this working?* Their teeth crack against each other's. The scent of wet tobacco making him nauseated.

Kit hadn't been in the living room. She wasn't in the kitchen, where the white-haired girl was eating a bowl of cereal. She pointed Keith outside, to the unmoving gardens. Birds-of-paradise hung their spiked heads, the bougainvillea posed as if waiting for a photo op. Not even a tremble from the palms. Everywhere was gray and blue until a kaleidoscope of color. Hundreds, thousands—maybe millions of butterflies all black and gold. Up, up, he followed them out to the hotel lawn, where they collided with his wife and Sean Flores, embracing on the street.

"Do you want a cigarette?" Ilka Beaumont asks, her body pink, hair askew.

They are lying on the floor. He'd finally been able to get his pants off but it didn't matter. Nothing she did, no amount of kissing and panting or caressing—no matter how much Keith clenched his jaw, determined, he'd remained limp. A gust of warm air blows in from the balcony.

"I'm sorry," he says, covering his face with his hands.

Ilka Beaumont has slipped the robe back on.

"It happens," she says, knotting the belt. "I'll make you a drink and then you should probably go."

A naked man collecting his clothes is a sad sight. A naked impotent man is pathetic. He worries someone in the mansions across the street is witnessing this lonely act of shame. Look at how timid and young this mustached man is as he joins Ilka Beaumont on the balcony, his clothes are wearing him. Panama hat crushed.

She hands him a screwdriver and they drink without speaking. There are several helicopters in the distance now. The wind is fiercer than it's been all week. A branch snaps off one of the banyan trees along Sunset Boulevard, the crack like a gunshot. Louie scurries back inside, whimpering.

"Do you want another? Or . . ." Ilka Beaumont is being polite. She's taken his empty glass and brought it inside to the bar.

"No, no, thank you," he says, flaccid and sticky from the dry wind. He attempts to adjust his pants without her noticing. "I should get going."

At the butler's door, her robe tied tight, she gives his cheek a light pat.

"Love," she says, lighting another cigarette. "I blame it all on love."

A maid bringing towels to Ilka Beaumont's room watches Keith Collins tighten his belt. She sees him run a hand through his hair, smooth and tuck in his shirt before trudging down the hallway, stopping every few feet to adjust his pants.

His shins are raw from falling from the bed onto the silk carpet. He pauses to look at the damage. The air making the wounds sting. How could something so luxurious slice right through his skin?

The elevator doors open and close. Look there, the reflection of a newlywed who has failed twice now to cheat on his new bride. What kind of man is he? He trudges down the hall toward the elevator, heading toward Suite 220, where Kit is waiting. Perched on the end of the bed. In her shorts and tank top and Converse again. Bags packed. The suite perfectly made up, everything clean and tidy, as if already waiting for its next guests.

She'd woken in Marguerite's bedroom at the sound of Sean's voice. The bungalow door shutting behind him. He was leaving and not coming back.

Everyone in this place has lost their goddamn minds, he said when she caught up with him.

Are those footsteps outside in the hall? Kit's fingers sneak up to her mouth but she stops herself. The sun cuts through the smoke outside, turning the suite golden brown. When the door doesn't open and the footsteps fade, she relaxes. Glancing at the packed bags.

Sean Flores had been the one to spot the butterflies, mistaking them for dried leaves from some exotic plant that had blown off in the wind. They'd walked through the construction site and everywhere were butterflies. Resting on the timber frames, fluttering among the pallets of cement and fertilizer. They stopped on their hair, their fingertips, the hood of his truck.

I guess they are migrating, he said with a sad little smile. The sun rising so that everything was black and gold and orange too. *They'll be dead by December.*

Maybe we'll have a warm winter, she said, and he reached out and pulled her against him.

Why do you let them treat you like that? he said, still holding her. *They dressed you up like you were a doll.*

It's easier to go with the flow. How nice his arms felt around her. *Not to make a fuss.*

Easy doesn't always mean best.

Then he was driving off, that loose piece of sheet metal rattling beneath his truck. When she returned to Marguerite's bungalow everyone was awake, the DJ playing out by the pool, mimosas and Bloody Marys already ordered. Marguerite complaining that someone had stolen her crystal ashtray. *It's as heavy as a bowling ball, who would take it?*

Keith wasn't in the bedroom. He wasn't in the kitchen or courtyard, where the twins were teasing two caracals with tufted black ears. Laser pointer pointing here and there. The cats leaping after the red dot until one caught a bird in its jaws.

Kill it! Kill it! the twins chanted, already dressed in tuxedos and simple black dominos. Their phones out and broadcasting.

She could hear them hunting for another bird as she hurried through the gardens. *A wren lives over there.*

Kit paces their suite, trying to retrace how they've come to this moment. The drugs, the alcohol, the ceaseless wind—it's a series of dead ends and foggy memories. All she knows for sure is that if they want to save their marriage they have to leave right now.

The lock on the suite door clicks and there is Keith.

But you'll think this scene cliché: husband and wife

standing in front of each other. His shirt creased, lips swollen. Her suitcases packed.

The wife asking, "Where have you been?" The husband throwing the question back at her, his voice rising so that she jumps.

They lack the language to express themselves. Words fail, as they often do. When she says, "Why are you being like this?" she's looking for solace, she's asking for reassurance. But he hears a plea for mercy, outrageous when *he's* the one in pain.

"Does it matter?" His voice aloof because he knows it will hurt her to feel untethered and distant from him. Driven by guilt and jealousy and a deep fear that eventually she will leave him. Never mind that all he wants in the world is for her to hold him and say, *You're okay.*

"Why did we get married?" Kit's voice cracks. "Why did you marry me?"

They've circled the room and come to the fainting couch, the little art deco coffee table. He's flipping through one of the luxury magazines fanned out on its glass surface.

"You know why."

The men looking back at him from the pages are mostly white and good-looking. They're on sailboats or climbing into private jets, behind the wheels of pricey sports cars.

"Say it. I want to hear you say it."

"Christ, Kit, what has gotten into you? Because I love you. You know I love you. I really dislike it when you get like this."

His palms are sweaty. That ache in his joints has returned tenfold. Maybe he's ill, a virus is attacking his cells. He finishes one magazine and picks up another, moving away when she sits beside him.

Every single man in these pages could be him. Why isn't

one him? He's flipping through them with such venom. "I'm trying to get this job," he says, his voice betraying him. "For us. I want this for us."

"Do you? Because I think we should leave. I think you should pack your bags right now and we should get the hell out of here."

"Have you lost your mind?" he scoffs. "I'm too close. We're too close."

She shakes her head. "I don't think you know what love is, Keith."

"Me? *I* don't? That's rich."

"Is it a noun or a verb or an adjective? Do you love me the same way you love this goddamn hat? 'Cause it's been crushed." She touches where Ilka Beaumont had rolled onto it, cracking its toquilla straw.

He slams the magazine down, ripping the hat from her hands.

"What about you? You and that construction worker? Going off with him like that—"

"You were working. Did you expect I'd stay in the hotel room all day?"

"I didn't expect you to fucking betray me."

She rolls her eyes. "I didn't betray you."

He's livid. How could she not understand? Of course it was a betrayal. His Kit would never have gone on some private adventure with another man. And to be so flippant as to roll those dark eyes, waving her hand as if he were a pesky gnat.

He's watching the scene unfold as one would from afar. It's as inevitable as a car swerving into oncoming traffic. The husband grabbing the wife's face—husbands shouldn't do that. They don't hurt the ones they love. Yet how crushable it is, with its cheekbones and eye sockets and mandible. The little whimper that escapes her mouth. He could break it open. Instead some horrible noise comes out of him and he's punching a hole in the palm-paneled walls. Her packed suitcases are next. He kicks them, over and over, until their zippers burst and her clothes come spilling out.

27.

A scene is developing at the hotel front desk. Tigran is supporting Mrs. Lacey, her face blanched and drawn.

"We've been robbed! Robbed!"

All the attention is on them. Someone pulls up the news on their phone. Images of trash floating in the Lacey's infinity pool, graffiti on the walls of their cliffside mansion: *We're coming for your money.* Cabinets pulled from their hinges, refrigerator and stove both stolen; mirrors and paintings and sculptures destroyed.

"Who would do this?" Mrs. Lacey is beside herself. Tigran is making phone calls, shouting to double security.

"All my things!"

"You'll stay with her until she's calmed down," Tigran says to Ilka Beaumont, who's only just descended from the presidential suite. She's in a raw silk pantsuit, stiff and shimmering. Her arms full with a small train case and Louie.

"I can't," she tells them, dropping Louie, who goes running off, barking feverishly. She rests against the counter. "I'm leaving."

Mrs. Lacey and Tigran look at each other. The other hotel

guests murmur among themselves. The looting of the Lacey house has suddenly become old news.

"Mrs. Beaumont, you can't smoke in here," one of the front desk managers says.

Her features seem to rearrange, her brows arching higher, the little lines around her nose deepening. She laughs so loud and long that Mrs. Lacey takes a step back, Tigran signaling to someone to find Mr. Beaumont.

"Oh, there's no need to radio my husband." She stubs her cigarette out on the counter, smoke billowing from her nostrils. "Just get me a car to the airport."

"Mrs. Beaumont," the front desk manager says. "I don't understand—"

"A car." She taps her manicured nails on the counter between them. "I want you to get one that will take me to LAX so I can fly the hell out of here—and I want someone to pack my things and send them here." She holds out her husband's business card, an address in Christchurch scrawled across the back.

More hotel guests have gathered to see what the fuss is about, Louie barking and sniffing and dashing around their legs. He stops to urinate on a large potted monstera.

"Ilka?" Mr. Beaumont strides across the lobby just as his wife is reaching over the counter to dial the number herself.

He forces an easygoing smile. "Why do you want to go to the airport?"

Ilka Beaumont sighs, taking another cigarette from her clutch purse.

"You really shouldn't be smoking in the lobby—"

"Oh, give it up, Richard." She blows the smoke toward the chandelier in the center of the room. "You don't have any real authority."

He tries to steer her toward a more private area but she shrugs him off. A couple dozen hotel guests are watching now.

She waves to a few of her friends. "I'll send you postcards, my loves."

"From where?" he asks, dabbing at his upper lip.

She fixes his flipped collar, brushes some lint from his shoulder. "You need a shave."

"I don't understand what's happening."

"I'm divorcing you, Dickie. My lawyers will contact your lawyers and it will all be perfectly amicable."

Mr. Beaumont has paled. His hands are shaking, his limbs are shaking. He's thinking of their wedding—it seems so long ago now. A big church service, with prominent politicians and minor celebrities. All her family, of course. He didn't come from money or power. Marrying Ilka was the best thing to happen to a midwestern boy with a grueling work ethic and a seemingly bottomless well of charisma.

Such a pretty young bride in white lace, her train fifteen feet long. There are lines around her mouth now. At the corners of her eyes, too. Had he caused them? They are chiseled into her forehead, mostly invisible because she's had a fair amount of Botox, but he can just make them out. A geologist staring at strata, realizing just how short and long time can be.

"Ilka, please, I don't understand."

"You want to have it out right here? In your precious hotel lobby? All right, then. I'm tired of our arrangement. It doesn't work for me anymore. No, don't look embarrassed. That is so pedestrian. Christ. I want you to know, it's important that you know, it's not your fault." She gestures to the grand domed ceiling and wavelike walls, the fireplace where flames leap soundlessly over fake wood. "It's this place, nothing *real* can survive."

A crowd has formed now. Coco, in her tennis uniform, among them. She calls to Louie, who is sniffing another potted plant in consideration. *Louie, Louie, Louie*, she sings quietly, patting her tender thighs. His fluffy white head comes to attention. He prances across the room and into her arms.

Ilka Beaumont watches this, a sad half smile on her usually hypermobile face. "You can keep him," she shouts to her. "He likes you better, I think."

Mr. Beaumont is desperate now. He grabs for his wife's hand. "I love you," he says, the words sounding hollow and tinny even to himself.

She lowers her voice. "I could hear Keith and Kit from my balcony."

"Yes." He strokes her hand, confused but hopeful he might be able to salvage the situation. "We've had some complaints. She's overtired, anxious about the fires. But the concierge doctor is with her now."

Ilka Beaumont withdraws her hand.

"Yes, it would be her fault," she says, tapping away on her cell. "There. I've ordered the car myself."

The elevator dings and the entire lobby follows Ilka Beaumont's eyes. There is a freshly showered Keith Collins, stylish in his dove-gray suit. Curls darling, eyes bright and blue.

"Make sure the hotel ships my things," she says, looking back at her husband. She stubs her cigarette out in one of the orchids on the counter. "Goodbye, Dickie."

Hot air rushes into the lobby as the doorman steps aside for her to leave. There's a sharp, electrical scent on the wind, its sudden dryness so abrasive that Mr. Beaumont recoils. But then the massive sliding doors shut and it's cool once more.

Someone, Tigran maybe, steers him into the Polo Lounge

bar. One of the hedge fund managers or chain store conglomerate CEOs or the aged jazz drummer—probably all three, one after the other, supply Mr. Beaumont with whiskey. Rounds and rounds, accompanied by stories of their first, second, and third wives. There are Elizabeths and Karens, Joans and Marys—how can there be so many failed marriages, how can love go wrong so many times? Chantel, Myrna, Ji-hoon, Eloise, Paloma. The list goes on and on. All beginning with those tenderest of emotions that search for human connection. Then always, always it turns suffocating, to husband or wife or both.

"Love is a fantasy," a high-profile attorney argues.

"Nonsense," a Hollywood exec rebuts. "I've been in love with every starlet since 1982."

In a whiskey haze Mr. Beaumont listens, wishing Coco would appear with Louie so that he might cry into her hair or his fur. He doesn't mind which. They would bring him the same comfort. He thinks he hears Louie's bark and sits up, looking around the room.

A medium-sized cat is looking at him from over one of the leather booths. It hops up, leopard-like but with a smaller, more triangular face, and struts toward the potted plants. Everywhere he looks are exotic cats. There's a rust-red one with black eyes atop the bar, another slinking between glasses as the bartender dries them—they're curled in planter boxes, hiding behind large-leafed palms and ferns, licking themselves beneath white-cotton-covered tables.

"I didn't think they should be kept in cages," Tigran explains. "Besides, they're harmless little creatures. All hybrids. Very well trained."

Had he asked the question aloud? Mr. Beaumont reaches out to pet one with pointed ears, long black tufts at the end.

"That one there is a cross between a Chausie and a Pixie-bob. I let the boys have caracals, but they know how to handle them."

The cat's lips pull back. Such sharp canines.

"Ah, I forgot," someone is saying. "Our Mr. C. is newly married."

"Have we sufficiently terrified you?"

"Kit." Mr. Beaumont swings his attention back to the table. "She's different. Keith is a lucky man."

Keith Collins is drunk. He plans to drink heavily for the foreseeable future. Anything to keep his argument with Kit in a fog. The look on Kit's face. How she'd backed toward the bathroom, her hand on the knob. Eyes steady but voice shaking. *Is this what you're like when I don't do what you want?*

He was breathing heavily, limbs weak. The suite a mess around him.

What if I told you I want nothing to do with this place? Or any place like it? That I'm going to drop the somm class.

What are you going to do instead?

I don't know, maybe I'll write.

His reply was a reflex. The words practically spat out: *Please, you're not that good of a writer. You'll end up like your mother.*

She might have been frightened and hurt before, but her face took on a new emotion. The exact counter to the girl in Tahoe. Pale and shaking, she screamed at him to get out. He tried to apologize, he didn't mean it—he was sorry. *Please, Kit, oh god, I'm sorry, wait a minute.* But she'd already locked herself in the bathroom.

"*Wife*," Keith says, draining his whiskey glass and waving to the waitress to bring another. "Such a small word for something with so much bite."

28.

Marguerite's bungalow is a bouquet of haute couture and dollar-store products. The white-haired girl is in a black feathered gown, a paper plate with cutouts for her eyes fastened to her face. A wave of ivory lace cocoons her girlfriend, who uses a cheap plastic kaleidoscope to watch Coco cross the room, through brunettes and blonds and redheads in damask and silk, petals floating about their shoulders, butterfly wings attached to their lashes. How plain she looks among them, in her white tennis uniform, wheeling a beverage cart into the kitchen.

Even Ethan is already dressed for the black-and-white ball. His suit embroidered on the shoulders as if he were a matador. He lifts a gold tray from the counter, lines of white powder racked in neat rows across its glossy surface.

"Do you want some of this?" he asks Coco, as she restocks the fridge and collects used glasses. He gestures to all the beautiful creatures in the sunken living room. "Before the kiddos dig in."

She sighs, neck aching.

"Why not? How the hell else are we going to get through this."

It's rare that Ethan will look serious about anything. Yet the boyish blond brows sag, his eyes cloud. He rests his hand on Coco's shoulder.

"Are you okay?"

A series of booms gently rattle the windows. The chandelier over the dining room table flickers.

She looks across the kitchen at Kit, who'd arrived at Marguerite's bungalow visibly upset. *I can't be here*, Kit cried. *I want to go home.* The honeymoon was over, she claimed. Maybe their relationship too.

There were no flights available to Sacramento. None that made sense for Kit to take. Did she really want a four-hour layover in Vegas just to go home? They were set to leave tomorrow anyway. Just one more night, Coco reasoned, offering her own bed in the staff quarters. She tried calling around to nearby hotels. Most were closed to outside reservations. The Bel-Air, the Kimpton, the Mondrian. Chateau Marmont's phone just rang and rang and then disconnected.

It doesn't matter, Kit said. Because what she really wanted was not to go back to present-day Boonville but the one before the Pink Hotel. Back to when Kit and Keith's apartment was new and full of promise, when their hotel and restaurant—with owls in the pines and elk crossing the road—was everything either of them ever wanted in the world.

It seems so long ago, Kit said, her lip trembling until the anger set in and Coco watched as Kit and Marguerite popped champagne and drank straight from the bottle. Music cranking on the television. *Just stay here with me,* Marguerite squealed, spinning Kit around and around until they both fell over laughing.

Now Kit's swiveled back to sadness, her face buried in Louie's kinked curls as she searches the cupboards for something to eat.

"Why don't we get you dressed for my uncle's party," Marguerite is saying to her. "I'm never sad in couture."

Coco rubs her temples. "No, I'm not okay, not really," she tells Ethan.

"Why don't you ask Mr. B. for some time off?"

"I can't leave, not after his wife left him."

"Coco," he says, rubbing cocaine on his gums. "I'm only going to say this once because it's none of my business, but you're so much better than that."

He pivots on his heel just as the glamorous horde in the living room call out for him. "Coming!" he drawls, and they all giggle and play-fight over who gets the first line. "I'm the one who bought it," the feathered girl whines.

Marguerite is tapping her yellow-and-green nails on the marble countertops, watching Kit destroy a bag of stale bagels.

"Coco," Marguerite says, turning to her. "Kit refuses to dress up, and she can't go dressed like this."

"I don't want to see *him*," Kit says, mouth full with a sesame bagel. "Go without me."

Marguerite stomps her foot. "I don't want to."

Every day Marguerite looks more and more like her mother, Coco thinks. Sometimes she even takes on traits of her uncle or cousins. That phony laugh, the way she will strut across the Polo Lounge or party with anyone who will give her attention. But occasionally—like at this moment—time reverses, and there are those big nine-year-old eyes again, filled with a childish insecurity that makes Coco want to weep.

A caracal is rubbing against Kit's legs. She leaps away.

"Aren't you on edge." A Lacey cousin posts up, touching Kit's arm with a whip. His brother pokes Marguerite in the sides until she jumps away, making him cackle.

"He's just marking you."

There are dark spots splattered across the front of their tuxedos. Bits of feathers and bird bones on their sleeves. They'd arrived with newly appointed security guards, a consequence of their home being robbed and Mrs. Lacey's anxiety. The last hour's entertainment was the twins getting the cats to attack the security guards' shoelaces, claw at their pants. One of them had already quit.

The twin with the whip lightly snaps it at the remaining two. "Begone."

"Yeah," the other says. "You're harshing our vibe."

He turns his attention back to Kit, watching her chew another bagel.

"Wanna see something cool, Kitty?" He produces the laser pointer from his tuxedo pocket and makes the cats chase the security guards. The group in the living room cheering.

"In Iran," he's saying, his clean-shaven face moving close, "caracals are trained for bird hunting. You put them in an arena with a flock of pigeons and place bets on how many they can take down."

The security guards have fled, the heavy front door slamming shut from the wind.

The twin's lips are practically touching Kit's cheek. She tries to move away but he catches her arm. "Who should we have them go after next?"

Coco swats his hand. "Knock it off."

"Yeah," Marguerite pipes in. "Kit's had a bad day."

He cracks the whip hard enough that Marguerite jumps.

"Haha," he says. "Scaredy *Margie*. What will you do once Coco isn't here?"

"Don't call me that. I hate it."

"Where am I going?" Coco asks, hands on hips. She has just about had it with the twins. Their kink and cruelty—how they mercilessly tease Marguerite. *Haha, Margie's drinking a cosmopolitan, you're such a poser.* Their parties always cover for some dark whim or desire. They're the kind of toxic rich she holds her breath around, and she's tired. It's been a whole damn week of grin and bear it. Now they're going after Kit Collins because of course they are. They can sense the weak and injured, are excited by vulnerability.

"Why don't you run along to the ballroom," Coco says. She's angled the beverage cart to create more distance between the twins and Kit and Marguerite. "Your dad spent *so* much money, it would be a shame if you didn't get to harass at least one shit-faced model."

One twin whistles. "You've really turned into an annoying bitch."

"It's 'cause she's aging out," the other says, flicking that whip at her. "Not Pink Hotel material for much longer, are you?"

Ethan looks over from the living room. He doesn't like the glint in the twins' eyes. This week hasn't been as much fun as he'd thought it would be.

"Hey," he calls out. "Mr. B. is supposed to be here any minute."

Coco knows what he's trying to do. Defuse the situation by mentioning the boss, the man in charge of this whole circus. The Laceys know about her and Mr. Beaumont. She's in a different class than the other employees. *Hands off.*

"Last time I checked," she says to the twins, "this wasn't your bungalow."

She's shoved the beverage cart so they stumble into the living room, one of them slipping on the Persian rug. This is when the laser is pointed at Coco's chest.

The caracals leap from the kitchen to the cart. Wine and champagne bottles clatter against the floor, dirty glasses shatter. The brunettes and blonds and redheads in their damasks and silk scream.

"What's going on here?" Mr. Beaumont is standing at the front door.

Coco's red-faced and breathing hard. Ethan had jumped over the sofa but is now pretending to be concerned with the empty gold tray.

"You little Hoover vacuums," he says to the group. "I'll get a refill."

Mr. Beaumont steps around the mess on the floor, touching Coco's hand lightly.

"You aren't dressed," he says.

"What?"

The twins snicker. They fall back on the sofa and plush chairs. One paws at the feathered girl's paper-plate mask, making her giggle. The other cracks that whip against his own thigh. Caracals circling the living room before purring around a redhead with gemstones adhered to her forearms like the scales of some lustrous reptile.

Mr. Beaumont smiles at Marguerite in the kitchen, waves to Kit Collins just behind her.

"I thought we'd go to the ballroom together but you aren't dressed."

Coco motions around the room, to the broken glasses on the ground. "I've been busy."

"Ethan, you can take care of this, can't you? That's a good lad." He's pulling Coco outside.

She can feel his arm trembling. His hand is slightly damp too. Is he unshaven? She's never seen him unshaven before. Always immaculate, a shining example of how he wants his staff to present themselves.

"I understand you're loyal to your guests," Coco starts. They're standing in the entryway, the lamplight making the

bungalow walls look jagged and rough and very pink. The
fires must be close. Ash swirls around her sneakers. "But I
don't understand why you're letting them run us—you—
ragged like this."

Mr. Beaumont smooths back his hair. An owl somewhere
in the gardens is screeching.

"I know, I know." He kisses her, hoping the sweet salt
taste of her mouth will ground him, but it only sets him more
at sea. That guiding hand has slipped. Poof. Gone. Ciao.

"You're drunk," she says to him.

His mouth twitches, eyes shutting briefly. He says, "I'm
making you my assistant manager."

She steps away from him. "What about Keith Collins?"

That owl will not let up. He thumbs the bottle of anxiety
medication in his pocket. He'd found it when he'd gone back
up to his presidential suite. Ilka's name faded on the label.

"What about him?" he says, shrugging. "He's not cut out
for this place. It's too much for him. He can stay the big fish
back in Doonville."

"Boonville."

"Whatever, does it matter? The position is yours. I should
have given it to you from the beginning." He's thumbing the
pill bottle, peering out into the dark gardens. Have they
grown? They look twice as big, twice as thick.

"Why didn't you?"

He blinks at her.

"Give me the position from the start?" But she knows the
answer. It flashes on his ring finger as he pops the top of
the prescription bottle and crunches on two blue pills.

The orchestra in the ballroom has struck up a waltz.

"Shit, I have to get over there." He brushes his lips against her forehead because he cannot handle kissing her mouth again. "I'll see you there. You will change first, though, right? Okay, love you. Thanks."

29.

"Excuse me," Keith shouts, following security in their cheap dark suits as they turn from valet parking and head for the hotel's entrance.

"Excuse me, how many times are we going to walk the perimeter?"

The dark suits don't answer him. They continue up the asphalt drive, the night air heavy with gardenias and gun powder.

"Mr. Beaumont is waiting for me," he tries again, his foot slipping on the red carpet as they reach the entrance. He catches himself on one of the pink pillars. Muffled orchestra music coming from beyond the hotel's sliding doors.

They've stopped to talk to a police officer dressed in heavy tactical gear. His radio crackling. The officer shines his flashlight at Keith.

"He's with us," the dark suits say. "Babysitting."

"All right, all right," Keith says, covering his eyes. Whiskey burning in the back of his throat.

"Are you going to puke?" one of them asks. The police officer snickers.

Keith straightens himself. Adjusting his suit jacket. How many drinks did he have? Those small wild cats slinking around the Polo Lounge, hiding behind potted palms, preening on the grand piano—Tigran and Mr. Beaumont and all the others grumbling about their ex-wives. The sun setting so that the whole restaurant was muted and golden. That look on Kit's face haunting him until he was sure his heart was breaking. So he walked behind the bar and grabbed the bottle of Jameson. *Just bring me a ginger ale and a glass of ice*, he told the waitress. It never came. Maybe he'd failed with the staff too.

Christ, he's sobering up. If he doesn't get another drink soon he'll start crying again. Mr. Beaumont had pulled him from the restaurant booth before Tigran or the others noticed. *Get it together*, he said, nostrils flaring. Too late, Keith was sobbing right there in the Polo Lounge bar where Frank Sinatra or Madonna or some other celebrity did something better and more important than anything he'll do in his whole damn life. *Kit doesn't want me*, he hiccuped as Mr. Beaumont flagged down security. *Mr. Collins needs some fresh air.*

The orchestra is playing a waltz, the music spilling from the hotel as someone comes outside to smoke a joint.

"Excuse me," Keith manages, pushing past those cheap dark suits, the police officers—there's a group of them now. More and more are showing up. A bang in the distance rattles the hotel windows but then Keith is inside, the glass doors sliding shut behind him and he's embalmed once more in the hotel's hedonic atmosphere. Hotel guests everywhere, all of them dressed in extravagant black-and-white costumes. One woman's headdress sweeps across the bottom of the chandelier as she crosses the room, her child a miniature replica in tow.

No bedtimes tonight. Nannies have made themselves scarce. Children in couture and tuxedos chase after one another, sparklers in their hands. The sulfur scent making Keith's eyes water. There isn't an employee in sight. No one to tell them to behave. One boy punches another in the face and then both roll around on the ground until a dog in a tux comes sniffing. Then they're off, the boys chasing the dog down the grand staircase toward the Crystal Ballroom.

More guests spill across the foyer, packing the lobby. Keith is a fish swimming upstream. He pushes through the perfumed frenzy to the elevators. A dog barks, a child cries out. A peacock answers, sharp and guttural from somewhere inside the Crystal Ballroom, where that full orchestra is playing. The swelling of violins, the dulcet tones of a bandleader.

He smacks his lips together, flexes his tongue against the back of his teeth as he rides the elevator to the second floor.

Everywhere hotel guests drift in and out of each other's rooms. Their doors propped open by anything heavy and portable. Buckets of ice, paintings pulled down from the walls, bedside-table lamps, even an armoire. Men in tuxedos run down the maze of halls, their dress shoes slipping on the carpet. Women in gowns chasing after them, bottles of champagne in their hands. Their faces obscured by feathers and rhinestones and glass beads. Keith can make out only their smiling teeth, their glittering eyes. Everywhere a hysterical scent of mock orange and gardenias and gunpowder. He twists the wedding band around his finger, feeling his heartbeat thumping away in his chest.

The suite is exactly the way he left it. Hole in the wall, suitcases and clothes strewn about.

"Kit?" he asks, his tongue heavy in his mouth. "Are you in here?"

He flips the lights on just to be sure. Then slowly picks up her clothes, zipping the suitcases and storing them in the closet.

Another boom, closer now. What might be animals in the gardens or animals in the hallway.

Something is scratching the other side of the door. He

stands there, unsure if he's imagining things. Suddenly he feels very drunk. Another crack out in the night followed by a series of *crack-crack-booms*. The lights flicker. The clawing on the other side of the door is frenzied now.

Only a group of youngsters. They're running up and down the hall with coat hangers. Dragging them across the banana-leaf walls, over any closed doors.

"Go find your parents!" Keith shouts after them. A ginger-haired kid turns and chucks a firecracker at Keith's feet.

Made you jump, made you jump, they chant as they disappear around the hall, that terrible scratching raking up and down Keith's spine.

The elevator is taking too long, so Keith takes the stairs, which spit him out into the gardens. Darker and quieter than just a few minutes ago. His ears ringing from the sudden change. Where are the lamps? Their golden glow should be lighting the way. Bats swoop overhead, crickets in the wet foliage, an owl's piercing scream. The sprinklers must have run again. His dress shoes squish into mud. He's wandered in the wrong direction. No bungalows here. Just trees rustling above him and on either side. The stars blotted out by smoke, wildfire or otherwise. Another *boom*—it bounces off the mountains, echoing in the canyons.

"Kit?" he hears himself say, which is stupid, because why would she be here.

He follows those distant flashlights, the music. The sounds of a party in full swing. Reptiles in the nasturtiums, the hydrangeas, the swollen camellias. Their eyes iridescent as opals—but then the orchestra. It overwhelms the sirens, the helicopters, the creepy-crawly things unseen in the night. His heartbeat evens out, that tickling along his spine disappears.

The Crystal Ballroom unfurls before him, as bright as a

cruise ship in the night. Jubilant with laughter, ablaze with torches and that massive chandelier. The gardens have been brought inside where it's safe and controlled—magnified into a tropical jungle. Dukes and principessas mingle beneath gigantic strangler figs and rubber trees; ex-presidents and global superstars swap stock tips beside towering corpse flowers, the spadix gracefully erect. Half obscured by ferns and bromeliads and bright heliconia, shipping magnates and oil men talk trade; the Hollywood and Bollywood execs nearby weave between cascading fuschia and orchids, showing off their bejeweled wives to anyone who will look, which is everyone beneath this unnatural canopy of green.

A banquet waiter hands Keith a tropical cocktail and a little vial of something that he pops and inhales. *Pow!* The blood in his veins is electric. It could power the heavy Venetian chandelier somewhere in the middle of the room, hidden under the weight of creeping vines and pitcher plants. Keith Collins, son of two nobodies—nobody to these exquisite creatures—has made it into those glossy pages, *finally*.

Tigran is saying something about Keith's reemergence. "I win," he tells his cohort of moguls. "Pay up."

"That's the natural order of things."

Keith jumps at Mr. Beaumont's voice. The ballroom is so thick with tropical plants, he didn't realize they were standing shoulder to shoulder.

"Sorry about earlier." Keith leans closer to him. "I'm good now. Better than good."

Mr. Beaumont's easygoing smile is lopsided. He's staring at a peacock and its harem.

"Men aren't meant to be with only one woman," he mutters. The tail feathers are fanned out now, eye spots lustrous and rattling. "We're animals too."

"Are you okay?" Keith has to shout over the swelling of violins and cellos.

Mr. Beaumont nods. "No, not at all."

"I can't hear you over the music."

"Yes, I feel great." Mr. Beaumont pulls his smile together like pieces of a smashed Tiffany lamp, taking those anxiety pills from his breast pocket and chewing them between his molars.

The Beverly Hills wives have found them, they climb up Keith's arms, ignoring Mr. Beaumont. *Have a drink, you darling boy,* they're saying to him. *We heard your poor wife is ill, it's such a stressful time.*

"We managed to get through the week," Mr. Beaumont continues, despite knowing no one is listening to him. "Cheers to us." He downs his cocktail and throws the glass at the peacocks. Over the crowd and the music he doesn't hear it break, which frustrates him further. Just once he'd like to make a mess. He tilts forward, caressing a cassava shrub. *How did they get this in here?* It's practically touching the ceiling.

"What are you looking at?" Coco asks, following where he's staring off.

She's still in her tennis uniform, a smudge on the white skirt.

"Courtney," he says, angling her into a grove of fan palms and taro. "Why haven't you changed? I got you that belted Max Mara evening gown."

"I'm not staying," she says.

Tigran and Mrs. Lacey have waved Keith over. Mr. Beaumont watches as Keith flops onto a pile of oversized pillows, Mrs. Lacey laughing at something he said. A large Siberian tiger pacing in a cage behind them. Titans of industry, politicians and foreign dignitaries, the real estate developers and shipping magnates—hotel guests Mr. Beaumont has cared for these last two decades. He believed in a rigid hierarchy, never questioned it, yet they're welcoming Keith Collins with open arms, offering wine, cigars, that vibrant redhead.

"Did you hear me?"

Mr. Beaumont turns back to Coco. Such thick beautiful hair. He reaches out but she steps away.

"Richard," she says, her eyes softening. "I'm leaving in the morning."

His hand drops. *Please, Coco, please.*

She's motioning to him, to Keith, to the ballroom-turned-jungle.

"I'm better than this. I deserve better than this."

Mimi Calvert backs into them, brandishing her poker at a small wild cat eyeing Norma Jean. "Shoo, shoo!"

She turns to them, that magnificent pomp of silver hair electric in the mirrored light.

"Mr. Beaumont, I'm surprised at you," she cries. "Letting wild animals loose like this. I'd return to my bungalow but I'm terrified to leave. Coco, darling, is that you? Who would have guessed, someone not in costume. Someone *sane.* Don't touch her hair." She slaps Mr. Beaumont's hand away.

"You're perfectly safe," he says. How half-hearted he sounds. He tries again: "They're well trained."

The orchestra has struck up a quick-tempo swing. He tries to take Coco's hand but she moves away again. His upper lip is damp. He wipes at it, realizing, horrified, that he's forgotten to shave.

"Perfectly safe," Mr. Beaumont repeats, still fingering the stubble on his chin and cheeks.

Mimi's expression remains displeased, becomes disgusted

when she sees Tigran feed pieces of chicken to a cockatoo. Keith laughing maniacally beside him.

"Where's that one's wife? Never mind, I don't want to know. Is Ethan here?" She strokes her pet capuchin. "I want to go back to my bungalow."

"I can take you," Coco tells her.

A small whimper escapes Mr. Beaumont.

"Leave it to the women to watch out for one another," she says, steering Coco away. "Of course you will, thank you, darling. But before we go, can we find the bar? It's somewhere in this grotesque menagerie. I do so want to drink as much gin as I can on Mrs. Lacey's dime. Did you hear what she said to me?"

Mr. Beaumont lunges for Coco's hand. "You can move into the presidential suite with me."

Mimi's eyes widen but then Norma Jean is being harassed by some animal and she's swinging her poker again.

Coco shakes her head. "I don't want that promotion either."

The plants and trees quiver from some mysterious breeze. She removes his clammy fingers before Mimi returns from defending her capuchin, and then they're walking away, pushing through the crowd and jungle.

Coco does not look back, she does not pause or slow, even though she can feel him staring after her, slack-jawed, eyes glistening. She marches right out the ballroom doors. Gulping down the warm, noxious air. Her blood humming. She's done staying still, letting weeks, months, years slip by. Done being mined for love and labor, always confusing the two. She misunderstood the transaction. It didn't matter how much she gave, there was no *real* power in the return. There wasn't even love. And they always wanted more. Well, too bad. Shop's closed. From now on she'll be a solace only to herself. Maybe she'll go back to school—maybe she'll call one of the dozen record producers whose card had been pressed into her hand with a wink and a nod.

"Christ, child, what's the hurry?" Mimi says, out of breath. "Is this even the right way?"

The big band in the ballroom has struck up a lively rendition of "Begin the Beguine." Guests have spilled out into the ballroom garden, dancing in the orange glow.

"I have no idea." Coco's laugh is unrestrained and deep, making the little capuchin skirt up its mistress's dress. "But it's better than being in there."

30.

An exec calls out, "Hey, Mr. B., grab that banquet waiter. We have a proposition for him."

Mr. Beaumont whips around, startled at hearing this iteration of his name. A nickname given to someone much younger than he is now, hungrier and more carefree. Someone who says *yes, sir*, and smiles with his whole being. Always in control. He slips on some monkey shit and collides with the emir and his entourage. *Sorry, my apologies, excuse me.*

"The man is losing it," the exec says in an aside to Tigran and Keith just as Mr. Beaumont approaches them.

"How is everything, good?" Mr. Beaumont asks, signaling the banquet waiter, who comes scurrying over. He constructs his lips and teeth into a grin. "Excellent, excellent."

Maybe just one more pill. He likes the chalky acidic taste. It reminds him of Ilka. He's sipping another cocktail without pleasure, thinking about the indentations his wife's slingback pumps left in the lobby carpet. They were there after that boozy lunch, even after the sun had set and he was running around making last-minute checks that everything was ready for the Laceys' ball. Small divots in the carpet, permanent scarring on the Pink Hotel.

The exec is propositioning the banquet waiter.

"Stick your hand in the tiger's cage and I'll give you five grand."

There's heckling from the others. The wager increased to twenty, then fifty. Someone must have opened all the ballroom doors because the enormous philodendrons are waving in a warm breeze. They could be in a faraway jungle, on some other continent. Or an island. It's unbearably humid. Cycads drip with dew, insects mate in the tall grass. Mrs. Lacey fans herself with her mask.

"I have a second job," the waiter laughs nervously, glancing at Mr. Beaumont. "Painting houses with my brother-in-law. If I lost a hand my wife would kill me."

"Boooo," one of the domino-masked businessmen complains.

"I'll do it," Keith interjects. He'd been sitting there listening to the plants around him grow. He was sure he could hear their stalks creaking, their foliage unfurling. That massive chandelier blotted out so that it's nearly dark. Hundreds of tiki torches have been lit, flames flickering over their faces. This experience of finally making it would be more satisfying if he had someone to share it with. Where is Kit? She should be here, dressed in a translucent caftan, or a silk pantsuit, some hand-sewn couture.

He loosens his collar, takes off the domino mask one of the Beverly Hills wives gave him to wear.

What if she doesn't come? What if she's left him? No, no, her suitcases were still in the room. He rubs his chest, remembering the year he lived in Los Angeles, the one he did not tell Kit about. Everything was going wrong. No callbacks, no auditions, his bank account running low. At a party, the night before he tried to learn to surf, the girl he'd been seeing laughed in his face and went home with someone else. He'd gone to the beach to try to console himself and on a whim rented a surfboard. One moment he was paddling out, another the current was too strong. A riptide pulled him under and out to sea. His leash snapped, the board disappeared. A lifeguard had to rescue him.

"I'll do it," Keith says again, getting up from the plush oversized pillows. He forces a breezy, charming grin, and saunters toward the tiger's cage. How humid and dark it suddenly seems. As if there were clouds above the canopy. Maybe they've created their own weather system. Soon it will begin to rain.

He can barely see the tiger's cage. He senses the weight and size of her. Head rising, her entire body tense. The orchestra has taken a break. There is only his breathing, the dripping of water onto plants. "You can do it," Mrs. Lacey offers, nearly crushing the fan in her hands. "Shhh, shhh," Tigran says to her.

Keith's heart is thumping in his chest. He thinks of the moment Kit walked into his restaurant. Her perfectly open smile. His hand trembles. The cat becomes nervous, displaying its teeth. Part of him hopes it will rip off his face, but nothing happens. The latch falls away, his hand enters the cage, and the tiger looks at it curiously, sniffing the wedding ring, before licking his fingertips, the pink tongue rough as sandpaper.

The group welcomes him back as if he were a hero gone to

war. Tigran offers him a job, the shipping magnate wants to hire him too. Mr. Beaumont gulps his drink.

"Nerves of fucking steel," Mr. Beaumont hears the Hollywood exec say.

"Have you considered acting?"

"Kid's got a chin like Clark Gable."

The alcohol catches in Mr. Beaumont's throat. He coughs violently, a burning in the pit of his stomach.

"My turn," he shouts, turning so quickly he kicks a tier of oysters, sending them scattering across the floor. Macaws and parrots diving for the bivalve mollusks.

Another boom, the chandelier, all the wall sconces, everything electrical goes dark. The massive ballroom is lit only by torches and candlelight now. There's a cry from the hotel guests, terrified but delighted. The little hairs on their arms tingling. Is this the moment they've been waiting for? Has it finally arrived? In the ambient lighting there are throaty purrs, low growls, wings beating. When the pygmy elephant moans a haunting wail, there's a collective sigh of euphoria.

"Maybe wait until the lights come back on," Keith suggests.

"What, you think you're the only one with balls?" He smacks his chest. "Watch this. You don't even have to pay me. Not one fucking cent."

His hand is on the latch, upper lip dripping. "See?" he calls to the group. "I'll put my whole fucking head in."

It happens fast. A swipe and a nip. That's all it takes to detach tissue from bone. Mr. Beaumont's ear is half severed from his skull. Damp heat, the wind coming from outside— the sensation of wetness is cool, almost refreshing. Keith and the banquet waiter are there with an armful of cloth napkins, he shoos them away.

"Don't fuss, I'm fine." Mr. Beaumont yells over the music, "What's happened to the lights?"

The banquet waiter just stares at him. Keith stepping away as blood pools around their shoes.

"I'll take care of it. You clean up this mess."

He turns to the others, who seem not to have noticed his injury, or otherwise don't care. Tigran is talking to his private security, the other businessmen listening in. Only Keith is watching him with concern.

"Let me help you," he says, slipping a little in the blood.

Mr. Beaumont jerks away. "I have to do everything around here," he says, or possibly only thinks it, stumbling away into the dark forest.

"It's all up to me," he tells the emir when he passes him at the door. His security stepping between them.

Everything, he thinks as he makes his way outside. The air turning rancid with sulfur and dry heat. Hardly any oxygen anymore. The world has run out of that, too.

He cuts through the back of house, which is completely empty. No one in the locker rooms, no chefs in the kitchen, the cafeteria empty of food, the tables and chairs tipped over. A beguiling shut-up smell reminiscent of summer camps and churches. Even the elderly Mexican woman who is a fixture in dry cleaning is not behind her counter. The uniforms hang in their plastic garment bags like ghosts. The emergency hotel lights along the floor are the kind in airplane aisles, flashing red and white, urging Mr. Beaumont forward.

Pop! Pop! Pop! He emerges in the Cabana Cafe. Children are playing with fireworks in the pool area. If he turns his head in the right direction he can hear their peals of laughter. They are dressed exactly like their parents. Tiny tuxedos and dominos and gowns embellished with gemstones and feathers, masks obscuring their faces. *Pop! Pop! Pop!* They're throwing fireworks at the woman from dry cleaning. Why can't he remember her name? He prides himself on remembering everyone's name. He reaches out to steady himself.

The old woman is chastising the children in Spanish. They throw more fireworks. Not just small bang-pops. Larger ones—Roman candles, Catherine wheels. One girl holds out her sparkler, catching the woman's uniform on fire. Coyotes nearby call and the children scatter. Mr. Beaumont tries to shout. He manages to get as far as a chaise lounge before the old woman stops screaming and falls into the pool. Mr. Beaumont still struggling to remember her name. *She was always very sweet, had a grandson.* He strokes his temple, fingers brushing the soft goo where his ear should be.

He slaps his cheeks, trying to focus. Nonsense, that cannot be the old lady from dry cleaning, half submerged beside a beach ball. Night is deceiving him. What was her grandson's name, Pico? Kato? Cute little tyke. He'd asked if he could work at the hotel when he was old enough. Jobs are passed down and down and down again. *Legacy.* Tomorrow Mr. Beaumont will come into laundry and the old woman will be there and he'll say, *Job well done, remind me, what is your name?*

He just needs to get the lights working again. Confirm everything is okay. That the guiding hand is still in control.

The electrical room is behind the lobby office. If he can just make it up the staircase. *One, two—up the wooden hill.* Only in this case pink concrete, and stairs as steep as a funicular in Lisbon. The only recent trip he can recall taking with his wife—soon to be ex-wife. They drank beer in a park like a couple of teenagers. He attempted to order in Portuguese and a whole fish arrived, head to tail. He was picking small bones out of his teeth the rest of the night, Ilka laughing like the tinging of a bell. He stumbles and pauses his ascent to catch his breath. His cheeks and chin wet with tears.

A medium-tempo swing drifts out from the ballroom. He recognizes it. Pictures himself as Fred Astaire. A stately minuet, Fred approaching Ginger, bowing and kissing her hand, like so. He imitates it. They come together, Ilka rests her head on his shoulder, and the music swells. *Your lips whisper so tenderly, her eyes answer your song.* They always did like to dance. A jolting two-step, *la-de-da-da-da.* He taps with his imaginary partner, resuming his climb up the stairs. *For it's a song of romance and love,* he whistles. A foxtrot as he twirls—missing a step. Down, down, down he falls. Tumbling head-first, crashing against concrete and stucco and finally the Cabana Cafe hostess stand.

The coyotes sniffing the burned lump in the pool turn their attention to him. They yip and howl. Ilka in her wedding dress flashes in his mind—her train had been fifteen feet long! The way she smiled at him. They had been in love once. But what he lands on in his final moments, as the trumpets in the ballroom blare their finale, is whether management would approve.

31.

When the power went out, Marguerite regressed into that frightened little girl who'd clung to Kit in the hotel garage. *Don't leave, no one leave!* she commanded. Her friends slinking away in the dark, eager to get to the party. The Lacey twins smug and satisfied, then indifferent because one of them was watching live feeds from the protests. *Rioters Storm Police Lines.* A youth midstride, tennis racket in hand. Face obscured by a mask and goggles. Night surrounds him, dotted by burned-out vehicles still cooking, the broken storefronts along Rodeo Drive, the neon Versace and Gucci and Louis Vuitton signs glowing their teals and pinks and golds, palm trees illuminated by a helicopter's sweeping light. And this lithe young body stretched gracefully, swinging his tennis racket like he's playing a match point, returning a smoke grenade to the riot police who disperse as smoke plumes up and toward a Starbucks coffee shop. *Fucking animals*, the twins said as they left for the ballroom. *Billionaires are people too.*

Ethan was the only one who remained. He'd miscalculated his dosages, was too high, too drunk to move from the couch. So when the lights went out it was up to Kit. She lit as many candles as she could find, Marguerite clutching at her.

"Will you hold my hand?" she pleads.

They huddle together in the center of the living room. Candles burning atop the oak and mahogany tables, the marble countertops and travertine mantels, wax puddling onto the carpet. The bungalow turned shrine, a monastery. Shadows flitting over the crown molding and vaulted ceilings. A faint din coming from the ballroom; dried leaves scattering across the ground; that pepper tree dragging across the roof shingles. Coyotes howling over a kill. Those helicopters draw closer and then farther away. Cracks that could be fireworks or gunshots or trees snapping in two.

"I hate the dark. Nothing good ever happened in the dark."

"It'll be okay," Kit says more to herself than to Marguerite. Her hand absently stroking Marguerite's fine short hair. The shock of Keith's betrayal has abated. Perhaps she'd always expected him to be unfaithful. But the pain that followed should have killed her—if love is the foundation of life, then when it breaks, everything should break with it. Yet here she is. She had not floated away, nor been sucked into an abyss.

"You're okay," Kit whispers. She imagines her mother there. *Hush*, she'd say while slowing her heartbeat. *This is only temporary.* Her mother's words. They'd found an orchid in the greenhouse of a local botanical garden one arid summer and she was holding it and crying.

Marguerite kisses the tears that have slid down Kit's cheeks. "Keith doesn't deserve your love."

There must be a better word to describe it. A more adequate description. No poem comes to mind, no verse. The failure of language is as painful to Kit as her failure at becoming *Kit Collins*. She'd been seeking transformation when the metamorphosis occurred the moment she said *I do*. She's already Kit Collins, wife, daughter, woman—a thousand other things too. When she thinks of Keith—*her* husband—besides the hurt and anger, another emotion is rooting around. Understanding, yes. Forgiveness, maybe. It's too early to tell.

The wind howls against the window. Marguerite's nails dig into Kit's arm.

"You're okay," Kit breathes. It occurs to her she could spend an entire lifetime trying and failing at loving. Women like Mimi Calvert suddenly make sense. Abandon this painful search. Gin martinis, animal companionship, and faith in yourself could be enough.

Flashlights sweep across the ceiling, their orbs growing brighter and brighter. Marguerite stifles a cry.

"It's probably just someone coming to check on us."

"Boo!" one of the Lacey twins cries as he throws open the door. The other has his flashlight beneath his chin. His features exaggerated. Like a gargoyle, like a demon.

"Marggggggieeee," he howls.

She's up and slapping their arms.

"You bastards." That artificial laugh bouncing around the room.

"The ballroom was too sweaty," they say, peeling off their tuxedo jackets and throwing them on the sofa where Ethan is conked out. Their caracals investigate the cocktail peanuts on the dining room table before slinking around Kit's legs, sniffing her Converse.

"Plus we know how you're scared of the dark." They've brought gas camping lanterns, placing them around the room.

"I'm not afraid," Marguerite declares, shrugging her shoulders. "Kit and I were just having a good cuddle since Keith cheated on her—oh, ma petite chou, if housekeeping knows, everyone knows. We're all on your side. I mean, this was supposed to be your honeymoon."

One of the twins snaps his whip. "And with Ilka Beaumont. *Gross.*"

"That's why he'll never work at the Pink Hotel," the other says from the kitchen, which is now flushed with light. "Oh good, you still have gin."

"What do you mean?" Kit says, incredulous. She's surprised by how furious she is. "It's all he wants, why wouldn't he get the job?"

"Ughh," the other twin says, puffing on an e-pen. "Don't be stupid. He was never going to get the job. He's a fucking pleb."

His twin snorts. "Googling cigar brands isn't going to change that."

"Maybe it's a good thing?" Marguerite suggests, chewing her lip.

Kit shakes her head. Keith will be humiliated, which he deserves, she supposes. He's brought it on himself. Part of her wants to be there when he finds out. To see his face when he realizes what he sacrificed for a job he was never going to get. But another part of her understands the throbbing empty center of him, the void he tries to fill with expensive pretty things in the hope that he will feel whole. This will destroy him. She's overwhelmed with pity. *Poor Keith, poor darling stupid Keith.*

The Lacey twins have paused from teasing their cats to snort whatever someone left racked on the coffee table.

"Oh shit, that was Adderall. Whew!" He nudges Ethan, who props his head up, a thin line of drool connecting his mouth to the couch pillow.

"You only get like this on ketamine," they shout at him. "Is there any left?"

Ethan points to a pillbox purse, its rhinestones glittering. The Lacey cousins rifle through it.

"Oh shit, I forgot you had this, Margie."

They're holding up a small pistol. Gold damascene, the handle inlaid with pearl. "Can I have it?"

"No." Marguerite reaches for it.

"Come on, I want it."

"Well, it's mine, Grandpa left it to *me.*"

One twin flops onto the sofa where Kit is sitting. "Don't look so surprised," he tells her. "Everyone in Beverly Hills is armed."

Marguerite lunges for the gun but it's tossed to the twin sitting beside Kit.

"Don't worry," he tells her, tapping the cold grip against her arm. "It isn't loaded."

Click. He cocks the pistol, brushing Kit's collarbone with its cold barrel. *Snap.* He pulls the trigger.

The other one has found the ketamine and is cutting a neat line across the dining room table. He beckons to the caracals. "Hey, cat, you want a taste?"

"Don't feed them drugs, you idiot," Marguerite cries. "It's bad enough you have them off-leash."

"So," the twin beside Kit says, his breath sour and damp on her neck, "do you want to get back at that husband of yours?"

When he strokes her thigh with the gun's barrel she jerks away, making him laugh. "Haha, okay, too soon. I'll wait." He switches his attention to Ethan. "Hey, wake up."

They whistle and clap at him. A blow-up unicorn bounces off Ethan's head. Marguerite giggles from across the room.

"Hmmm?" Ethan raises his head.

"You can get us anything, right? Get us some bullets."

Ammoooo, the other twin mouths.

Ethan rubs his face. "What is that, a thirty-two? Mimi's got a Saturday Night Special too."

"That ain't no Gabilondo. This is real fucking gold."

Marguerite has moved closer to Kit. "Ouu, let's have gin and tonics," she is saying, tapping those clawlike nails together. That diamond eyetooth catching the light. "That was grandpa's favorite drink, wasn't it?" she asks her cousins, but they're ignoring her. "I never met him," she tells Kit. "But Maman says I have his nose."

"A hundred bucks says I'm a better shot than you."

"Pffft, make it a grand."

"You're fucking on."

Already they're taking candles and moving them to the courtyard, camping lanterns too. Kit is checking her phone to see if Keith has tried to reach her. The Wi-Fi must be down, she has no service.

"I've always thought I'd make an excellent sharpshooter," Marguerite is saying. She makes a finger pistol and fires.

32.

The orchestra has not paused between songs, and the guests continue to dance, oblivious to Mr. Beaumont's fate, to Guadalupe's body, a crisp lump of meat and bone at the bottom of the pool. The underwater speakers still playing French electronica.

Keith is drifting in and out of consciousness, awakening when macaws cry out or when he hears those animal sounds humans sometimes make when they think no one is listening. A gust of wind rustles the thick-leafed plants and trees so that it's warm and balmy like a bell-jar rain forest.

He twitches, then relaxes as a woman's hand caresses him, her nails raking against his scalp. He and Kit had gone wine tasting for their honeymoon after all. This is only a menagerie on one of the estates Kit had told him about. *Giraffes and zebras and pinot noir, can you imagine?*

"You're safe, sweetheart," the woman says.

His eyes snap open and there is the vibrant redhead. He blinks, struggling to sit up from the oversized silk pillows. The heavy scent of her perfume, the hypnotic fragrance of thousands of orchids holding him down.

"Seven stitches." She raises her bangs to show him the gash on the side of her forehead, something flashing on her ring finger.

The confluence of time collapses as easily as an accordion. How long since her enormous diamond ring had caught the sunlight out by the pool, making him self-conscious of Kit's plain gold band? Was that the same night this gorgeous woman was trampled by Louboutins and Manolo Blahniks and Jimmy Choos? Strobe lights crossing the pool, a mountain lion approaching.

"It didn't hurt that much," she's saying, her hands reaching for his hair again. "With the right plastic surgeon no one will even see it. I love these curls."

"They said you'd understand," he slurs, wanting to explain why he had carried her, half-conscious, to the loading dock where a taxi was waiting to take her to the hospital. Why hadn't he thought that odd? The discarding of a human being so casually. *Get her out of sight*, Mr. Beaumont had said to him. *I'll call a cab.* At the time it made sense—an ambulance at the Pink Hotel would upset the guests. But now, seeing her smiling and blinking up at him, fingers in his hair—*who are these people?*

He looks around at the dozens of champagne bottles upside down in ice buckets. The ground littered with crushed oyster shells, a heel dangling from a philodendron. Mrs. Lacey is reclined on Tigran's lap, both of them looking drunk and ordinary. Nearby, Peggy Nasar vomits in a potted kentia palm before wiping her mouth and disappearing back into the crush of partygoers. Everywhere men and women roam about, red-faced and squealing. A group of women point and laugh at two Chausie hybrids fornicating in the branches of a rubber tree, their evening gowns slipping from their shoulders. He looks around for Mr. Beaumont. The swinging motion of his head making him woozy.

How much had he had to drink? What drugs had he done—*where is Kit?*

"Hey," the redhead is saying, twisting a curl around her finger. "Take it easy. I forgive you."

He rubs his face, remembering how heavy her body had been. He will probably remember it all his life.

She's caressing his jacket lapels. "I bet they cleaned your suit real good. I lost quite a bit of blood."

The orchestra is playing a waltz. A peacock struts by, its feathers fanned out, thousands of eyes watching them. He rolls onto all fours and heaves himself onto his feet.

She's standing too, her smile dazzling.

"Good idea," she says, following him into the jungle. "Why don't we dance?"

Through the jungle Keith glimpses half-naked hotel guests, rutting like animals in the brush. A Bengal cat hisses and swats at his pant leg as he passes.

"Aren't you an adorable little leopard," the redhead says, squatting to feed it a caviar-and-crème-fraîche tartlet. "I want to make you purr."

"Look," he says when she reaches for his curls again. "I'm sorry, but I need to find my wife and get the hell out of here."

He moves away, making her stumble. Hotel guests are watching. He doesn't care, how marvelous that he doesn't care.

She's already gesturing to someone behind him. *Baby, where have you been? I've been looking for you all night.*

Keith pushes past the menagerie of animals and plants. Climbing halfway up the grand staircase so he can scan the crowd for Kit.

There's the stage where the orchestra is playing, the conductor sweating from the lack of air-conditioning. Everyone on the dance floor is off tempo. He laughs at how they bump into one another or slink off into the thick surrounding forest, the artifice of which he can see from here. Thousands of potted plants arranged to create the illusion of hidden depths.

Someone in plain clothes catches Keith's eye. No gown or mask. His heart swells.

"Kit!" he yells, but his voice is lost in the cacophony. Back down the stairs, he moves to where she was standing with Tigran and the others. The tiger pacing in her cage behind them. He wants to tell Kit he understands—or rather that he *doesn't* understand. Not a thing about how to love. But he'll beg her to teach him. Or ask her to stay, and he'll learn on his own. Sweaty, grinding bodies brush up against him as he charges forward. He could not be more disgusted. The jungle heavy with humidity and rank body odor. Love as a redemptive, radical act. Yes, that's what he'll strive for, and as he reaches Tigran, panting and sweating, he repeats his wedding vows. *I do, I do.* The chugging engine of a train forever going uphill.

It's not Kit. A boy, maybe sixteen, svelte in a tank top and baggy pants. His coarse curls tight and shining. Restraint zip ties cutting into his wrists. He's standing between Tigran's security, in their sleek suits, and police in body armor and riot helmets.

"They ran," one of them is saying. "But this one wasn't fast enough."

"What should we do with him, Mr. Collins?"

For a moment Keith doesn't realize who they're talking to. His eyes are adjusting, his brain taking in the riot police in their big military boots; their canisters and shotguns and semiautomatic launchers. Guns in their holsters, grenades on their belts.

Someone suggests taking the boy to a command center.

"Command center?" Keith repeats. When did they set up a command center?

"Yes, in the Rodeo Ballroom."

Mrs. Lacey is inspecting the boy. Her face so close to him that for a moment Keith wants to shove her away.

"Ask Mr. Beaumont."

"Nobody can find him."

Mrs. Lacey is fingering her necklace, considering something.

"It's up to you, Mr. C.," one of the masked businessmen says.

The riot police are showing Tigran a backpack. Empty except for a hammer. Mrs. Lacey presses her polished fingernail into the boy's chin, forcing his face one way and then the other.

"Tigran, do you think he was one of the hoodlums that looted our house?"

Her brother is busy weighing the hammer in his hands. A man in a Tom Ford tuxedo takes it from Tigran, examining its worn rough handle. He pretends to hit the boy in the face.

"Ha, he flinched."

"What were you going to do with that?" Tigran asks the boy. His smile easygoing, body relaxed.

The kid's arm is yanked back until he winces in pain.

"Smash in your skull."

Tigran lets out a bellowing laugh, slaps a tanned hand on the boy's shoulder.

"Put him in with the tiger," a man in Givenchy says, tickling his thin erect back.

More laughter. The boy keeps his eyes lowered, jaw pulsing.

Keith leans forward. "Did one of you hit him? He's got a black eye."

"He resisted." They shrug.

"Why do you want to smash in my skull?" Tigran hasn't

dropped his hand. It's still clamped on to the boy's knobby shoulder.

Keith clears his throat. "Maybe we should let the officials handle this."

"No, I don't think that's what you wanted to do," Tigran continues, ignoring Keith and steering the boy to the mountain of oversized pillows. "Why the empty backpack, then? No, you were going to use the hammer to break in. You were going to steal." He sits the boy down. "Where are you from? Never mind, I wouldn't know the neighborhood anyway. But I'm guessing this isn't the first time you've stolen, am I right? Otherwise why would you be here? Were you protesting? Good for you, I admire that about the middle class. It's a very specific kind of naïveté. Easily exploited, always a price." He traces the boy's wrist with his finger. "In the old days, repeated theft would mean amputation of the right hand. And an aggravated theft—one where a hammer might be involved— would mean a hand and a foot."

He taps the boy's sneaker, the boy jerks it away.

"Relax, we're not going to cut anything off. I *understand*. That's what I'm trying to say. You see how much we have and you think, why not me? Why can't I have that too? Here," Tigran says, producing a slim leather wallet. "See this card? It's titanium. Virtually indestructible. And its purchasing power—you could buy a jet with it. Do you live in an apartment? A house for your family, then. Go on, take it."

Keith can feel the blood throbbing in his ears. He's watching Mrs. Lacey press her nails into her own palms; the Hollywood execs and trust fund managers, politicians and real estate developers, the CEOs and heiresses are gathered around, straining over one another for a better view.

"Go on, I'm giving it to you."

The kid hesitates, then raises his bound hands.

Tigran shakes his head. "Open your mouth."

The orchestra has switched to a jazzy foxtrot. One of the peacocks cries out.

"What?"

Mrs. Lacey claps her hands. "You have to eat it. Swallow it whole."

"I can't cut it," Tigran says apologetically. "Titanium, remember?"

The kid tries to move away. He clamps his mouth shut. Someone is holding him down. The sound of metal against teeth, gagging. Encouragement from the other hotel guests. The reed and string instruments swaying, that peacock sounding like a cat in heat.

"Tin snips!" Keith shouts. He'd been standing there unsure whether what he was watching was really happening. Tigran, dressed impeccably, silvery beard neatly trimmed, a magnificent silk handkerchief bursting from his breast pocket. Standing over a boy, tears and snot running down his young face, a bit of blood from where someone bopped him on the nose until his mouth opened. *This will stop*, Keith had told himself. *This has to stop.* When he shouts they let up, and for one horrible moment Keith thinks the boy is dead. But he struggles to sit up and spits out the card as if he were an ATM.

"There's a pair of tin shears in the office," Keith lies. He shifts his weight, trying for casual. "From the construction site. Why don't I set up something in one of the conference rooms? Something with a little more privacy."

Tigran is wiping his hand on the kid's tank top.

"A hundred grand says this little shit can't get it down cut in half."

Keith collects himself. "Champagne or something stronger?" He manages his breezy smile. "The little shit can help me set up the bar."

They decide on an array of Japanese whiskeys and single-malt scotch. Keith pretending to write it down.

"Don't forget the cigar cutters." They laugh, pretending to snip the boy's fingers between their teeth.

Keith leads the boy away by the neck. Security in tow. Their radios crackling. He walks quickly, and when they get to the thicker, darker parts of the indoor jungle he ducks behind giant monsteras.

"What the fuck," the boy says, tripping and falling onto his hands and knees.

"Be quiet."

"There's a fucking leopard looking at me."

"It's an ocelot, and shhh."

There will be no Pink Hotel job now, Keith muses as he watches the security in their slick suits ascend the grand staircase. He's surprised by his relief, by his sudden longing for the Old Boonville Hotel, for their apartment, where their wedding gifts are waiting, unpacked and spread across the living room. As soon as security is out of sight he rushes the ballroom doors.

"You've got to get out of here," Keith says, cutting the zip ties. "Run—"

The boy kicks him in the shin, right where the rug burn scraped away a good portion of his skin, pink and raw as steak tartare.

"Ah, fucking Christ!" Keith doubles over in pain. "Shit."

"*Pinche güero cabrón*," he spits. "Fuck you."

Keith stays crouched on the ground, breathing through the pain. There are tiny white lights strung up in the small courtyard garden, a gazebo at the other end. Towering syca-mores and oaks lit up like Christmas trees. It would be an enchanting place for a wedding.

There's a series of loud blasts. Guests file from the ball-room to watch fireworks over Sunset Boulevard. *Crack!* They explode. Red, white, and blue.

Oooh, the guests say.

Ahhh, the guests cry.

Keith slips back into the ballroom, careful not to let Tigran and the others see him. He needs to find Kit. It'll be light out in a few hours and then he can figure out how to get to the airport and get the hell out of here. His leg aches, he limps up the grand staircase.

The heavy tables in the lobby hall have all been overturned to block windows. Massive floral arrangements spilled onto the ground. Everywhere the smell of lilies.

Are they police? National Guard? Private security? Their helmets and gas masks and heavy body armor reveal alle-giance to no one. They're showing off their riot shields to ad-miring hotel guests, who have brought up tiers of oysters from the ballroom.

You must try a Kumamoto! They slurp them together. Toss-ing the pearly shells onto the carpet.

The hotel guests want to fire off canisters from grenade launchers; shoot pepper-spray guns. They want to pull the fuse levers off flash-bangs and see if the protesters outside will be made temporarily blind and deaf. There is dancing to the or-chestra, and posing for photographs. One of the military men has a beautiful baritone.

Cheers, they say, and clink their delicate flutes of cham-pagne, which someone has pilfered from the Polo Lounge bar.

As Keith passes the lobby doors, they slide open and he's

hit by a burnt-plastic smell. He pauses to let the wind dry the sweat beneath his suit jacket. There are blinking emergency lights along the red carpet, the candy-striped awning is torn from fallen palm fronds. It's as if he were on a different planet, some other timeline. Maybe there's been a crack, a fissure that only quantum mechanics can explain. In a parallel universe he never left Boonville and he and Kit are asleep in their bed, or maybe the asteroid that killed the dinosaurs missed, and humans don't exist at all.

He's hobbled outside, turning to look back at the hotel's infamous entrance. The one he's seen in countless movies, on postcards and magazines. Scorch marks brand the red carpet. Someone has shattered a beer bottle against the pink pillars, written the words *hi-de-ho* in bright lipstick beneath the hotel's name. A lone baggage cart near the front desk is missing a wheel. The bellhops and valets long gone.

A canister rolls down the red carpet.

At first Keith thinks he's dying, he cannot breathe. He's gagging and stumbling inside, blinded by tears and mucus. *Kit*, he tries, but can only gag and listen to laughter and delight at his pain. *Please.* His entire face is burning. He cannot see anything.

Someone has taken his groping outstretched hand.

"Shame on you." Mimi Calvert's voice. He can hear Norma Jean screeching. "This poor boy has been nothing but good to us all week."

She's leading him away from the hotel. Out into the bungalow gardens where it's cooler and darker, the dampness of a greenhouse enveloping them.

"Hold still." Coco's voice. "Stop touching your face."

He's sobbing now—or would be if he could catch his breath. *Kit, where is Kit?* One of them is pouring something cold and thick over his face. The scent of artificial cherries reminiscent of childhood stomachaches and sick days spent at home.

"Oh my god," he finally manages. "Oh my god. They shot me."

"You're going to be fine." Coco's opened a water bottle and is rubbing a bar of hand soap onto his hands. "You're not the first person to get pepper-sprayed."

"Where . . ." He coughs and spits into a hydrangea bush, then goes on coughing and spitting. "Where is Kit?" He wheezes.

"Probably still at Marguerite's."

"How puffy are my eyes? They burn like hell."

She laughs, shining a flashlight at him so that he squints and puts up his hands.

"You look like shit."

Mimi Calvert pats him on the arm. "Good thing old ladies live off gin and antacid, eh?"

The gardens are pitch-black besides Coco's flashlight, which illuminates only a few feet ahead of them. Their progress is slow, serenaded by crickets, the steady staccato of pops coming from the lobby, louder booms in the distance.

Mimi snorts. "The Laceys will dance all night and still demand breakfast in the Polo Lounge in the morning." She's leaning on Coco, Norma Jean perched on her shoulder.

Coco glances at Keith. "I don't think there will be any Bloody Marys tomorrow."

They walk cautiously, Mimi too old and frightened to go any quicker. Every couple of steps she stops to swing her poker into the darkness.

"Watch it," Keith says. "You almost whacked me."

Mimi snorts again. "Maybe it'd knock some sense into

that handsome head of yours. Get those gears turning in the right direction."

He can feel his face blush. A gust of wind pulls at the trees above, dirt and ash pelting their legs.

"No response? Typical. Disappointing but typical."

"Respectfully," Keith says, rubbing his eyes because they still sting, "it's none of your business."

Mimi's laugh is gruff and quick. More like a bark.

"Love not my business. Courtney, did you hear that? *Hilarious*. Child, the only thing I know anything about is love. Five husbands and I loved every single one."

"No one true love for you, then."

"Oh no, no, no. That's a child's definition of love. There are many types of love, but only one way *to* love. It's a verb, not a noun. But you're young, you'll learn." She thrusts her poker into a wall of oleander. Moths flit from within it, passing through Coco's cylinder of light.

"I suspect you're learning already."

A series of gunshots ring out. Then a chilling stillness, quiet but for Norma Jean's whimpering.

"Where did that come from?"

Several more shots echo across the hotel grounds.

Coco points. "Bungalow Five. Straight ahead. You go, we'll catch up."

Keith jogs the rest of the way, his chest tight with fear.

33.

"My turn, my turn!" Marguerite cries from a rattan chaise lounge. Her cousins are always doing this to her. They'll come up with a game and then won't let her play. When she was little they'd include her only if she guessed who was who. *Wrong again, Margie.*

Even now she gets them mixed up. Premier is quicker to laugh, Deuxième following along. But sometimes they'll swap roles. Especially if they're trying to mess with her—and in the poorly lit courtyard, the wind so strong it's blowing small eddies of dirt across the pool, they could be doing just that. Both are smiling the same wicked grin. Premier or maybe Deuxième snickering. She reaches out for Kit's hand.

"Promise you won't go anywhere without me," she says, flinching when shots ring out. "You said you were loading it for me!" She gets up.

Her cousins shrug. "Okay, okay," they say, camping lanterns hissing beside them. Caracals restless and pacing. "Don't freak out."

Candles surround the hot tub and pool, a nimbus of gold flickers in the wind. There is no moon.

Two gin and tonics, one bottle of champagne, a few bumps of coke, and half a chocolate—Marguerite calculates how vulnerable she is, how susceptible she is to tricks her cousins might play on her. But they hand over the pistol without pulling her hair or poking her sides, both of them stretching out beside Kit, who's holding her knees against her chest, pretending not to be frightened. She must be pretending, no one is that brave around her cousins except for maybe Coco.

Ethan has dragged a bedside table and a box of empty Dom Pérignon and Veuve Clicquot bottles to the other side of the pool. Only two bottles have been nicked. One fell over from the wind.

"Ethan," Marguerite yells so he'll stir from his perch by the bar. "Move the table farther into that corner."

"Oh-ho," the cousins taunt. "*Margie* thinks she can shoot better than us."

A gust of wind blows through the courtyard, extinguishing some of the candles. That laser pen sweeps across Marguerite's ankles, and she's kicking at the cats when something bursts through the side gate. Marguerite is so frightened, she almost drops the pistol.

"Kit!" Keith pants. "Where are you?"

Fucking guy ruins everything, she hears her cousins say— that's Premier's sneer for sure. And Deuxième has unbuttoned his dress shirt, she can see the Arabic word for twin above his left pectoral. Premier has his on the right.

Marguerite moves closer to Kit and Keith. She likes seeing how their heads bend toward each other, like flowers or swans. The softness with which Keith takes Kit's hands and her grace in allowing this. No broken dishes for the maids to sweep, no divorce attorneys on speed dial.

"What are you trying to say?" Kit is asking. "I can't understand you, what happened to your face?"

"He's apologizing, ma petite," Marguerite says, the pearl handle hot from her tight grip. "And I think he might be crying."

"Pepper spray," Keith says.

Her cousins roar with laughter. "You were protesting? Figures."

Keith ignores them. Marguerite watches him kneel beside Kit.

It's brighter where they are, by a camping lantern, in each other's arms. Marguerite moves closer. A moth to a flame. She watches Keith kiss Kit's hands, her fingers. *Please*, she hears him whisper.

Deuxième has aimed the laser pointer at the wall behind our newlyweds. The cats are suddenly upon them, tearing through Keith's pants, catching and ripping skin.

He leaps onto a chair. The red dot following him, the cats too.

"Play with the kitties."

Bottles of alcohol go crashing to the ground. Keith is cursing, trying to kick the cats away.

Kit waves the pool skimmer, attempting to fend them off.

"Marguerite, do something," she cries.

But Marguerite cannot tell what's happening. The rest of the candles have gone out. A camping lantern too. There's only the shattering of glass, the horrible sound of cats attacking, her cousins cackling, Keith swearing and yelping somewhere in the dark. She backs away from the commotion, toward the remaining camping lantern where it's safe.

Coco's voice is calling out now, and there's Mimi Calvert, her magnificent silver hair shimmering in what little light there is.

Coco will fix it, Marguerite thinks just as wind turns over a courtyard chair with a heavy crash. She yelps, pointing the pistol into the darkness. Somewhere Norma Jean is squealing, a horrible, panicked sound. Are the cats hurting her?

"I'll sue your whole goddamn family if anything happens to her," Mimi Calvert shrieks, swinging the fireplace poker at Deuxième, Coco trying to calm her down.

"Fucking hag," Deuxième roars when Mimi wacks him. "Give me that."

The cats have chased the monkey across the courtyard where Ethan has managed to reignite one of the camping lanterns.

"Shoo, shoo, go away!" he shouts at them, Norma Jean on his shoulder. The cats nipping at his fingers.

Someone's yelling to get the leashes, get the leashes! Which is pointless because there aren't any. When have her cousins ever kept anything on a leash?

Snap! A whip cracks. Premier raises it again. *Snap!*

Ethan stumbles backward. Black dripping from his eye.

"I can't see," he starts to wail. The monkey goes running into a tree. "Coco, I can't see anything."

"Well, if you'd only stopped moving." Premier shrugs. "You did it to yourself."

The caracals are more excited than before, one grabbing Ethan's sleeve. Their silhouettes are large and terrifying. Cats on top of boy. Attacking face, exposed neck.

"Help him," Coco screams, moving away from the scuffle between Mimi and Deuxième. "Stop recording and help him."

How strong she is, taking the whip from Premier and hitting him with it. Over and over until he rushes her.

"Don't . . ." Marguerite chokes out. Tears in her eyes. "Please . . . leave Coco alone."

Deuxième is on the ground with Mimi. The poker easily intercepted and discarded. He'll use his bare hands. He wraps them around her throat.

Marguerite can't catch her breath. The tears are hot on her cheeks, the sharp stucco wall at her back. She's had nightmares like this. Horrible nightmares where no one can hear her calling for help. *Stop*, she tries, but the word will not come out. She's watching Keith pull Deuxième off Mimi, using the poker to beat him back. The two of them struggling for control of it, Mimi gasping and limp on the grass. Kit's used a camping lantern to scatter the cats away from Ethan's limp body. Marguerite catches sight of his grotesque face. A wad of fat exposed in his cheek, blood pulsing from the wound. *Stop, please.* She squeezes her eyes shut, the pistol raised in front of her.

Coco screams. Premier has managed to restrain her against a rattan chaise. His pants unbuttoned.

Stop it, stop it! Stop it! Marguerite is saying in English, in French, in Persian when the wind kicks up and blows out every candle, every lantern, every torch in the courtyard. Everything dark, dark, dark. Marguerite fires. She shoots until someone has tackled her to the ground. The sudden silence ringing in their ears.

34.

Kit finds an abandoned tiki torch beside the jacuzzi and manages to light it. The wind so fierce with dawn approaching, it blows the flame sideways, sending embers up into the dry bougainvillea above them.

Ethan moans, his hair dirtied with blood and grit.

"You're okay," she says to him. "You're going to be okay."

The sky turning gray, the courtyard subdued. As if the pink had been drained from it, the green from all the palms and banana plants too.

"Norma Jean." Mimi Calvert's voice wobbles and she coughs lightly, hands to her throat. She's sitting in the grass. Dress ripped, hair flattened. "Where's Norma Jean?"

"We'll find her," Kit tells her.

Coco is helping Marguerite up, doe-eyed and trembling.

Her gown's puffs of taffeta and satin squished and streaked with ash.

"Let me see you," Coco says, examining the blood coming from her mouth.

"Oh my god, ith he dead?" Marguerite points at Premier floating in the pool.

Coco turns her away. "Don't look, shhh."

The embers in the bougainvillea have caught the dried leaves on the bungalow roof. They pop and crackle.

Kit helps Keith upright.

"It's not my blood," he assures her. The front of his gray suit stained crimson. "Most of it anyway."

His hands are slick. The smell of blood in his nostrils. Deuxième stares up at him, the poker sticking out of his chest. It was self-defense, he tells himself. Sirens grow closer. They whine over the music still coming from the ballroom. Blood plumes from the twin's gunshot wound turning the pool pink in the early predawn light.

Marguerite is wailing. "Why wouldn't they thtop?" She sobs. "I juth wanted them to thtop." A dark hole where a canine and incisors used to be.

The fire is moving as quickly as the approaching sunrise. It's reached the pepper tree, climbing its dry branches.

"We have to get out of here," Keith says.

Someone whistles. Short then long. As if trying to get their attention. Are you there? it asks. Where are you?

Kit recognizes it. She'd heard it on the construction site.

"Back here." Coco has recognized it too. The relief in her voice palpable. "Sean!"

He'd come back for them. His pickup truck rattling out on the street.

"I tried to get here sooner," he says, hugging Coco tight.

Kit reaches out to touch the smudge of dirt on his arm. There's a cut above his brow. His hand bandaged. Is he really here?

Something like an earthquake rumbles, sloshing the pool water. Sirens swell. The orchestra in the ballroom thunders. They can hear reeds and strings and a French horn.

"It's crazy out there," Sean is telling Keith, who's standing beside Kit, face blanched and tired. "They're going to storm the hotel. Everyone in the ballroom is fucked."

Coco nods. "We need to get Ethan to a hospital, he's hurt really bad."

"Maybe somewhere in the Valley, if they're still letting people through the canyons."

Kit waits for Keith to say something, to help Sean and the others get through this, but he just stands there, his expression unreadable. Hands clutched to his sides.

"I'll find a blanket," she says, her voice firm. "Something to wrap Ethan in."

Coco directs her to a stack of towels beside the pool. Out from the singed brush beside them races a small capuchin.

"I knew you wouldn't abandon me." Mimi straightens herself, the monkey taking its perch on her shoulder.

Kit returns with the towel, laying it beside Ethan. She'd been ready to forgive Keith, believing there was a new balance in their relationship. An understanding that they could be equals. That their love could get them past this. Something they would strive for, and probably often fail at, together. But now she's helping Sean shift Ethan onto the towel, thinking she was wrong, all wrong, and no one is getting over anything. At the last moment Keith bends to help them.

"On the count of three," she says to him.

The fire has reached the bungalow roof. The pepper tree fully engulfed. A large branch snaps off and crashes onto the roof as the group leaves Bungalow 5. They trudge across the vibrant green lawn, birds beginning to chirp, church bells drowned out by flash-bangs and firecrackers. Ethan is lifted into the back of the truck with what's left of the Pink Hotel staff, a dirty bichon frise yapping at their heels.

"Louie!" Coco cries, making the little dog bark with pleasure. "You want to make a run for it too? Get up here."

"How hideous am I?" Ethan asks as Coco tucks another towel around him, Louie trying to lick them.

"There go the big tips."

"Don't," he says. "It hurts to laugh."

She squeezes his hand.

Marguerite's climbed into the truck, her eyes puffy from crying.

"Nothing my plathtic thurgeon can't ficth. He'ths a geniuth."

"I'm so sorry about your tooth," Coco tells her, sitting between her and a dazed banquet waiter.

"It'th okay, I didn't like that diamond anyway."

Coco laughs. "You've got quite a lisp."

"A hundred buckth thayth I make it fathhionable."

"Thanks for coming back for us," Keith says to Sean, who nods. They both know he didn't return for him. Keith winces, leaning against the back of the truck, a searing pain in his stomach to match the one in his heart. Lifting Ethan had been a bad idea. He holds his side, watching his wife say thank you to the man who came to their rescue.

"I hate to state the obvious," Mimi Calvert announces, her hair somehow magnificent again. A discarded tuxedo jacket draped across her shoulders as if it were a trophy pelt. "But you won't all fit in that truck."

Keith clutches his abdomen where his blood is seeping through his fingers, disturbingly warm. He has the sudden urge to give Kit and Sean Flores his blessing. It wouldn't be so terrible. Husband redeemed. He'd die a hero. Those booms are so close. Soon they'll overtake the orchestra, which is still playing an up-tempo swing in the ballroom. And more than one bungalow must be on fire. He can smell burning plastic and paint. It will close off their only escape, those in the ballroom are trapped. He wonders what Tigran is doing. That titanium credit card cannot save him now.

"Kit, go with them."

"Don't be a dramatic idiot," Mimi huffs. "My Cadillac is well maintained—Christ, it better be for how much I pay this damn hotel. The keys are in the center console."

"You're staying?" Kit takes her hand.

Only young girls have eyes that inquiring and innocent, Mimi muses. She thinks she's learned something—they all do. She should tell them their revolution won't be the last. It never is. But the weight of Kit's life stretching before her with all of its horrors and disappointments and beauty is too much. Mimi nods, staggering a bit. The construction worker catches her arm.

"The hotel is on fire," he says.

Mimi does a delicate, practiced shrug. "Darling, the whole world is on fire."

"Kit?" How faint Keith's voice sounds as he reaches out for his wife. He's changed his mind. He doesn't want to die a hero; he doesn't want to die at all.

35.

Inside Mimi Calvert's bungalow, everything is exactly how it should be. The rooms are dimly lit to prevent migraines, the plush white sofa has its plethora of throw pillows, the Louis XV writing desk, tables, and chairs are all illuminated by the pale slanting light coming from the bay window—Guerlain Shalimar and stargazer lilies and Gauloises cigarettes blend together to create the reassuring bouquet of European theaters and opera houses.

She'd left Kit Collins standing on the hotel lawn, between a wounded husband and a construction worker. That pickup truck idling behind them, waiting for her to make a decision. Mimi was too exhausted to care. Bone tired. Love, this thing she'd professed to know so well, is a lie. There's no decision for Kit to make because love doesn't exist. Human beings are incapable of it. For fuck's sake, that Lacey boy—whom she's known since he was a toddler—had tried to kill her tonight.

There's a dull roar from the sudden quiet. The air-conditioning switches on. She lets the little capuchin out into the caged courtyard and changes into a bright silk caftan. A welt already forming on her hip. Bruises on her forearms and neck. She picks up the room phone, finger hovering over the in-room dining button, dial tone in her ear. She sets it again in its cradle.

It's been a long time since she's made a martini herself. Nausea sweeps over her at the thought of Ethan, the poor boy's face. The right surgeon and he should be okay. After this drink, in a few hours once she's had a rest, she'll make some calls. He'd been good to her, more friend than lover. She enjoyed the rumors, though. *Mimi Calvert*, outrageous and eccentric and untouchable. The stuff of Pink Hotel legend.

The ice is difficult to get out of its tray. She takes a knife, then, thinking of the Lacey twins dead in the courtyard where Liz Taylor spent all those lovely honeymoons, she exchanges it for a fork. Even this seems too violent. She uses the handle of a spoon. Three parts gin, half an ounce of vermouth. Like riding a bike, really.

Her fifth husband had been a lot like Ethan. Wicked and impish, but oh so much fun to be around. Perhaps she should accept his invitation to spend a summer with him and his longtime partner at their villa in Sicily.

She sips the martini, the gin easing the tension in her thin body.

Her only living husband and he's gay. How depressing. No, she won't go to Sicily. Best to keep things the way they are. Occasional emails and deposits into her account and the hotel bill always paid on time.

Dropping onto her sofa, she kicks off the throw pillows and stretches across it, watching Norma Jean play in her large enclosure.

At first she hadn't been interested in Kit Collins. So many come and go at the hotel. Then the girl had passed by her bungalow in a dreamy daze as if being drawn to something. Curious, Mimi followed her. The construction worker wasn't a surprise, in fact she had almost turned around, disappointed. Then she noticed Kit's hands were balled into fists. This she recognized. Hidden behind fan palms and hydrangeas, in the blistering wind, she stood with Kit, watching the men break apart asphalt, pulverize the earth and trees, destroying something so much larger than themselves. Pollen and seeds and tiny flowers tangling in Kit's damp hair. She hurried back to her bungalow, anxious not to get caught, and slipped in a patch of soft grass.

Was that a truck engine? The window in the dining room overlooks the hotel lawn. She'd only have to move the heavy tasseled curtain to the side to know.

She was younger than Kit when she first married, but just as romantically inclined. And a sucker for a man in uniform—an airman nonetheless, *ou la la*. Married in Honolulu and dead a year later. A midair collision during a routine drill. Senseless and stupid.

A sweet, wistful love grips her. Directionless, with no outlet, no one to share it with. She retrieves the shaker from the kitchen, topping up her glass.

Husband number two was an actor. *Forget housewife*, he said. No white picket fence or grocery store lists for Maeve Dwight, who was rechristened Mimi Calvert. Auditions and backlots and late-night parties with bohemians and movie stars. But she had outpaced him, and he'd grown resentful and bitter. Men like that always do. Years later, when she was settled into marriage number three, she learned of his death. His son hadn't checked on him for several days. Squirrels and racoons had gotten to the body.

A tender grief clings to her ligaments. Her bones are heavy, her chest too. More gin, a cigarette, the lighter trembling in her hand.

Things got ugly with number three. Thinking of him, a coldness comes over her. She'd loved him deeply; he loved his secretary more.

And number four—is that smoke? She sniffs the air but there's only the tobacco from her own cigarette, the herbaceous notes of gin.

Number four was the longest of any of her marriages.

Much younger than her, he should still be alive, but an embolism took him at forty. Their union had produced her only child, an estranged daughter—ah! Mimi clutches her chest. How can one heart contain so much?

Tears roll down her cheeks.

"Ridiculous!" she says to the empty room. The pale pink carpet stiff under her feet. She's being sentimental and ridiculous.

That heavy tasseled curtain glows from the sunrise.

Kit Collins will have chosen her husband because she's young and it's the right thing to do. They're probably in the Cadillac already—a gift from husband number three—on their way to whatever backwater little town they're from. Promising to do better, *be* better. Ha!

Or he's dead. The wound had looked pretty bad. He could be lying out there on the damp grass, alone. Something for the protesters or firefighters to find, it doesn't matter which. Not really. The world has gone mad.

She does like the idea of being saved by a firefighter. She can hear the sirens approaching. That would be lovely. Possibility for husband number six. The gin has muted her pain. Defiant and stubborn, she refuses to look at the curtain, now gleaming with orange light. A lifetime of loving should have taught her not to believe in love any longer.

She drains her martini and chews on the olive. Norma Jean staring at her.

"Don't you judge me. These are cruel, ugly times. I have nothing left to give."

A girl struggling with her rage. That's what she'd recognized when she saw Kit at the construction site. Learning how to be so filled with anger and hurt, sadness and fear—all the horrors life can throw at you, and still somehow offer love. Because how else could any of this work? Love despite the monster. Without it there's nothing.

She steps out into the caged courtyard, the air stinging her eyes. Norma Jean watches her unlatch the gate, pushing it open.

"Go on," she says. The monkey squeaking and chattering and then it's gone. An empty cage larger than most Los Angeles apartments. Mimi drops back onto the sofa, sniffling into her gin.

The wind has pushed the fire toward the construction site. A flame, whooshing. Like a slack sail snapping taught. The wooden structures crackling, embers and flames whirling toward the Pink Hotel, where the orchestra in the Crystal Ballroom hastily pack up their instruments and slip away just as protesters cross the red carpet threshold. More gusts blow smoke from the hotel fire, carrying cinder and ash to anoint the city.

Just a peek, Mimi Calvert thinks. Martini glass empty, the dining room window brilliant. Her fine manicured hand reaching out to draw back the tasseled curtain.

ACKNOWLEDGMENTS

This book has been a long time coming. My profound thanks and gratitude to my editor, Daphne Durham, for believing in this deranged vision from that first cocktail at the Polo Lounge. My love for everyone at MCD is fierce: Julia Judge, Lydia Zoells, Devon Mazzone, Na Kim, and of course the inimitable Sean McDonald. Your support means the world to me. Special thanks to June Park for turning this book into stunning visual art, and Christine Paik for whipping it into shape. Love to Brooke Ehrlich and Marya Spence, Natalie Edwards, and everyone at Janklow and Nesbit.

Shout-out to those who visited while I did *Pink Hotel* research: Susan Ruskin, Katie Orphan, Douglas Wood, and Eileen Shields. I'm in your debt. My deep appreciation and respect for the staff at the Beverly Hills Hotel, who in no way resemble any of the characters in this fictional book. They welcomed me with open arms and are a credit to the hospitality profession.

But also, fuck the Sultan of Brunei.

Thank you, Timony Siobhan Ramos, your photography was (and continues to be) an inspiration; Nina Gregory and Kemper Bates for many things but especially for street taco delivery and getting us into Beefsteak; John Brady for the insider intel; Janelle Brown and Sara Sligar for their literary wisdom and affinity for fine cocktails; the 360 Xochi Quetzal Residency for giving me somewhere to write while my world burned; and Mark Haskell Smith, Tod Goldberg, and David Ulin for their continued guidance and support.

I could not have gotten though the last couple of years without the following people: Yanina Spizzirri and Michael and Imaan Fitzgerald, Gallagher Lawson and Timothy Walker, Linde Brady Lehtinen and Karl Lehtinen; my husband, Jordan; my sisters Ariel and Rachel; my brother, Willy; my other sisters, Heather and Jessica; and my nieces and nephew, who are a daily reminder that there is hope for the future: Ava, Jack, Soni, Gemma, Fifi, and lil' Georgia.

I also want to acknowledge some social movements that inspired much of this book. The Women's March. We Are the 99 Percent. Black Lives Matter.

Get out there and vote. Or burn it to the ground.

A Note About the Author

Liska Jacobs is the author of *Catalina* and *The Worst Kind of Want*. Her essays and short fiction have appeared in *Literary Hub*, *The Millions*, the *Los Angeles Review of Books*, and *The Rumpus*, among other publications. She divides her time between Berlin and Los Angeles.